Can't Hurry Love

"Using humor and heartrending emotion, O'Keefe writes characters who leap off the page. Their flaws and foibles make for an emotional story filled with tension, redemption and laughter. While this novel is not a direct continuation of the first in the series, it makes the reading richer and more interesting to devour the books in order. Readers should keep their eyes peeled for the third book and make room on their keeper shelves for this sparkling fresh series."

—*RT Book Reviews*

"Have you ever read a book that seeped into your soul while you read it, leaving you feeling both destroyed and elated when you finished? *Can't Hurry Love* was that book for me."

—Reader, I Created Him

"*Can't Hurry Love* is special. It's that book that ten years from now you will still be recommending to everyone because it is undeniably great!"

—Joyfully Reviewed

"An emotion-packed read, *Can't Hurry Love* . . . is a witty, passionate contemporary romance that will capture your interest from the very beginning."

—Romance Junkies

BANTAM BOOKS BY MOLLY O'KEEFE

Can't Buy Me Love
Can't Hurry Love
Crazy Thing Called Love

Praise for

Moll[y

"Reade[...]
pick up[...]
touching book that is 'unputdownable.' Her story is a roller-coaster ride of tragedy and comedy that is matched in power by believable and sympathetic characters who leap off the pages. Best of all, this [is] just the beginning of a new series."

—*RT Book Reviews*

"From the beginning we see Tara's stainless steel loyalty and her capacity for caring, as well as Luc's overweening sense of responsibility and punishing self-discipline. . . . Watching them fall for each other is excruciatingly enjoyable. . . . *Can't Buy Me Love* is the rare kind of book that both challenges the genre's limits and reaffirms its most fundamental appeal."

—Dear Author

"*Can't Buy Me Love* is an unexpectedly rich family-centered love story, with mature and sexy characters and interweaving subplots that keep you turning the pages as fast as you can read. I really enjoyed it. It's also got some of the most smooth and compelling sequel bait I've ever swallowed."

—Read React Review

"If you love strong characters, bad guys trying to make good things go sour, and a steamy romance that keeps you guessing about just how two people are going to overcome their own angsts to come together where they belong, then I highly recommend *Can't Buy Me Love* by Molly O'Keefe. You won't be disappointed."

—Unwrapping Romance

"A stunning contemporary romance . . . One of the most memorable books I've read in a long time."

—Deirdre Martin,
New York Times bestselling author

"Molly O'Keefe is a unique, not-to-be-missed voice in romantic fiction. . . . An automatic must-read!"

—Susan Andersen,
New York Times bestselling author

Crazy Thing Called Love

Molly O'Keefe

BANTAM BOOKS
NEW YORK

Crazy Thing Called Love is a work of fiction. Names, characters, places, and incidents are the products of the author's imagination or are used fictitiously. Any resemblance to actual events, locales, or persons, living or dead, is entirely coincidental.

A Bantam Books Mass Market Original

Published in the United States by Bantam Books, an imprint of The Random House Publishing Group, a division of Random House, Inc., New York.

BANTAM BOOKS and the rooster colophon are registered trademarks of Random House, Inc.

ISBN 978-0-345-53369-2
eBook ISBN 978-0-345-53370-8

Cover design: Lynn Andreozzi
Cover photograph: George Kerrigan

Printed in the United States of America

www.bantamdell.com

9 8 7 6 5 4 3 2 1

Bantam Books mass market edition: February 2013

For Adam, for everything

Crazy Thing Called Love

prologue

Maddy was going to beg. She'd start with an apology. Heartfelt, of course. Desperate mostly.

But after the fight last night she was scared that they were past apologies. She and Billy were already way past reason. Compromise was long gone.

Which left her with begging.

I'm sorry. I shouldn't have said those things. I don't want to leave. I don't want a divorce. We can do this. I know we can. I . . .

She put her head against the door, feeling through the wood the bass line of the music being played in his hotel room.

I'll go back on the road with you.

Resentment sizzled through her, burning holes in her purpose. Other professional hockey players didn't need their wives to babysit them. To keep them out of hot tubs with strippers. Away from bar fights and the mercenary puck bunnies.

But that seemed to be exactly what Billy needed. Two years ago he was a second-round draft pick, the bright young homegrown star of the Pittsburgh Pit Bulls. Eight months ago he was finally called up from the minors and he'd promptly lost his mind with the excitement.

But her husband was a twenty-two-year-old enforcer with a temper, a slap shot that could dent metal, a whole bunch of cash, and no clue how to handle the world he'd been thrust into.

He was easy pickings for puck bunnies.

I'm not his mother, she thought bitterly. But she was his wife and maybe . . . sometimes being a wife meant being a mother, too.

Dad had died three months ago, and Mom was selling the house to move down to Florida with Aunt Lisa, so there was nothing keeping her in Pittsburgh full time anymore. She could travel with Billy.

Some wives did that. It wouldn't be weird. Or exhausting. Or boring.

What about college? She asked herself because she was the only one who still remembered that she used to have her own plans and dreams before Billy's career and then Dad's sickness had taken over everything. She was twenty years old, had been married for two years, and sometimes it felt like her life was over.

What about journalism school?

Stop, she told herself. She lifted her head from the door.

You married him, honey, her mom had told her. *Now you gotta try living with him.*

She loved Billy Wilkins. Down to her bones, she loved him, which was the only reason she was outside his hotel room in Detroit. Ready to beg, if that's what it took.

Enough, she told herself, and knocked on the hotel room door.

"Just leave it outside," Billy's voice called out. The Pit Bulls had lost tonight, she'd heard it on the radio in the cab she took from the airport.

He was going to be prickly.

She closed her eyes and prayed for strength. "Billy," she called back. "It's me."

Almost immediately, the door was yanked open and

Billy stood in front of her. His thick brown hair was damp from the shower and curling at the ends. He was shirtless, the muscles of his chest and shoulders bathed in low lamplight from the room behind him.

And it was all there, everything he felt was on his face. His surprise. His love. His joy—in her—it illuminated him, the hallway, her entire world. He'd been looking at her like this since they were kids, and she felt an answering spark inside her.

They could do this. They could make it work. It was worth fighting for. *They* were worth fighting for.

The relief was profound and her heart threw itself wide open.

But he closed right down, no doubt remembering every awful thing she had said to him the night before. A chill rolled off of him, and he lifted the beer bottle he was holding to his lips.

Where the scar pulled his mouth into a terrible sneer.

The sight of him—his scar, his body, his virile strength barely restrained—rippled through her, as it always had. As it always would.

Maybe she would have been able to walk away if she didn't want him so badly.

"What are you doing here?" he asked.

"Can I come in?"

He pulled the door a little closer to his body.

That would be a no.

"You're going to make me do this in the hallway?" She tried to make it a joke, but he just stared at her. Immutable.

Right. On with the begging.

"I'm sorry for those things I said. I was mad. Hurt."

"Yeah? Well, it's my turn now. And screw your apology, Maddy." He stepped backward as if to shut the door, but she reached out her hand, nearly touching him. They both froze.

"Don't, Billy. Please. Let's talk. I'll come back on the road—"

He blinked. His eyes flared and the sneer spread briefly into a smile. "You will?"

A bittersweet happiness flooded her. It wasn't perfect, but what was?

"Yeah," she said. "I miss you."

"Oh my God, baby. I miss you so much, I—" He reached for her.

"Billy?" a voice called from the hotel room behind them.

A female voice.

A woman in a hot pink dress slunk toward the doorway, glowing malevolently in the shadows.

"What are you doing out here?" the woman asked, her voice strangled by the breasts pushed up to her throat.

Bittersweet happiness curdled to a bitter rage. And right at that moment Maddy hated Billy more than she'd ever loved him. It was a terrible rending, from which there was no going back.

Hating him like that changed her on a molecular level.

And the pain . . . the pain was shocking. She couldn't see or breathe. She couldn't think. Her whole landscape was pain.

"Maddy," Billy said, blocking her view of the bitch in the pink dress. "It's a party."

"Yeah? For two?" The words spilled from numb lips.

"No," the stupid stupid woman said. "My friend is here, too. Are you delivering the champagne?"

"Gary and Ben are coming over," he said quickly, acting like she was a fool for imagining the worst. A fool for doubting him.

Well, she wasn't going to be his fool anymore.

Speechless, she shoved him as hard as she could. Punched him. And then again. Both hands. Wanting to pull his heart out through his chest. Wanting to take out his eyes.

He grabbed her hands, his brown eyes slicing through her skin to the muscle and sinew of her.

Look at what you've become, she thought, horrified by her violence.

"You said you were leaving." There was an apology in his voice but there was pride there, too. He was the star athlete who didn't have to explain his shit to anyone. Not even his wife.

"And I am, asshole," she snapped. "Enjoy your whore."

"Hey!" the woman cried, but Maddy ignored her, stomping down the hallway. She was sweating under her winter coat and shock and nerves made her sick to her stomach. Her hands shook as she pressed them to her lips.

What was she going to do? Where would she go? She had nothing outside of what Billy had bought for her. She had no money of her own. No car. No home.

How did I get here?

A soundless sob broke out of her throat and she held her fingers to her mouth to push the despair back.

Think, Maddy. Think.

Billy grabbed her elbow by the elevator and she jerked herself sideways out of his grasp. Barefoot and shirtless, in his black athletic shorts, he was the tide just before a storm—barely contained.

"Don't touch me!" she cried. "You never get to touch me again."

"Come on, Maddy. You know these things are nothing."

"Do you really believe that?" she asked, searching his face for the boy she'd known because this Billy was a stranger to her right now. "Or are you just hoping I'll believe that?"

"You're overreacting!"

"Don't talk to me like I'm a child."

"Come on, forget about that." He threw his arms out, as if he were a magician pulling a screen between them, making the woman in the pink dress and his final betrayal disappear. "You came here to make this work. So let's do it. We'll make it work. You . . . you wanted to go see a counselor. We can do that."

He was months too late. And suddenly her anger deflated, leaving her wounded and bleeding. And tired. So damn tired she couldn't fight anymore. "There's no fixing this, Billy."

"Don't say that. We—"

"No. No, we're broken. All the way."

"We made promises!"

"Promises?" She jabbed her finger down the hallway. "She wasn't in any promise I made."

"You know nothing happened."

"I don't know that, Billy. And I feel like a fool taking your word for it!"

"You're not a fool." He tried to touch her and she smacked away his hand. "You're my family, Maddy."

"And what are you to me?"

He flinched at her words, but she couldn't stop them. Couldn't help hurting him. This is what they'd come to. Every conversation was a fight, a chance to hurt the other. "I can't keep giving you everything you need and get nothing in return. Nothing."

It was unfair, she knew, it's not like anyone had shown him how to be a family. Without her, he'd probably slide back into the dark hole his sisters lived in.

Not your problem anymore.

But it was still hard. They would eat him alive, his sisters.

"Once the season's over—"

"How many times have I heard that? No, Billy.

You . . . you just absorb me. You need me and you suck me in until there's nothing left for me. You always have. I don't believe you anymore. I have no more faith in us. I have nothing."

"Yeah?" He was getting angry, his default position, all his doors closing. They'd start yelling just like his parents had. It was so ugly, so not the way she'd thought their life would be.

I will never be in this place again, she promised herself as Billy yelled, "That new house in Ben Avon Heights? The clothes? The car? That's nothing?"

"I don't want things. I don't want money. Why can't you see that? I want you and I've lost you. I've lost me. I can't do this anymore," she whispered, dry-eyed and hollow. "This sport is turning you into someone I don't know."

"Bullshit—"

"No. It's not. Just because you don't agree doesn't mean it's bullshit. And being married to you is turning me into someone I don't know. I can't do it anymore, Billy. I just can't."

Maybe because she wasn't screaming, wasn't crying and trying to hurt him, he finally got the message.

His face, so handsome, so very dear to her—despite the scar, or maybe because of it—crumpled.

"Please," he whispered. He *begged.* If her heart weren't already cracked, she might actually have felt something.

But she looked at the boy she'd loved since she was thirteen and felt nothing.

There was a God—the proof was that when she pushed the button the elevator doors opened immediately, and she stepped in.

Don't look, she told herself, staring at the white salt stains on her boots. But as the elevator door started to close, she looked up and saw her husband, all alone. Nearly naked. Tears in his eyes.

But he wasn't fighting. And she knew, right then, that it was over.

Really over.

"I'm sorry," he said.

And the doors closed between them.

chapter 1

Fourteen years later

Billy Wilkins sat on the bench, bone dry. He might as well have been wearing slippers. A freaking robe. All he could do was sit there and watch as the second-rate team he'd been traded to blew their shot at the play-offs.

If the coaches weren't going to play him, all of it was totally useless—the skates, the pads, the stick in his hand—worthless. Just like him.

"Pull Leserd!" he shouted over the screaming in the Bendor Arena. "He's done. That's the fourth goal he's let in in five minutes."

But Coach Hornsby wasn't listening. He never listened to what Billy yelled during the games. Hornsby wouldn't even look at him, much less reply.

But that was Coach Hornsby. Stubborn, righteous, and probably deaf.

Billy waved off the water bottle one of the trainers offered him. No need to hydrate. He hadn't even broken a sweat tonight.

And what was worse, worse than the dry pads, the clear visor, the body he'd recuperated back into prime shape only to have it sit unused on the bench, was that he didn't care. He didn't care that the coach didn't listen to him. Didn't care that the kid in the net was totally overwhelmed and the Mavericks' rally to get into the play-offs was going to die a pitiful death right here. Right now.

"If you stopped being an asshole, he might listen to you," said Jan Fforde, their injured starting goalie, his consonants blunted by his Swedish accent.

"Not much chance of that." Whether Billy was talking about being an asshole or their coach listening to him, he wasn't sure. Being an asshole was his way of life: it was why hockey teams had been paying his way for over sixteen years. The sport needed assholes and Billy was the best. Used to be anyway.

Until he landed in Dallas, with a coach who preached respect and integrity.

Someone should tell Hornsby that respect and integrity didn't win games. Didn't turn momentum. A good fight did that. Let Billy get out there and drop gloves with that big Renegade center, Churov, and then the game would turn around. The crowd that was booing them would cheer.

The Renegades, who were beating the Mavericks on their own ice, would have blood on their faces and they'd know their opponents had gone down swinging.

The Mavericks' first line, O'Neill, Blake, and Grotosky, surged back into Renegade ice, skating their hearts out. Blake wound up and hammered a slap shot that ricocheted off the post. A mob in front of the goal scrambled for the puck and everyone on the bench stood up screaming. A goal right now would tie the game and they'd have a shot in overtime.

"Come on!" Billy whispered, willing his fight into those young guys out there with the fast legs and the strong arms and barely managed talent. "Come—"

The buzzer silenced the crowd for a moment and then the few Boston Renegades fans in the arena roared.

The Mavericks were out.

Disheartened, silent, the team skated back toward the bench, knocking fists, defeat riding their young shoulders. This team had fought longer and harder than anyone had expected, keeping the play-off dream alive for a community that barely cared. Despite losing tonight, they'd fought like demons.

Hornsby was silent and Billy could think of a thousand better coaches. His grandma for one. And she was dead.

"Good effort, guys," Billy said, slapping shoulders. His teammates grunted, unsmiling.

Blake, their captain, finally led the team onto center ice to shake hands. Billy stood at the end, the only guy besides Fforde who hadn't seen ice time. Who hadn't felt the sweat and blood and heaving lungs of play. For a second the grief nearly took out his knees. It was a sucker punch that his career was going to end this way.

As he shook hands with the Renegades, who were about to go into the first round of the play-offs and get slaughtered by the defending champions, not a single one of them looked him in the face. It was salt in the wound.

Billy Wilkins, second-round draft pick sixteen years ago, was a non-fucking-issue.

Might as well be dead.

Bullshit, he thought, and his temper roared through him in a brush fire, burning lesser emotions into dust. Everything about this was bullshit.

Churov, the freakish Russian giant, was the last guy in line. As he skated past, barely touching Billy's outstretched hand, Billy—a good foot shorter and thirty pounds lighter, but blessed with a temper that leveled every playing field—coldcocked him. Snapped the big man's head back so hard Billy could see his third-world dental work.

For a moment, Churov wobbled in his skates, and

Billy braced himself to be crushed, but then the big man went down on the ice with a thud.

The arena roared.

Victory was sweet but short-lived. Grisolm, the hard-working Renegade captain, landed a right hook across Billy's face. Billy swung back, feeling the satisfying pop of nose cartilage under his fist. Someone wrapped him up, using his kidney as a punching bag. But out of the corner of his eye he saw that the Mavericks were skating back from the dressing rooms, dropping gloves and sticks, throwing off helmets, all their defeat melting into raw bloodlust.

Billy smiled before someone punched the back of his head and bells started to ring in his skull.

What he'd done to Churov was dirty. A cheap shot after the game was over, just the sort of thing that made the sports journalists go crazy. No doubt Billy would get suspended. That pussy Hornsby would probably send him to counseling or some shit.

But he didn't care about what was going to happen when this fight was over. Because for guys like Billy Wilkins, there would always be another fight.

An hour later, after the mob scene with the press in the locker room, he sat in front of Hornsby's desk, showered and changed, with Kleenex shoved up his nose to stop the blood from dripping on the collar of his shirt.

Billy arranged the ice packs on his knuckles while the coach paced the hardwood floor behind him.

Coming up in the rep leagues, Junior A's, and then the minors, half of Billy's coaches had been not just old-school hockey, but old-school *Eastern Bloc* hockey. Giant men with forests of hair in their ears, who kept bottles of vodka in their desks and would have bought

Billy a steak dinner after the fight he'd just caused. And a hooker.

His first coach in the NHL, Georges St. Bleu, a French-Canadian force of nature, would have told the press that he was embarrassed and that steps would be taken to reprimand Billy. But behind the locker room door, he would have shaken Billy's hand, applauded him for knowing how to return pride to his defeated team.

But over the last fifteen years the league had changed. The last five especially. Concussions had changed the game. All this talk of taking the fighting out of the sport? These were not friendly times for guys like Billy.

Outside the big window to his left he could see the departing crowd. The few hundred stalwart hockey fans left in Dallas stood on the sidewalk, hailing cabs, storing away their play-off excitement until next year.

Suckers, he thought. This team wouldn't get any closer to the cup next year, or the year after. Front office called it "rebuilding." Billy called it "being a shitty team."

"What were you thinking?" Hornsby asked. Billy would have rolled his eyes if they didn't hurt so bad. "You're suspended. You know that, right? You'll be out at least the first four games of next season. Maybe more. Barry wants to trade you."

"How is that any different from the end of this season?" Billy asked past his fat, cracked lip. Barry, the GM, had wanted to trade him practically since the moment he'd arrived. Billy had no idea why the hell they had brought him here in the first place.

Hornsby stopped pacing and the silence changed, got all loaded, like Billy had fallen into Hornsby's trap. Billy pressed one of his ice packs up to his lip, wishing he'd kept his mouth shut.

"You don't like sitting on the bench?" Hornsby asked questions like he was a six foot four, slightly balding Oprah.

"I don't like watching my team lose."

"And you think you would have stopped that?"

"Yes."

"By what? Fighting?"

"Maybe."

Hornsby sat down behind his desk, a sleek metal and glass table he kept annoyingly clean. Desks were supposed to be cluttered, covered in coffee cups and scouting reports. Hornsby clearly didn't read the NHL coach handbook.

"You know why I wanted you here?" Hornsby asked, adjusting his glasses up over the bump of his broken nose. Billy didn't like the guy, but he'd never have been able to trust him if it weren't for that nose. Men who'd never broken their noses shouldn't lead men who barely had cartilage left in their faces. It was a rule.

But then the guy went and ruined that broken nose with turtlenecks. Tonight it was a black one under a gray coat. Made him look like a sissy.

"Do you know why I worked so hard to convince Barry that an aging enforcer with more penalty minutes than shots on net needed to be a part of the team?"

"I have no idea, man," Billy said, twisting the toilet paper higher into his nose.

"I wanted a leader. Some experience on a young team."

"Yeah, well, put me on the ice and I'll lead the shit out of these guys."

"No, Billy. You'll fight. You'll shoot your mouth off, you'll piss everyone off."

"Sometimes that's what a team needs."

"Sure. Sometimes. But what I need all the time is someone who uses their brain, someone who'll show these kids how to play their way out of a 3–1 deficit."

Blood trickled down the back of Billy's throat and he coughed it up, leaned forward, and spit it into the garbage can beside his feet. He'd learned at an early age how to walk the very fine line between rude and insulting, between disgusting someone and getting the crap kicked out of you. And spitting blood into Hornsby's fancy garbage can rode that line pretty hard.

He looked right into Hornsby's eyes so the guy could make no fucking mistake and said, "I'm not that guy."

"You used to be."

Billy laughed and wondered when. Because he'd missed it, entirely.

"I've watched you, Billy. And you know, you used to play like a high scorer with thug tendencies—somehow that balance changed over the years."

Oh Jesus. This Oprah shit had to stop. "You want me to pay a fine or something for starting that fight? Do some community crap?"

"I want you to grow up and be the player I need."

"I've got one year left on my contract, Hornsby. Keep me on the bench next year, let Barry trade me, do whatever you want, but I am who I am. Nothing's changing that now."

"That's too bad, Billy." Hornsby folded his hands over his lean stomach. "Most players wouldn't want to go out that way."

Billy's temper snarled and spat and the urge to tip that desk right over was a tough one to control, especially since he wasn't used to trying to control anything. "We done?"

Hornsby sighed. "Yep."

Billy stood, turned, his kidneys throbbing, his eye swollen, and walked out of the office. The concrete hallways under and around the arena were still full of staff. Most of Hornsby's minions shook their heads as they passed him, like they were so disappointed in him they could barely stand it.

Billy smiled real wide at each of them.

Mike Blake stepped out of the PT room, his eye swollen shut and already going black. Even with the eye, he was still a good-looking kid. Farm-raised somewhere in the hinterlands of Canada, Blake had the blond hair and blue eyes that women were interested in, and a cocky smile that sealed the deal.

Blake never went home alone.

"Hey, man," Blake said, stopping in the doorway to button his shirt. He had to tilt his head sideways to see the buttons out of that busted-up eye. "How's the nose?"

"Fine." Billy yanked the Kleenex out of his nostrils, balling it in his fist. "How about the eye?"

"Doc said I need to have it checked out when the swelling goes down."

"Ah, shit, man, that's not right."

Blake laughed. "I'll live. That fight was the best part of the whole damn season. Hornsby give you a hard time?"

Billy shrugged.

"Look, we're heading over to Crowbar tonight, it'd be—" Billy rejected the idea, shaking his head, before Blake could even get it out. "Come on, man, the guys—"

"Don't need another fight." And that's what he felt like right now, the anxiety spinning his guts into a ball that wanted to put fist to face one more time.

"I don't know about that. You should come."

"Thanks, Blake. But I'm just gonna head home." He honestly wished the kid would stop asking him to go out with the guys. He was so tired of refusing; it made him feel old. In fact, the only thing that would make him feel older would be actually going to the damn clubs.

"You know, if you weren't living like a monk—"

Oh God, last thing he needed was a conversation about his sex life with the team slut. "Good night, Blake," he said, and made his way to the locker room to grab his stuff. Security had cleared out the press awhile ago, but somehow he wasn't surprised to find Dominick Murphy lingering around.

"Thought I smelled something bad," Billy said, grabbing his stuff from the locker. The insult was a weak one, but he just didn't have it in him to try and match wits with Dom.

The air was thick with the slightly nacho chip odor of sweaty hockey pads. The equipment manager had switched on the fans, but modern technology just hadn't solved the problem of stinky gear.

"It's your jock," Dominick said, sitting on the bench in front of Fforde's locker.

Billy's lip curled despite his best intentions. It was hard not to like Dominick.

"I've given you my quote."

"What did Hornsby say? Is he fining you?"

"He's buying me a steak dinner."

"Somehow I doubt it."

Billy sighed and pulled his duffel bag up over his shoulder. His kidneys didn't like the twist of his spine but he managed to swallow a wince. Dominick watched him through thick glasses. His salt and pepper hair was looking a lot more salty these days, and his beer belly had a good thirty years' experience.

Dominick was freelance, a hired pen, usually for *Sports Illustrated,* sometimes *Esquire* and *Rolling Stone.* As far as sports journalists went, they didn't get any better than Dominick. He could make you look like a hero in less than ten words. Of course, he could publicly castrate you with just as few.

And for some reason, the guy liked Billy.

Maybe because they were both dinosaurs. And dinosaurs had to stick together.

"You want to get a drink?" Dom asked. "Tell me a little more about that fight?"

"I'd rather let the Renegades have another shot at my kidneys."

Dom smiled and heaved himself to his feet. That beer belly could pass for a pregnancy from the side. Truly a commitment to poor health.

"I'll take it easy on you, Billy."

Billy didn't think much about his feelings. Except anger, which he made a study of. He was a professor of rage. The rest he ignored, but tonight it was hard to pretend not to feel anything about the sad state of his life.

Which was the only reason he opened his mouth and asked: "Why you so interested in me? Lots of guys go out the way I am, injured and old, sitting on a bench. Why you want to buy me drinks?"

"Because the best fighter in the league gets traded to a coach who's leading the charge for change in the NHL. Hornsby has supported every anti-fighting rule that the league recommends."

"So?"

"So? What's he supposed to do with you?"

Hornsby was probably right now cleaning out his garbage can and wondering the same damn thing.

"Nothing," Billy said and it was so much the truth it depressed him. He waved good-bye to Dominick over his shoulder, relieved that Dom was gentleman enough to let him go without further hounding.

The season was over. No early morning training to keep him honest anymore. The off-season stretched in front of him, a spring and summer pleasantly empty. His boat down on Padre Island was gassed up and ready to go. Maybe he'd finally teach his buddy Luc how to fish. Tomorrow he'd think about that.

But tonight loomed ahead of him, endless with its darkness and recriminations. Regrets came out with the moon, looking for their pound of flesh.

"I need a drink," he muttered.

He thought about picking up a woman. Someone soft, with sweet-smelling skin. Someone who would whisper all the right things. He tugged on his ear, his fingers brushing the thick ridge of scar tissue that curled from the corner of his lip halfway across his cheek.

There were women who liked the scar. Who had expectations of what sex would be like with a man like him. And usually he could go with that particular flow. But playing the marauder in bed wasn't something he wanted to do anymore.

Not since he'd seen Maddy.

The thought of her, the memory of her in that hallway three months ago, made him suck in a breath, like he'd taken a fist to the stomach. The shock on her face fading slowly to horror at the sight of him, just as he was fighting back a smile, the urge to run at her, throw his arms around her . . . ah, it gutted him every time he thought of it.

And he'd thought of it plenty over these past months.

She'd come out of nowhere like a lightning bolt illuminating how dark his life had become. And it was pitch black.

He'd run into her at the opening night party for the Crooked Creek Spa. Some friends of his owned the resort and Maddy had been there to do a story. Running into her had been an accident. An unexpected gift. He'd only been in Dallas for a few months at that point, and he hadn't even known she was in the city, let alone that she hosted a big-deal morning TV show.

She was famous, his Maddy. Accomplished and respected and more beautiful than he had words for.

And she had taken one look at his ugly mug and run away. Left him in that hallway, feeling the shame of the past like fire over his skin.

As a rule Billy didn't believe in fate, but having her

come back into his life when it was at its very darkest, that seemed important. Like something he shouldn't ignore.

Something he didn't want to ignore.

So he'd watched her show every morning for a month. Studied her face on his big screen, marveling at the hard stamp of her beauty. Parts of the girl he'd known were missing—the wild curly hair, those full womanly hips that she'd despaired of and he'd adored with unholy love. She'd gotten her teeth fixed and changed her name.

He'd grown up with and been married to Madelyn Baumgarten.

But the sparkling intelligent whiskey eyes, the laugh that could turn away every black cloud, those long legs and strong arms he still remembered wrapped around him—those parts were there.

He'd tried to contact her through the studio, but she hadn't returned his messages, and after a while he stopped trying, and a little while later it had started to hurt to watch her. It stung until he'd decided to turn off the TV and pretend like he'd never seen her.

And his life . . . it just got darker. This was his worst season of hockey, his career was in the toilet, and he was alone. Not the kind of alone he'd been for the last fourteen years, since she got into that elevator in Detroit, but *alone*.

Down to his gut alone.

Maddy was out there in the city somewhere. And the mere thought of her smothered the worst of his instincts. There weren't any more nameless women asking him to do terrible things to them. There hadn't been since he'd run into Maddy and been reminded that he used to be a better man. That he used to *want* to be better.

Punching open the door to the players' parking garage, he felt the wet heat of the Dallas spring night wrap around him like a slimy towel, and his white shirt immediately stuck to him. Fforde kept making fun of him for buying such cheap clothes. With his salary he could buy the kind of material that would never stick to him, no matter how hot it got. But he didn't give a shit about clothes.

What do you give a shit about? He could practically hear Hornsby's voice.

Nothing, he realized; hadn't for a long time. And if he was bored and slightly sickened by that fact—well, too bad.

He was Billy Wilkins and this was what he'd done with his life.

chapter 2

"Let me get this straight." Gina, Madelyn's hair and makeup goddess, met Madelyn's eyes in the mirror. "You still don't watch *The Bachelor*?"

"Why is this such a big deal to you?" Madelyn asked, distracted by Gina's half a bagel sitting on her dressing table. She was trying to prep for the show, but that bagel . . . it had lox on it. Salty lox on top of fatty cream cheese on top of a carby pumpernickel bagel. A trifecta of things she tried to pretend didn't exist.

"Because it's the best show ever?" With a little too much enthusiasm, Gina combed the ends of Madelyn's hair so that they rested flat and silky over her shoulders like obedient eels.

Beauty was painful, and Gina carried the whip.

Madelyn picked up her script, blocking the lox from sight. "Marriage isn't entertainment."

Gina blinked. "You got a point there."

"Ladies, can we focus?" Ruth, *AM Dallas*'s associate producer, sat curled up like a comma in the white chair in the corner. Behind her thick black glasses, her equally black eyes glittered. It kept with her whole monochromatic black-on-black look. Ruth had aspirations for New York and she practiced by dressing the part. "We've got changes to the script in between the Decluttering Your Junk Drawer segment and the one with Pierre, Cutting Your Own Bangs."

"Got it." Madelyn flipped past the change she'd read an hour ago. She liked to work as if every college professor who had ever doubted her journalism skills while staring at her chest was looking over her shoulder. It made her very, very good at her job.

Well, that and Ruth. She and Ruth had pulled *AM Dallas* out of the ratings basement, where it had been living under Phil Montgomery's care for years. In some ways they were like two polar opposite peas in a pod.

Very single, very limited social lives, very focused type-A personalities. They were a match made in a.m. television heaven.

"We've replaced the—"

"Section on sexual health with that stupid thing about gluten-free cheese?" The script rustled when she smacked it down in her lap. "All cheese is gluten-free. Always has been. What are we doing here, Ruth?"

Madelyn had worked hard, and in her game plan, *AM Dallas* was her last stepping stone to the network. To the *Today* show. And because that was her goal, there was a bar she was straining to hold herself and this show to. And even if she'd said it a million times, it bore repeating:

"Matt Lauer wouldn't do it."

Gina groaned. Ruth rolled her eyes. "What *would* Matt Lauer do? Really?"

"We want network jobs, we need network stories."

"They can't all be Day Care Fraud." Ruth arched a black eyebrow at Madelyn, reminding her of last month's fantastic success.

"I know," she agreed, both proud and sad of that fact. "But shouldn't we be trying?" Ruth didn't say anything and Madelyn regretted her outburst.

Richard, the station manager, liked to remind her that they hadn't hired her to be a journalist. They weren't changing the world on *AM Dallas,* they were informing it.

AM Dallas needed her to be the trusted, knowledgeable, well-dressed, and skinny best friend every woman in Dallas wanted to have. She didn't have opinions, or outrage or passion.

She smiled and told people about the delicious wonder that was gluten-free cheese.

Madelyn waited for Ruth to get up and leave, or to start barking orders into her headset. But she sat still. A little black cloud in Maddy's modern white dressing room. And that was odd. Ruth wasn't a lingerer. Which meant something was cooking under that black hair.

"I have an idea." Ruth pulled a newspaper from the bottom of the stack of papers in her lap. "Something Matt Lauer probably would do."

"I'm intrigued."

"But it's tricky."

"That's why they pay you the big bucks," Madelyn said. No one laughed at her joke—no one ever laughed at her jokes.

"They pay you the big bucks to fit into that Calvin Klein dress," Gina whispered, and Madelyn scowled at the hateful woman.

"What do they pay you for?" she asked Gina.

"Well, originally I was supposed to keep you skinny, but that's not working out so well, is it?"

"You're fired. Go tease someone else's hair."

Ruth snapped open the newspaper, the sound as effective as a whistle, and Madelyn and Gina shut up, watching as she folded the paper and flipped it around to show them the picture on the front page.

Madelyn's heart climbed into her throat and stuck there.

"Lord Almighty, that man is ugly," Gina said. "All the way ugly, too. You can see it in his eyes. That man is mean." Gina pointed a teasing comb over Madelyn's shoulder toward Billy Wilkins' bloody face on the front page of the sports section.

Yes, Madelyn thought, a chill settling into her bones. *Yes, he is mean.*

"Well, he's also the biggest news in sports right now. He caused a huge fight after last night's game against Boston." Ruth put the paper down in her lap. "He's a total Neanderthal. Unrepentant, too."

I have nothing to be sorry for, baby. This is hockey. You knew who I was when we got together.

"Madelyn?" Ruth said and Madelyn realized she was staring at her hands, her head in the past.

"Why are you bringing him up? Sports stories don't work on our demographic unless they're for kids," she said, pleased her voice was calm and solid, when inside she felt like quicksand. "You want him to talk about helmet safety?"

The idea was ludicrous and at least Gina laughed.

"You're hired again," Madelyn whispered and Gina patted her shoulder.

Ruth leaned forward in her chair, her eyes shining. "I don't want to do a sports story. I want to do a makeover story."

There was silence for a moment, the minute hand on the clock over the dressing table clicked backward and thundered forward. And then, thank God, Gina howled with laughter, bracing herself against Madelyn's shoulder.

"On that man?" she said. "It's going to take more than hair and makeup to fix up that mess."

"That's my idea." Ruth stood, paced to the rack of clothes lining the far wall and then back again, stopping in front of Madelyn like she was proposing the cure for cancer. "Let's do clothes and etiquette, table manners, maybe even anger management stuff. We could do cooking classes. The idea is to take this total piece of coal and turn him into a diamond."

"We can't," Madelyn said.

"Well, it might not work, but even that would be good television," Ruth said, misinterpreting Madelyn's words. "Could you imagine that man making cookies? It would be classic—"

"No." Madelyn stood up, practically towering over Ruth and Gina. Her dressing room was small and with the three of them standing, it seemed even smaller. Claustrophobic, almost. Or maybe it was the idea of Billy being on her show that was making it hard to breathe. "I mean, we can't do it. Our audience—"

"Will love it!" Ruth cried, and much to Madelyn's horror, Gina was nodding along. "This is a good story, Madelyn, and you know it. Phil would green light it—"

"No." Madelyn pulled off the tissue paper collar that was protecting her clothes from powder and hairspray residue. She shoved her feet into the red heels wardrobe had picked out to go with the gray pencil skirt, lace patterned stockings, and black gauzy blouse she was wearing today. The naughty-librarian look tested well with women. Go figure. "I don't like it."

Ruth blinked at her. "Why?"

Oh, for so many reasons, which would never see the light of day. "Because I bet he's terrible on camera. We've all seen post-game interviews with these guys. They're like . . ." She lifted her hands, pantomimed the robot dance. "Cyborgs or something. Totally lifeless. And I'm not spending the energy it would require to make him interesting for a fifteen minute segment."

"I was thinking a series. Once a week for a month."

A month of Billy? Not happening.

"A month? That's insane."

Ruth and Gina shared a look that Madelyn ignored.

She never played the prima donna. Ever. This was a first for all of them.

"And frankly," she said, lifting the paper, turning the picture up and holding it out at them so she wouldn't have to look at it. "This is not a face made for television. You want to make over a jock, great, get one of those pretty basketball players. But this," she shook the paper, "is a bad idea."

Ruth sniffed and pulled her shoulders back, the picture of slighted pride, and Madelyn didn't have the luxury of feeling bad for pooping all over her idea. Because the alternative might put her right back in Billy Wilkins' orbit.

"I won't do it, Ruth."

"Fine." Ruth grabbed the paper and gathered her work from the corner of the dressing table where she'd left it. "Be on set in fifteen minutes."

She left, turning down the hallway toward the *AM Dallas* set, where the live studio audience was filing in.

"What is wrong with you this morning?" Gina asked, folding her arms over her giant shelf of a chest. At times like this Gina was every disapproving Italian momma in the world, and she was a hard wall to walk into. "It's a good idea."

"No," Madelyn said, leaning over to apply her own lipstick, which pissed Gina off to no end. "It was a terrible idea. Trust me."

At six-thirty Monday, Madelyn walked into the morning meeting, fresh from her three-mile run. Her legs felt wobbly in her boots, but she'd been religious with her diet this weekend. And wardrobe wasn't going to be looking sideways at her any longer about fitting into that Calvin Klein dress for the spring promos they were shooting next week.

She had also brought donuts.

A peace offering to Ruth. Not that Ruth would eat them. As far as Madelyn knew, Ruth didn't eat anything but coffee and air. But donuts woke the staff up during the morning meeting and that made Ruth happy.

It was the first morning meeting of the month, so Phil Montgomery was sitting in. Wearing a Snoopy T-shirt. Snoopy, on a full grown man. An executive producer, no less. It went past ironic and into ridiculous.

And it was getting pretty obvious around the office that he was sleeping with Sabine, one of the segment producers. It made sense for Phil—Sabine was young and beautiful. But if Sabine thought sleeping with Phil would further her career, she had picked the wrong producer.

Light-headed from her run and high on the smell of donuts, Madelyn smiled at the idea of Sabine trying to seduce Ruth to further her career.

Hey, baby, I thought you might like to look at this New York Times *piece about online advertising budgets. Oh, and I brought you some coffee and air.*

"What's so funny?" Sabine asked, walking in behind her.

"Nothing. Sorry."

Both Sabine and Phil could get fired for sleeping together. Which seemed like a pretty risky move for Phil, who had two adultish daughters and an ex-wife who had taken him to the cleaners.

Maddy had often wondered how Phil managed to keep his job, but then she remembered the guy could maintain a budget like no other producer she'd ever worked with. Even the ones in public broadcasting.

And he was great with the crew.

Way better than Ruth. Every time Ruth had to deal with the unions there was talk of a strike and Phil, with his dumb T-shirts and shit-eating grin, would be sent in to smooth things over.

Where Phil did not shine was at Monday morning meetings. Every idea that she and Ruth had to carefully talk him out of was deeply tabloid in nature.

Phil liked the chair-throwing shows. And that was a problem. But usually Ruth could handle him, getting him to support her. Because if the two of them voted yes, the story idea got passed.

So the two producers made a strange yin and yang. Ruth was the brains, Phil was the . . . hypoglycemic kid hopped up on Coca-Cola.

"Morning, all," Madelyn said, sliding the dozen assorted into the center of the table, where the staff fell upon them like wolverines. "Good weekend?"

She vaguely listened as Sabine talked about the new club downtown. She had a hickey peeking up over the edge of the turtleneck she was wearing in an attempt to hide it.

You are a grown woman, Madelyn thought, embarrassed for her. Embarrassed because she knew Phil had given her that hickey. The two of them ignored each other with such force that they might as well throw off their clothes and have at it on the conference table.

Maybe you wouldn't get all nunlike at the sight of hickeys if you actually had some sex, she thought. But that wasn't going to happen unless on one of her early morning runs she stumbled onto a man and his penis entered her vagina in some freak accident.

Phil mentioned the new restaurant he'd tried. He said "filet mignon" like he wanted to personally wound her. But that might just be the diet talking.

"How about you?" Sabine asked and Madelyn made up a lie about a baby shower. These guys didn't want to hear about a weekend spent running and calculating the calories in croutons.

Slipping into her usual spot in the corner, she kept her eyes on Ruth, who was making notes on the forms in front of her.

Madelyn felt bad about the smackdown last week.

They were a team. Friends. She shouldn't have snapped like that.

"Our ratings are soft," Ruth said. "We're getting some pressure from advertisers to bring them back up, so we need big ideas, right now."

Pressure from advertisers made everyone sit up a little straighter and Madelyn took out the list she'd made while on her recumbent bike last night.

"Let's do a spring garden makeover giveaway," she said. Makeovers were huge ratings hits, as were giveaways. "We'll get viewers to send in videos and then we'll take the worst of the lot and totally revamp their backyard."

"Some of our advertisers will like that," Ruth said. "What else?"

Other ideas flew around. Madelyn was relieved when the idea of her going to Comic-Con in an Ork costume was shot down. She didn't even know what an Ork was and had no desire to dress up like one.

"I have an idea," Phil said and the room went silent.

Uh-oh, Madelyn thought, preparing to talk him out of midgets.

But then Phil opened his mouth and mentioned the words *four-part series, Billy Wilkins,* and *makeover.* All in the same sentence.

As a whole, the room loved it. Sabine clapped her hands like a little girl.

"I agree," Ruth said. "Let's chase it down."

Numb with fury and shock, Madelyn turned to Ruth, who decidedly did not meet her eyes.

chapter 3

An hour later, Madelyn stormed into Ruth's office, slamming the door so hard behind her it bounced off the casing and rebounded to bump her in the ass.

"What's the big idea, Ruth?" she demanded.

Ruth feigned innocence, but Madelyn wasn't having it and she glared at the other woman until she broke.

"Shut the door," Ruth murmured and Madelyn slapped the door away from her butt.

"It's a good idea," Ruth said, "and you know it." She sat back in her chair, crossing her arms over her thin chest. "You and I have not been shy about our plans for moving up into network."

"Right. But I thought we were working together."

"So did I. We both know this is a big story. A national story. A story that will get us noticed if we do it right."

Oh, God, Ruth was so right. Every word she said was totally right.

"Not if he's awful."

"He won't be," Ruth said. "You're too good at your job for him to be awful."

Ruth wasn't kissing ass. She'd always been totally up front about why she was hitching her wagon to Madelyn's star, and the two of them had served each other well.

"I said no."

Ruth stood up, stretching her hands out. Supplication

looked so fake on her, Madelyn nearly rolled her eyes. "Tell me why. Give me one good reason to throw away an idea like this and I'll do it. If it's that big of a deal, I'll do it. But so far, your reasons don't hold water."

He broke my heart. He devastated me. He's my past. He's every single skeleton in my closet.

But she couldn't say those things. She'd gone to incredible, drastic lengths to leave the old her behind. Changing her name was the least of it. And there was no way she was going to confide in Ruth that she'd been a doormat to a professional thug.

"I said no," she repeated, and Ruth sat back down. "That should be good enough for you."

"It isn't. But Phil said yes and that is good enough." Ruth shrugged her shoulders, bony and thin under her black scoop-neck shirt.

"There's no chance Billy Wilkins will agree to do this," Madelyn said, resisting the urge to pace. Ruth's office was so small she'd probably only get dizzy. But she had a window, while Madelyn had the bigger office and no window. The two of them had rock, paper, scissored for the offices when they were both new.

Don't you remember that? she wanted to howl.

"You might be right," Ruth said. "But it's worth a shot."

Madelyn bit her tongue, her lip. God, she wanted a bag of chips right now. A big salty bag of potato chips, the kind with ridges. And dip. Oh, yes, sour cream dip like her mom used to make. She wanted a pound of that.

"I thought we were friends."

Ruth seemed confused and Madelyn wondered if maybe she simply had the wrong idea about friendship. She never seemed to get it right. It was as if she thought she had a real banana in her hand and someone always had to point out that it was just a picture of one.

"It's business, Madelyn. Nothing personal."

Nothing personal? Oh my God, it was almost funny. Ruth had no idea what she was talking about. Because between Billy Wilkins and Maddy Baumgarten, it was all too personal.

"Fine, but I'm not helping you. You want him. You get him."

She walked out, hoping that was enough. Hoping that the proud, selfish, childish boy she'd known was still living in that terrifying man she'd seen at Crooked Creek. Because the Billy she'd been married to would never agree to do this show.

"We've talked about this before and the answer is still no." Billy should have known that his best friend's girlfriend had ulterior motives when she asked him to help her paint.

"I never pegged you for a coward, Billy," Tara Jean Sweet said as she cut the corners around the door with her white paintbrush.

He didn't dignify the insult with a response. Even if it was the stone-cold truth.

Painting was not Tara Jean's strong suit—there was white primer all over the trim, floor, her hands, her shirt—but she was gung-ho and Billy appreciated that.

"I'm reminding you of your civic duty. You have to go."

"I gave you a bunch of money, and I'll keep giving you money. You don't need me at some fancy party." Billy worked his way across the wall with his roller, trying to repair the worst of TJ's mistakes.

She threw her hands up, splattering primer across the floor. "Do I have to remind you that this school was your idea?"

"No. You don't. I've had the idea about the school for a long time, but that's all it was—an idea. You're the one who went nuts and hired consultants and started working on charter applications and fund-raising stuff."

"Because it's a great idea, and you're a great advocate for it. For crying out loud, Billy, you convinced Luc and me to commit to a charter school with a sports focus. Over beers. Imagine what you could do in a room full of people ready to spend money."

Tara Jean was a sweetheart, but this determination she had to see the best of him was getting a little old. "No one will believe it, TJ. Me, funding a school? I'll put people off."

"What bullshit." She turned back around and started priming the wall with a vengeance. "You're going. Like it or not. And you're getting a new tux and because you're being so dumb about all of this, I might even make you give a speech."

"TJ—"

"Did it ever occur to you that Luc and I might need you there? As a friend. The foundation is new and we've never done anything like this before—"

"Okay." He held up the brush, knowing when he was beat. If she was going to play the friend-in-need card, he had no defense. "I'll be there. Whatever you need."

She radiated pleasure. "I knew you'd see it my way."

Talk about a snow job. He rolled his eyes at her, just so she knew he was on to her. Oddly, though, he was not all that upset. He'd given his share of money and time to charities over the years, but he'd never been attached to something so big, something so . . . personal from the beginning.

The New School. The name was lame, but he hadn't come up with it.

Truthfully, he was amazed at how far Tara and Luc had taken this idea he'd had in his head for years. Though, considering the way Tara Jean was railroading him, he was sort of surprised she wasn't the governor of Texas by now.

The phone in Billy's back pocket vibrated and he dragged it free, wincing when the scabs on his knuckles broke open again.

"I'm not paying you to talk on the phone." Tara Jean eyed him sideways.

"You're not paying me at all." Billy sucked on one of the cuts. "In fact, I urged you to pay someone else."

Her blond ponytail, speckled with white paint, shook as she laughed. He totally understood why Tara Jean wanted to paint her own house despite having Luc Baker's fortune at her disposal. She had never had a house before and she intended for every inch of it to be her own. Including the paint on the walls of the living room.

The phone buzzed again and he glanced down. Relief that it wasn't Hornsby made him answer a bit more cheerfully than he usually would have.

"Hey, Super-Agent Man," he said.

"Do I have the wrong number?" Victor asked.

"Very funny. What's up?"

"Well, clearly paying thousands of dollars in fines and being suspended for the first four games of next season agrees with you, Wilkins," he joked.

"I'm just hoping you're calling with a big time endorsement deal. Surely someone wants my face to sell something."

Tara Jean scowled at him before walking out of the room to give him privacy. She didn't like his jokes about his looks—a little squeamish, clearly.

"No, actually, but I do have an opportunity for you."

Billy returned the roller to the tray at his feet and turned around to face the window. Luc and Tara Jean had bought a pretty farmhouse on an acre of land outside of Dallas. The stream in the backyard was surrounded by big cottonwood trees, perfect for a tree house in a few years. And that stream actually had fish in it.

Maybe he wouldn't teach Luc how to fish after all. Then he'd have an excuse to come over and spend time with the kids his friends would one day have. He smiled at the thought, even as he rubbed away the stabbing ache in his chest.

Upstairs there were four empty bedrooms just waiting for kids to fill them with all the crap kids came with. Diapers and toys. Little shoes. Bikes.

It was a house with a future.

A million years ago, he'd wanted that kind of future. Fishing, tree houses, painting rooms, a pretty woman to boss him around.

In fact, Luc's life was a lot like the life Billy had had in the palm of his hand.

Until he'd ruined it.

And now he only had visitation rights.

"What's the opportunity?" he asked. He wasn't all that interested, but if it could fill some of his empty off-season hours, that would be good. Though with his reputation and looks he couldn't imagine what opportunity would come looking for him.

"A morning show wants to give you a makeover," Victor said.

Billy laughed. "You're hilarious. Be serious, man."

"I am serious. A producer called my office wanting to talk about doing a four part series on you."

"A makeover? Have they seen me?"

"They have. And it's sort of a lifestyle makeover. Manners, clothes, they want to do a cooking segment, an anger management—"

"I hope you told them to fuck off." Billy turned away from the window as his temper started to simmer.

"I didn't, Billy—because, frankly, you could use something like this."

"Like what? Public humiliation? No thanks."

"It doesn't have to be humiliating. It could actually be humanizing. You could show the rest of the world the softer side of Billy Wilkins."

"I don't have a softer side," he said, thinking of that fight last week. With both hands he'd thrown away the last year of his career, because he'd been mad. Because he'd felt insulted.

"What are you doing right now?" Victor asked.

"Helping paint Luc Baker's house. Tara Jean wanted to do it herself and doesn't have the slightest idea how to hold a paintbrush."

"So you decided to help a friend."

"Yeah, but—"

"That's soft, Billy. And people would love to see that."

"Bullshit, Victor." He groaned. "No news show—"

"It's *AM Dallas,* that morning show on . . ." Billy heard Victor flipping through his notes over the sudden pounding of blood in his ears.

AM Dallas. Maddy. That was Maddy's show.

"Is Madelyn . . ." *What the hell was her name? Cornwall?* No, that wasn't right. *Cornish?* That was it. "Is Madelyn Cornish still on that show?"

"I don't know, man, I don't watch this stuff."

"Tara!" Billy yelled and she ducked back into the room. "Is Madelyn Cornish on *AM Dallas*?"

"Yep," she said.

"I'll take the meeting," he said to Victor. There was a moment of stunned silence. "Victor? You still there?"

"Yeah, I'm just . . . surprised. Hornsby is going to love this."

"I don't care, I'll still take the meeting."

"All right, I'll set it up and text you the details."

Billy hung up and looked back out the window, his

chest heaving as if he'd run six miles at a dead sprint. There was a good chance Maddy had some very public, very vindictive and humiliating revenge plan in the works.

"Billy?" Tara Jean stood in the doorway. She was beautiful, blond and stacked, blue eyes that could eviscerate a man with one glance. But to Billy, she was a poor second to Maddy Baumgarten on her worst day. And he'd seen that day. Caused it.

"You all right, Billy?"

Fourteen years ago he'd ruined everything. They were supposed to be a family—that was the promise they'd made to each other, and he'd broken it. Smashed it under heavy, callous heels. Because he hadn't known how to keep that kind of promise.

But he'd had some practice now. He thought of Luc and Tara Jean, all the guys on the teams he'd played with. He knew more about what it meant to be someone's family, the two-way nature of it.

Despite what had happened, how they'd crashed and burned and failed each other and hurt each other, all these years later, when he thought of family—real family, not his parasitic sisters, not his messed-up parents—he thought of Maddy.

Of her arms around him at night. Her strength and support.

"Let's get back to work," he said, stepping up to the empty wall and the paint.

"You know, if something's bothering you—"

"Don't you go all Oprah on me too, Tara."

He could feel her watching him, debating whether or not to press the issue, but then she sighed and went back to messing up the trim.

"Why did you ask about Madelyn Cornish?" she asked.

"I think I'm going to do her show."

Billy smiled when he heard TJ's paintbrush clatter onto the hardwood floor. She swore, using the edge of her Toronto Cavaliers hockey T-shirt to clean it up.

"I told you we needed drop cloths," he said.

"Billy, you always said those shows were humiliating."

"They are."

"Then why do it?"

His past, particularly the part about Maddy, was such ancient history he never talked about it. No one ever asked. A childhood failed marriage wasn't interesting to the sports journalists, who only cared about his penalty box minutes. And the guys on his team didn't even know.

But suddenly her name was on his lips again and it felt so good. It brought the worst of his past back to him, but it also brought the best.

It wasn't a mystery that he'd lost part of himself when she left. The part that cared what other people thought of him. The part that wanted to be worth something—namely her.

And with her absence, he'd pushed away what was left of his family, his friends from back home. His childhood. Because he couldn't stand his past without her there to make it tolerable.

When he finally ruined what had been left of them, she took his future, his past, and the best of him with her.

"Maddy and I grew up together, down the street from each other actually, and we . . . we used to be married."

Tara Jean's mouth fell open and he held up his hand, stopping the barrage of questions he could see coming. "We were like ten years old and I . . . I ruined it."

"What did you do?"

"Not your business, Tara. I'm sorry, but it's not." It

was Maddy's business and he knew that she'd kept it a secret, so he would, too.

"So is she just going to ask you questions? Or have you play hockey with kids? What?" Tara asked, looking small—but never frail—in her boyfriend's big T-shirt. He remembered Maddy like that, the sight of her brown legs under one of his T-shirts the hottest thing he'd ever seen.

"A . . . a makeover. Teach me how to dress, how to act. That sort of thing. She's gonna shine me up for Dallas."

Tara's eyes narrowed and he knew how it sounded, how the show would be debasing at best.

"You gotta admit, it's good TV and the Mavericks' PR folks are going to love it."

"Billy," she sighed, her eyes so sad on his behalf, which was sweet, but unnecessary. She had no idea how much he was looking forward to this. To seeing Maddy again.

"Don't worry about me, Tara," he said, spreading the last of the primer over the wall. "I can take care of myself, and if Maddy wants to humiliate me, I owe her that."

Tara Jean nodded and went back to priming her section of the room. In that silent moment he thought about his future and how, when you least expected it, the past came all the way back around.

Dressed up like a second chance.

chapter 4

The photo shoot for the spring promo was in full swing. Gina had done miraculous work, and when Madelyn looked in the mirror she didn't even recognize herself. She looked perfect. Airbrushed but breathing.

Which was exactly how you wanted to look when you were going to be on a billboard overlooking the North Central Expressway.

The blue Calvin Klein dress fit like a second skin from her chest down to her knees. Ironically, when she had stepped out of the changing area, Gina had clucked her tongue and told her she was too thin.

"What do you want?" Gina had asked in response to Maddy's incredulous look. "I'm Italian, part of me just wants to feed you manicotti until I can't see your hip bones."

Madelyn had thought about manicotti for a good twenty minutes.

"Less teeth, more eyes," Jerome, the photographer, said over the Beyoncé song on the sound system.

"Can we kill the wind?" she asked, doing exactly what he'd requested, closing her lips and smiling with her eyes, which were getting dried out from the fan blowing in her face.

"Yeah, let's try a few that way," Jerome agreed.

She tilted her head back, shifted her hips forward, crossed her arms, dropped her arms. She smiled. She looked serious. She laughed, tipping her hair back off her shoulders.

On the table next to the yellow and green screen they were shooting against, her BlackBerry rattled into her bottle of water.

All work stopped. Such was the power of a buzzing BlackBerry.

"Just a second," she said and Jerome nodded, already reviewing the digital shots they'd taken.

The latest message, from Ruth, bloomed on the screen.

Billy Wilkins meeting tomorrow morning after the show. 11:30.

Her own Brutus hadn't even had the decency to stab her in the back in person.

In a sudden panic, she began to sweat and it was so hard to breathe. So hard to pull in air past the anger and hurt that rolled through her.

Oh God, she thought. *I'm going to be sick.*

Forcing herself to calm down, to close her eyes and open her lungs, she yanked away the negative emotions like they were leeches.

The emotions belonged to the old her, stupid Maddy Baumgarten, the fool. The idiot who'd cared about Billy Wilkins despite his casual cruelty. Who had given him everything, only to be repaid in regret and embarrassment.

You are not that girl, she reminded herself. She'd shed that persona like a too tight skin. Lost all that irrelevant guilt and concern and worry, just like the twenty extra pounds she'd sweated off since divorcing Billy.

Losing the girl she'd been for twenty years hadn't been easy, but it had been necessary.

"Jerome?" she said, without looking up. She wasn't sure she could, her muscles felt frozen. Her entire body chilled to the marrow of her bones. "You get what you need?"

"Actually, I'd like to shoot a few more with the yellow backdrop."

Good. Great. Work would keep her focused. Work would remind her of who she was and, more importantly, who she wasn't. Work had pulled her from the black hole her divorce had sent her into, it had given her a new identity that had nothing to do with Billy Wilkins. With that useless girl she'd been.

As she stepped back under the lights, the blue of her dress glowed.

Every morning in this city people woke up needing weather and traffic and morning banter. Women sat down with their coffee, looking for a distraction from their screaming children. The population of Dallas was hungry to learn how to redecorate on a budget, find a pediatrician or make the perfect summer cocktail.

And they looked to Madelyn Cornish for all of that.

The girl outside that hotel room door fourteen years ago didn't exist anymore.

Thursday morning Madelyn was Patton, leading her morning show troops into battle. Joe the Cameraman's segment about racing through a local Target trying to get all the stuff for a spring break trip was funny and sweet. Every time the man opened his mouth, the female studio audience audibly sighed.

Bringing him up in front of the cameras had been one of their finer ideas.

Even the snake segment went better than expected. A reptile company was going to be touring local schools next week and *AM Dallas* had brought them in to air their highlights. The owner was so engaging and exciting that Madelyn didn't have to pretend to be scared, or get pooped on, just to make it interesting.

"Nice show," Joe said when the lights went cold.

"Thanks, Joe, and thanks for taking one for the team with that shopping segment."

"I'm not kidding, Madelyn, I'm too old for that shit." Tough as his words were, he grinned while he said them, his soft white face creasing into likeable wrinkles. "If it weren't getting me laid—"

She covered her ears with her hands. "No no no no, I can't hear you, Joe."

On the run, Madelyn grabbed her post-show water from Ramon. She guzzled it as she headed toward her office. There had been a snake around her neck for the last twenty minutes and she wanted to shower, change, and re-do her makeup. Before meeting with her ex-husband in half an hour.

"Good show," Ruth said as Madelyn turned the corner from the studio, toward the offices.

Screw you, Ruth. "Thanks."

"Meeting in—"

"I know." She glared over her shoulder as she rounded the filing cabinets and cubicles. "I'll be there for your meeting."

Ruth didn't even have the good grace to appear chagrined. She looked self-righteous, standing there in her three-year-old black wrap dress and boots.

We'll see, Madelyn thought, pushing open the door to her office with her butt. *We'll see who's self-righteous after this meeting.*

She turned in to her office, slamming the door shut behind her, and for a long and confusing moment her brain sent panicked messages to her body to run.

Dressed in an ill-fitting sport coat and a red golf shirt, Billy stood in the middle of her tiny office, not two feet away from her, taking up too much space and air. Space and air she needed.

Inwardly, she reeled, the earth lost beneath her feet.

Numb, she watched his eyes run down her body, taking

in the purple sweater and the black slacks. Her straight hair.

Obscenely, she was pleased that he wouldn't see much of the girl he'd married in her appearance. She was a stranger to him. But he—with his broken nose, that terrible scar, and the forward-thrust jaw, daring all comers to take a swing—he was all too familiar.

Wearing her indifference like a suit of armor, she tossed her water bottle onto the chair Ruth usually sat in.

"You can't be in here."

"I just wanted a chance to talk with you before the meeting."

She arched her eyebrow, fighting with super-human strength the desire to bite her thumbnail. "About what?"

"Maddy . . ." he sighed, as if disappointed that she wouldn't play along.

That sigh's effect on her composure was cataclysmic—the world went red. Her heart pounded behind her eyes and she wanted to push him through the wall.

But, instead, because she was better than what he wanted her to be, because she'd worked too hard to succumb to the controlling influence of anger and hurt, because, damn it, he couldn't do this shit to her anymore, she reached behind her and calmly opened the door.

"I think you should leave. I'll see you at the meeting."

He blinked, waiting as if she might change her mind.

You will get nothing more from me, she thought. *Not one more thing.*

The words echoed in the room, echoed between them as if she'd screamed them.

"I'm doing this show," he said.

She swallowed the growl lodged in her throat, where it joined—in the pit of her belly, where nothing ever vanished, where every slight and pain and injustice was kept and preserved—the millions of screams she'd swallowed during her short, disastrous marriage.

"That's your prerogative," she said, managing to keep the sneer from her voice.

Careful not to touch her, he slipped out the door.

Billy sat in what had to be one of the messiest conference rooms—in the middle of the stupidest goddamned meeting he'd ever been in—waiting for his chance to fight.

Victor sat beside him and Billy took some comfort in the man's quiet, sharklike demeanor.

The producer, wearing a Darth Vader T-shirt, kept grinning at Billy. He filled every gap in the conversation with questions about the fight at the end of the last game, like every other bloodthirsty hockey fan who met him on the street.

Maddy sat at the head of the table, her hair slicked back in a tight ponytail, surrounded by newspapers and magazines and women without half her shine.

She'd changed her clothes, taken off the pants and put on a blue dress that showed off how thin she was. She smiled at him, polite and removed, as if he were selling something cheap. And unwanted.

But beneath that chill, she was bothered.

She had to be. Right? Not that she'd seemed bothered in her office. But he had been . . . and he was now. Flop sweat, sticky and rank, ran down his sides in spite of the air-conditioning.

Back when they were married she would have been screaming at him. Throwing plates, coming at him with curled fingernails. She'd be hurling insults, vicious and true.

Somehow, she'd figured out how to curb all that. The ice queen at the top of the table didn't look like she ever screamed, and she certainly didn't look like she'd faced off against Kevin Dockrill in the cafeteria of Schelany

High School or destroyed every single CD in Billy's extensive Bruce Springsteen collection.

No, in fact, the woman sitting there looked kind of stupid. And like she barely gave a shit. She was pretty, sure—but she cultivated a certain emptiness. A cool distance.

For a stark and stomach-spinning moment, she seemed like a stranger.

Incredulous, he glanced at everyone else in the room to see if they bought this act of hers. And it didn't seem like they found anything strange about that vapid empty smile on her face.

He stared at her, waiting for her to break, to catch his eye. They might have had one of the worst marriages in the history of the world but they'd had years of incredible friendship preceding it.

Finally, while someone droned on about positive PR, she looked at him. Right at him.

What gives? he asked with the lift of his eyebrows.

And those eyes of hers flashed, her lips went taut.

Fuck you, dick-wad.

The room was suddenly electric with her fury. Everyone shifted awkwardly, glancing sideways at one another as if to see who'd farted.

Somewhere under that sleek hair and flawless face and anemic body was the woman he remembered. The woman who'd fought with him, fought for him, when no one else in the world would.

And this was his chance to fight for her. A chance to make right what he'd gotten so wrong.

He cracked his knuckles, ready for his opening.

"It's a series of five spots," Ruth, one of the producers, said, with a smile that was thin as melting ice. "First an introduction, we'll talk to some of your teammates and family—"

"My family?" he asked. "Why?"

"To hear stories about you as a kid," she answered smoothly.

"Really?" He glanced over at Maddy, but she was calmly inspecting her manicure like she had no idea who his family was. Or what they were. Like she hadn't been friends with his little sister, Denise, the two of them thick as thieves for a chunk of their childhood.

He shrugged, having made peace with where and how he'd grown up years ago. Of course, that peace came a whole lot easier with a thousand miles of distance between him and Pittsburgh.

"Feel free," he told Ruth, "but I'll warn you. I'm like Prince Charming compared to them."

Maddy laughed, once through her nose. Practically a snort.

"Well, then that will be interesting, won't it?" Ruth said, brightly. But it was hardly convincing. Ruth clearly wasn't used to being "bright." "We'll also talk to your teammates and friends in order to lay the groundwork for the makeover. For the second episode, we'll bring in a tailor. A manners expert—"

"Fine." He agreed quickly, a slap shot they weren't expecting. "Is there something I have to sign?"

"Let her finish," Maddy said. "You should know what you're signing up for."

"I get the gist."

"I don't think you do," Maddy shot back.

"Let them finish," Victor said, leaning forward as tensions were getting stranger in the room.

"As I said," Ruth cleared her throat, glancing sideways at Maddy, "we've got a tailor—"

"I understand."

"No," Maddy said. "I don't think you do."

Silence echoed. People leaned back in their seats.

"We're going to talk to your *family*, Billy." She arched an eyebrow but he didn't even flinch. "We will get your friends and teammates to tell us what a barbarian you are. How you can't dress and you act like a buffoon in social situations. How all you're good for is fighting." She paused, waiting for a reaction and even though he felt blood rise up in his neck, making the skin itch under his collar, he didn't give her an inch.

Her eyes narrowed and she leaned over the table. "And about that tailor. It will be a man—probably flamboyantly gay, because how funny will it be to watch the hockey bruiser get uncomfortable when the gay tailor flirts and measures his inseam."

"Madelyn—" Ruth said, but Maddy cut the woman down with a glance.

"Oh, Ruth, don't for a minute pretend you have any motive but making good television." Ruth was silent, looking sideways at the dude in the Darth Vader shirt, who simply shrugged. Maddy was melting down. The girl he knew was emerging, her hands sweeping the air in front of her, sarcasm dripping from every word. This was the street fighter inside her and no one in this room knew it but him.

Smiling to egg her on, he sat back and watched the show.

She stood, her chair screeching across the floor behind her.

"And the very best television you can make for us, Billy, is letting us rub your nose in your barbarianism. Letting us poke at you and laugh at you, letting us, in fact, get one million viewers to laugh at you. At what an animal you are. Letting us trot you out like a trained ape. And then when we try to clean you up and it fails—which it will, spectacularly!—we're going to need you to just take it, Billy. You can't fight. You can't walk away. You can't just leave when things get hard."

Silence boomed through the room.

"Madelyn?" Ruth said, louder and sharper this time,

and Maddy's mouth clicked shut. Everyone, her colleagues and her boss, were looking at her as if she'd turned into a werewolf.

And she knew it. Hives broke out on her neck and she lifted a hand as if she could feel them. Could hide them.

Too late he had doubts. *This is how you're going to use your second chance? Driving her nuts like this? You think it will endear you to her?*

This was a mistake. Once again he hadn't thought his shit out and she was paying the price.

"Perfect," Victor said. "That's exactly the kind of situation Billy needs."

"Needs?" Billy asked.

"Yeah, you need to prove that you aren't just a fighter. That you have a sense of humor."

"I don't."

Victor laughed. "See right there, very funny."

"Victor—"

"We're in."

"Excellent. So are we." The station manager leaned across the table and shook Victor's hand and then Billy's.

Maddy straightened, a tall goddess, her thin, manicured hands in fists, the blotches like wounds on her neck. "Welcome aboard, Billy," she said, calm once more. "It will be a pleasure having you on the show. Excuse me, but I have to get some work done for next week."

Everyone took a big sigh of relief when she left the room.

The producer in the stupid shirt droned on and on about new sponsors. National and local. The room seemed to buzz, and Ruth was suddenly animated, and almost pretty. But Billy's eyes were fixed on the spot where Maddy had stood, the blue of her dress seared into his brain.

Finally, Victor pushed to his feet, his phone in his

hand. "Let's go get some lunch," he said, not looking up from whatever crucial business was happening on his phone.

Billy had done it, he was back in her life. Now he had to make sure he didn't mess it up the second time around.

chapter 5

Madelyn drove slowly down Mulberry Lane, trying to find house numbers on the mansions that were set back from the street.

Having a research team at her disposal was a helpful perk, particularly when she wanted to find the addresses and phone numbers of people who didn't want to be found.

And in the suburbs, apparently addresses were a big secret. Lots of famous rich Dallasites were out here and for a minute she couldn't believe that Billy Wilkins had landed in this green suburban neighborhood. Preston Hollow was a long way from 12 Spruce on the Hill in Pittsburgh.

She checked the address on her BlackBerry and looked back up at the discreet numbers on the side of the giant garage attached to a glass and stone mansion.

The flower beds were empty but the grass was green and lush despite the spring heat.

This was Billy's house.

Getting Billy to back out of the show at this point was an impossibility. The station manager had sent a congratulatory fruit basket to everyone in that meeting. Unheard of. Advertising, giveaways—it had all been set up nearly the minute she walked out of that conference room.

If Billy backed out, they'd all be in trouble.

So she was here to find out what his motives were for doing the show. Because her freak-out in the meeting had to be a one-off. Her reputation, cultivated and groomed like prize roses, required her to be generally emotionless. Other than interest, surprise, and pleasure, she was a blank slate.

Anger, righteous though it might be, was a card very rarely played. Outrage, resentment . . . people didn't attach those emotions to her, so she couldn't afford to show them.

Which meant she and Billy had to come to an understanding. If he was going to do this, he was going to do it her way—which meant they were strangers to each other.

She pulled down the passenger-side mirror and checked her lipstick, fluffed her hair. Camera-ready on a Sunday morning.

As she walked up the stone path to the front door, the muffled sound of music thrummed up from the ground. The glass window in the door rattled in its casing.

Billy still listened to his music like a teenager trying to piss someone off.

He's never going to hear me, she thought, but she pounded on the door anyway before ringing the doorbell. She waited a few moments and then rang again. Frustration mounted as she stood there, knocking like an idiot, getting angry on about twenty different levels.

Sweat gathered in her armpits and trickled down her sides under the light cotton of her peasant blouse. Her makeup was going to run in this heat.

Suddenly, the door burst open, that muffled bass line coalescing into a familiar Bruce Springsteen song.

"Where's the damn fire?"

And there was Billy. Big, shirtless, and smooth. Sweat ran down the hills and valleys of his chest and shoulders, the ridged planes of his stomach, connecting the dots of his freckles and the scars from at least a dozen different surgeries across his pale white skin.

She swallowed the gasp that rose up in her throat.

Between the sweat and the daylight and that skin, which he'd inherited from his Irish mother, Billy gleamed. He was marble in sunlight.

There weren't a lot of people who could say they lived in their bodies the way Billy did. The way he always had. He wore his skin with the kind of confidence she'd never felt in her life.

Except with him, she thought. *With him you felt like the most beautiful woman in the world.*

"Maddy?"

She pulled her eyes away from a bead of sweat navigating his collarbone and glared at him. "Could you turn down the music?" she yelled.

And put on some clothes?

"Yeah . . . ah . . ." He stepped back awkwardly, suddenly boyish. The moment collapsed upon itself and it wasn't just now, it was twenty-eight years ago and she was going to her new friend Denise's house for the first time and Denise's big brother, eight to their six, had answered the door. Without a shirt over his concave little-boy chest.

And then it was summer and they were going to the pool and she was picking him up at his house in the car she'd gotten for her sixteenth birthday, and he was eighteen and fresh from a World Junior Championship. He didn't wear a shirt that whole summer.

And she was meeting him at the Rochester arena, her wedding band gleaming on her finger, his still hot body steaming in the cold air as he walked to her car.

"Put on a shirt," she'd cried as he got into the car. "It's freezing out!"

"I'm hot, baby," he'd said, kissing her with cold lips.

She'd seen him like this countless times in her life,

shirtless and sweaty, and every time—every single time—the sight of him boomed through her, the echo touching everything visceral and sexual in her body.

Madelyn loved Billy Wilkins' body.

And that wasn't just in the past tense.

Oddly enough the realization did not cheer her up.

"You want to come in?" he asked, still yelling over the E Street Band.

"No. I want to stand out here and sweat."

He smiled at her sarcasm, which was the opposite of her intention, and vanished down one of the hallways leading away from the foyer. And then, despite the wild dogs of her doubt and pride growling at her not to put one foot into Billy's house, she stepped inside.

In front of her was a big and airy room, with a brown leather sectional on one wall and a giant television on the other. There were pictures on the walls, but she ignored those. She wasn't interested in the memories Billy chose to treasure.

She did not step past the stone foyer, instead, she braced herself there and waited.

The music stopped and Billy came back down the dark hallway, toward her. Still no shirt, but he ran a towel over his head and down his face, leaving his silky brown hair a mess.

The past threatened to swamp her and she looked away. Focused instead on the view out of the floor-to-ceiling windows of the great room.

It was an ocean of green out there. Apparently he'd never heard of the water ban.

"Sorry," he muttered. "I was working out. Can I . . . can I get you something? Water? Beer?"

Beer. If he knew how long it had been since she'd had a beer, he'd probably die.

"I'm fine."

"Okay." He threw the towel over his shoulder and

braced his hands on his waist, his fingers catching on the elastic waistband of his gray workout shorts. Briefly pulling it down over that thick ridge of muscle at his hips. She used to kiss that muscle. Test her teeth against it until he groaned.

She yanked her bag up higher on her shoulder. "We need to talk."

"Yeah. I'm sorry about that meeting," he said.

That took her aback, made her recalculate her route.

"I didn't mean for it to go that way."

"Really? How did you think it was going to go?"

"I don't know. I guess I didn't think that far ahead."

"Classic Billy. Tell me, why are you doing this show?"

"My image. You heard Victor—"

"Oh please, Billy. You don't give a shit about your image. You never have."

"A guy can't change?"

"Not if he's you."

That grin, macabre and strange, pulled and twisted by the pink knot of his scar.

She knew there were millions of people in the world who believed the scar made him ugly. In her eyes, however, it was one of the most beautiful things about him. Maybe because she knew how he'd gotten it. She looked at that scar and remembered him leaning out the window, telling her everything was going to be fine.

"It's been years, Maddy. I might surprise you." He walked away, down the beige steps into the great room and then through it to the kitchen.

"What are you doing?" she asked, her purse falling from her shoulder.

"Getting a beer," he yelled back, out of sight. "Come on in."

She stared at the carpet, the stacks of athletic shoes by the door, as if they were snakes waiting to bite.

The feel of her colleagues' eyes—Ruth's eyes—staring

at her with horror and fascination in that meeting had kept her up for three nights.

Like a knife at her back, the memory forced her to walk into his kitchen, even though everything in her gut told her to leave.

It was getting darker outside, the brilliant blue of the Texas sky bruising at the edges, and the kitchen was shadowed when she stomped into it. Billy sat at a round mahogany table, his body a muscled curl. He looked so brawny in his clothes, but naked he was sleek.

She used to love touching him. Could run her hand down his back for hours.

The memory started unpleasant fires in places in her body that had grown used to being cold.

No, she thought, resisting, denying him and his brute appeal. *Not him. Not again. We like sophisticated men,* she told her unruly hormones. *We like men with class and dignity. Men who like art and culture. Who drink wine and wear shirts.*

Her hormones weren't listening.

He held up a beer, at home in the surprisingly warm kitchen with its granite countertops and pretty red tile backsplash. His house looked surprisingly like a home.

"You sure you don't want one?"

"I'm not here to drink."

"You changed your name."

She blinked at the sudden shift in subject. "Baumgarten isn't exactly made for television."

"You were Maddy Wilkins."

"Did you think I would keep your name?"

His indifferent shrug sent her into some dark, angry places. He'd used that indifference against her for the last year of their marriage, making her feel crazy. Like her suspicions and worries were insane.

She stared at him, her reasons so obvious a child could see them. Or even a man as rock-headed as Billy.

"That's what I figured," he finally whispered.

"So you can imagine why I'm concerned about you doing this show."

"You think I'm planning to go on air and tell everyone your real name? Imagine the scandal."

"None of this is funny, Billy. I have no idea what you're planning. That's why I'm here."

"Well," he rubbed his chin, the sound of his hand over the scruff of his beard loud in the quiet house. "I don't know if you saw my last game . . ." He paused as if waiting for her commentary. She used to do that, years ago, help him analyze his game, find the places where he could improve. Hockey had been something they shared . . . before it tore them apart.

"I haven't seen a single minute of hockey since our divorce."

"Really?" Why he sounded sad was beyond her. "You used to love it."

No, asshole, she thought. *I used to love you.*

She slammed her bag down on the table.

"Cut the crap, Billy. This isn't about your image, or that fight—"

"You did see it." Only he would sound proud. She ignored him.

"You're coming onto my show, ready to debase yourself, willingly. The Billy I knew would never do that. Why," she enunciated each word, "are you doing the show?"

For a long moment his fingers pulled at the edge of his beer label.

"Because I wanted to see you. Because after seeing you at that spa thing, I . . . I missed you."

Oh. Unable to look at him, she turned away, wanting to leave. Desperately wanting to get out of there. She'd expected this, but not really. Not with that naked honesty in his eyes.

"You don't get to miss me," she told the stainless steel fridge. "You don't have that right."

"I know." He took another sip of beer, somehow forlorn and resigned. "Believe me, I know."

She grabbed her purse, clutched it, a life raft in turbulent seas. "You miss having someone who makes your dinner, keeps your stats, rubs your shoulders after a loss. You don't . . . you don't miss me."

"No?"

"You don't even know me. You barely knew me when we were married."

"How can you say that? We grew up together! You were my best friend, and I'm pretty damn sure I was yours."

"Oh please, Billy. Our whole marriage was about you. About hockey. Your career." Distantly, she realized she was falling right back into her role with him. The nagging wife. Shrewish and hurt.

"That's not how I remember it."

She stared at him until she crushed that twinkle in his eyes. Until nothing remained but the hard rock and grit of the past. Of who they'd been to each other. And what they'd done.

Rising from the table like some kind of gladiator, he braced his hands on it, the outrageous musculature of his chest flexing, the veins and sinew standing out in relief. She was suddenly breathless with anger and *want*.

"I didn't cheat. Ever. From the homecoming dance until I signed the divorce papers, I didn't cheat."

She'd had fourteen years to pull herself back from the wild ledge of emotions their marriage had put her on. Now she was able to be calm. "I know. But that wasn't the point, was it?"

"That night . . . the hotel room."

She held up her hand. "I really don't want to talk about this."

"You think I do?"

"Then why are we doing it?"

"Because it's here!" He pointed at the table as if that night was sitting between them on its mahogany surface, that girl in the bright pink dress and all that heartbreak, right there. He pointed to his head. "It's in here. And it's been killing me for a lot of years."

"I had told you I was leaving. The night before, I told you I didn't want to be married, that it was over." The things she'd said echoed through the years; she still felt bad. "I don't know what I expected, flying to Detroit like that."

"That night . . . the hotel . . . I swear nothing happened."

She was suddenly so tired of all of this. Of carrying this anger around in hidden pockets and secret compartments for years. Perhaps that was why she was here, really, to finally set this burden down.

"It doesn't matter anymore." She meant what she said—she wasn't sure if this was forgiveness, or just weariness, but she was ready to be done with this old madness. "We were kids, Billy. And everyone knew what we were too blind to see; we were too young. Your career was just taking off."

"No. Maddy . . ." He stepped toward her and she shifted back, wanting the distance. Needing it. But Billy kept walking, until he was a foot from her. She could smell him, salty and raw.

It made her breathless, dizzy.

"You . . . you were right, all those years," he said. "I was selfish and disrespectful. An idiot. And yeah, I was a kid, but I loved you. Christ, Maddy I loved you so much and I treated you like an afterthought. You were so sad and so angry after your dad died and I didn't know how to handle it. How to make you feel better.

And I'm more sorry than I can say for the way things ended. You deserved better. You always did."

The words blew holes right through her chest, tearing through bone and muscle and blood, and it hurt. It hurt so much she gasped for breath. He'd apologized a million times, the words so easy for him, because he never really applied his guilt to them. It was easy to say sorry if you didn't actually mean it.

But now he sounded guilty. Agonized with it.

"Maddy," he sighed, more naked in front of her than he'd ever been in their marriage. He touched her fingers, slowly gathering them into his giant palm. His skin was hot and that heat sizzled up her arm, spreading through her body, frying her nerve endings. Her skin recognized his touch, his heat. Like an old code she'd forgotten, her body remembered him, and responded. Opened.

She snatched her hand away.

"Nothing will ever happen between us, Billy. You have to know that." Looking into his eyes, she could tell that he didn't see. "You can't screw around with my show, thinking you can change my mind."

He leaned back against the granite counter, a bowl of apples behind him. Apples. Honestly, in a warm wooden bowl. It was like he lived in a catalog. "I won't use the show, but is it impossible to think that this might be fun?"

"You've taken a few too many shots to the head."

"We used to have fun."

"We were different people, Billy."

He rolled his head on that thick neck of his, and she heard tendons pop. "I feel the same. Older, maybe. But I still feel like the kid who grew up down the block from you."

"That's your problem." She laughed. "That's always been your problem. You don't change, Billy. You're the same reckless, single-minded, selfish kid you always were." He absorbed her words like blows and she wished she had more to fling at him.

But that wasn't why she was here.

Professional. She needed to be professional.

"And my name is Madelyn. No one calls me 'Maddy' anymore."

That was as good an exit line as she would get.

"We'll be in touch," she called over her shoulder and left. Out the door and into her car and she didn't look back, not once. Not until she was sure he couldn't see her.

But where it clutched the steering wheel, her hand still felt him. Like a brand, it burned.

chapter 6

Sixteen years ago

His blood hummed in his veins and despite the shower and the Gatorade he couldn't calm down. His first NHL game and he'd nailed it.

He'd fucking nailed it.

"Press conference," Georges St. Bleu growled as he walked by Billy, who was still wearing only a towel. Still sweating. "Five minutes. Get dressed."

"Yes, Coach," he said and started to throw on his clothes.

"Good one out there, rookie." Oh God, it was Vincent Larue, the goalie. The legend. Future Hall of Famer, two-time Olympic gold medalist, three-time Stanley Cup winner. Vincent hadn't said one word to Billy since he'd gotten called up from Rochester. Barely looked at him.

But after Billy's two assists and . . . well, that fight, now the guy was talking to him. Billy had turned the momentum with that fight.

"Thanks, Vincent. You too. I mean, I thought Jackson had you there at the end; but man, you were like a wall, nothing could get past you."

Vincent's smile was razor sharp. "Doing my job. How is your face?" Vincent pointed to his own face and Billy felt the cuts and the swelling from his fight. His eye was the worst. And he had a tooth that felt a little loose, but all of it was secondary compared to the long scream of jubilation in his gut.

"It's fine."

"Good. Some of the boys, we all go out afterward. Steaks, some drinks, we unwind. Montreal is a fun city."

"Are . . . are you inviting me?"

Vincent smiled, revealing his own missing tooth. "Yeah, Billy. We're inviting you."

"Of course!" His voice cracked—oh God, his voice actually cracked. "I mean . . . yeah. That would be great."

"Here's the address." Vincent handed him a card and Billy tucked it into the pocket of his coat, which was hanging behind him.

"Wilkins!" Georges hollered from the door leading to the press room.

"Crap!" Billy pulled his shirt over his head, his hair still dripping from the shower.

Ten minutes later he was in front of a wall of cameras, trying not to blink every time a flash went off, but it was hard.

"Billy!" someone cried, a faceless voice behind the lights. "How do you feel after that game?"

"Great." He laughed. "Who wouldn't feel great?"

"Popov is out with a possible concussion," someone else said. "Any comment?"

"Popov dropped the gloves. Not me. And he's got a hard head, I'm sure he'll be back tomorrow night."

Georges laughed beside him and clapped his shoulder. "Billy's fight turned the game around for us," he said. "Pulled our boys' heads out of their asses. I've never seen a player get pulled up and make such an impact on a game."

Billy felt like his head had lifted off his body, like he was looking down at some beaten-up, nobody kid getting his whole freaking life handed to him.

In the corner, where the lights didn't blind him, was Maddy. His Maddy.

He'd done it tonight. All that faith she had in him, the sacrifices she'd made for him—tonight he felt worthy of them. The smile on her face was beautiful and radiant and proud—so damn proud, it was like looking into the face of the moon.

I love you, he thought, willing it across the room and into her head.

I love you, too, her eyes said right back.

There were a few more questions about the fight and then some suit from the front office cleared the room. When the guy put his hand on Maddy's arm to try to push her out, Billy stood.

"That's my wife!"

Everyone who was still in the room stared at him, openmouthed. She looked young, he got that. And his marriage wasn't common knowledge. But he scowled at them just the same.

The suit lifted his hand from her elbow and she nearly ran toward Billy and he would have jumped over the table to get to her if every single square inch of his body didn't hurt. He was starting to feel those body shots. He circled the table and met her in the empty space between the chairs.

Her arms went hard around him and he crushed her to his chest.

"You did it," she whispered fiercely into his ear. "You did it, Billy."

"I can't . . ." He felt tears well up in his eyes and she seemed to know it, turning them slightly so no one could see his face buried in her beautiful hair.

"I'm so proud of you, baby," she whispered. "So

proud. Although," she leaned back, smiling up at him, "I don't know why all they asked about was the fight. You had two assists and twenty shots on net. You were more than just that fight."

"But the fight was pretty awesome."

She touched his face, the bruises and swelling, the cut at his lip. "I hate watching you get hit."

"Just doing my job." He took Vincent's line and tried to smile, but his lip stung so much that he stopped.

"Oh, honey, let's take you home."

"Hey, no . . . actually, Vincent asked me to go out with him and some of the guys."

"Oh." She blinked and then mustered a smile, his beautiful girl. "You should totally go. Celebrate."

"Come with."

"Billy, I'm twenty—"

"No one will care if you come in with a bunch of Pit Bulls. And it's Montreal, I don't think they care about that here. Come on, it will be fun. Vincent said something about steaks."

Her eyes lit up at the mention of steak. His little carnivore would do just about anything for a good steak.

"Let's go!" she cried, her happiness making her buoyant. She curled her hand around his arm and they headed out the door, into what felt like a brand new life.

The taxi dropped them off in front of a building sandwiched on either side by what could only be strip clubs. The letters *XXX* meant the same thing in French. He checked the address on the card. They were in the right place.

"Billy," she said, staring up at the building. "This is the red light district."

"Yeah, I bet the guys come here because there's no press and they don't get hassled." Or something.

"I don't know."

"Let's just check it out." He knew she didn't want to be here, just like he knew she'd roll with it if he pretended not to understand that. She was good like that.

"You really want to go in there?"

"I got invited, Maddy. I said I'd come. I'll bet there are other wives here. You'll be able to make some friends."

It took her a second but she finally agreed.

They walked up the stairs to an old brick and stone building that didn't have a name on it. If it weren't for the red light above the door, you wouldn't even think it was a club. You wouldn't even think anyone was there.

His skin prickled at the thought. It was so exclusive it practically didn't exist. How cool was that?

A giant man with no neck opened the door for them, the sound of music pouring out all around them. But not that cheesy dance stuff—which gave him hope that there wouldn't be naked women dancing inside.

"Who are you?" the giant asked, his voice so low the ground practically shook. It took Billy a second to wade through the man's French-Canadian accent to understand what he meant.

"I'm . . . ah . . . I'm Billy Wilkins."

The guy stared at him, tilting his head to look at the scar, and then his dark face split into a grin. "Nice game tonight. Hell of a fight." He clapped Billy on the shoulder, ushering him inside. But then he held up a hand, stopping Maddy.

"She's with me," Billy said.

"I'm his wife," she clarified and the bouncer glanced between them and then shook his head, chuckling like he knew a punch line they didn't.

"Go right ahead," he said and Billy stepped into a dark alcove shuttered by thick curtains. Music thumped and boomed in the small space. When Maddy reached his side, he pulled back the dark fabric.

Instantly, his heart plummeted.

There wasn't any stripping, per se. But the girls were wearing practically nothing and were curled up on the laps of his teammates, looking like they would take off what little they had on without much asking.

All the guys sat in low, leather chairs, a big table between them, covered in food.

"There's your steak," he said, brightly, hoping she might be blinded by the steak and not see the girls.

"Billy?" she whispered, her eyes wide.

A beautiful woman wearing a blue dress that hugged every curve and hollow of her body came up to them. He didn't look, he honestly didn't. He kept his eyes on the woman's. Beside him, Maddy stiffened.

"Can I take your coats?" she asked in a French accent.

"No," Maddy said, quickly. Too quickly. She wasn't mad, she was just nervous.

The woman in blue left and Maddy pulled on Billy's hand.

"It's French, babe," he said, trying to calm her down, because he wanted to stay even though she was uncomfortable. "It's just the way things are here."

Vincent, at the table, stood slightly, waving Billy over.

"Come on," he whispered, pulling Maddy along with him. They got to the table and he shook hands around the table. It was Vincent and five other guys. Christ, talk about being invited into the inner sanctum.

Belznick; Reed; O'Hare; Bern, who didn't play tonight because he was injured; and Murphy. All of them with Stanley Cup rings.

So. Fucking. Cool.

"Who is the girl?" Vincent asked in his ear.

"My wife." He turned to introduce her, but Vincent stopped him.

"Wife?"

"Yeah. Maddy."

"Dude. Do you see any other wives here?"

"Uh, no."

"That's right. We don't bring wives."

"But . . . she's cool. I mean . . ." He didn't know what he meant.

"So's my wife," Vincent said. "But she sure as hell isn't here."

Vincent leaned past Billy and looked at Maddy, his smile sincere. "Your husband was awesome tonight," he yelled over the music. Maddy's face lost some of its stern white lines.

"Yes." Her eyes rolled over Billy with hot familiarity and pride. "He was."

"Have a seat," Vincent said, pulling out a chair for Maddy, acting all chivalrous, and Billy felt like he was getting a lesson in lying. A lesson in living two lives. "You want some steak? There's not much else on the menu tonight."

"Steak is perfect."

Vincent lifted his hand and made a gesture to the woman in the blue dress, who vanished behind another set of dark curtains.

Their steaks arrived. He ordered two beers and gave one to Maddy; no one batted an eye at her being underage. He touched the neck of his bottle to hers, but she didn't smile. She drank like she was dying.

At the front of the table one of the girls took O'Hare's hand and led him away to a dark corner. In the shadows he saw the flash of her white skin as she peeled off her dress and danced for him.

He tried not to be turned on, but it was impossible. The game, the invitation, the shadowy corner where the girl was dancing: all of it made Billy's blood pound.

"Billy," Maddy whispered. "Let's go. You want a dance, I'll dance for you. But this place isn't us—"

"Billy!" Reed yelled from across the table. "You put

Popov down tonight, man." The other guys started talking about the fight and Billy felt himself expand under their praise. These men, these veterans of the game, they accepted him. They'd invited him into their world. Their party.

He glanced back at his wife, whom he loved with all his heart.

Next time he wouldn't bring her.

chapter 7

Ruth didn't let any moss grow under her ass—they were scheduled to tape Billy's introduction episode on Friday.

On Wednesday afternoon Madelyn declared a temporary and necessary detante and knocked on the door of the editing suite.

"Go away!" Ruth yelled, which is what she yelled at everyone, so Madelyn walked in anyway. The room was dark, a series of cubicles off a long center hallway, with editing equipment tucked into each one. She followed the flashing lights and the dim hum of audio to the back cubicle where Ruth was sitting with James, their senior editor.

On the screen was Luc Baker, former NHL player and one of Billy's friends from way back.

"How's it coming?" Madelyn asked.

Ruth pulled off her dark-rimmed glasses. "Good. Really good. The guys love Billy but they love making fun of him, too."

Madelyn crossed her arms over her chest. "Sounds great." Her sarcasm was unmistakable.

"It's good-natured. Honestly. We had to find an ex-girlfriend to get anything concrete. I think you'll have a lot to work with on Friday." Ruth was clearly trying to extend some kind of olive branch, but Madelyn wasn't interested.

"I came in to see if you'd found his family."

Ruth put her glasses back on and turned toward the screen. "Trim that up a little," she told James. "Let's cut him off after the laugh. And use the headphones, would you?" Ruth asked James and then came around the partition to stand in the dark, a foot away from Madelyn.

"Phil's handling the family—he said he couldn't find any of them."

Maddy blew out a long sigh. Thank God.

"Why do you ask?" Ruth's eyes were black and sharp behind those glasses. "Ms. Baumgarten."

Of course, Madelyn thought, *I'm just surprised she didn't find out earlier.* Ruth was a search-under-every-rock kind of woman.

"Spill it Ruth, I can tell you're dying to."

"You and Billy were married for two years," Ruth said.

"A long time ago."

"Why didn't you just tell me?" Ruth asked. "When I brought up the idea—"

"Because it's not something I talk about. Ever. And I don't want to talk about it now either. Promise me it's not part of the show. Do me that courtesy."

"I wouldn't have pushed if I'd known."

"Yeah, Ruth, you keep telling yourself that. Just promise me that my marriage won't be part of the show. And if Phil finds Billy's family, you let me know. They're bad news."

"How bad?"

For a moment she thought of how Denise's addictions had made her blank. Empty. And Janice had been all too full of jealousy and resentment. Madelyn hadn't seen them since before the divorce, but she had a hunch they'd probably only gotten worse. People like that usually did.

"Very bad."

"Okay. I promise."

Madelyn wasn't sure she could trust Ruth, but it wasn't like she had any choice. "Thanks. See you tomorrow."

"This is going to be great. I know it might be hard to see that right now, but it's going to be amazing. For all of us."

"I hope you're right."

Billy was mad. He was mad because it was five a.m. on a Friday morning. Which was ungodly, really. Unless he had to be on the ice, there was no reason to be up at five a.m.

And he was in a suit. Which he hated.

Plus, the little impish teenager person in charge of his makeup had been smoking crack. Clearly.

"You're kidding, right?" Billy asked the girl when she came at him with mascara.

"Nope." The girl advanced, the little black wand thing outstretched, and Billy shook his head. "Trust me."

"No."

"Mr. Wilkins . . ."

"Back off," he said and put his hand against the girl's forehead like kids do.

"Gina!" The girl screeched and Billy dropped his hand just as Maddy and a formidable Italian woman rounded the corner.

"What's wrong?" Maddy asked, putting her hands on her lean hips. She was wearing green today and her eyes glowed. She looked gorgeous. Though a couple of steak dinners wouldn't hurt her.

"Tell me," the makeup imp flung her hands up in his direction, "what am I supposed to do with him?"

"Charming the crew already?" Maddy lifted an eyebrow, watching him in the mirror.

"Powder is fine. I don't need anything else." He shrugged, his skin flushed at her nearness. He could touch her if he wanted. Just reach out and stroke her face. Her hair. He wondered what she would do if he tried to hug her.

Because truth be told, he could use a hug right now. There was no way this show was going to be anything but painful. Even if he didn't end up a laughingstock, he still had to wear makeup, and get his hair fussed with. And that didn't even include the lights and that set out there. The stools where he guessed he and Maddy were going to sit and talk.

Talk. For like twenty minutes. About something other than hockey.

Could he do that?

Should have thought of that before, huh, Wilkins?

The makeup girl laughed. "You need a whole lot more than powder, buddy."

He looked at her, slightly incredulous. "I could squash you. You get that, right?"

"Okay, Sue," Maddy said, stepping in. "Let Gina finish up with Billy."

"Fine!" Sue stomped off and the Italian woman leaned over his other shoulder. She and Maddy stared at him in the mirror.

"I feel like a bug," he muttered.

"We can't hide that scar," Gina said, ignoring him.

"The point is *not* to hide it," Maddy said.

"You want me to highlight it?"

"No. Lord, no."

"That nose is going to cause a problem," Gina said.

"You know," he muttered. "I'm sitting right here."

"Blush and powder," Gina said, her eyes darting down his body. "What about that suit? I'm pretty sure wardrobe's got to have something from when Hugh Jackman—"

"What's wrong with my suit?" He'd spent a couple hundred bucks on it. Granted, he might not have tried all of it on, but still.

The women just laughed over his shoulders.

"Did you iron that shirt?" Maddy asked.

"It's new."

"I can tell." She pointed to the crease where the shirt had been folded. "Do you even own an iron?"

"This is bullshit." He pulled the paper towel thing from around his neck and shifted to stand.

Maddy put her hand on his shoulder and he stopped. All of him just stopped, completely reined in by her touch. His heart would have stopped if she'd asked it to.

"This is what you signed on for," she said.

"Out there." He jerked his thumb over his shoulder at the set, where people were testing lights. "Not here. Not . . ." He sighed, hands on his hips and then finally blurted, "Not you."

He watched her in the mirror. Her cool imperial beauty. Would she give him this? Any sane man would have his doubts.

"Can you give us a second, Gina?" she asked and Gina vanished into the shadows behind the set.

"You can have your pound of flesh, Maddy. I owe you. But Christ, it's going to be hard enough going out there—"

Awkwardly she patted his shoulder. "Okay. You're right."

She tucked her hands out of sight, like secrets she had to keep. Her gaze touched his face, and he would have given anything for her actual touch right now.

"Have you seen the video footage?" he asked.

"Yeah. Ruth found an ex-girlfriend."

"Ex . . . ?" He couldn't for the life of him figure out who would be an ex besides the woman standing behind him.

"Sandra Marks."

He groaned. Sandra had been a black six month period in his life about three years ago. "Ruth must have really dug to find her." The wood grain on the arm of his chair was suddenly fascinating. "What about my sisters?"

"Apparently we couldn't find them."

"That's too bad." The bitterness and sadness tasted like chalk in the back of his throat. "They'd make good television, wouldn't they? Very Jerry Springer."

"I don't do that kind of television, Billy."

"Of course not. Did . . . did they find out about us?"

Maddy nodded. "Ruth did."

It was so strange to feel bad for her because of her association with him. "Even if she put it on the front page of the paper, no one would believe you were slumming with a Wilkins."

"I was never slumming."

He pointed at their reflections in the mirror. "Look at us."

Both of them came from nothing, and he still carried the dirt of 12 Spruce under his nails and in the seams of his suit. But she looked like her dress cost more than the house she grew up in. Like she'd ridden in limos down Spruce on her way to someplace else.

"Where is your family?" she asked. "Do you know?"

"Mom died ten years ago. Dad . . . well, Dad never came back after the . . . accident."

"I'm sorry, Billy. She was a good woman—I know she tried."

That she understood how complicated Mom was, how hard it had been, broke his heart all over again. "She always liked you."

Maddy laughed. "Because she knew I was on the pill and wouldn't let you knock me up."

"That, and you made me do my homework."

"A mother's dream, clearly. What about your sisters?"

"Last time I saw either of them was at Mom's funeral. Denise has been in and out of rehab a few times."

"Oh, Billy. I'm sorry." The way she said it, she wasn't surprised. Denise had started down the road to destruction when she was sixteen years old.

"She went twice. I stopped giving her money about five years ago. She was messed up again. I told her I'd pay for her to get better, but I wouldn't give her money for more drugs." He crossed and uncrossed his legs, unable to get comfortable. "She told me to fuck off."

"And you haven't talked to her since?"

"All she wanted was money, Maddy. I couldn't keep giving it to her knowing she was killing herself." That wasn't all of it, but he couldn't quite bring himself to say it. He cleared his throat, wishing things could be different, but after all these years he was so damn tired of not being able to figure out how he could change anything.

"I know," she said, shocking the hell out of him. "I talked to her about two years ago. She called me up out of the blue."

"And?"

Maddy shrugged. "She asked me for money. I sent it."

Her guilt on top of his own was crushing, and taking a chance, a huge one, he took her hand, slipping his fingers through hers. Holding his breath, he waited for her to pull away. Stealing the moments to memorize the silk of her skin over the hard knots of her bones.

"I stopped answering her calls after that." She pulled her hand away, and he released it one piece at a time. Palms, fingers, crimson nails.

"Don't beat yourself up, Maddy."

"I could say the same to you." How strange that she still saw him so clearly, especially the guilt and worry he carried over the decision to sever ties with his family.

"It's not the same. I was their brother. All they wanted

was money, how hard would it be to just give it to them?"

"I remember what they were like," she said. "Even before you got drafted they treated you like you were their own private bank. Like you owed them, when all they'd ever done was take from you, their whole lives."

"Denise has a kid. A three-year-old at the funeral." The words erupted from the guilty place they lived. "And I walked away from that kid, knowing . . . knowing what her life must be like. I set up a trust fund for her, but I can't trust my sisters to manage it. So, I'm . . . Oh hell, Maddy. I'm ignoring them because I don't know what else to do."

Their eyes met again, this time without the mirror between them, and it was the most intimate, most real moment he'd had with a woman in years.

Blood churned through him, thickened with the desire he'd always felt for her.

Like he was a damn kid again, he got a hard-on—because Maddy Baumgarten had turned those whiskey eyes his way.

Remember when we'd kiss for hours? The words were burning on his lips. *Remember how we'd touch each other?* Love had made them gentle. Tender. No lover since then had wanted his tenderness.

"Hockey is all you have left, isn't it?" she asked.

His dick deflated, the desire vanished.

Reality was as good as a cold shower any day.

He sat back in his chair, not even meeting her eyes in the mirror. Instead he stared at his hands, the scars and scabs his life had left on him. "You gonna call Gina back, or do my makeup yourself?"

"After the break we're going to reveal our top-secret guest. Trust me when I say you do not want to miss this.

It's the segment everyone is going to be talking about." Maddy smiled into the camera until the red light on top went black.

"Commercial. We've got ninety seconds," the stage manager called out and suddenly the set erupted with activity. She closed her eyes and let Gina brush powder over her nose.

"We gotta stop the sweating around here," Gina muttered.

"Please, I haven't broken a sweat on air in five years."

"Yeah, well, maybe you can give some tips to Billy. He's looking like he's fresh off the ice."

Gina vanished. A chair appeared to her left and the big screen was unfurled behind her, where they would show the clips of Billy's teammates and his ex.

As she flipped through her cards, she was aware in a very distant way of Billy sitting in his chair, and she leaned away. She needed distance from him.

Strangers, she reminded herself. *We're strangers.*

"Watch it, cold hands," Billy muttered as Peter mic'd him, clipping the small lavaliere mic between the buttons on Billy's shirt.

"Test," Peter said and then waited for the response from the booth through his headphones. Finally he nodded and backed away.

Billy blew out hard through his mouth like he was about to dive into deep water.

"Nervous?" she asked, still not looking at him.

"I might throw up."

She set down the cards and took a quick sip of water from the bottle Peter handed her. "Wait until commercial break."

"You're cool as a cucumber, aren't you?"

No, she wanted to howl. *No, I'm wrecked inside. I can't look at you. I can't stand to smell you. I don't want to remember any of the good parts. I don't want to remember what we shared. What we had. A life and a history. I don't want any of it.*

She steeled herself to look at him. To lock herself down tight, to remain unmoved at the sight of his nerves, the bead of sweat at his hairline.

It was humanizing, his worry. The scary hockey player was freaking out under the lights.

Not. Cute.

"This is my job." She hoped her smile wasn't as blank as it felt. "And I'm good at it. Don't worry."

"Right." He used the sleeve of his jacket to wipe his forehead, leaving a streak of sludgy powder on the dark fabric.

"Really, Billy?"

"What? I'm losing my mind."

"Ten seconds." Peter slipped back behind the camera.

"Oh Christ."

"Breathe."

Again that deep sucking breath—somewhere in Oklahoma there were cyclones.

"Five. Four." Peter held up three fingers. Two. And then as the light glowed red Peter pointed at her and she felt that sudden rush, the sudden spasm of excitement and ownership.

I am Madelyn Cornish, she thought. *And I own this.*

"Welcome back, everybody. All week long I've been talking about our mysterious makeover guest. And today all will be revealed. Does everyone recognize this man?" Beside her, Billy awkwardly waved and the studio broke out into polite applause.

She rolled her eyes.

"Who are you kidding? You guys have no clue who he is. Here, maybe this will help." She grabbed the prop at her feet and handed Billy a Mavericks' hockey helmet.

This is a joke, right? his deadpan eyes asked in the moment before he took it and put it on.

"Anyone? Ring any bells?" Three people cheered wildly, and she laughed. "Looks like we have some hockey fans in the studio today. Let me fill in the rest of you. Sixteen years ago Billy Wilkins was a second-round NHL draft pick. Since then he's won Olympic gold and silver, and he's been in the Stanley Cup play-offs no less than seven times. In 2002 he was voted one of the most important NHL players on the ice by *Sports Illustrated.*" Madelyn rattled off the rest of Billy's very impressive resume and found herself reluctantly connecting to the stats.

Billy Wilkins, that rough wild boy who'd lived up the street from her, had followed his dream and his skill right out of the nightmare he'd been raised in.

This sudden *pride*? In him? In this man who'd hurt her? It couldn't be a good thing.

Distance, Maddy, she thought. *Distance.*

"All of that incredible success aside, Billy has been the NHL leader in penalty box minutes for three different seasons. He's been suspended and fined and hospitalized more than any other player in the league. Some of you remember this headline." She held up the newspaper Ruth had opened that day weeks ago when she pitched this idea. Billy's face, bloody and maniacal, grinned out at the audience, which appropriately gasped and groaned.

"He's been called 'the unrepentant bad boy of the NHL.' He's the Dallas Mavericks' own Billy Wilkins and he has agreed to be a part of our very special five part series, the Billy Wilkins Project."

This time the crowd applauded with more enthusiasm.

"Can I take this thing off?" Billy said when the applause died down.

He was still wearing the helmet.

"Yes," she laughed. "Go ahead."

He took off the helmet, patted down the worst of his hair, and grinned. Part little boy, part prison escapee, with that scar.

"Billy we're so excited to have you here."

"I'm pretty excited to be here, too."

Now, that's a lie, she thought.

"*AM Dallas* has done some incredible makeover shows, but you're going to be our first man."

"I'm honored."

"You should be. We don't take this stuff lightly around here. My question is, do you think you need a makeover?"

He blinked as if stunned that she'd asked. "I guess so."

"You don't sound convinced."

"Ahh . . ." The air was empty and dead between them. Panic was a halogen light behind his eyes. He watched the audience as if they'd suddenly all appeared in his bathroom while he was peeing.

He had that trapped hamster look she'd seen in plenty of her guests' faces.

It was in moments like this that she earned her substantial salary.

"Well, Billy," she reached over to squeeze his hand. Lord, he was sweating. "Let's see what your teammates have to say about you getting a makeover."

The lights dimmed and the screen behind them sparked to life. Jan Fforde, the young Swedish goalie, filled the screen, looking handsome and boyish.

"Does Billy need a makeover?" Jan asked, clearly unsure of the word's meaning. His eyes flickered to someone behind the camera who translated the term. Jan started howling with laughter.

The audience loved it.

The video cut to the captain of the Mavericks, Mike

Blake, who had the black and yellow remains of a shiner on his right eye.

"I'm not going to tell Billy Wilkins he needs a makeover, are you crazy? He'd kill me. Billy, if you're watching this, I think you're perfect just the way you are."

They cut back to Jan Fforde, who was still laughing, but now he was wiping his eyes.

Coach Hornsby appeared in a dapper sports coat, his thin glasses catching the camera light as he nodded, definitively. "Yes, Billy Wilkins needs a makeover."

"Good God, you asked Coach?" Billy said. The mic picked up his mumble. "Don't tell me you talked to my mother."

Only she knew that was impossible and the crowd laughed at his joke.

"Better," she said, rubbing her hands together. "An ex-girlfriend."

A woman with short, cropped black hair appeared on the screen, her arms crossed over her chest as if she was waiting for a late bus. "A makeover?" she asked. "Billy?" She slapped her hands on the arms of the chair. "Oh, let me count the ways. One," she ticked on her fingers, "he doesn't own a decent suit. Two, he's probably wearing white athletic socks with black shoes right now."

Billy lifted his pants to reveal white athletic socks over the tops of his black shoes.

The crowd roared.

He glanced up at Madelyn and winked.

Quickly, she turned her attention back to the screen.

Luc Baker, dark-haired and devilish in a sublime navy suit, filled the screen, and the mostly female audience sighed. Estrogen filled the air.

The future Hall of Famer's sharp features were made even sharper by a scowl. "Billy Wilkins is one of the best men I've ever had the pleasure of skating with. He's a fighter in the best sense of the word. He's loyal, he's fierce, and his hockey IQ is through the roof. No one knows the game like he does and no one—I repeat, no one—loves the game like he does."

There was a scuffle off camera and then a beautiful blond woman leaned into the frame, her blue eyes sparkling.

"Tara!" Billy cried, clearly surprised.

"The fighting thing," she said. "It's a problem. You can tell he doesn't love it like he pretends to."

The blonde darted back off screen, revealing a wincing Luc.

"Sorry, Billy," he muttered.

Back to Sandra, who was still ticking on her fingers. "Three: chews with his mouth open. Four: opens beers with his teeth if he has to. Five: he's a full-grown man and all he knows how to cook is toast."

"That's not true," Billy protested. "I make great pot roast."

Maddy stared at him incredulously.

"What?" He shrugged as if it wasn't the strangest thing. "My mom taught me."

She knew firsthand that his mother's pot roast was barely edible, but she turned back to the screen.

The clip went on for another forty seconds, players talking about how rude he was. The Mavericks' manager told a story about Billy getting into a fight at a restaurant.

Jan just kept laughing.

Finally, the lights came up and Maddy could see that the people in the crowd were grinning at one another as if they were all in on the joke.

Gold. This was pure gold.

As good as she was at her job, this feeling, this moment, was rare. Rare because it was effortless. Over the years, there had been some great segments, but they had required a lot of work. That was her job, making the difficult look easy. But this . . . this was simple.

This was fun.

Whatever was outside the studio was irrelevant. She needed none of it. All she needed was the audience, her staff and crew, and a story to tell.

Billy.

It was like she was thirteen all over again, and he was magnetic. So compelling she couldn't look away. He was sweeping her back into his tide.

"Well," Billy said, looking as abashed as a man with such a scar and such a twinkle in his eyes could, "I guess I need some help."

"And we're here to give it. Are you ready?"

"Will you be gentle with me?" he asked, taking her hand in his giant mitt.

Careful here, Madelyn, she tried to warn herself, but instead she gripped his hand right back. Diving headlong into the contact. A firm shake. Partners, teammates, whatever. For the segment, she'd commit.

For this feeling she'd do anything.

"Sorry, buddy, there's nothing gentle about it." She turned to the studio audience and winked. "Makeovers are a brutal business, aren't they?"

They roared and Billy hung his head.

"This is going to be bad," he muttered.

"Join us next Friday," she laughed and told the cameras. "For day one of the Billy Wilkins Project. We're going to bring in a tailor and get this hockey player a new suit and some black socks." Shaking her head she glanced over at Billy. "Really? Athletic socks with dress shoes?"

"At least the socks match."

"Tim from the Man Room Spa and Salon will give

Billy an updated look. Tell me, Billy, have you ever heard of manscaping?"

Billy didn't have to fake his fear. He shook his head. "No."

"That's what I thought." She rose from her chair, still holding Billy's hand, and he stood up with her. The two of them facing a wall of excited women. "Join us on Friday, guys. This is going to be fun!"

The theme music swelled up around them and the red lights on the cameras went dark.

"We're clear," Peter called and the stage was swarmed.

She immediately dropped Billy's hand, but he wouldn't let go. As she pulled away, he yanked her toward him, holding her in his arms, surrounding her with his size and strength, the warmth and smell of him.

Her eyes closed and before she could stop herself, she squeezed him right back. Holding him hard against her body in sheer jubilation.

She could feel the sweat under his jacket, smell it on his neck. He'd been nervous, but he'd managed to keep his shit together.

"You did great," she whispered.

"You are amazing."

His breath teased her neck, setting off alarms in her body. The adrenaline of the show was a powerful aphrodisiac and she wanted—for one wild, breathless moment—to kiss him. Press herself full-tilt against him. Test her nails and her teeth and her sex against his strength.

Lust roared through her, opening up every nerve ending, every synapse, every pore. Her skin was a giant receptor and she twitched with sensation. Shook with it.

Sex. Oh God, suddenly she wanted to have sex. With Billy.

She tore herself away from him, pushing him back.

He gave her a confused look, his arms by his sides. "Maddy?"

Without another word, she turned and left. Leaving all that victory, tainted now, colored by her foolish lust, on the set behind her.

Billy watched Maddy walk away, half aware that three people were surrounding him. Someone took off his mic. That Ruth woman was telling him what a great job he'd done. Phil shook his hand. And still Billy was barely paying attention.

If the last ten minutes had proven anything, it was that he'd been right to come here. He'd been right to think this show might be a second chance for them. She might not see it that way right now, but it was clear to him. Obvious. As obvious as the lust she'd been feeling just seconds ago.

Maddy was right, she was a different person than the girl she'd been. More exciting. More interesting. More realized. Like all the promise in that young girl had not only been fulfilled, but surpassed.

And they were still good together, better than good. They fit, when the whole rest of the world chafed, she fit him perfectly.

In the shadows past the set he could see the green of Maddy's shirt as she made her way back to her office.

Where she was going to fix the cracks in her armor. She would convince herself that what just happened between them on the stage—the connection they'd felt—was nothing. A mistake.

"No," he muttered.

"Sorry?" Phil asked.

Billy shook his head, "Sorry, man, give me a second, would you?"

Maddy could pretend all she wanted, but they were good together. There was magic between them. And he wanted her out of that armor. He wanted her naked and real and in his arms.

He took off after her.

chapter 8

He nearly threw the door to her office off its hinges when he pushed it open.

"Whoa, what's the rush, Billy?" Maddy asked from where she sat in front of her mirror. Her hair was pulled back, her face slick and free of makeup. Her eyes empty of all that fire . . . that excitement and lust she'd revealed just a few minutes ago.

Every ounce of anger he'd swallowed since agreeing to this ridiculous proposition roared through him.

Finally. Thank God. A fight. A fight he could win.

He kicked the door shut.

"Holy—"

"Maddy, you can't pretend that wasn't great."

"I told you,"—her smile was bright, fake,—"you did a great job. The segment—"

"Fuck the segment, Maddy."

Maddy stood, heading for her desk. "It's Madelyn."

"You are Maddy. You'll always be Maddy. And what was great out there was us. We did a great job. We . . . Christ, Maddy, I know it's scary."

"Scary? It's my job."

Frustrated, sweaty, and miserable, he grabbed her. Her shoulders fit the curve of his hands so perfectly. Like always. Like a key he'd lost somewhere along the way.

Her gasp was kindling to what burned inside of him.

She didn't fight him. Thank God—he didn't know what he would have done if she had.

She put her hand against his chest and it burned right through his clothes, past his skin and muscle, down to his blood and bones. She was in him.

And then like some kind of miracle, like some kind of divine gift, she was kissing him.

After years of being out of his life, Maddy was kissing him again. Her lips were soft and full, lush against his. Her hands were urgent, but never cruel. Never rough. They threaded through his hair, holding him close. Closer.

His tongue touched hers, old friends finding each other after years apart. Her hips were so thin under his hands, but no less exciting. No less her. His Maddy.

Relaxing into the kiss, into her, the years fell away and it was better than everything that had happened on the ice in the last decade and a half.

It was perfect.

"Madelyn, I've got your water and some—" The door flew open and Madelyn shoved him away. He stumbled back into a chair and whirled toward the doorway.

"Sorry," a startled brunette said, putting the water down and making a rapid retreat.

The door shut behind her and the silence was profound. Choking.

Billy didn't have the words to convince Maddy not to freak out, that it was okay to trust him. That he wasn't the boy he'd been. He was a man, and he could take care of her. He could honor her. The past was gone, burnt and buried, but right now, at this very moment, they could change their future.

Carefully, knowing how thin the ice was beneath his feet, he touched her shoulder, curled his hand there, a finger resting patiently against the pulse in her neck.

Please, he thought, *have a little faith. A little faith in me.*

But then she shrugged him away, crossing to the other side of the room.

"Leave," she whispered. "Please."

"Maddy—"

She took a deep breath and looked at him dead center. Right into his black soul. "It's Madelyn. Now get out of my office."

It was the Snuggie that did it.

A six mile run. A long-distance phone conversation with her mother about the weather in Miami. An hour of yoga. None of it put a dent in her fever.

But the Snuggie was the tipping point.

As Madelyn waited to give her credit card number to the woman on the phone at three o'clock in the morning, she knew that the empty pint of mint chocolate chip ice cream on the floor and the Bumpits hair accessory she'd ordered twenty minutes ago were all flash. Distraction from the real problem.

Just watch some porn and be done with it, she told herself.

Now that she was mentally and physically exhausted from trying to banish the desire still rumbling through her body, she could be honest.

She didn't want porn.

She wanted Billy.

And she could order all the Kenny Rogers greatest hits CD sets in the world (CDs? Who bought CDs anymore? Besides . . . well, her, obviously), but it didn't change the fact that she wanted to have sex with her ex-husband.

You're better than this, she said to herself, trying to start a rally, but her heart wasn't interested in rallying. Her heart was interested in sex.

And since sex wasn't available, she'd make do with more ice cream . . . and possibly a Magic Bullet food processor, because she'd cook more if she had something that made fresh restaurant-style salsa in less than ten seconds.

That was how these infomercials got her, they found the cracks in her perfect life and turned them into chasms.

And kissing Billy Wilkins and getting caught by her segment producer? Oh, the cracks in her life were deep and plentiful.

Thank God Sabine would keep her mouth shut.

This—this kissing, this teenage mooning, this fever in her blood and ache between her legs—it was the first step in a terrible pattern.

It started off with kissing. And he was so utterly irresistible, so totally exciting, that the kissing would lead to sex. And the sex . . . the sex would be epic. Addictive. And he would look at her like she was the only person in the world that mattered. And she would slowly, a piece at a time, start giving herself away to him. Bits of her time and her energy, things she'd convince herself she didn't need. And from there it would grow. Until suddenly Maddy would find herself all alone, a stranger to herself.

Again.

But God, she wanted to have sex with him.

Shifting on the couch, her foot kicked over the ice cream container. She glanced down at the congealed green fat in the bottom of the pint and felt her stomach turn. She'd eaten herself sick.

Gina was going to have a conniption.

"This is your idea of professionalism?" she muttered.

You need a new plan.

Tilting her head, she looked at the green ice cream in a new light.

Okay, so she wanted to have sex with Billy. Badly. Every woman who had sustained a diet for as long as she had knew that sometimes you had to give in to the craving. You had to eat the ice cream until you didn't want it anymore. You had to eat it until your tongue was coated with milk fat solids and artificial sweeteners. You had to eat until your teeth hurt and your stomach rolled and you were filled, utterly filled, with the disgust that came free with each pint.

The key was making sure it was only one pint of ice cream. Not a lifetime supply.

Excitement and confidence coiled and danced through her. She could do this.

He might have come back into her life under the delusion that there was a future for them, but she knew that was impossible.

And having sex with him was not the same as agreeing with him.

Making sure he saw that, that he fully understood it, was probably easier said than done, but she was a full-grown woman now. Not a love-struck teenager.

And she had to have the ability to say no. To say stop.

This affair would have to happen on her terms.

"Ma'am?" The Snuggie-pusher on the phone was getting persistent. "I need the expiration date on your credit card."

"I've changed my mind," she said and hung up.

Unsticking the bare skin of her arms and shoulders from the leather couch, she stood, her knees protesting the sudden work required of them.

It wasn't as if she was in jeopardy of falling in love.

The sparks of feelings between them were residual, or the result of adrenaline from the show. Either way, they weren't real.

Madelyn watched Dallas wake up outside her windows and calmly and rationally prepared the rules that would allow her to sleep with Billy, and keep her heart safe and far-removed.

* * *

Billy's fame didn't often come in handy. Most of the time drunk men just wanted to fight him. "You're not so tough," they'd say, just before taking a giant swing at his head.

But every once in a while, he'd find a hockey fan in just the right spot.

For instance, Lou, the security doorman at Maddy's fancy Turtle Creek condo building was a huge Mavericks fan. Thank God.

"She's out for her Saturday morning run," Lou said and checked his watch. "She'll be back in about fifteen minutes. You can have a seat." He pointed to a small couch surrounded by potted plants in the corner of the lobby.

"Thanks, man," Billy sat. Oddly enough, it had been pretty easy for him to find out where she lived. The receptionist at the studio had a boyfriend who was also a fan. Two Mavericks fans when he needed them was nearly unheard of. The promise of a couple of tickets to the season opener had bought him Maddy's address. Which made him worry about security on that set.

"You want a drink or something?"

Billy smiled. "I'm good. Thanks."

"I saw the Mavericks' last game." Lou whistled through his teeth and Billy smiled, knowing which way this was going. "That was some fight."

"Thanks."

"Good to see the boys with some fire in their eyes again."

"That's what I thought."

"I tell you," Lou shook his head, the sunlight in the lobby sliding over his bald scalp like oil. "It's a shame what they're doing to your sport."

"How do you mean?" Billy asked and glanced down

at his watch. Fifteen minutes of hockey talk. No problem.

"Getting rid of the fighting."

"You think that's a problem?" He shifted one of the plants so it partially hid his face, trying to avoid the possibility that Maddy might take one look at him and keep on running. Only one of the many worst-case scenarios he'd thought of this morning.

"Fighting is the life of hockey. The guts."

"I thought goals were the life of hockey."

"Without fighting it's just soccer. Who likes soccer?"

"Millions of people in every other country but this one. How long does Maddy usually run on a Saturday morning?"

"An hour or two. But she's always back at ten."

An hour or two, no wonder she was so skinny.

Ten to ten now. He had ten more minutes to figure out what to say to her. He'd spent a sleepless night working out arguments, but none of them really seemed to hold water.

So he'd come here planning to just let her scream at him if that's what she wanted. He'd take her anger on the chin, because he'd never done that in their marriage.

And she probably had plenty of anger.

Oh, the screaming he was going to get.

"If you ask me," Lou said as he sat back in his chair. His red jacket with the security badge on the breast pocket was a size too big. Made him look like a kid dressing up in his dad's clothes. "Coach Hornsby isn't using you the way you should be used."

"Tell me about it," Billy muttered. This was usually his favorite conversation, but he was so damn preoccupied with looking for any sign of Maddy.

Just as Lou was really getting warmed up on penalty kills, Maddy ran up to the glass door in sleek black running pants and a gray T-shirt, stopping at the edge of the wide red mat in front of the door.

Her chest heaving, she pushed a button on her watch and then pulled out her earbuds.

Maddy, his entire body sighed.

A week ago she'd come to his house, swearing there would be no second chance for them, but the whole time enough sparks had traveled between them to light Arizona on fire. And yesterday . . . God, yesterday she'd been in his arms again. After years. Cold year after cold year.

The time for pretending was over.

Somehow, he just had to show her he had changed and that the chemistry between them on her show was proof she *hadn't* changed, not as much as she thought.

She waved at someone over her shoulder and then pulled open the door, using all the weight of her lean body. Panicked, excited, he stood as she came in.

"Hey, Lou." Her voice was husky, and sweat poured down her face, turning her gray T-shirt black in places.

It turned him on. The athlete in him wanted to sweat with her. Wanted to lick her, taste the salt and heat of her. Oh God, he was getting hard. He shifted a little more behind the large plant.

"Got a guy here waiting for you." Lou smiled and jerked his thumb over at Billy, who felt more and more like a prom date who was about to be rejected.

That loose, easy, post-run look on her face vanished. She boarded herself up tight.

"Hi." He lifted his arm, waved it limply like an idiot.

"Billy." That was it. His name and nothing else. Then she turned and kept walking through the granite foyer, toward the elevators. She punched the up button and the wooden elevator doors opened.

That's it. She's leaving. What's your move now hotshot?

"You coming?" she asked, without looking at him.

Like he was charging toward a play in front of the net, Billy crossed the foyer to get in that elevator with her.

Once inside, the doors closed behind them.

"Maddy—"

"Don't say anything." She dug her iPod out of the band around her upper arm, her face turned away as if managing her playlist was the most important thing in the world.

Poised on a knife's edge, he clenched and unclenched his fists, listening to a tinny, instrumental version of Elvis' *Hound Dog*.

The elevator binged, the doors silently swept open, and Maddy turned left down the hall. He followed, trying not to stare at her ass in those pants, but Lord, it was hard.

Using a key she untied from her shoelace, she opened a door at the far end of the hall, and he stepped into her home behind her.

The walls were filled with art and photographs, and a white leather couch covered in bright pillows sat across from a wall of windows. Outside, the city glimmered in the sun. He wanted to inspect every inch of the room, stare at every photo, connect every pillow to the woman who had bought them.

"Take off your shoes," she said as she kicked off her runners.

He toed off his beat-up tennis shoes. The small trash can under the bright pink hall table was stuffed full of red roses.

"I see you got my flowers."

She was silent.

"We need to talk about yesterday."

Looking up at him through her lashes she said, "Is that what we need to do?"

That put him off his stride and he felt the room

shift under his feet. She tossed her iPod on the pink table under a silver mirror and then pulled the rubber band out of her hair. Her curls, brought back by the humidity and the sweat, fell around her face, against her shoulders.

There was something happening in this room, something totally unexpected, and he wasn't sure what to do.

He wanted to touch her hair so badly, his fingers twitched.

He was lost. Lost in her bright, cheerful home, the scent of her sweat, the sight of those curls. Arms at his sides, heart hammering in his throat, he just stood there. Obviously she had some kind of agenda, and he'd wait to find out what it was.

"How'd you sleep last night, Billy?"

"Uh . . . fine."

"Well, I didn't sleep very well at all." She stared out her window, the city like a steel carpet at her feet. "And sleep is pretty damn important to me. My routine makes my life do-able. Without control, everything falls apart."

She looked at him as if expecting a response, so he nodded. He saw the steel locks all over her. The chains around her life. He got it. This was a woman who owned her days, attacked them.

"You want to control me?" he asked, eager for it. Well, if not eager, then at least ready. Ready to try.

Her low laughter burned through the room. "Please, Billy. No one controls you. Not even you."

"Then . . . what do you want?"

"To control myself." She faced him fully, her eyes like lead. "To control my reaction to you. To get rid of this *shit* I feel for you."

Hurt by her words, he flinched. "Shit?"

Her long legs ate the distance between them, and somehow this pristine condo, its white walls and clean scent, suddenly felt dirty. He knew what she was going to say before she said it, and he knew he wouldn't be able to say no.

"We're going to have sex," she said, a foot from him. His blood pounded in visceral reaction to the smell of her. His wife. His woman. "Until I can't stand myself anymore."

He shook his head, trying to talk himself out of this. Even as his body roared in approval of her plan.

"Stop." She was undeniable. "You'll agree because you want me. However you can get me."

"And you don't want me?" he mocked.

"I want you out of my head."

Furious that she had pegged him so easily while staying so damn aloof, he let his temper go.

He reached for her hands, yanking her into his arms, where she fit so perfectly. If she wanted a demon to exorcize, fine. He could be that demon.

He leaned down to kiss her but she turned her face away. "No kissing."

"What?"

"You heard me."

"Why?"

She blinked up at him, her lips tight, her face tighter. A stranger in so many ways, and now she was going to fuck him and keep that distance. Brutal game.

But brutality had been his bread and butter for a long time—how different was this going to be?

But I wanted it to be different, he thought, mourning even as he was jacked up on the power in her.

"I don't want it to be like what we had," she said. "That's over. Gone."

"You think you won't feel anything if we don't kiss?" He laughed, but she reached down between them, her hand cupping him through his jeans, and he hissed.

The heel of her hand pressed hard against the tip of

his erection, and he staggered back against the door, seeing stars.

Her fingers flew over the buttons of his pants. "Take off your shirt," she murmured and he whipped it over his head. Her smile was feral, mean and satisfied all at once.

It was familiar, that look. Plenty of women since her had looked at him that way, like they couldn't wait to bite him. To use him.

"Maddy—"

"Shut up." And then she leaned forward and bit him. Her teeth clamping down on the flesh of his shoulder, the muscle underneath, and it felt like lightning.

He groaned, his head hitting the door behind him, and she bit him again, his pectoral. His dick surged against her hand and he hated this. Hated it as much as he loved it.

This was Maddy. His Maddy. Back in his arms like some kind of nightmare, and he wanted to walk away. Wanted to be better than the sick, twisted way she was going to use him, but he couldn't.

"Touch me," she whispered against his chest. "Billy—"

He lifted her, his hands holding her upper arms as he twisted and pushed her up onto that little hallway table, keys scattering down around their feet.

She was panting, her eyes heavy, dilated.

Somehow she was still the most exciting woman he'd ever touched. He leaned down to kiss her but she pushed him away. "No. Kissing."

Angry and turned on, he arched against her, the edge of his erection finding the sweet hollow between her legs. He curled his fingers around the corner of the wall, grinding himself against her so hard, it had to hurt. But she only gasped, spread her legs farther. Clutched at the belt loops of his jeans, holding him with all her strength.

With one hand he reached down between them, found

her breast, the hard ridge of her nipple utterly foreign under the layers she wore. He let go of the wall, stepped back slightly so he could rip off her shirt, the red sports bra under it. Her belly was lean, muscled, her breasts smaller than he remembered.

But still breasts.

"Will you let me kiss you here?" he asked, crudely, roughly cupping her breasts in his hands. His thumbs rubbed over and around her pink nipples. Gasping, she nodded.

"How about here?" He thrust his hands down the front of her pants to find the wet heat of her. The incendiary dampness. She cried out, pain, pleasure, acceptance, denial. All of it was in that gasp and he laughed, low and dark in the back of his throat.

She wanted to control her reaction to him. Fuck that.

"Can I kiss you here?" he whispered again into her hair, sliding one finger along the furrow between her legs. She jerked against him as the calloused edge of his thumb found her clit.

"Maddy?"

"Yes," she gasped, swallowing as if she couldn't get enough air. As if she were drowning. Rough, without gentleness, as if she had asked for it this way, and hell, maybe she had, he didn't know what was going on anymore—he thrust one finger inside of her.

She screamed, her nails biting into the skin above his pants.

Fuck, he thought. *What am I doing?*

She jerked, slipping off the table, and he caught her, shoving her back up onto that narrow ledge. Her muscles were shaking. All of them, the tiny ones under her skin, the larger ones in her arms and legs. Everything inside her was trembling.

Memories rolled through him. Thousands of them.

He closed his eyes and braced his forehead against the wall, beside her head.

The night after prom, the first time they had sex, that startled gasp in his ear when he took her virginity. "It's okay," she'd whispered when he tried to pull out, agonized by the thought of hurting her. "I'm glad it's you," she'd said. "I love you."

That time they'd watched porn in Chris Alfano's basement and she'd tried to give him a blow job in his car. She'd laughed and choked and finally he told her to stop, but she wouldn't until she got it right. And she had. She really had.

Their wedding night, she'd been eighteen and he'd been twenty. Their first anniversary in the hotel room down in Atlanta, when they'd had too much champagne and nearly drowned in the heart-shaped hot tub.

After every fight that last year, when she would come apart in his arms and then sob curled up on her side of the bed and he'd stare up at the ceiling, feeling worthless and angry, wondering if this was how marriage was really supposed to be.

He pulled his finger out of her body, the electric heat slipping across his knuckles.

"What are you doing?" she gasped, clutching his wrist.

"Not like this," he whispered, kissing her ear. "Not with you."

"What . . . what do you mean?" she blinked up at him, lost in that haze. Everything about her was twitching, so close to orgasm. He'd seen her like this enough to know. The knowledge was its own kind of pain.

He scooped her up, one hand under her legs, the other under her shoulder blades. Startled, she slung an arm around his neck.

"I don't want it like this," she snapped.

Silent, because what could he say, really? He laid her down on the couch.

"Condoms are in the bedroom." Her voice had hard edges that he tried to ignore.

"Shhh," he whispered and ran a hand over her breasts, down the muscles of her belly, which twitched and jumped at his touch. His fingers slipped under the waistband of her pants again, into the curls between her legs.

One knee fell open and her arm lifted. For a moment, breathless with an agonized hope, he waited for her touch—against his neck, the side of his face, anywhere—but she only flopped her arm over her head, her palm lying open against an orange pillow.

He smiled down into her eyes, and for one breathless moment, it was just them. Like it used to be.

But then she closed her eyes.

On his knees on the floor beside the couch, he leaned down, pulled one long hard pink nipple into his mouth, and she arched up against his face. A long slow undulation of her whole body, lithe and beautiful.

Using his fingers, that callous on his thumb, his teeth against her nipple, he urged her higher. Pushed her further. Fresh sweat broke out on her body, and her small gasps turned to moans.

"Yes," she cried.

Yes, his body answered, throbbing in his pants. *Yes. Yes.*

But he kept his pants on. Thought about ice. Empty arenas. The look on her face years ago outside that hotel room.

For her, he told himself. *Once in your life, just for her.*

"Billy," she groaned, curling herself against him, her hand sliding up under his arm to his back. The skin, so sensitized, his body so full of want, he flinched from her touch.

Too much. It was too much.

"Come on, baby," he groaned against her skin, licking the lower curve of her breast up to her nipple.

He slid in another finger, higher into her body.

She pulled herself taut against him, every muscle engaged in the act of reaching for orgasm. "Yes," she chanted. "Yes. Oh God, yes."

One jerk, then another. Her legs clamped hard against his hand. Her fingers raked the skin of his back. He hissed, arching away even as his dick throbbed. He let her nipple, wet and hard, fall from his mouth.

God, he thought, looking at her. *God.*

"Billy," she sighed, half-smiling. For just a moment, she looked exactly as he remembered and he reached his limit.

Awkward and clumsy he pulled his hand free from her body, the scent of sweat and woman—musky and so fucking erotic he couldn't stand it—followed and he lurched to his feet. Away from the couch. From her.

She sat up, her breasts wobbling at the motion.

Stop looking, he told himself, but he couldn't.

"What are you doing?" she asked, slipping one foot down onto the floor. The muscles in her stomach clenched and released—and honest to God, he'd never seen anything hotter.

Though she could be wearing a clown suit and juggling and he'd still want to fuck her.

But he had some standards. And one of them was that he wouldn't use his wife like a puck bunny and he wouldn't let her use him like some kind of Gladiator dildo. He'd had enough of that for three lifetimes.

"Stop." He held up his hand, warding her off like she was trying to mug him.

"But . . ." She gestured limply toward him. Toward the erection raging in his unbuttoned jeans. "Don't you want—"

"Yes," he growled, suddenly furious with her. "I want.

But not with your rules, Maddy. You want me, you take me. All of me. I can't fuck you and pretend to be strangers. You're my wife."

"Ex." She stood, stepping toward him, her eyes on fire. If she touched him, he'd take her down on the carpet, he'd push himself so far inside her, she'd scream. And she'd get her wish, there would be no tenderness. Everything that had made them special would be ground to nothing beneath their bodies.

He stepped away, his back hitting the wall of windows. Her eyes gleamed like she had him.

"No, not like that."

"Please," she scoffed, running a hand from her collarbone, over her breasts down to the waistband of her pants. "Like you're really going to say no to pussy."

Oh God, he hated how she was trying to demean what they had. How she was trying to tear apart something that had been so special, so important to him.

"Fuck you."

"I'm trying," she laughed.

She reached for him, her lips parted, and he could feel her, the inside of her mouth, the lick of her tongue. He imagined her on her knees in front of him, his hand cupping the back of her head, and he nearly came right then.

He grabbed her hand, holding the fingers hard, while he used his other hand to slip inside his unbuttoned jeans to cup his erection. Palm it. He was rough, but terribly, horribly ready. Looking right into her eyes, it took three strokes hard and fast and it was over. The orgasm came and went with a whimper.

The air went cold in the room. His penis soft in his messy hand. Desire turned to stone in her eyes.

Yanking her hand free, she stepped away. Every muscle and bone in her back stood out in rigid relief against her skin when she bent to grab her shirt off the floor and pull it over her head.

"The bathroom is just down the hall," she murmured and walked in the opposite direction, around the half wall and into the kitchen.

And what was that? he asked himself as he walked down the shadowed hall. *You feel noble?*

There was no answer, inside he was empty, cleaned out. Being with Maddy always pushed him off his skates. He felt constantly one second behind with her.

A dumb body struggling to decipher her complicated heart.

In the dark he cleaned himself up, peed, and flushed the toilet.

He didn't look in the mirror, ask himself any questions, because there wouldn't be any answers.

At the front door, he pulled on his shoes, listening to her throw shit around the kitchen like she was at a Greek wedding.

He leaned around the corner, watching her in her white and stainless steel kitchen. Modern and sleek, like her.

You remember our first kitchen? he wanted to ask. The stove with only one burner that worked?

But he was smart enough not to mention it.

"Maddy?" he said instead.

"Hmmm?" she hummed without turning around, as if he were the cleaning staff and of no consequence.

It had been a mistake pushing her away like that. Even as he tried to convince himself that she'd be different on Friday, he knew the set of her shoulders.

She was hurt. Offended. Righteous and stubborn in her anger.

Because he hadn't played by her rules, she'd keep him at arm's length forever.

And I don't have forever, he thought. He had one day a week for a month.

There would be another chance, he knew that. He could orchestrate it and next time he'd play by her damn rules. To a point.

But for the first time he realized that getting what he wanted was going to cost him. Self-respect was getting harder and harder to drudge up when he needed it.

"See you Friday," she said. He waited one more second and when it was obvious she wasn't going to face him, he turned to go, pausing for a second to spread his hand out on that pink table. As if he could still feel her heat. As if he could still, through wood and paint and years and pain, touch the heart of her.

chapter 9

Monday morning, Maddy walked out of the early programming meeting feeling like she needed a shower.

Furious, she waited outside the door for Ruth.

Phil came out first and the sight of him turned her stomach. It wasn't just the T-shirts anymore. He was stooping to new lows. This Billy makeover segment had gone to his head.

"I know they're radical ideas," he said when he caught sight of her, continuing to press his case despite the fact that everyone in the meeting had shot him down.

"They're not radical, Phil," she said. "They're tabloid. I'm not doing a story about college girls stripping for tuition money. I'm not."

"Huge ratings, Maddy."

She clenched her teeth at the sound of her nickname from his mouth. Fucking Billy.

"Think about it," Phil said as he walked away and Maddy stared after him, her blood boiling.

Finally Ruth came out, reams of paperwork held to her chest.

"Don't," she said, when she saw Maddy waiting for her.

"Don't what?" she asked, following Ruth toward her office. "Don't talk about the fact that our producer has clearly lost his mind?"

"They're just ideas," Ruth said, slapping her files

down on her desk. Undeterred, Madelyn followed her in and shut the door behind her.

"Not when he says them," Maddy said. "What the hell is going on?"

Ruth collapsed back into her chair, as if blown by a big wind. "We'll handle it. Like we always do."

"Maybe we need to talk to Richard?"

"You want me to tell on my boss?" Ruth asked. "This isn't kindergarten."

"Yes it is, if he's lost his mind. I'm not sure you've noticed, but he's acting like the Billy Wilkins Project was his idea!"

"What am I supposed to do, Madelyn?"

"Man up!" she cried and Ruth started to laugh.

"You're one to talk, Madelyn Baumgarten." The silence boomed between them. Recriminations on both sides. Then: "I . . . think he might have made contact with Billy's sisters."

Maddy's mouth fell open. "What do you mean?"

"He's talking about adding a segment to the series. I'm pressing him for more information, but so far he's been cagey."

Phil? Cagey?

"We can't let that happen!" Maddy said. "We can't."

Ruth leaned forward and checked her watch before starting to sort through her paperwork—her not-so-subtle way of dismissing her. Maddy had seen Ruth do it a thousand times to other people. But never her. Betrayed and now blown off. Awesome.

"I'm not sure how we stop it," Ruth finally said. "He's the executive producer."

Madelyn opened the door to leave but turned around at the last minute.

"I get it that we're not actually friends," she said. "But I thought we were at least teammates. I thought we were in this together."

Ruth didn't look up from the papers on her desk, and Madelyn, who'd put herself out there enough, decided to take the hint.

She slammed the door behind her.

"We're going to need you to take off your shirt," said Tam. Behind his thick, cool-guy glasses, the small tailor's eyes gleamed.

Friday morning's studio audience cooed with scandalized delight.

Billy glanced over at Maddy for support but she only grinned and shrugged, as if his sudden role as a stripper was beyond her control.

"If Tam says off, I guess you take it off, big boy," she said, her tone settling into that sweet spot of familiarity, like they were old friends.

But her eyes were dead cold.

Walking in this morning, he hadn't expected anything less.

The audience didn't seem to notice, because they were responding to her every cue. Every joke was hilarious. All of Tam's innuendos were met with gasps and laughs of titillation.

Working it like a Chippendales dancer, he gripped the hem of his gray Mavericks workout T-shirt and slowly, firing up every muscle in his core and chest, eased it up, then whipped it over his head.

The crowd cheered.

"Oh. My." Tam sighed.

The tailor was flirting with him, just as Maddy had predicted. But in a flip of expectations, Billy was flirting right back. Maddy, with her chilly control, her icy distance, was way more threatening than Tam.

He swung the shirt in a circle over his head and tossed it toward Tam, who caught it with a grin. The man was wearing a pink shirt and a gray and black striped vest. He should look like a circus performer, but somehow he pulled it off. He looked masculine and feminine all at once.

Pretty cool trick for a guy who didn't come up to Billy's shoulder.

Billy didn't look at Maddy, hating to see her dead eyes while he stood half-naked for the studio audience's enjoyment.

Earlier in the segment, he'd gotten his hair cut and even he had to admit it looked good, short on the sides, longer on top, not the buzz cut he usually got twice a year.

Tim from the Man Room had scrubbed Billy's face and put gunk on it and now his skin was pink and tight, the scar not quite so grotesque.

Skin care, go figure.

There had been an awkward moment when Tim had asked about the scar.

"Bar fight." It was his standard answer and he didn't elaborate. He never elaborated. The silence had echoed for a moment as everyone in the audience probably imagined the fight. It took everything in his guts not to look at Maddy.

Tim had quickly filled the awkward moment with talk of shaving creams.

Now, half-naked and freezing, he wondered if Maddy remembered the night he'd gotten that scar, or if she'd boxed it up like the rest of his things and left it out on the lawn like garbage.

From the corner of his eye he saw the monitor. The scars on his chest and back looked very red under the lights and his muscles looked very cut. He dared a quick glance at Maddy, and was gratified to see that she couldn't hide her reaction.

While Tam took the measuring tape off his shoulders, and talked about shoulder measurements, and where cuffs should hit wrists, Billy watched Maddy in the monitor. Her eyes were a different measuring tape, following Tam's movement across his body. Tracing every curve and line and scar.

Tam dropped to one knee in front of him, stretching the tape to measure his inseam.

"Watch it," Billy said, arching an eyebrow at Tam, who only laughed.

But Tam was a consummate professional and he jumped back up after taking his measurements.

"You buy pants that are too big for you, don't you? Around the waist?"

Billy blinked. "Yeah, I guess."

"Because of your sport, your thighs and butt are bigger than most men's and getting a proper fit off the rack is difficult."

"Tell me about it," he muttered. Only one of the many reasons he hated shopping.

"It's why God created tailors."

"I thought it was why he created belts."

The crowd chuckled and Tam shook his head. "I've had a few pieces tailored to your measurements and I think you'll be amazed at the difference it makes."

Tam turned to the audience, his black hair sleek and shiny under the lights. "Now the fun begins. This spring is all about tailored, light and luxurious fabrics that are both sensual and masculine. Billy, I swear to God, is going to be a new man."

"Can't wait for that," Maddy said to the camera. "Come back after the break."

The lights on the cameras went dark and Sabine, the woman who had walked in on him and Maddy kissing last week, led him offstage to dress him in some of those luxurious fabrics.

"You're doing great," Sabine whispered, quickly pulling a white button-down shirt over his shoulders. She started to button it, but he nudged her hands aside.

"I can do that," he whispered. He'd tried to turn the tempo of this game with Maddy this morning, but she hadn't responded to his small talk. His questions about the show. Nothing. Until they got on the set, and then she livened right up. All sorts of false intimacy between them. Which rankled and left him off balance. He wasn't very good at faking things.

And he didn't want to fake anything with her.

But that's all they'd have unless he played by her rules.

Sabine pulled a tan linen vest from a hanger while he finished with the shirt. The inside of the vest was red silk with big giant sunbursts of yellow and green on it. He'd never worn anything like it in his life.

There was even a little scrap of red silk in the pocket over his heart.

"You're supposed to roll up the shirtsleeves."

He did so and shrugged into the vest. It was tight across his stomach and chest.

"Jeez, Billy, careful. You're going to pull off the buttons." She pushed his hands aside and finished the buttons on the vest. He looked over her shoulder at the red exit sign above the doorway that led back to the offices.

"Sorry," he muttered, though he really wasn't. This thing with Maddy had him pissed off at the world.

"I'm sorry, about the other day. I didn't know—"

We'd be making out in her office?

"It's okay. Don't worry."

"I haven't told anyone. Maddy was really worried about that."

"I'm sure she was."

"So are you guys, like . . . ?"

He shot her a shut-the-hell-up look and it worked pretty quick. She silently handed him a pair of pants, light brown and tight through the crotch and thigh. Utterly lacking modesty from years in locker rooms, he changed in front of her. "Holy crap, are they supposed to fit like this?" he asked, doing up the button and zipper.

The boots he slipped into were brown and worn but so soft they felt like butter.

"Do I look ridiculous?"

Sabine's eyes were round in her face, her mouth open.

"Oh God," he muttered. "This is a huge mistake—"

"No. No, Billy." She stopped him from taking off the vest. "You look incredible! Honestly . . . incredible."

Oh. He felt himself blushing and he ran a hand down the vest. It did feel nice, the fabric. And the pants. He turned to glance in a mirror beside the rack of clothes.

His package looked awesome! He shifted, not too bad in the butt department either.

"She won't be able to keep her hands off you," Sabine whispered and he caught her eye in the mirror.

"You think?"

She laughed, knowing and feminine.

That would certainly make the next step of getting back together with Maddy easier.

No kissing. God.

"Ten seconds," Peter whispered from the edge of the set.

Billy was remic'd and one of Tam's assistants gave him a few finishing touches, pulling and tugging and tucking. "You look great," the man said, a pin in his mouth.

Billy ran a hand down his vest again, and now that silly scrap of red in the breast pocket didn't seem so silly—it seemed kind of cool.

Maybe I do look good, he thought, for the very first time in his life.

"Welcome back," Maddy said from the stage, the bright lights hitting her face and hair, making her sparkle.

"For those of you who are just joining us, Billy Wilkins—hockey player, bad boy, and unrepentant fashion disaster—is backstage changing into the most stylish of this spring's fashions."

Tam started talking again about vests and V-neck T-shirts, and Billy, in the tight vest and the tight pants and the slick boots, felt the very same surge of confidence that he usually felt just before going out on the ice.

He felt like he could do anything and it was so weird that a new set of clothes would give him that confidence.

Gotta hand it to Tam, he thought.

"Let's bring him out here," Maddy said and turned toward where he stood in the shadows.

Here we go, Billy thought as he stepped out into the lights.

Oh. My. God.

That was the crowd's reaction. That was the reaction in a million homes across the Dallas/Ft. Worth area. And that was the reaction detonating in Maddy's chest.

Billy looked . . . delicious.

Menacing, sure, he was always going to look menacing with that body and that scar. He was a powerful, dangerous man, but he looked . . . sophisticated. Rough and urban at the same time.

In the last few years, after every failed or lukewarm date she would lie alone in her big bed and think about what kind of man she wanted, and it was impossible, utterly impossible, but Billy as he stood in front of her right now wasn't far off the mark.

Utterly masculine with just the right amount of civilization.

Not like last weekend, she thought. He didn't look a

thing like the ill-kempt and angry man who'd been in her house on Saturday.

And she'd been crazed for that version of him.

Internally her body clenched, as if holding tight to the memory of his fingers inside of her. His thumb against her. Rough and then gentle.

Maddy put her hand against the chair, trying to restore her balance, her equilibrium.

This version of him, cleaned up just enough—this Billy could ruin her with a look, a raised eyebrow, one of his naughty boy grins. There was no end to the dirty, depraved things she wanted from this Billy.

"How do you feel?" Tam asked him.

"I honestly can't believe I'm going to say this." Billy looked both vulnerable and strong at the same time and the reaction in the room was amazing. He was shrinking the studio down to an intimate space. Every woman in the room felt like he was talking just to her.

Including Maddy.

Especially Maddy.

"I feel different. Good. I really do," he said, looking down at himself.

"This is a new look for you, isn't it?" Tam asked quietly.

"Well, I've got new socks, so yeah," Billy joked, but then shook his head. "Most of my life has been dedicated to hockey. I've let everything else slip away, including who I am off the ice. And with my scar . . ."

Don't, she thought, wishing she could block out the words, the utterly human way he was relating to Tam, and the audience of women who were falling a little in love with him.

"Well, most people don't see past it. But this?" Billy laughed. "I mean, holy shit, this is great." He winced. "Can I say that on TV?"

Tam laughed. "My job here is done."

"I'll say," Maddy chimed in, forcing herself to get it together. She looked into the camera "Join us next Friday for a new installment of the Billy Wilkins Project."

For the life of her she couldn't remember what the segment was; it was like the sight of Billy in that vest had short-circuited her brain. Fumbling slightly, she thanked Tam and as she did, Billy interrupted and shook the tailor's hand with both of his. "Thank you," Billy said, earnest and sincere, a combination that was utterly devastating with that face of his. "I mean it."

Tam took the gratitude with poise and the red light on the cameras flickered off.

She pulled off her mic and left the stage. Rattled and flustered, she grabbed her water and went to her office.

Thirty minutes after the studio audience left, Billy bought all the clothes. The tight jeans, the vests, the sweaters with collars. He bought the button-down shirts and the T-shirts that were so soft they felt like he'd had them since Juniors.

And all the footwear. Even the loafers, though he doubted he could wear them without the team laughing.

And the pièce de résistance: the overcoat. Because it made him feel like an English gangster and he always wanted to feel like an English gangster in one of those Guy Ritchie movies.

"Oy, guvner," he said, looking at himself in the full-length mirror.

So in love with his whole look, he wore it to Maddy's door. If he was going to be a Gladiator dildo, he was going to be a sharply dressed one.

"Come in," her voice called and it sounded exactly like the whistle before the puck drops at the beginning of the second period. One of the best sounds on the planet.

He pushed open the door.

She'd changed from the clingy sweater dress she'd been wearing to a pair of jeans and a plain white T-shirt. It was his favorite look in the whole world, only slightly better than her wearing one of his T-shirts and nothing else.

The thought made his pants even more uncomfortable.

"Look at you," she said, watching him over the top of her white laptop. Her smile was soft. Indulgent. Fleeting.

"I bought it all," he said.

"You look like an English gangster."

"You think?" He looked down at himself as if surprised and she laughed.

"Please, you've probably been practicing your cockney accent."

He shrugged. "Maybe."

The silence sizzled, electric awareness filling the small space.

"What are you doing here, Billy?" she whispered, stopping the pretense.

"I'm not giving up."

She sat back, her arms outstretched. "This isn't a game."

"Now, that's ironic, coming from the woman who is setting all the rules."

She shook her head, his puck going wide.

"I'm not something you can win back just to prove you can."

"You think that's what I want?" It hurt that she thought his affection was so fleeting, but he realized she was telling herself these things as a way to keep him at arm's length.

"Saturday was a mistake, Billy. Let's just forget about it."

"Not possible. Sorry, Maddy, I'll go to my grave remembering how you felt."

He shrugged out of the coat, because suddenly it was so damn hot in the small office. Suddenly it was a sauna.

"I have been thinking about you every minute. The way your skin felt, the way you smelled, how you looked when you came apart under my hands."

This is what he'd come in here to say, the ball he was ready to set in motion. He wanted to change her mind about him, wanted to get back into her life, and the only way to do it was by following her rules. Otherwise she would keep them apart forever.

The buttons on his vest slipped open almost before he touched them. As if the English gangster clothes were in perfect accord with his plan for seduction.

"What . . ." She licked her lips. "What are you doing?"

"Whatever you want." From his back pocket he pulled a foil-wrapped condom and tossed it on her desk. His vest hung open over the shirt hugging the muscles of his chest and stomach.

Silent, agonized, he waited. The seconds pulled and stretched, bleeding his courage, gaining him years.

Until finally:

"Lock the door," she whispered.

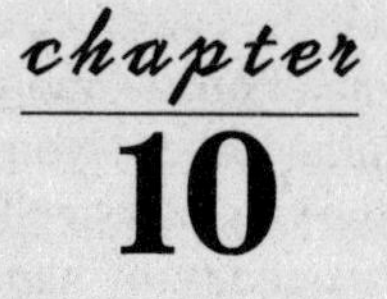

chapter 10

***What are you** doing?* The clipped, judgmental voice of Madelyn Cornish, host of the top-rated Dallas morning show, screamed in her head.

But the jungle drums beating between her legs drowned out the sound of anything rational. No time for judgment. Not when Billy was looking at her like he wanted to eat her.

His white silk shirt hugged every muscle in Billy's arms, every twitch and twist as he reached behind himself and turned the lock on the door.

Her mouth went dry, her core wet.

Click.

"My rules," she said.

Face like granite, he nodded.

Power erupted in her. Power she'd never had in their marriage.

Without a word from her, he continued taking off his clothes. Undressing for her pleasure.

That vest and shirt should look like a costume on him. They should make him ridiculous, but they didn't.

Madelyn liked clothes, and she knew their effect, and Billy, whether he knew it or not, wouldn't be able to hide in his rough, ill-fitting clothes anymore. People would look at him differently now. She couldn't help but look at him differently.

It was as if the new clothes were highlighting aspects

of himself that he usually reserved: his intelligence, empathy, and generosity; his loyalty and fierce heart.

Stop, she thought. *Don't think of him like that.*

The whiteness of his skin gleamed in the lights of her dressing room as the shirt fell off of him, the pants, the boots. He stood, nearly naked in front of her, his erection straining against his black briefs.

His scars, the evidence of his brutality, all of it was starkly on display.

Better, she thought. This was the man she knew. The man whose hold on her needed to be broken. She walked around her desk to that small space between the desk and the dressing table. Too late she realized her feet were bare.

His eyes on her toes felt more intimate than anything they'd done on Saturday.

Everything they'd done on Saturday, until that moment at the end when he'd made himself come rather than have her touch him, had been about as intimate as a car crash.

What do you want? she asked herself. *What possible outcome are you looking for?*

She didn't have an answer. Didn't want to waste time thinking about it. She felt slightly drunk with lust, out of her head with desire, and she liked it, wanted more of it. So she banished Saturday from the room, from her head.

Stopping inches from him she reached out and touched the strong, hard ridge of his erection. Tracing the edges with her fingertips, she relished the way he shook and trembled, but didn't touch her. He stood there and he took it.

Control. It was hers.

Her fingers reached below his erection and cupped the heavy bulge of his sack. Her fingers tightened, just enough, just until he hissed.

Her eyes lifted to his and she was transfixed. Immobile.

"Why are you letting me do this?" she whispered.

He didn't say anything, he didn't have to. Everything he felt was right there in his face. His eyes. That lack of boundaries that she used to love about him was in full effect.

This, for him, was about being loved again.

Boundaries, Billy, or you'll get hurt.

Reflexively her fingers twitched around the tender flesh held in cotton and he winced.

Stupid Maddy, she thought, *you are the one who wants to hurt him.*

Fast, she undid her jeans and pushed them down her legs, taking the scrap of blue lace that was her underwear with them. She kicked her legs free and wrapped her hands in the hem of her shirt to throw it over her head.

"Leave it," he whispered, his fingers running up the muscles of her legs, making them twitch and dance. "Leave the shirt."

My rules, she thought, and pulled the shirt over her head.

He closed his eyes as if saddened. But then she took his hand and put it between her legs, where the heat and the wet were already gathering. Already pooling.

With one hand between her legs, the other on her shoulder, he shifted, easing them around until her back was to the wall and he was pressed against her. His warm flesh, his thick muscles a living blanket from shoulder to hip.

His fingers found every curve of her, every recess and hill. The small places where pleasure hid, electric and difficult. She gasped, arching her neck, trying to suck down enough air to keep her balance, to keep her grounded. But his fingers knew her secrets. His breath, hot and damp, feathered her shoulder. His lips found that place behind her ear, and then his teeth, and she shook against him.

"Yes," she sighed. She lifted a leg around his hip, giving him more room, more territory to conquer. Her hips beat against his and he leaned harder against her, keeping her still.

This was what she loved about him. About sex with Billy. He could fold her up in a ball with the pleasure he gave her. All that confidence with which he wore his own skin he applied to hers. To her body. She didn't have to work for her orgasms, he delivered them to her. Served them to her. They came effortlessly.

One finger reached inside her and she arched against the wall, swallowing her cries. Suddenly, though, that warm strength of his body was gone and she couldn't help but cry out. But he'd only dropped to his knees.

What a sight, Billy, in all of his muscled glory, on his knees in front of her. She'd missed this.

He lifted her leg, throwing it over his shoulder, his fingers opening her for his tongue. His teeth.

As good as this man was at hockey, he was better at *this*. He'd spent a summer between her legs, studying her response, figuring out all of her secrets, all the ways he could make her scream with his tongue and fingers. Small touches, bold licks, hard, soft, quick, and agonizingly slow.

No one went down on a woman with as much intent and pleasure as Billy Wilkins. And he'd ruined her for other men. The few that she'd let between her legs since him had been sad disappointments. Not worth the effort of the bikini wax.

But Billy . . .

Yes, she thought, curling her fingers through his hair, feeling his jaw move against her. *Yes. This. There. Now.*

Seconds, less than seconds, between one heartbeat

and the next. She was herself and then she was shattered, a thousand glittering pieces on a jet-black horizon.

He kissed his way up her body until he was on his feet, his mouth hovering over hers. His lips damp with her. Her eyes met his and she wanted to kiss him so badly it hurt, but she turned her face away, denying herself because it denied him.

"Get the condom," she whispered. He crossed the small room, the muscles of his back, his round tight skater's ass flexing as he walked over to her desk. His back to her, she watched as he used his teeth to open the wrapper. Head bent, he put the condom on, and then, without turning around, he walked over to her desk chair, an armless wooden antique that she'd picked up from who knows where.

He sat, his erection vulgar and crude. Exciting.

"Come here," he whispered.

My rules, she thought, but she could feel him between her legs, could feel how she'd be able to control it all from that position. Her pleasure. His.

She stepped up to him, placing her legs on either side of him. Careful not to touch him, though her fingers burned to do so, she curled her hands around the top of the chair.

The sensation of his hand on her hip was searing and she almost told him not to touch her, but then he pushed her down and the head of his dick was stretching her, testing its welcome into her body.

She dropped her head forward and closed her eyes, taking him inch by delicious inch.

"Maddy," he groaned. "Oh God, you're so . . . ah . . ."

Tight. Hot. Wet. Yes, she was all of those things.

And in control.

She curled her hips and sat, taking all of him inside her so fast and so hard, they both cried out at the riot of sensations. His hands clenched at her hips, a small pain.

"Shh," she whispered as he arched up higher into her. "We have to be quiet."

"Move," he groaned into her ear. Slowly, she rocked on him, pressing her groin against his, until she felt the heightening pressure on her clit. Back and forth again, a long, slow rock and curl.

He was whispering, groaning filthy things in her ear, and it drove her higher. Faster. His hands skated across her flesh, cupping her breasts, her hips, curling around her neck, pulling at her hair. All of it added to the pleasure building low in her belly.

"Maddy," he groaned and she lifted her head to look at him.

And then, like an insect in a web, she couldn't look away. Billy, tortured with pleasure, holding himself back for her, was mesmerizing.

"Baby," he sighed, his face splitting with a luminous smile. He leaned forward to kiss her and she lurched back, turning her face away.

"No."

"Look at me," he growled and she closed her eyes, unable to look at him. Unable to see him so happy just because they were fucking.

"Look. At. Me." She shook her head and he grabbed her waist, lifting her slightly away from him, holding her still. "Maddy."

"My rules," she gasped.

For one long moment she wasn't sure what he was going to do and knew she wasn't strong enough to make him do anything. She tried to break his hold, but he wouldn't budge. Pleasure grew thorns and jagged edges and she groaned with the agony of it all.

In one easy, graceful surge he took them down to the floor behind her desk. He braced one hand against the wall so she wouldn't hit her head and then slowly, inch by agonizing inch, thrust into her and then retreated.

"Look at me."

Every breath she sucked in tasted of sweat and sex. She dug her nails into the muscles of his hips, his back.

But no way would she look at him. Scared of what she'd see, scared of how she'd feel, she kept her eyes closed, holding on to her pleasure with a fierce grip. He hissed and thrust back into her, setting a rhythm that wasn't enough. Not even close.

"Look at me, Maddy. Please. God . . ."

Her rules. Honestly, who had she been kidding? It would always be his rules when it came to this. Furious with him, with herself, but helpless with lust, she opened her eyes.

"There you are," he whispered.

There you are. She curled her fingers into fists against his back so she wouldn't touch his face, trace that scar, the curve of his smile.

Beloved, so beloved to her once.

What are you doing? she thought, suddenly cold with panic. Her hips stilled, her arms fell to her sides. *This isn't uninvolved! This isn't arm's length!*

He paused, as if sensing her sudden change of heart and then, without looking at her, he shifted, leaned down to her breasts, breathing across the tips. He kissed her nipples, the curve of her breasts as his hands shaped her waist, cradled her hips.

Those places on her body, unobtrusive and quiet, she loved to be touched. The back of her knee, the crease of her elbow. He knew all of them, like a map he'd committed to memory.

He stroked and touched until the fires came back.

Until she forgot who she was and who he was and what a huge mistake they were making.

Dropping his head to her neck, he picked up the rhythm, drove them headlong as fast as he could, as if he knew she was a reluctant passenger, as if at any moment she could come back to her senses, right into pleasure.

Awkwardly, Madelyn picked her clothes up from the floor, slipping on her underwear and pants, all too aware of her naked ass and his interest.

"So," he asked and she looked over her shoulder at him just in time to see him working on the middle button of his shirt. With the scarred half of his face hidden, he looked like one of those men on the underwear ad billboards. "Are you just using me for sex or can I get a meal out of it, too?"

Smiling at her blank expression, he pulled the shirt from her limp hand and slipped it over her head. Dressing her tenderly, as if she were a child. "Can I take you out to dinner?" he asked, his heart in his eyes.

"What?" she snapped, slapping his hands away.

"Food. Some steaks. Frankly, I don't think anyone is feeding you these days."

"No. Billy—"

"Okay." He shrugged, totally nonplussed. "Thought I'd give it a shot."

"We're not . . ." Awkward, she pointed to the office chair they'd just defiled. "Dating."

"Trust me." He also pointed to the chair. "I know what that's called."

He pulled the vest on over his untucked shirt, leaving the buttons undone. The jacket, slightly wrinkled, was picked up from her office floor.

"You have big plans this weekend?" he asked and then laughed when she just gaped at him. "We can't even make small talk? Maddy, come on. Throw me a bone."

"I . . . I have a charity thing tomorrow." She put on her shoes.

She'd gotten picky the last few years about which charity events she attended because she wanted to enjoy the events and in her position she got asked to a lot. But this one had sounded interesting, a sports-based curriculum for inner-city kids.

"Charity? Sick kids or poor ones?"

"A new charter school for inner-city kids." She dug through the drawers of her dressing table for a hairband. It seemed like Gina kept taking all of hers and leaving them on the dressing tables backstage.

Billy was quiet, so she glanced at him to make sure he wasn't staring at her butt. He wasn't. He was grinning at her like he had a secret.

"What?"

"You need a date?"

Back in the far corner she felt something rubber band like.

"No. Billy, I just told you we're not dating."

"I bought a tux from Tam. I'll be pretty slick. Maybe I'll get you a corsage and we can make out in my truck after. Just like old times."

"This isn't going to happen again."

"What?"

"Us." She yanked her hair back in a ponytail, pulling it extra tight as if to punish herself for the pleasure she'd just had. "And what in the world do you need a tux for?"

"I go to charity things, too." He was grinning at her and she forced herself not to grin back, but it was hard and he seemed to know it.

"All right." He grabbed a pencil and a Post-it from her desk. "But if you"—he smirked at her, an eyebrow raised—"change your mind and want a little man candy on your arm . . ."

Laughing would only encourage him but she couldn't help it. She would blame it on the sex.

He waggled his eyebrows. "Here's my cell phone number."

"A booty call?" Again, she laughed.

"That's what the kids call it."

He was totally unhinged. Deluded. But as she stood there, counting the ways he was a fool, even as she laughed, he leaned over and pressed a soft, sweet kiss on her cheek.

She felt every crease of his skin, inhaled the spicy scent of him, part new clothes, part sex, all Billy.

Those fires, put out just moments ago, flickered back to life.

Again, her body moaned. Just one more time.

She pulled back. "I won't call you," she said, making it clear to both of them.

"All right."

His acceptance made her nervous and she was reminded suddenly of the Monday morning meeting. And Phil.

"Billy, I think . . . I think Phil may have found your sisters."

"They're not hard to find," he said. "They've lived in the same neighborhood their whole lives."

"I know, but . . . maybe you should call them. Talk to them."

"And say what?"

" 'Don't do the show.' "

His face went blank and her stomach dropped to her feet. She knew he had to feel the same way, embarrassed and horrified at the thought of having them on the show, and embarrassed and horrified that he felt that way.

But Denise and Janice weren't happy unless they brought the world down to their level.

"You've worked so hard—" she said, trying to twist the screws her direction.

"Don't," he lifted his hand. "Just . . . don't."

"Fine." She swallowed the taste of vanity and snobbery. "For me, Billy. Try to convince them not to do the show, for me."

"Okay." His immediate agreement surprised her and made her feel worse. Made her feel self-important and crass. *Remember,* she told herself, shoring up the weak spots in her resolve, *remember what they're like. Dogs with a bone. Do you want your show to be that bone?*

"Thank you," she whispered, because the answer was clear. She would do anything to protect her show. Her life.

"Ah, baby," he whispered, his fingers touching the side of her face, brushing a hair behind her ear, turning her skin to electricity. "Don't feel so bad."

She let his touch absolve her. Let his words wash away the worst of her regret about Denise.

He dropped his hand and unlocked the door, swinging it open as if nothing had happened.

Does it smell like sex in here? Panicked and embarrassed she grabbed the hairspray from the corner of her dressing table and filled the air with the masking scent of aerosol.

Now it smelled like sex in a junior high girls' locker room.

He stopped, leaned against the door frame, the smile gone, his eyes serious. "I missed you. I missed—" he glanced sideways at the chair, the floor, "—us. Like that."

So did she. Painfully. But she would rather eat her foot than reveal that to him.

I won't lose myself to you. Not again.

"Good-bye, Billy," she said and closed the door in his smiling face.

chapter 11

Seventeen years ago

Maddy stamped her boots, trying to keep her feet warm. Her toes were like little frozen peas in her socks. She could be in the car, the heat blasting as she waited for him, but she was too nervous. Too excited to sit.

It had been two months since she'd seen Billy. He was playing in Rochester in the Junior A's and had been billeted with a family up there. He hadn't been able to come home for Christmas or her birthday, but now he had a three day break and was hightailing it back to Pittsburgh.

Billy had been busy lately—he'd been signed by an agent and they'd submitted his name for the draft in June. Last year had been the first he was eligible, but his shoulder surgery had kept him out of the action.

So this was his year.

Her stomach lurched at the thought and she bounced, trying to find a balance between excitement and worry.

Excitement that all his hard work was about to pay off and worry that he would be taken away from her on the wings of his big NHL dreams.

He's going to leave at some point, her mom had told her. And in her head Maddy understood that. But in her heart she believed Billy was hers, NHL or not.

A car pulled up, white exhaust clouding the cold cold air. And then Billy spilled out of the passenger seat, his eyes on her.

Her body shook at the sight of him. Her nipples were hard, her skin on fire. So long. It had been so long.

She waited, breathless, as he got his gear, and said good-bye to the guy who'd given him the ride. Then, as the car drove away, she couldn't stand it anymore. She ran, launching herself onto him.

Hockey sticks clattered to the frozen asphalt, his bag falling with a wet thud. And then he was there, his arms hard around her. His breath in her hair.

Through their coats and sweaters, she felt his heart. And it belonged to her. No question.

"Maddy," he sighed, as if slipping into a hot bath or a warm bed. "I missed you so much."

Holding his head between her mittened hands she kissed him. She kissed him like she wanted to put a mark on him, and maybe she did. He was going to get picked up by the NHL in a few months, and his life would change dramatically. But the world should know she got here first. She had known the power of Billy Wilkins before everyone else.

She opened her mouth, her tongue slipping in against his. She licked and sucked at him.

Billy liked that, always liked it when she got carried away. When she took control. He lifted her slightly and in his jeans she felt his dick, long and hard, and she pressed up tight against it, let one of his legs slide between hers.

His groan matched hers as their bodies pulled and pushed toward each other.

"You're killing me, baby," he whispered.

"I've got Dad's keys." She lifted them from her pocket, the old Pit Bulls keychain catching the streetlight and gleaming like silver.

His grin, cockeyed and dangerous, sent sparks of excitement through her body. "Then let's go," he said.

They grabbed his stuff and headed for the back door of the arena, making sure no one was watching.

She opened the old purple door and they slipped inside.

It was dark and cool. Emergency lights made red splotches on the cement, and the ice glowed bone-white in the shadows.

"I missed you," Billy whispered, unzipping her coat. She shook off her mittens and then she started work on his coat. Heat from his car ride was trapped inside his clothes and as she mined for his skin, digging through fabric and buttons for the smoothness of his chest, her fingers got warm. Her body even warmer.

He pulled her turtleneck over her head, and at the sound of his moan she was glad she'd put on the fancy bra he'd sent her for Christmas.

He bent, lifting her breasts together, the mounds coming up high out of the lace, and he licked and kissed her. Sucked her nipples through the fabric as she curled against him, shaking with pleasure. She forgot about his shirt. Another time, maybe. Right now she was too desperate. Too hungry.

She reached for his pants, her fingers finding him under the warm denim. Long and thick and hard.

Mine, she thought. *Mine before anyone else's.*

He backed up and turned, pushing her against the wall. The concrete was hard and cold against her back but she didn't care. Not as long as he was there, hot and hard against her front.

"You missed me?" he asked, laughing a little. Teasing her. This was new, this teasing thing. Like she had to prove how much she wanted him every time they saw each other.

"So much," she gasped, licking his neck. "So much, Billy."

"Did you think about me?"

"All the time."

"Did you think about having sex with me?"

She leaned back, meeting his eyes, his face bathed in the light from the red exit sign above their heads.

"Yes," she whispered, her heart pounding around her chest like an elephant.

"What did you think about?"

Embarrassed, she tilted her head, looking away. He kissed her cheek, the corner of her mouth, and she turned again, trying to kiss him for real, but he leaned back.

"Billy—"

"I thought about kissing you," he said. "I thought about going down on you. I thought about the way you look in that red swimsuit and that sound you make when I push my dick inside you. Every day, all day long, I thought of how hot you get. How wet."

"Billy," she groaned, arching against him, restless and hurting.

"Feel me," he said and she reached between them and undid his zipper. Enough of these games. Enough of trying to convince him with words.

She stroked him hard and he hissed. The tip of him was wet. He didn't bother to remove her tights; he reached down and tore a hole in the crotch.

She groaned, so excited she couldn't help it. His fingers, rough and big were there. Right there. Billy was the only guy she'd ever slept with, but when he made her feel this good, when he made the world fall away and the lights start spinning, what in the world would she need another guy for?

"No one but you," she said, because he always seemed to need the words.

"Me too," he said and then he pushed down his pants and pulled up her denim skirt. She wrapped her legs around his waist, and rested her back against the wall.

When Mom first caught wind of her and Billy dating, she marched Maddy to the doctor and got her a prescription for the pill. Even though they weren't having sex yet.

But now they were. They were having lots of sex. And Billy was really happy they didn't need condoms and she felt grown up and excited with his skin against hers.

Hot and hard, he speared into her. Through her. Changing her every time, making her more and more his.

She cried out and he groaned. He wrapped his hands around her back, over her shoulders, holding her still with all his strength while he moved in and out of her, dragging himself slowly against her wetness. It felt like someone was bunching her up, crumpling her together, and she held on, held on, tighter and tighter, until finally she let go in a wild, crazy burst and flew high and bright into the dark.

Billy rested his head against her shoulder, panting and thrusting, and she could feel him. The tension in his back. His arms.

"Baby," he groaned. "Oh God . . ."

"I love you, Billy."

And then he was flying, the skin over her collarbone caught between his teeth, and she sighed and winced at the same time.

She held him as he shook, laughing when he wiped his sweaty forehead against her neck.

"Wow," she sighed, unlocking her legs from around his hips. Her boots hit the floor and he slipped out of her, she could feel him wet and soft against her belly.

He curled his arms around her back and now that the

storm was over, he just held her, swaying slightly, his pants around his ankles. Her skirt around her waist.

This was her favorite. As amazing as all the other stuff was, this was her favorite part. When he was tired and sweet and they'd made each other feel so good and there wasn't any other world or person or thing they had to worry about.

At peace, she burrowed her face into his shirt, the chest strong and warm beneath it.

"Marry me."

She laughed and shook her head. Billy had proposed about a hundred times. Usually after sex.

"I'm not kidding."

His voice was different and she glanced up at him, only to find him staring at her. Earnest.

"What are you talking about?" she asked.

"I want us to get married. I hate being apart."

"I do too, but Billy—"

"I'm going to be drafted. Victor said there's a lot of interest." The draft was a sure thing in Billy's head and she didn't have the heart to say it wasn't a done deal, no matter what his agent said. Good players didn't always get drafted. But she wanted to believe he'd be drafted just as much as he did. "And what if I go to Phoenix or Canada? What do we do then?"

"Let's worry about it later."

"I don't want to worry about it at all. Let's get married and it's taken care of." His grin was so sweet, the only argument he needed most of the time. But this was serious.

"I just turned seventeen."

"Next year, then. Your birthday is right after Christmas. We'll get married then."

"What about school?"

"There are schools everywhere. Even in Canada." He winked. "I think."

He kissed her cheek and helped her get dressed again. She loved it when he took care of her, the big tough hockey player, straightening her torn tights over her hips, tucking her turtleneck into her skirt.

"I could just move with you," she said. "Wherever you go."

"Right. Your parents will love that."

"Well, I don't know that they'll love me getting married either."

Billy cupped her face in his hands, her hair pulled slightly under his palms but she didn't say anything.

Pain and pleasure. With Billy you couldn't have one without the other.

"You are the only person that matters to me," he said, kissing her cheeks, her eyelids. "The only family I need."

She sighed and closed her eyes. Why was she fighting?

"After my birthday and the draft."

He reeled back, joy all over his face. "Really?"

"Really."

He whooped, picked her up, and spun her, her feet clanging into the garbage can that her father emptied every night.

"But—" she said and he stopped. "We have to talk to my parents."

He set her down, the first storm clouds entering those brown eyes. "After we elope?"

"Why are we eloping?" she asked, dropping her arms from around his neck. It was getting cooler in the arena.

"You want my family at your wedding?"

No. She didn't. But she didn't want to lose the white dress and her dad walking her down the aisle either. "I want to tell my parents about this. I can't just surprise them with it."

"Why does it matter?"

"Because my family is important to me."

"They won't like it, Maddy. They don't like me."

"That's not true, Billy. They don't know you. You don't let them." He groaned and stepped away. Now it was freezing. She grabbed her coat and shrugged into it.

"I don't want to fight," she said, pushing her hands into her mittens.

"Me neither," he said, like it was all her fault. She reached out and stroked his back while he zipped up his jeans.

"It means a lot to me," she said and he sighed. "That you would try to get to know them better. Not every family is like yours. And not every dad—"

"I get it, Maddy."

She nodded and backed off, knowing it was such a sore subject for him. They could never talk about his family without getting into a fight.

"Are you hungry?" she asked, changing the subject for everyone's sake. Because he would just stew and get moodier and the night would be ruined.

"Starved!"

"Primanti Brothers?"

"Oh my God. Yes!" he groaned and they both collected his things. When they stepped out into the cold night, he wrapped his arm around her shoulder.

"I'm sorry," he breathed into her hair. His breath fogging the air in front of her, obscuring her world.

"I love you."

"I love you, too."

And really, what more did she need? As long as he loved her, they could make anything work.

chapter 12

After Maddy had divorced him and moved down to Florida with her mother, Billy had been unable to stay in that big house he'd bought. So he went back home to his mother. To his sisters.

They weren't the family he hungered for but they were what he had. And at that moment, it had been enough.

Their vileness, their small hearts, their cruelty. It had fed the poisonous weeds growing in the place where all his love had been.

They drank together. Cursed Maddy. Cursed their lives. And when he woke up one morning and decided that he'd had enough, they'd held on. For money. For fame.

They sold information to any gossip magazine. Ugly details about his childhood, his marriage. And if the tabloids didn't want the truth, his sisters made up terrible lies. It had been embarrassing, angering, frustrating, until finally he just shut and locked the door between him and them. Effectively ending his relationship with the only family he had left.

However, Tuesday night Billy sat in his dark kitchen thinking about opening that door again, even though he was certain nothing good would come of it.

The shadows lay like cats over the furniture, over the bare skin of his arms and chest. And he was cold—no warmth was to be leeched from the shadows, from his empty house.

On the table, his cell phone sat in a bright puddle of moonlight beaming in from the window behind him.

You said you would do it, he told himself, and then, before he could talk himself out of it, he picked up the phone and dialed a number he knew by heart.

The number to that black home where he'd grown up.

"The number you have dialed," a robotic woman's voice repeated the familiar digits, "is no longer in service. Please check your number and try again."

He hung his head, the phone clasped between his praying hands. "Thank God," he murmured. He'd tried. He had no other number for his sisters, there wasn't much more he could do.

Bullshit, a voice inside of him said.

Out from under the locked door slipped the memory of that three-year-old girl at the funeral. Wide-eyed and stoic. A bright red ribbon in her hair.

Swearing, he pushed the speed dial button for his lawyer's office. He wasn't sure if Ted was the right guy to call; he probably needed a private investigator, but at least it was a start.

After the voicemail beep he explained the situation with his sisters and asked for help tracking them down.

When he hung up he felt sick, pursued.

He hoped that the poison of his past wasn't going to ruin his future.

"I've got the world on a string," Billy sang under his breath as he walked into the glittering red and gold ballroom at the Four Seasons.

He wasn't a huge Sinatra fan, but when a guy looked this good in a tux, Springsteen just didn't cut it.

It was Saturday night and Billy had put in a little extra

effort getting ready for the New School fund-raiser. He'd moisturized, for crying out loud. Underneath his new tux, he was soft as a baby.

But it was all working for him. Women were giving him second looks as he walked by, and the men he passed smiled, nodding their heads, like putting on a tux and slicking back his hair elevated Billy into a certain club.

Hell, maybe it did. It's not like he'd ever done this shit before.

As a rule Billy avoided these black-tie charity functions like the plague. He donated plenty of money, so he got invited to a lot of them, but he never went.

He was breaking that rule tonight—in a big way. Tonight, he didn't want to be anywhere else in the world.

Maddy was going to die when she saw him.

In a good way, he hoped. Die in a good way.

Thanks to the stupid bow tie, he was a little later than he'd expected and wasn't sure if he was still able to get to the hotel before her.

Scanning the room, he saw plenty of black ties and sequins, and the requisite ice sculpture in the corner—an open book, how fitting. Under the crystal chandeliers, waiters with trays circulated among the crowd, but no Maddy.

Thank God. He blew out the breath he'd been holding. He needed a few minutes to find something to eat and get his skates under him. Across the room, Luc—looking dapper as always—waved him over to join the small crowd of people he was entertaining. Billy swore to himself.

He was going to have to mingle and shit. In his excitement to see Maddy, he'd managed to forget that small detail.

Maybe he'd just grab something to eat before heading over there. He tried to catch the eye of one of the waiters who was carrying a tray of appetizers, only to catch the eye of Coach Hornsby instead.

"Hey, Coach," he said, trying to be polite. Friendly, even. Coach Hornsby was big on charity, and he'd probably open his wallet pretty wide tonight.

"Billy." They quickly shook hands as if it were a chore. "Luc was telling me that this school was actually your idea?" Coach said it like he couldn't quite believe it, and Billy laughed.

"Sounds crazy, huh?"

"Uh . . ."

"It's okay, Coach. Actually, it was an idea I've had for a long time and last summer I ran it by Tara Jean and Luc, who had started up their foundation to help kids. The next thing I knew they were getting this whole thing organized. So I can't claim much more than the idea. The rest is all them."

"Well, no matter what, I'm pretty impressed."

And that, Billy thought, *is because I have set the bar so low.* God, this bow tie was too tight. He lifted his chin, stretching his neck.

"You know, I've also been impressed with you on that show," Coach Hornsby said. "That morning makeover thing."

Oh, this was getting out of hand. He could feel his whole body flushing. "Yeah?"

"You're doing great. Front office has had a lot of calls about you."

So was Billy's agent. A men's soap company wanted to talk to him about doing an ad. With leprechauns. It was ridiculous.

"What kind of calls?"

"Good ones." Hornsby grinned at him like a proud father and it rankled so hard, so suddenly, Billy had to take a step back. It was a knee jerk reaction, he knew that, one he'd been having with people all his life.

Don't get close. I'll only fail you.

No other coach had expected this much from him. Billy did his job on the ice and they were happy. There was none of this heart-to-heart, I'm-proud-of-you nonsense.

"I'm impressed, Billy. I'm impressed by how honest you are on that show. None of the bullshit I usually see."

"It's only clothes," he snapped, even though that hadn't been his intention. Hornsby blinked, surprised, like the friendly dog he'd been patting had just snapped at him.

And whatever normalcy there had been between them was ruined. Another one of Billy's special skills. "I need to . . . ah . . ." He pointed vaguely toward Luc.

"Sure. Nice talking to you." Hornsby walked away, probably grateful for the escape.

I'm no good at this, Billy thought, watching the guy go.

Luc approached with a plate full of appetizers and Billy's stomach growled in welcome.

"Hey, buddy." He pulled two shrimp off Luc's plate.

"Here," Luc handed him the plate. "You look good, man."

"Thanks. Took me forever to tie this stupid tie."

"They're tricky."

"So . . . you think it's going well?" Billy asked, dipping a crab cake into some spicy white sauce. Awesome.

Luc nodded. "Yeah, I do. Tara Jean is excited because the consultant we hired says the fund-raiser is better attended than expected. We've got the education commissioner here and she seems pretty fired up about the whole thing, talking about a citywide program. I think you've really started something."

"It wasn't me," Billy said, catching sight of Tara Jean walking toward them. "It was your girlfriend."

Luc and Billy watched as TJ approached, glimmering like a disco ball.

"She is something, isn't she?" Luc murmured, a private smile that spoke volumes on his face. Billy focused on another crab cake.

When she finally reached them, Tara Jean kissed Luc and gave Billy a hug.

"You ready to say a few words?" she asked.

"Who? Me?" Billy pointed to himself.

"Yes, you."

He looked to Luc for help, but his friend only shrugged.

"She said you promised."

"Not yet," he said. "Let me eat and have a drink. Loosen up."

Billy pinched a broken crab cake between his fingers and tipped back his head to drop the crumbs into his mouth. Tara and Luc stared at him.

"What?" he asked.

"Why don't you just lick the plate?" Tara asked.

"Very funny."

"When is your manners makeover?" Luc asked.

"Friday," he said, and caught a piece of crab cake in his hand as it fell out of his mouth.

"Not soon enough," Tara muttered.

"Come on, it's enough that I get harassment from Maddy."

"Maddy . . ." Tara drew the name out like a five syllable word.

To counteract the blush roaring up his neck Billy took a bite of a spring roll.

"You guys are so good together on that show," Tara said.

Oh honey, he thought with an internal grin, not unlike Luc's external one a second ago, *you don't know the half of it.*

What happened in the office Friday was like a dream he kept getting lost in. The memory of her touch was so immediate it was as if she were right there, at his shoulder, her palm against his cheek.

He couldn't help but smile. Was it ideal? No. But it was better than nothing.

"So . . . I take it things are going well?" Tara Jean and Luc exchanged slightly baffled looks.

There were things on the tip of his tongue that he didn't even realize he wanted to say, but suddenly now in this moment, in a tux with crab on the jacket, he needed to get them off his chest.

"I love her." The feeling exploded in his body, blowing him wide open. He pretended to wipe off his hands in an effort to expel the energy that rippled through him, nervous and wild.

It wasn't a revelation to him. He'd loved Maddy since he was fifteen. Divorce hadn't changed that. Fourteen years apart, her anger and resentment, even as she had sex with him—all of those obstacles were minuscule compared to his feelings.

And those feelings had been in storage for a long time. It felt good to dust them off and set them up in the sunlight, where things like love belonged.

"Does . . . does she love you back?" Luc asked. "Are you getting back together?"

"No," he laughed. "Not . . . not anytime soon."

"Why are you laughing?" Luc asked.

"Because two weeks ago, I would have said 'never.' So, you know . . . progress."

Someone stopped at Tara's shoulder, distracting her, and Billy felt Luc's eyes on him.

"I've never seen you like this before."

"Dressed up?"

"Happy." Luc clapped him on the back. "Looks good on you."

"Hey, Billy?" Tara asked, turning around. "Now's the time, they're setting up the microphone."

His stomach erupted with butterflies, battling it out with the crab cakes. "You sure it's necessary?"

"Just say what you said to us that day on the patio." Luc pushed Billy toward a little stage.

"Fine. Fine. Stop pushing." He shrugged off Luc's hands and jerked his jacket straight.

Always composed in front of a crowd, Luc stepped up to the microphone like it was no big deal.

Billy could feel the sweat beading in the small of his back and at his hairline.

"If I can have your attention, please," Luc said. "I'd like to thank everyone for coming tonight, and for giving so generously to the New School. Ever since Hurricane Katrina, our city's public schools have been running at capacity and the needs of many of these students—who were already behind educationally and who have suffered astonishing trauma—have not been met. The New School, in its efforts to educate students by integrating sports into standard curriculum"—Luc held a hand to his chest—"is, I think, a step in the right direction. Now, before we begin the silent auction, I would like to invite a friend to say a few words. Most of you know Billy Wilkins from his reserved seat in the penalty box—"

There was a chorus of laughs and Billy shook his head, taking the teasing good-naturedly.

"But the idea for the New School was actually his. Billy?"

Billy stepped to the podium and shifted the microphone with hands that ran with sweat. He almost lifted his arm to wipe his forehead with his sleeve but he remembered Maddy giving him a hard time about that and he stopped.

"I . . . uh . . ." The microphone buzzed and squealed and Billy pulled it away from his face. What the hell?

"Step away from the stand," Luc whispered and Billy backed up and tried again, his confidence totally shaken.

"I grew up in a pretty tough neighborhood," Billy began, "under . . . well, some pretty tough conditions." A nervous tic, he touched the side of his mouth, the scar, and then dropped his hand, hoping no one would take too much note of it. "I went to school in the days before everyone understood, much less diagnosed, ADHD or post-traumatic stress disorder, but there's no question that I had it. Sitting at a desk all day didn't make sense for me. I honestly couldn't keep my body still, or stay focused for long enough to absorb what my teachers were saying. But once I got on the ice, things made sense. And not just hockey. Math made sense, geometry. Science. I could think when my body was moving. Sitting still, I . . . I was lost. And I've known a lot of athletes over the years, not just hockey players, but across every sport, who had the same experience growing up."

Everyone was staring at him and he tried to pretend they were in their underwear, but that made the butterflies even more restless. So he was staring over their heads, toward the back door, when a tall, beautiful woman in a purple dress walked in.

His brain was such a mess, it took him a moment to recognize her.

And when he did his heart filled his chest to capacity, and his lungs collapsed with pleasure and delight.

Maddy.

chapter 13

Maddy winced and slipped in along the side of the room. She'd come in during a speech and she didn't want to distract the audience or the speaker.

"I . . . ah . . . I heard about this school in New York City using art to teach kids who had . . . special needs, I guess is what they call it," the speaker said and her head snapped up at the sound of his voice.

Billy?

Quickly she crossed the empty space near the door, joining the small crowd around the stage.

It was. It was Billy up there. Speaking. In a tux.

The first time she saw him skate, she'd been ten or something. She'd gone to the arena after school to meet her father, and Billy had been on the ice, working drills with his team.

Skating in and around pucks and then sprinting up and down the length of the ice.

She'd sat in the stands, breathless with surprise. Awed by his talent. He was faster than everyone, more clever, quicker. The sound of the puck coming off his stick was like a gunshot. He'd been awesome in her eyes.

This moment was not all that different.

"And I wondered," he continued, "if there wasn't a way to use sports in the same way. Kids in parts of the city live through trauma every day. Trauma many of us in this room can't even imagine. And if the kids can't deal with it, they get stuck. Lost. Like I was. I shared this idea I'd had running around in my mind for a few years with Luc Baker and Tara Jean Sweet, and they've found the people who can put the whole thing together so we can reach those kids. And . . ." He chewed on his lip, looking so uncomfortable but so earnest at the same time that the effect he had on the crowd, on her, was magical. She was so spellbound by him she couldn't breathe. "I believe it can work. With the right help—and by *help,* I mean money."

The crowd laughed and he smiled, his fingers brushing his scar. His nervous tic. She pressed her fist to her stomach, above the ruche fabric at her hip, just to remind herself of who she was, where she was.

He opened his mouth as if to say something else but stopped, smiled, and then laughed. Awkward. So damn cute she could barely stand it.

"Thanks," he said and shrugged, looking for a place to put the microphone.

The crowd erupted with cheers and she felt the applause ringing through her body. He'd just shown these people the side of him she'd loved.

"Quite a speech, huh?"

She blinked and turned to find a man standing next to her in a suit that worked hard over the swell of his stomach. He watched her with warm, intelligent eyes from behind a pair of thick glasses.

"It was," she said, smiling. He was the kind of guy who got smiled at. Like Santa Claus.

"I've been following that guy's career for the last ten years and just when I think he can't surprise me anymore, he does something like this."

Buddy, she thought, *you don't know the half of it.*

"I'm sorry." He switched his champagne glass to his left hand and held out his right. "I'm Dominick Murphy. My friends call me Dom."

"Madelyn Cornish."

"Oh, I know who you are. You're the one giving Billy some soul on daytime television."

She laughed, trying to downplay her pride in the show. "So far it's just been some new clothes."

"I like your modesty, but I think something big is happening on your show."

"Thank you," she said, not immune in any way to flattery. The guy's crusty charm was pretty effective.

"This guy bothering you?" Billy appeared at her elbow, and the relief and happiness she felt upon seeing him made her awkward. She crossed her arms over her chest as if to make sure they wouldn't touch.

"Not at all," she said.

"Well done up there," Dom said, shaking Billy's hand in that hard, swift way of men. "I can barely recognize you in that monkey suit."

"Thanks." Billy rolled his eyes toward Maddy. "I think. And thanks for coming. So . . . what do you think?"

"I think the school is interesting. But what's more interesting is you and your involvement in it. Those tough circumstances you mentioned—"

Billy held up his hands in surrender. "You don't give up, do you, Dom?"

"No. Not on you, Billy. Here." He handed Billy a business card. "If you change your mind, I promise I'll be gentle with you."

"I've heard that before. But here . . ." Billy took a pen from the inside pocket of his beautiful tux jacket, and Dom handed him another card. Billy wrote on the back of it. "This is my cell number and email address if you're interested in talking about the New School."

Dom took the card and lifted his glass in a salute toward Maddy. "You are even more beautiful in person," he said and then turned back to Billy. "I can't say the same about you."

"Very funny." Billy shooed him away and as soon as the old reporter disappeared, Billy's magnetism increased. Her body felt the distance between them and protested, trying to force her closer. An urge she had to work hard to resist.

"Who is Dom?"

"A freelance writer for a bunch of magazines, like *Sports Illustrated* and *Esquire*. He keeps harassing me to do a story."

"About the school?"

"About me. My life."

Panic skittered across her skin like bugs.

"About your past?"

About me? That's what she really wanted to say and he picked up on it, watching her carefully as if she might run.

"That's probably part of it."

Immediately the walls began to close in on her. Between this and the threat of his sisters showing up on her show, she felt her whole world slipping away. Everything she'd worked so hard for could be destroyed. By him.

"Hey, hey," he said, touching her wrist and she wanted to jerk her hand back, protect herself, keep up the walls that allowed her to feel safe. And as if he read that, as if he knew, he dropped his hand. "I didn't say I was going to do it."

"It's not just that story. It's your sisters."

"I'm tracking them down."

That brought her up short. "You are?"

"I called my lawyer on Tuesday, and yesterday his secretary called me with the name of a private investigator. Don't worry, Maddy. I won't . . . I won't let you get hurt."

In all their years together he'd never said that. He'd never offered that to her. For so long, in so many ways large and small, she'd been his protector. The one constantly watching for hidden dangers. Rocks just under the surface of the water.

The temptation to lean back in that support, to allow him to care for her in that way, was bittersweet.

Their little corner of the ballroom was suddenly the most intimate place in the world. In the shallow curve of his neck she could see his heart beating and she imagined kissing him there.

"I like the way you're looking at me," he whispered.

"Billy." That was all she could say in the face of his desire, her marshmallow arms were useless. Part of her—a larger part than she was prepared to admit—wanted to wrap herself around him and leave. Go to that surprising home of his and make love to him. Be made love to by him.

But again, he showed this surprising understanding—this heartbreaking empathy—and stepped back, granting her some distance.

He grabbed a glass of champagne from a passing waiter and handed it to her, giving her a second to pull herself back from that surprising cliff.

Half the glass went down in one swallow, something she'd regret when it hit her empty stomach, but it gave her the chance to get her feet back under her.

And once she did and the walls crept back into place, she remembered how she'd been duped.

"Wait a second. You're behind the New School?"

He held out his arms. "Surprise."

"Did you send the invite?"

"I didn't lick the stamp—"

"You could have told me." She narrowed her eyes at him. "Yesterday in my dressing room."

"If I had told you, you never would have come."

There was no point in denying it. Because with forewarning, she would have done anything to circumvent this unwelcome attraction. And she thought he understood that. He was supposed to be playing by her rules.

This couldn't be happening between them. Not now. There was too much that would be ruined if they were to take their tentative reconciliation any further.

The show.

Her identity.

"I told you we aren't getting back together, Billy. Ever."

"I know."

"You say those words, but look at what you're doing." She gestured to the ice sculpture, the black-tie waiters, the glittering women and handsome men. "You keep trying. You keep pushing. The same old Billy."

How foolish she'd been to think that she could keep her distance with him standing right next to her. Arm's length? What nonsense.

She could lose weight, change her hair and her name, but none of it mattered. If Billy was around, she got sucked back into his orbit. A willing moon to his life.

It wasn't him.

It was her. She was the one who couldn't be trusted.

"I need to leave." She put her glass down, and without looking at him again, she left.

This was not how this night was supposed to go, Billy thought.

She was walking out.

Before she got too far, he stepped in front of her—not touching her, because that wouldn't go well, but forcing her to stop. She huffed, her long hair blowing back.

"Listen. You can leave, but I want to answer your

question. I invited you because . . . I've been thinking that you might be right about something."

Her laugh was loud and round. Several men turned their way, interested speculation in their eyes when they looked at her. A beautiful woman with a laugh like that? Priceless. He wanted to kick them.

"You think I'm right? That's a first," she said.

"I don't know you. Not really. Not Madelyn Cornish." As he talked, she sobered. It was as if she'd dropped her mask for a moment. And he saw her—the real her—nervous and worried but pleased, somehow, even though she didn't want to be. "And I want to know you. I really do."

"So you sent me a ticket to a charity fund-raiser, dressed up in a tux, and braved my anger, just to get to know me?"

"I know, I amaze myself sometimes. But you amaze me all of the time. My whole life, I've been grateful for the chance to be with you and now isn't any different. I want to know you, Maddy. The real you. Not the reflection of me you were for so long."

She was gaping at him and he pulled back, suddenly brutally uncomfortable with all that he'd said. But it was honest. He could stand by it, even if she walked away, he could say he went down trying.

"Stay," he said. "Please. Think of the poor kids."

"Oh! Cheap shot, Wilkins."

"I'm a desperate man."

She blew a raspberry, letting him know what she thought of his desperation. Those men looked over again and he glared at them.

And he waited, aging a year with every second.

"Okay."

"Okay?"

"I'll stay. For a while."

"I'll take it." He resisted the impulse to fist pump and take a victory lap.

A waiter went by with a tray of champagne flutes and he grabbed two and handed her one. "You look beautiful, by the way. I always liked you in purple."

"You liked me in anything," she laughed. "But thank you." She pressed a hand to her waist and tilted her head; her hair, brown and gold and red, picked up the low lights and gleamed. "You look . . . amazing."

"You think?" He ran a hand down the snowy white shirt, preening for her.

"Tam created a monster, didn't he?" she asked. "You and clothes, who would have guessed?"

"Not me."

Another waiter went by, this time carrying little cracker things with black stuff on them. He grabbed two of them and handed her one.

"You like caviar?" she asked as he threw the whole hors d'oeuvre in his mouth and began to chew.

No. Decidedly no.

"Is that what that is?" he asked around the disgusting salty ball things, which weren't delicious at all.

Laughing, she handed him a napkin. "You gotta stop just puttin' stuff in your mouth."

Turning his back to the crowd, he spit out the caviar into the napkin.

"Are you hungry for something else?" he asked, happier than he'd been in years because she was here and laughing. He was giddy with memory and delight. "There's some shrimp and I know how much you like shrimp—"

"I'm fine."

"You sure? Because there are these crab cakes going around that are seriously delicious." He craned his neck, looking for one of the waiters with the crab cakes.

"I'm not hungry."

"Are you lying?" he asked. "Because . . . you look great, don't get me wrong, but you're . . . skinny. Seriously, very skinny."

"Wow. How could I possibly take that the wrong way?"

"No. I'm just—maybe it's just one of the things about you that's so different now."

"Billy, I'm on television five mornings a week. If I gain three pounds, it's all over the Internet. I've worked hard to look like this. It's a part of my job."

Man, that caviar taste was not going away. He took a sip of champagne and tried to pretend he liked that, too.

"Did . . . did you always want to be on television?"

"Not television. Not exactly. But I wanted to be a journalist. Remember?"

He nodded. He did. Her career, her passion for writing, had been one of the things that had gotten left by the wayside when his career took off. She'd traveled with him as much as she could at the beginning. And then her dad had gotten sick, and that had started to eat up the rest of her time. That was when the fighting had started.

"I'm . . . I'm really sorry I didn't support you more with that. I knew you wanted to go to school, and I was . . . I was selfish, wanting you on the road with me."

They just looked at each other, the events of the past a winding line of dominoes long since toppled.

"Well, in the end you did. The divorce settlement paid for my tuition." She drained the rest of her champagne.

"I'm glad something good came out of it."

"Are you bullshitting me right now, Billy? Because," she dropped her voice, "I'm already sleeping with you."

"I told you, I want to get to know the new you." He brushed her wrist with his thumb and felt the ripples in the air around them. It was powerful, what they shared—the attraction, past and present.

He wanted to ask her if she'd ever felt this way with another man, but he wasn't sure he could handle the answer if it was "yes."

Because no other woman came close to affecting him the way she did.

She made him want to be better. And she made him regret every single time he fell short. And that had happened a lot in the years of her absence.

She pulled her hand from his, rubbing her wrist as if to wipe away the sensation. They couldn't keep standing here like this. People, namely Tara Jean, were going to start staring. He set his nearly full glass of champagne down on the table. "Let's go cause some damage at the silent auction."

She seemed to be in the process of solving a difficult equation. As if having fun with him at the silent auction might be some unsolvable mistake.

But then that wrinkle between her eyes vanished and her smile spread across her face like a brand new day, and he had to suck in a breath at her beauty. "Let's go."

chapter 14

There had been a surfeit of champagne. A plethora. And that wasn't Maddy's style. Nope. Not anymore. Champagne had calories. Lots of them. Delicious, delicious calories.

And now, tipsy, unable to drive, all she wanted was french fries.

She stood out in front of the Four Seasons, her green pashmina slipping over her shoulders, letting the warm Texas breeze travel across her skin like a sigh. Her skin felt alive tonight. She wanted to open her arms and feel everything.

The doormen were handling cabs and she waited for her turn, smiling at the young valets, who tried to flirt with her in Spanish.

"You shouldn't encourage them," a voice whispered over her shoulder and she nearly closed her eyes in relief.

Billy.

Toward the end of the night, when things started to get fuzzy, when her loneliness became too heavy to carry, she'd avoided him. Because she was a little drunk and he'd been . . . he'd been so fun. So silly and charming and she found herself wondering if maybe he was different after all. If maybe she was wrong to hold all those crimes against him. They'd been young after all. Neither of them without blame.

And she knew, in the sober part of her brain, that those thoughts were dangerous. They were best left . . . unthought. And frankly, she was slightly scared of being this loose around him, this weak.

Billy made his livelihood taking advantage of weaknesses.

She should have left at the beginning of the night.

But at the same time she was so glad she'd stayed.

Because more than french fries, she wanted Billy.

"You need a ride?" he asked, taking his keys from the valet and slipping the guy a tip.

"I can take a cab."

His eyes burned through the night, all coy flirtation gone. All the careful boundaries they'd established and adhered to all night eradicated.

The pashmina slipped from her limp fingers, trailing on the ground.

"Let's go, Maddy," he breathed, winding the pashmina in his arms, uncovering her as he did it. It was as if he were unwrapping her—a present. And then he slipped a hand under her elbow and led her over to where his car crouched at the curb. Not his SUV, but an erotic, low-slung sporty beast.

Even his car looked like sex.

He opened the passenger door for her, waiting until she slipped in before giving her back the pashmina and shutting the door.

The car was small and dark and intimate. And it smelled like Billy—and when she took a breath, the air tasted like him, too.

This was a very very big mistake but she couldn't really get herself to care.

After all, she did need a ride home.

The car roared to life and he shifted it into gear, his legs flexing under the material of his lovely tux. She rolled down the window, letting the Texas night inside.

"Congrats on your boat." She tipped her head against the headrest to watch him. The street lamps and car lights illuminated his face in flashes and slices, vivid and jagged.

"Oh my God," he groaned. "That was totally your fault."

"Hardly." She laughed, resting her hand out the window ledge where the wind, that soft air, feathered over her skin.

She felt so alive—on this night, with this man, the possibilities all around them like magic.

"You told me the guy I was bidding against was going to call it *My Fair Lady.* It would have been a crime for that boat to be called something so stupid."

"What will you do with it?"

"Give it to Luc and TJ, I guess." He checked his mirrors, flipped on his blinker and shifted again. She wanted to trace the muscles of his leg under those pants. "An engagement gift, for whenever they get around to that."

"I liked Tara Jean."

"I'm sure you did. You two are a lot alike."

She crossed her legs and leaned toward him, aware of how he was watching her when he wasn't watching the road. "Coach Hornsby seems nice, too."

"I suppose he is." In the years they'd been together she'd run into that tone of voice before. He didn't want to talk about the coach.

During the silent auction she'd watched the two of them talk and there had been a lot of tension between them. The reporter in her wanted to keep at him. Dig a little deeper. But it wasn't worth it. No point in ruining a great night over hockey.

"You want me to hit the drive-through?" he asked, his eyes glowing under the neon lights of Turtle Creek Boulevard.

"Very funny. No."

Still, he slowed down in front of the golden arches and she laughed.

"You want me to, I know you do, Maddy," he said, but after another grin he picked up speed and turned left, heading toward her condo.

Without warning, the magic in the night made her nervous. And she was very aware of how small this car was, of how badly she wanted him to come upstairs, of how scared she was that he would.

Once they stopped, she pulled her pashmina and clutch closer to her. "Thanks for the ride," she said, too loud. Too bright. Like she was talking to a bus driver.

He laughed. "My pleasure." And then he opened his door and walked around the car to open hers. Slipping out of the car, she was so close to him. A breath away. And then none. Her chest, her thigh, his thigh, his chest, they were a puzzle coming together.

"Do you want—"

"Yeah, Maddy, I want." His fingers brushed the side of her face, tucking hair behind her ear. But then he lingered, his thumb against her cheek, an electric touch she felt through her whole body. The night pulsed, her body loosened and tightened. Want and desire and worry and fear were dust storms inside of her and she could barely think.

Billy shifted closer to her, his other hand cupping her cheek, her whole head cradled in his palms. He was so big. So strong, and she didn't want to think about why this was a mistake anymore. She wanted him.

"Come upstairs."

"Can I kiss you?"

His thumb brushed her lips, teasing the corner. She sighed with pleasure, liquid and troublesome, a drug far too potent, and she tasted his thumb. The salt and heat of it.

"Baby," he groaned, his eyes locked on her lips, the thumb that played there. "Please let me kiss you."

She almost said yes. For a second she was so tempted to throw away that rule. But if she let that go, what would happen next? What part of herself would she lose?

His words from earlier rolled through her head, her heart. Everything she'd ever wanted him to say, ever dreamed of him saying, he'd said it.

All she had to do was believe it.

Looking at him, she could see that he was changing. The boy he'd been was vanishing.

But whatever the reasons—trust, fear, you name it, it was part of the messy stew in her heart—she couldn't open her mouth and accept him back.

Once, a long long time ago, she'd silenced the doubt in her heart. She'd ignored the fear and trusted that her faith, her love, would be enough to keep them together.

And she'd paid—brutally—for that.

She shook her head. Things had gone far enough tonight, boundaries erased at every step. She had to cling to something.

His smile was terribly sad but not surprised and he stepped away, lifting his hands from her skin as if he were a magician and without his touch she would just vanish.

And then he was gone, into his car, into the night.

chapter 15

Something was off. On Friday, all through the Cooking With Beer segment, Madelyn had been watching backstage. Sabine wasn't there, but Ruth was. A thin black shadow at the edge of the set.

Ruth was never backstage.

"Delicious," Maddy cried, trying a bite of stew cooked with Guinness while simultaneously calculating how many extra minutes on the recumbent bike it would cost her. Next up was a cheese fondue with ale in it. Just looking at it was making her fat.

On the other side of the stage, Billy—dressed in one of his new light spring sweaters, a gorgeous blue V-neck with a gray T-shirt underneath—waved at her. Grinning like the Cheshire Cat with all of her secrets locked away in that dirty little mind.

She was embarrassed by how much time she'd spent this weekend thinking about him in his tux.

The cheese fondue was served to her on an apple, which hardly reformed the fat content. She ate the apple and cheese and moaned in unfeigned ecstasy. Though at this point in her dairy-free life, it could have been a Velveeta slice on stale bread and she'd have loved it.

Wiping her mouth and fingers with a napkin, she turned to the camera. "All right, guys, next up, Billy Wilkins will go toe to toe with an etiquette expert." She leaned sideways, looking at Billy. "And I don't want to put too fine a point on it, but Billy looks good. See for yourself after the break."

"We're out. Ninety seconds," Peter yelled.

Instead of Gina rushing to her, it was Ruth. Instinctively, she stepped back, as if to protect herself. Ruth looked rabid.

This was getting very strange.

Ruth leaned close, way past any personal space limit established years ago. "Listen," Ruth whispered. "There's been a change."

"A change?" She glanced sideways at Billy, who was watching her.

"Shhh. Look at me. I need you to focus. It's not as bad as it seems, if you can keep Billy under control."

Panic clamped down on the back of her neck. Keep Billy under control? "What the hell are you talking about? And where's the etiquette guy?" She whirled around, looking for the formally set table they had planned on using. She'd seen it backstage before opening the show.

It wasn't there now.

"Twenty seconds."

"Read the teleprompter and . . ." Ruth blew out a long breath, and Maddy suddenly realized how much older her associate producer looked.

"Are you okay?" Maddy asked.

Ruth's smile was broken. "I'm sorry, Maddy. But I promise I'll try to fix it."

And then she was gone.

Gina appeared, brushed powder over her face. "What's going on, Gina?" Maddy asked.

"I don't know, baby, but it's bad news back there. Phil—"

"Phil?"

"That man is acting like a fool," Gina said and then was gone.

That instilled absolutely no faith.

Billy walked over and sat next to her, his face folded into concerned lines.

"What's up?" he asked. "Where's the table?"

"Do you know what's going on?" she whispered.

From one moment to the next, Billy . . . sharpened. Gone was the smile and the easygoing slump in the chair next to her. Now he was fully on guard. A warrior ready for a battle. "Why?"

"And five." Peter was giving her the finger countdown behind the camera and then the red light was back on and there was nothing to do but move forward.

"Welcome back. For those of you just joining us, it's day two of the Billy Wilkins Project. Last week, we cleaned the hockey bad boy up, and if I do say so myself, we did a pretty good job."

Billy stood, his muscular body shown to perfection in his sweater, the tight but not too tight fit of his gray slacks.

The crowd loved it. Unaware that every muscle under those clothes was tense, radiating a menace that made the earth uneven beneath Maddy's feet.

Calm, she thought—or rather, prayed—*keep calm.*

She glanced back to the teleprompter. "Well, today we were going to put Billy to the test with an etiquette expert, but we've had a change in plans."

A sense of irrevocability settled hard in her bones.

"Our producers have done some digging into Billy's . . . past," she stumbled over the word. Past? Her mouth kept talking, but she lost all connection to what she was saying; she knew she was just a face spitting out words. An automaton. But damn it, Ruth had promised her that her and Billy's marriage would have no part in this.

"And instead of Ms. Manners from the *Dallas Gazette,* I'd like to introduce Rebecca and Charles."

Rebecca and Charles? What the hell?

She turned sideways, waiting for the mystery guests to come in from backstage, but there were no chairs. No mics. No setup. Nobody had planned this right.

What the hell was going on?

From the corner of her eye she saw a commotion in the front row, right behind the camera operator, who swiveled quickly to catch the two children standing up.

Charles was a toddler, two or three years old. Red-faced and clinging to an older girl, brown-haired and undeniably militant. The kids were clean, the young girl's body hidden under a blue hoodie. Her long brown hair was pulled back in a ponytail.

But the look in her blue eyes was haunted.

Maddy caught sight of Ruth backstage, pointing frantically to the teleprompter, but Maddy was thunderstruck, lost.

Beside her, Billy came to his feet.

"Becky?" he asked.

The girl glanced to the left where Phil was standing, nodding so fast it was like his neck was broken.

Clutching the boy closer, the girl lifted her hand and waved to Billy.

"Hi, Daddy!"

The *AM Dallas* audience went ape shit. Rabid. Phones came out and people nearly fell over themselves trying to take pictures.

Anger roared through Billy. Justified and huge, barely controlled.

Maddy just stared at him, her mouth open, her eyes pleading, standing at the front of the stage, a giant chasm opening between them.

And he wanted to yell, *Did you lie to me? Did you look me in the eye and lie about my family?*

"I didn't know," she whispered.

He didn't believe her, or if he did he couldn't quite gather himself enough to actually say the words. The girl—God, could it really be Becky?—crouched to protect the now screaming boy in her arms as the crowd pushed in to get a closer look.

I gotta get them out of here.

Billy ripped the mic off his sweater, but it wasn't enough, his anger demanded more. He kicked Maddy's empty chair to the floor and the clatter and bang silenced the studio. Every eye was on him. Every cell phone lens.

Maddy jumped, startled. And he liked that. His anger loved it, his anger was like a dog rolling in a dead bird, so he kicked over his own chair. The shitty side table with the coffee cups on it shattered under his boot.

It was either that or strangle his ex-wife with her straightened hair.

The sound of that boy's cries cut through the mayhem like a knife and he charged off the stage toward those two kids.

"Come on," he barked, holding out his hand. The girl shook her head, her eyes wide.

Phil appeared at Billy's shoulder and Billy knew he would punch him in his smarmy face if he stood there one second longer. Without the patience or the words to make their exit happen any other way, Billy grabbed the girl's hand and crouched and picked up the boy.

The girl stiffened and the boy freaked right out. It was like pulling a two-by-four and carrying a wiggling puppy at the same time.

"Calm him down or I'm going to drop him," Billy muttered to the girl as he pushed his way backstage.

"Charlie," the girl whispered. "Charlie, chill out. It's like a piggyback. See?" Billy glanced sideways in time to see the girl pretending to smile.

How many times did I do that for Denise? Lip swelling, eye bleeding, he'd told her countless times he was fine. That everything was going to be fine.

He'd been lying.

The girl was lying, too.

"Billy!" It was Ruth. He ignored her, walking to the green room, where he'd left his coat. The keys to his truck were in its inside pocket.

"Billy!" She was following him. Stupid woman.

He continued to ignore her, turning the corner into the room where the small breakfast buffet was still set up. He set Charlie down and dug through the coats on the rack for his new overcoat.

"I'm sorry," Ruth said.

"Go. Away."

"Billy . . ." Ruth took a step closer and the chains keeping him in line strained. He yanked his coat from the rack, sending the whole thing to the ground. "Stay the hell away from me."

His phone buzzed in his coat pocket, like a living thing.

Good chance it was Victor. There was no time for putting out his agent's fires, so he let it go to voicemail.

He turned off the phone.

At the buffet, Becky was filling the pockets of her hoodie with fruit and muffins, stuffing snacks into Charlie's small hands.

"Let's go," he barked at the kids, who both flinched so hard granola bars rained onto the floor. They stood paralyzed.

"Come on. We gotta get out of here."

"No." Becky's face twisted into a sneer, her hands in fists. It was like looking in a mirror, and he knew this girl's back was to the wall and if he kept pushing, she'd start pushing back.

Charlie sucked back tears.

He sensed Ruth at his elbow and he jammed his hands in his pockets so he wouldn't grab her. Wouldn't shake her. God, the urge to hurt someone was overwhelming.

She was holding a plastic bag. "Diapers," she said. He yanked the bag from her hand.

"We're not done," he muttered.

"I know." She seemed resigned, like a woman on her way to the gallows. "Go out the back door. Apparently there are some camera crews at the front one."

Gratitude didn't even register.

"We need to leave," he barked at the kids. Ruth crouched on her knees in front of them, pushing the fallen granola bars into their pockets.

"We're not going anywhere with you," Becky said.

"Do you know who I am? Really?"

Cagey, Becky glanced sideways at Ruth. "You're our dad."

Ruth whispered, "We all know that's not true."

"Fine time for you to admit it!" Billy snapped at Ruth as the little boy started to cry again.

Behind him he heard the clickety-clack of high heels on concrete and he knew, with the terrible sixth sense that came with his love, that Maddy was coming.

The anger billowed back up.

"Billy!" Maddy came around the corner, panting, her hair a wild banner behind her. "Billy, oh my God, are you—"

"Leaving." He couldn't look at her, maybe not ever again.

He jerked his fingers at the kids. "Let's go."

Becky just reached down for Charlie's hand, their little feet rooted to the ground.

"Please!" he yelled, losing his mind. He just wanted to get them free of this den of snakes so he could figure out what was going on. Thinking was impossible in this place, where every touchstone of his anger was being fondled and rubbed and thrown against walls.

"Christ, Billy, stop scaring them!" Maddy whispered.

Unable to stop himself, he turned on her, so close that her breasts would touch his chest if she took a deep breath. His skin shrank to nothing, his anger pounded in his veins, not unlike lust. Not unlike love. Every emotion he'd ever felt was too big for his body and betrayal was no different.

She shrank back, her whiskey eyes filled with tears.

"Stay away from us, Maddy. I'm serious—just stay away."

"The show—"

Laughter, dark and rotten, churned in his throat. "You do not want to talk to me about the show."

Reining himself in, he crossed over to the kids and went down on one knee in front of them. He was in enemy territory without any help in sight and he didn't know what he was doing. At all.

With painful hindsight he wished that he'd called that private investigator about finding his sisters. But he'd forgotten, or decided it wasn't that important, and what a stupid decision that had been.

"I'm not your dad," he said, right into Becky's blue eyes. "You know that, right?"

After a moment she nodded.

"You're our uncle," she whispered.

"That's right. I'm your uncle. Your mom is my sister. We need to get out of here."

"Where . . ." She swallowed, so clearly scared and over her head and he suddenly wanted to kill Denise for coming up with this ridiculous scheme. Did she send two kids on a plane with no adult? Was she here? What the hell? "Where are you taking us?"

"My house."

Becky shook her head.

He took a deep breath, counting to ten. "I have video games."

The girl kept her mouth shut.

"Ice cream."

Nothing.

"I like ice cream," Charlie whispered and Becky shushed him.

"What can I do to make you leave with me?" At this point he would promise her the house, whatever she wanted just so they could go. "I'll pay you."

Somebody gasped, one of the traitorous women behind him, who had no business judging him after the shit they'd pulled, so he ignored them.

"How much?"

He didn't even blink. "A hundred bucks."

"Okay. And some clothes for Charlie. He peed through his diaper."

He ripped open his wallet, blindly pulled out some bills, and shoved them into her hands.

Carrying the bag of diapers, Billy led his niece and nephew out the back of the building to his truck.

He had no idea Maddy was following them until she said: "You . . . you don't have a car seat. For the boy."

"His name is Charlie," Becky said. "And it's okay. He didn't have one at home."

"That's . . . that's illegal, isn't it?" Maddy asked.

"Not if you don't have a car," Becky said, lifting Charlie up into the Audi.

Maddy looked at him, as if not having a car was the worst thing she'd ever heard of.

"You've forgotten what it was like," he said and climbed into the driver's seat. Shutting the door as hard as he could, a sad outlet for the violence simmering inside him.

Once he pulled out of the parking lot it hit him:

I've forgotten, too.

But that wasn't true. It was worse. So much worse.

I pretended to forget. I walked away because it was easier and I never looked back.

chapter 16

This wasn't good. Not at all.

Nothing was going the way Becky had planned. Aunt Janice had said she and Charlie would be taken care of once they got to Texas. That there would be people who were happy to see them.

No one—not that stupid Phil guy and definitely not Uncle Billy—was happy to see them.

She hadn't really expected Uncle Billy to be too happy, what with the daddy lie and everything. God, why had she listened to Janice about that? She'd known it was stupid, but Janice had told her that someone would pay her for lying. She'd been freaking out that the Phil guy would check up on her story, but he didn't seem to care. Like her word was enough.

But he hadn't given her any money either.

That hundred bucks Uncle Billy gave her burned in her pocket.

And now she and Charlie were going to Billy's house. Alone. And the dude was totally scary. Really scary. And big. Bigger than he looked on TV. Bigger than Aunt Janice's boyfriend. And the way he'd destroyed all the furniture on the set? Like the chairs were toys?

He was going to beat the shit out of her. The second they got into his house, he was going to turn around and just whale on her.

So much for that happy-family fantasy she had going.

It was time to come up with a Plan B.

Maybe it was because she was so tired, or because she hadn't had anything to eat in hours, but Plan B didn't come.

She picked at her chapped lips with shaking fingers.

"I'm scared," Charlie whispered.

Yeah, and what do you think I am? she wanted to shout.

Instead, she just took Charlie's hand. "Let's have a thumb war," she whispered.

Things would be better if that woman had gotten in the truck with them. The talk show host woman seemed nice. Way nicer than Uncle Billy, who looked like he couldn't wait to kill her and Charlie and hide their bodies.

Becky had recognized the talk show host right away. Aunt Janice had shown Becky a whole bunch of pictures of Maddy Baumgarten before putting her on that plane. Aunt Janice had called Maddy a stuck-up bitch. But Aunt Janice called everyone a stuck-up bitch.

Hard to believe that beautiful woman who looked like a picture out of a magazine had been friends with Becky's mom. Grew up in their shitty neighborhood. Not that Maddy looked that much like the photos Aunt Janice had shown her.

Maddy used to have really curly hair and a big ol' bubble butt. And her teeth used to be a little funky in front. Not bad, like Amy Winchester's, but pretty bad.

Must be nice, she thought, to have so much money. To get everything that was wrong with you fixed.

"I'm tired," Charlie whispered.

"Go to sleep, bud," she said and within minutes he was slumped sideways against her. She lifted her arm, and put it around him, letting him slide into her lap.

In the front seat, Uncle Billy picked up his cell phone, pressed a button, and held the phone to his ear. Almost immediately she could hear the tinny sound of the person on the other end.

"Victor," Uncle Billy said. "God. Yes. Stop yelling. I know. Man . . . I know. What? Everywhere?" Uncle Billy sighed and the tension in the truck rolled down over her, making her feel small. Smaller than she was. Folding her bones in half, squishing her skin, pushing her heart into her stomach, where she felt it pound and pound. "Tomorrow," Uncle Billy said, still on the phone. "No. My house. Yeah, I know, but it's gotta be my house. Just say 'no comment.' Isn't that what you're supposed to say? Okay. Bye."

Uncle Billy punched the buttons on his phone like he wanted to stab someone.

Again, he lifted the phone to his ear. "Hey, Luc," he said. "I know. I know. I was there! No." He laughed a little, a tired sound that made Becky watch him carefully. "I'm fine. They're . . . I don't know . . . scared. But listen, can you do me a favor? I need some clothes and stuff for the kids." He glanced at her in his rearview mirror and she stared back, even though she was practically wetting her pants. "You're thirteen, right?" He asked and she was so stunned he knew that she just nodded. "And the boy is like three. Thanks."

He hung up and looked at her in the rearview mirror again. She wanted to yell at him to pay attention to the road before he got them all killed in a crash.

"What's your mom's phone number?"

"Mom's?"

"Yeah."

"Why do you want her number?"

"So I can find out what the hell she was thinking putting her two kids on a plane and sending them to Dallas without telling me!"

He doesn't know.

Aunt Janice said he knew, but he obviously didn't.

"She's dead."

The big car swerved and Becky grabbed the door handle so she wouldn't squash Charlie, who put his thumb in his mouth and went back to sleep.

"What?" Uncle Billy asked.

"Mom's dead."

"When?" His voice was weird. Scary and thin like he couldn't talk.

"A few months ago." Seven months, one week and three days.

"Months? What . . . What happened?"

"Overdose."

Uncle Billy was quiet for a long time and Becky's heart felt like it was going to beat out of her chest.

"I'm sorry," he said.

"Whatever." She looked out the window and bit her lip until her eyes stopped burning.

"Where's your dad?"

"I don't know. Mom never said."

"And Charlie's?"

"Jail, I think."

Outside, the trees were a blur. Inside her heart was a bird flying her far away from here.

"So, you've been staying with Janice?" he finally asked.

She nodded and then realized Uncle Billy couldn't see her. "Yes," she said, her voice cracking around the word.

"What's her number?"

"You're going to send us back?" The thought clanged around her body, hurting her from the inside. This had all been for nothing. Nothing.

She clenched her hands into fists, her nails biting into the skin distracting her from the scream clawing up her throat, filling her mouth.

Did you honestly think something else would happen? she asked herself, pulling Charlie closer. *Like he would take one look at you and invite you into his life? Just because he was family? You know better than that.*

"I . . . don't . . . It's your home, isn't it?" he asked.

Instead of answering such a stupid question, she told him Aunt Janice's cell number and with one eye on the road he dialed and then lifted the phone to his ear.

After a moment he swore, banging the phone against the steering wheel.

Like Aunt Janice would answer the call, Becky wanted to say.

"Janice, it's Billy. You'd better call me or I swear to God the next call will be from my lawyer."

Uncle Billy threw the phone against the passenger window and Becky swallowed a startled shriek.

The car was silent for a moment and then Uncle Billy asked, "How did Janice pay for the tickets?"

"She didn't."

"Because the show did?"

That made her laugh. She wasn't sure what the story was with the Phil guy, but that dude wasn't paying for shit.

"No."

"It didn't?" he asked, glancing at her real quick in the mirror. "Maybe Phil did it on his own."

Becky didn't tell him that the money had been hers. Eight hundred dollars she'd saved from babysitting and doing Pauly McCormick's homework. Every single penny she'd had.

I am so stupid.

But she wasn't stupid enough to go back. Just because he meant to send them back didn't mean she would go. No way.

Outside, all the buildings and alleys gave way to streets and grass. Trees. Not just parks, but lawns that looked like parks.

She knew cities—Dallas, Pittsburgh, it didn't matter.

She knew back alleys and fire escapes and Dumpsters. She could find her way around those places.

But out here? In all this open space?

Oh God, she thought. She reached over to roll down the window but there were so many buttons she changed her mind.

Last year Mrs. Jordal had kept her after class and told her that pretending to be stupid wasn't going to get her anywhere. Mrs. Jordal had talked to her about college and scholarships and changing her life, and for a few minutes Becky had believed her.

She wondered where the hell Mrs. Jordal was now.

This was the one smart thing she'd done to change her life and it had blown up in her face.

She glanced at Charlie, his face red with sleep. His little eyelashes like feathers on his cheeks.

Her stomach rolled and she gagged.

"Can we pull over?" she asked.

"What?"

"I need . . . Can we just pull over?"

"I'm on the highway!" Uncle Billy cried.

"You want me to throw up all over your leather seats?"

"Okay, okay. Here. Hold on." He looked sideways and jerked the truck onto the shoulder. They'd barely rolled to a stop before she threw open the door and puked all over the concrete.

Eight hundred dollars, dragging Charlie thousands of miles, leaving behind everything she knew to take a chance on a guy who hated them. *This was supposed to make them safe,* she thought, squeezing her eyes shut. And everything just felt more dangerous.

The green room echoed with silence. It pounded with it. Or maybe it was Maddy's head, she couldn't tell.

I think I'm having a stroke, she thought.

For about a year after her divorce Maddy had lived in a state of deep freeze. Which was ironic since she'd moved to Miami with her mom.

But after the emotional smackdown of her marriage, the endless confrontations and arguments, the sustained emotional violence of being in love with Billy Wilkins, she'd been wrung out and empty. So for one blissful year she had let herself feel nothing—she'd been totally removed from the sludge of bad news and anxiety and depression.

She didn't care about Billy. The stories in the gossip magazines. She didn't care about whomever he was fucking. The divorce. It was all just background noise, echoes heard from far away.

Every night she laid her head down on her pillow and she slept like a baby. And every morning she woke up and, using the money from the divorce settlement, she went to school at the University of Miami and studied broadcast journalism.

There were no friends. No boyfriends. No rebound sex. Nothing. No one got close enough to touch her, close enough to hurt her. No one got close enough that she had to care about them.

All she had to care about was herself. She lost a shitload of weight, and maybe it was the vaguely distant and emotionless way she related the news, but she was good at it.

And her star began to rise.

Slowly, she'd started to feel things again over the years. Pride. Elation. Disappointment. Now betrayal, thanks to Ruth.

But she had lived in that deep freeze for so long that it had become her natural habitat and sometimes she had to force herself to feel something. To engage on a human level. To not treat the whole world and every person she met like it was a segment she had to get through.

But not right now.

The ice she'd lived in for so long had cracked and split and she felt it all. Every molecule of guilt, every inch of shame and anger and horror at what had happened on her show. On her watch.

Those children, they weren't Billy's. She didn't believe that lie for a moment. They were Denise's kids, or Janice's, there was no other explanation.

And her producers were responsible for that ambush.

Ruth's mic buzzed and she pressed the button on her headpiece. "He's gone," she said. "And not coming back. Put on that Jason Aldean special. No, Phil," Ruth glanced at Maddy, "she's not going on either. You screwed us all."

Ruth let go of the headset and stumbled back, one of the overstuffed chairs in the corner catching her as she fell.

"There go our careers," Ruth said.

"How much did you know?" Madelyn asked, unconcerned about her career. About the Jason Aldean rerun. All of it was a distant second to finding out how big a setup this had been.

Ruth didn't look at her, just stared up at the ceiling as if she were considering melting into her chair. "Nothing until this morning. Halfway through the first traffic segment I realized something was up."

"So Phil flew them down here behind your back?"

"No, actually. He's not that devious. I think Billy's sister got excited and sent them down here. One-way ticket, mind you. And Phil just capitalized on the situation."

There were so many problems, so many things wrong that Maddy couldn't settle on one long enough to form an argument. She was just a long scream of anger.

"You could have told me. You had time."

Ruth nodded. "I could have. And I could have told Billy and I could have put my foot down. I could have done a dozen other things to protect our show, our integrity, those . . ." She lifted her glasses, digging at her red-rimmed eyes. It was about the most raw Maddy had ever seen Ruth. "I could have protected those kids."

"So? Why didn't you?"

"He was like . . ." Ruth dropped the glasses and took a deep breath. "Like a cocked gun, and he threatened to fire me if I told Billy or you. And then . . . then you guys would have been totally unprepared."

"That little pep talk at commercial? That was you preparing me?"

"It was me doing the best I could without ensuring that you or Billy would walk off the show. The kids were freaked out, dirty. Hungry. Tired. Phil wasn't even going to clean them up."

"Is that supposed to make it all right?"

Ruth finally looked directly at her. And Maddy saw that she was a woman diminished, reduced to a puddle in last year's Anne Klein funeral line.

"I'm sorry," Ruth said. "For what it's worth, and I know it can't be much, but I really am sorry."

As if they'd conjured him, Phil came around the corner into the green room.

"The studio audience is getting rain checks, but they're not happy," he announced and then turned to Maddy. "You should have gone back on."

"And done what, Phil? Lie some more?"

"I wasn't lying," he said, a hand pressed to his chest. "I was doing my job, and doing it pretty fucking well."

"You can't be pleased with that show," Maddy said. "That was a train wreck. We're all going to get fired because of your stupid—"

Oozing smug satisfaction he held his hands out as if placating a jealous lover. It was hard not to punch him in the throat.

"Now, I'm sorry things played out like that during the show. There wasn't any way to warn you that would have protected the integrity of the surprise."

The top of her head felt like it was going to blow off.

"But before you get upset—"

"Get upset? *Get?*"

"Listen, the numbers are through the roof. Facebook, Twitter, the *AM Dallas* blog, that segment is all anyone is talking about in the tristate area. The clip of Billy kicking over that chair has gone viral, Madelyn. Viral! Ruth, tell her how great this is."

Slowly, like an ancient woman, Ruth got to her feet, uncurling vertebrae by sore vertebrae. And when she reached full height, she looked Phil in the eye.

"I quit," Ruth said.

"What?" Madelyn and Phil asked at the same time.

"I won't get dragged into your cesspool, Phil."

"What about the show?" Madelyn asked.

Ruth shrugged. "What about it? For three years we've loved this show like some morning it was going to wake up and love us back. Look at us, Maddy. What has our work gotten us?"

Richard stormed into the room, stopped dead center, and pivoted to face all of them, his hands at his hips. His short-sleeved plaid shirt stretched over his middle-aged man paunch. Normally, Richard looked like a mild-mannered high school science teacher. Not now. Now he looked like a man who was about to fire the lot of them.

"Can one of you explain what the hell just happened?" he asked.

Phil looked up from his phone, smiling like a smug rat. "I think we just became the most talked about morning show—"

"Stop." Richard held up a hand. "Who planned this?"

Maddy and Ruth pointed at Phil, who suddenly seemed to catch on to the fact that Richard was not pleased.

"I wouldn't say planned," he hedged. "It just sort of happened."

"You flew those kids down here?" Richard asked and Phil shook his head.

"I got a call this morning from Janice Wilkins saying the kids were on the red-eye."

"And that daddy bullshit?"

"They're his kids." Phil glanced at Ruth and Maddy, neither of whom jumped to his aid. "The girl said so."

"And you didn't check?"

"Why check, she said he was her father. Why would she lie?"

Oh, Phil, Maddy thought. *You lazy lazy bastard.*

"Right. Why would anyone lie? One phone call and I got the truth. One fucking phone call and I found out they're his sister's kids. Did you pay the girl?"

Phil shook his head, looking green.

"You're sure? No gifts?"

"Some diapers."

"You're fired."

"What?"

"Out. Immediately."

"You . . . you can't do that."

"Yes, Phil, I can. And considering the fact that Billy's lawyers are without a doubt going to land on us with both feet, I am delighted to throw you under that particular bus."

"But the show didn't make the accusations, we just provided the forum. That's . . . that's the law, right?"

"You weren't even sure?" Richard sighed and shook his head. "God save me from fools. I should have fired you when your wife left and you started wearing those stupid T-shirts. Snoopy does not make you look younger, Phil." Richard was in full attack mode and if Maddy weren't so terrified that she was going to be next, she'd actually be enjoying this. "All right, let's pick another reason to fire you from the many many I have. Are you schtupping your subordinate?"

Phil choked on his tongue.

"Sabine, right?" Richard looked around for confirmation and Ruth got very interested in her manicure, but Maddy knew a chance when she saw it.

"Yes," she said.

"Right." Richard nodded. "Explicitly against the station's HR policy. A policy we keep around so I don't have to think about any of my employees naked. You're out. Pack your shit and make sure I don't see you again."

Phil didn't move, his mouth agape. His Superman Says Stay in School T-shirt was sadder than ever.

"Do I need to call security?" Richard asked.

"My lawyer—"

"Won't help you. You'll get a package, Phil. Now leave."

Phil shook his head and slunk away, his proverbial tail between his legs.

"As for you two . . ." Richard pointed his fingers at Ruth and Maddy. And Maddy braced herself for the hit. ". . . you have one week to fix this."

"Fix what?" Ruth asked.

"The show."

What would Matt Lauer do? Maddy thought. *He'd pounce on this opportunity.*

"We've got some great ideas," Madelyn said, even though they didn't.

"We'll worry about great ideas after you get Billy back on the show," Richard said.

"He won't . . . he won't come back." Maddy looked

at Ruth, who was still white-faced and small. No help. "Not after that."

"Convince him."

Like it was that easy? Did he know nothing about Billy Wilkins?

"What happens if we don't?" Ruth asked.

"Well, Ruth, you'll be fired for going along with that fiasco this morning." He turned to Madelyn. "And you'll be doing weather at five a.m. in Omaha. We clear?"

Numb, both Maddy and Ruth nodded.

Richard left, taking all the air in the room with him, and all the strength from Maddy's legs—she collapsed onto the green room couch.

"What are we going to do?" Ruth asked.

"You quit, remember?"

"I know. Maybe I still will." Behind her dark glasses her eyes were alive. "I don't know about you, but I could use a drink. Or twenty."

They'd never done this, in their years together. Sometimes when they worked late, they'd order salads from the deli and eat in the conference room. But they'd never socialized outside of the office. Maddy didn't socialize with anyone outside of the office.

All part of her life on the iceberg she'd been calling home.

"Let's go," she said.

chapter 17

Holding two new toothbrushes and a tube of toothpaste, his pockets stuffed with water bottles and protein bars, Billy stood outside his guest bedroom door. The second he'd opened the front door Becky had run into this room with Charlie, acting like the devil was chasing them. Of course, the way Billy had been yelling, he couldn't blame her.

But it had been twenty minutes since she'd barricaded the two of them in the guest room and he was beginning to get nervous.

Beginning? What a joke. He was sick with worry, with anger and stress. What if they jumped out the window?

Carefully, he twisted the doorknob, planning to just look in on the kids, see if they were both sleeping. Or missing. Or dead.

But the door was locked.

What the hell? With sudden, exasperated anger, he lifted a fist to pound on the door, but he stopped himself, took a breath, and carefully knocked.

"Becky?" he called through the wood.

Silence. Lots of it. And then finally the door creaked open. Her little face poking through.

"Did Janice call?" she whispered.

He shook his head. "I thought maybe you'd want this stuff." He held out the toothbrushes and toothpaste and a bottle of water.

If he'd held out a snake she couldn't have looked more distrustful.

"I didn't poison it. I promise." He smiled, but the tension around the girl was too thick to even dent. One hand slipped out and grabbed the water. Another hand grabbed the toothpaste.

And then the door shut in his face.

Again, the urge to bang on it was pretty hard to resist, but stomping around like a bully wasn't going to help anything.

Denise. God. Denise was dead. Those poor kids in there.

It had been a long time since he'd felt so useless. The divorce. The trade to Dallas. He was nothing but a dumb body. There was no one in this situation he could fight. No opponent he could punch to the ground.

He wasn't even entirely sure what the situation was, since his sister couldn't be bothered to return his phone call.

Maddy would know what to do, he thought, but he instinctively rejected the thought of calling her, much less having her here.

He couldn't . . . he couldn't even stomach thinking about Maddy right now; the wound was too raw. The woman he'd known would never have done this. Never. And he was afraid that he might have only seen what he'd wanted to see. That he'd ignored the reality of this new Madelyn Cornish, that she had changed so much that all the things he loved about her were gone.

They had both walked away from their past, but if she'd done this . . . ?

Then he was a fool.

A fool who needed to figure out what to do next. Luc was going to come by and drop off groceries and some new clothes for the kids, but that left many many empty hours.

Realizing he couldn't stand outside a closed door all day, he walked down the hallway, through the dining room, and to the kitchen, where his cell phone sat like a loaded weapon on the counter. He'd turned it off a half hour ago, unable to keep up with the phone calls and texts.

He scrolled through the numbers until he found the one that Becky had given him in the truck and hit call.

"Leave a message." Janice's recorded voice jerked him sideways. That smoker's rasp she'd practically been born with reminded him all too clearly of being a little kid, following his tough, ball-busting big sister around with nothing but worship in his heart.

The beep sounded. "Call me, Janice," he said through clenched teeth. "This is your last chance." He spat out the numbers for his cell and home lines and hung up, his anger unspent, growing larger by the second.

As soon as he hung up his phone rang.

"Victor," he said, not even having to look.

"All right, Billy. We gotta talk. This shit is getting crazy."

"Okay." He sighed and collapsed into a chair.

"You need to make a statement. The Mavericks' front office is seriously up my ass right now."

Some of those messages on his phone had been from the head of the team's PR department. Hornsby too. They were not happy with him.

"Fine. Write it up."

"I think . . . I think it would be best to make that statement on *AM Dallas*."

"No."

"Billy—"

"No. Nonnegotiable, Victor. I'm not stepping foot on that show again."

"All right, all right. I'm just trying to do some damage control. What's the story with the kids?"

"They're not my kids. They're my sister's. She . . . she died a few months ago. As far as I know they've been living with my older sister."

"Man, I'm sorry."

"I don't want sorry," he said, rubbing his forehead, a useless effort against the giant thundercloud of pain building in his skull. "I want all of this to go away."

"Okay. I'll do my best. So, why did the kid say you were her father?"

"She was coached, it was a setup."

"By the show?"

"That stupid fucking Phil guy, Ruth too. Maybe Maddy."

"You willing to take a paternity test?"

"No!"

"I'm just trying to make this go away, Billy. You want me to get the lawyers on it?"

"They already are." He'd called his lawyer the second they entered the house.

"Okay, I think I've got enough to work with. I'll be in touch. Keep your phone on."

Billy hung up and his phone immediately rang again.

Coach Hornsby.

The fight, the anger, it all drained out of him and he was just too tired to hash out the details, too tired to defend himself against a guy who didn't understand him, much less like him.

A man who was undoubtedly back to being disappointed in him.

How was he going to explain that he'd left these kids behind with his addict younger sister. And his older, cold and brutal sister.

He couldn't even explain it to himself without wanting to throw up.

He ignored the call and within a moment a text bloomed on the screen.

Billy, Coach Hornsby's message said, *I need to hear about what happened from you. Management is out for blood and I can't hold them off forever. Help me help you.*

Oh, man, now the guy was quoting Jerry Maguire.

Billy forwarded the message to Victor. Let him handle Hornsby and all his disappointment.

The second the message was sent, an email took its place.

It's Dom, the email said. *You want to talk?*

No. No, he did not want to talk.

Ignoring Victor's command, he turned off the phone, and sat all alone in his house. He looked at his hands and wondered what he was supposed to do. What was right in this situation? Because he couldn't see it.

This was one of those moments that required him to be better, and it had been so long he didn't remember the steps up and out of the darkness.

But maybe . . . maybe he was already doing what he could. Maybe being better sometimes meant being patient.

Finding some comfort, some confidence in that thought, he sat back in his silent house and waited. For what, he wasn't sure, but whatever it was, he would handle it. Maybe not well. But he would handle it.

It was dark in the seedy little bar and no one recognized her. Which was great, because by the time she got done with her third vodka soda, Maddy didn't recognize herself.

"We have to get Billy back," Ruth said. Her hair was messy and the neckline of her dress had been pulled aside. There was a flash of a purple bra strap. Purple.

All in all, it kind of looked like Ruth had just been fucked.

"How?"

"You were married to the guy," Ruth said.

If only that had come with special knowledge. A guidebook. Something. Billy in his anger was as unpredictable as ever. But the one thing she was sure of was that he didn't want anything to do with her. Or the show. She had to think of a way to get past that.

Ruth's elbows hit the table. "I need another round." She bypassed the sullen woman who was supposed to be taking their orders and instead signaled to the bartender, who nodded.

It seemed like an oft-repeated conversation between the two of them.

"Do you come here often?"

"Twice a week," Ruth said. "A shot of Jack and I cry in the bathroom for ten minutes."

Maddy gaped at her producer.

"Swear to God, it was the only way not to hit Phil in the head with a hammer."

The waitress with the ill-fitting tank top and a put-upon attitude brought them their drinks.

"You have any more peanuts?" Ruth asked, lifting their empty bowl.

The waitress spoke volumes with the roll of her eyes.

"If this place weren't across the street I would never come here," Ruth said as the woman left.

"Come on, Ruth, we need to be thinking. We have an opportunity here to put together the kind of show we've always wanted to do. Let's forget gluten-free cheese and making the perfect cocktail, let's do the stories that matter."

"What would Matt Lauer do?" Ruth's sarcasm infuriated her.

"No! What would we do? If we had no restrictions, what would we do?"

"What about Billy?"

"I'll handle Billy." She thought of Becky's blue eyes, so like her mom's. The blue of a clear sky on hot days. Tomorrow she'd go over to Billy's house and see how they were. See if she could help.

Ruth stared deep into the ice of her fourth drink.

"Why are you so scared?" Maddy asked, the knowledge that fear was guiding Ruth right now only obvious after three drinks.

"I'm not scared, I'm mad. Mad at myself for thinking I was so clever to go to Phil behind your back. Mad at you for not telling me the truth about Billy. Mad at Richard for making us pick up after Phil. I mean, what are we doing here, Maddy?"

"Our jobs."

"Well, our jobs suck right now. I never dreamed about having a husband and kids or a house with a white picket fence. I couldn't give a shit about that. But I do want a life. I'd kill to have a friend to watch *Survivor* with. I'd kill to have sex. Real sex. With another person. Don't you want that?"

"This job is what I want," she said. It was the truth and at the same time not quite. Right now she wanted *more.* She looked down at her glass and blamed the alcohol . . . not Billy at the fund-raiser. Not Billy with those kids. Not Billy turning the lock on her office door.

"You know how I felt the first time I heard that Phil was banging Sabine? I was jealous. Jealous."

"You want to have sex with Phil?" Maddy gasped, she couldn't help it. The thought was repulsive.

"God, no." Ruth shook her head, appalled. "Gross. I have to scrub my brain now. No, I was jealous that Phil got to have it. Kinky sex in the workplace. It's not fair. I've worked myself right out of a social life. So have you."

"How do you know it was kinky? The sex."

Ruth shrugged, her collarbone a knife blade peeking

out of her shirt. "I don't. I just wanted someone to be having kinky sex."

Maddy felt herself blush, felt the burn of embarrassment flood her face. She was like one of those cartoon characters who catches fire and then is dust and ash afterward.

"No," Ruth gasped, because she was no dummy and Maddy was practically broadcasting her sex life. "In the office?"

"Just once."

"Okay. Okay." Ruth sat back, her arms spread wide, a strange grin on her face. "Spill."

Maddy chased down the straw in her drink and shook her head.

"Nothing?" Ruth asked and again Maddy wondered if this was what friends did. Ruth sobered and sat forward again. "Okay. Then tell me this, what are you so scared of?"

"About what?"

"Billy. Why aren't you at his house right now?"

"You saw him."

"Yeah, and I've seen him every other time he's been here. The man is crazy for you. You tell him you didn't know what Phil was doing and he'll believe you."

He would, Maddy knew that.

"And from there, isn't it just a hop, skip, and jump to getting him back on the show?"

"I don't want him on the show," Maddy said. "I never did."

"Because you were married?"

The marriage was the least of it. She set down her drink, lining up the bottom edge of her glass with the damp ring on the paper napkin in front of her.

"Never mind, Madelyn. I'm sorry. I shouldn't pry. And I know it's not like you should trust me."

"No. No, it's okay." She did want to talk about this.

She didn't have anyone else in her life she could confide in. And three drinks had made Ruth seem pretty trustworthy. Billy had always told her she was a terrible drunk, too trusting, too ready to believe the best in people when they were showing her their worst. "My mom signed her name Mrs. Doug Baumgarten," she said, because this, *this* was the root of it.

"So did my mom. It was a generational thing." Ruth shrugged like it was no big deal. Maybe because she'd never been married. Maybe because she'd never looked that decision in the eye and decided, just decided, to put aside her name for someone else's. Like everything she had been up until then didn't matter.

"I started doing that with Billy when I was thirteen. Thinking of myself as Mrs. Billy Wilkins." Ruth sat back, her black eyes surprisingly understanding. "It wasn't just my name. He was my life. My identity. And when we broke up, it wasn't just him that was gone. It was me too, in a way. I was defined only by his boundaries. Where he ended, that was me. That was what I got. And he had a way of filling every available space, every thought. Until I was nothing."

She wasn't making sense, but Ruth was nodding like she understood.

"And if word gets out that Billy and I were married," she snapped, "there goes Madelyn Cornish. I'm back to being Mrs. Billy Wilkins. And I've worked too hard to let that happen."

"So why are you having sex with him in your office?"

"Because part of me misses what we had together and part of me is weak and part of me is stupid and all of me is lonely."

For him. Lonely for him.

Ruth reached between them over the scarred black surface of the table, past their half-full drinks, and grabbed her hand.

"I'm sorry, but you heard Richard—Billy has to come back on."

"I know and I'll do the best I can to get him. Tomorrow."

Ruth nodded. "Tomorrow." It was a promise.

The silence between them was kind. Generous. The type of silence that gave everyone the privacy of their thoughts.

"But . . . about the show," Maddy said. "I have an idea."

"I'm listening."

Maddy leaned forward and so did Ruth.

"An hour show, one topic. Interviews, panels. It can be serious and fun. But no more traffic reports. No more weather."

"What about Joe the Cameraman?"

"Gone." It hurt to say it, he was so great in front of the camera, but the new show had to be totally different. A whole new animal.

It took a long moment, during which Maddy died about a hundred times, but finally Ruth sat back and slapped the table.

"I love it!" They pushed aside their drinks and got to work.

Maddy's soul, starved on a diet of snake segments, cheered.

chapter 18

Becky's hands were sweating. Everything was sweating. Partly because she'd put on every scrap of clothes that the Luc guy had bought for them.

Underwear, even; how totally embarrassing.

But mostly she was sweating because she'd never tried to steal a car before.

God, why hadn't she paid better attention when Jonah showed her how to do this? Becky panicked as she stared at the wires under the steering wheel.

"Becky?" Charlie asked from the backseat.

"Yeah, Char?" Was it the red wire and yellow wire? And what was she supposed to do with them? Did Jonah strip them? She remembered him doing something with his teeth.

"Where we going?"

An excellent question.

Pittsburgh was not an option. They'd left that place behind for good. And they obviously couldn't stay here. As soon as Luc and that nice Tara Jean woman had left after dinner she'd hustled Charlie back into the guest bedroom and waited until midnight before sneaking out.

"Padre Island." Padre Island was where all those MTV spring break shows were.

That seemed as good a place as any.

As long as it wasn't Pittsburgh.

She had taken the last of the pizza from dinner, the jumbo box of Goldfish crackers, and the gallon of milk in the fridge. This car had to be worth a whole bunch of money. And there was that hundred dollars in her pocket.

"Is Uncle Billy coming?"

"No. Just you and me, bud."

The pounding on the driver-side window scared the crap out of her and she screamed, jumping a mile.

It was Uncle Billy outside the door, the black night a dark curtain around him. It made him look scarier. Meaner. He was wearing sweatpants and no shirt and she'd never seen anyone with that many muscles.

Aunt Janice's boyfriend liked to pretend he was a big guy, but he was a fat bloated pig compared to Uncle Billy.

He was going to kill them. She just knew it.

Defeat strangled her and she bit her tongue until it nearly bled, to keep herself from crying. Charlie freaked out when she cried, and one of them freaking out was about all she could deal with at the moment.

Uncle Billy knocked on the driver-side window again and she wiped her nose on the sleeve of her hoodie before opening the door.

"Are you stealing my car?" he asked.

"Admiring the leather."

"You broke out of my house."

"I didn't know it was a jail."

It was weird, a surprise, and Becky didn't really like surprises, but Uncle Billy started to laugh.

Instead of hauling her out of the car, he leaned against the door like he had all the time in the world.

"Where were you going to go?" he asked, looking in the backseat at the pizza and milk and Goldfish box she'd taken.

"Away." She lifted her chin and settled on a plan.

"Look, you don't want us. Aunt Janice sure as hell doesn't want us. Why don't you just give us some money and we'll get out of your hair."

"Just like that? I'll never hear from you again?"

"Not even a Christmas card."

That made him laugh and she wondered if it was good or bad.

"How much money do you think you'll need?" he asked and she couldn't believe it, but it seemed like he was going to go for it. The guy was rich, so she pounced on the biggest amount she could think of.

"Ten thousand dollars."

He pursed his lips and nodded. *Ohmygod, this is happening.*

"I don't just have that lying around."

"We can go to an ATM."

The laughter faded from his face and she realized he'd been joking. Tricking her. She clenched her fists in anger, her brain shook with it.

"I can't let you go," he said.

"I won't tell. You know Aunt Janice won't tell—"

He put a hand on her knee and she jerked back, hissing. Immediately he lifted his hand.

"Don't touch me," she whispered through numb lips. She sounded scared and she hated that. It made her hate him even more.

"I won't. I swear, Becky, I won't ever touch you."

It took her a second to unclench her jaw, to relax every muscle in her body. To get her brain to stop freaking out.

"You . . . you okay?"

Hell no. "Sure."

"I can't just let you go."

She didn't understand him. She didn't understand anything anymore. Not since Mom died. Not since she and Charlie had moved into Aunt Janice's house.

"Why?" she whispered, blinking back the burn behind her eyes.

Uncle Billy swore and looked up at the sky. It had been so hot today, like an oven. Not now. A cold wind blew through the open window and she shivered in her sweatshirt.

"Because it wouldn't be right," he finally said.

"Right? What the hell does 'right' have to do with anything?"

Man, the guy made no sense. But it was obvious she wasn't going anywhere tonight. She'd try again when he went back to sleep.

Careful not to touch him, she slid out of the car.

She pulled Charlie from the backseat. His diaper was wet and he was so tired, he put his head down on her shoulder and didn't say anything. He was getting too big to carry. Too hard to keep safe.

In the dark, she walked back to the house.

Next time she'd find his keys.

Madelyn was putting an outrageous amount of faith in donuts. Stupid, really, chocolate cake donuts with sprinkles were not going to fool Billy. His old favorite, Boston cream, would probably only make him laugh at her. All dozen of them might end up getting thrown at her or her car.

But she didn't have a whole lot of choices at the moment. So, at dawn, hungover, the scent of fresh hot donuts on her passenger seat slowly making her crazy, she drove out to Billy's house.

As a peace offering in this particular situation, she knew the donuts were shamefully inadequate, but all they had to do was get her in the door.

After that she would just beg.

It was barely after six-thirty in the morning and there

was a really good chance he was still sleeping, but she knew Billy in the morning. A grump, yes, but sweet. Susceptible to all sorts of suggestions. He was like a little boy waking up happy from a long nap. All he wanted was a treat and a cuddle.

Her best chance at getting through the door was a dawn attack.

In the pearly light before sunrise, Billy's house—or the lawn in front of it—was a hub of activity. News vans from the local channels and ESPN were parked along the street. Camera crews were set up on the sidewalk, careful not to step foot on private property.

A spark lit in her chest, chasing away some of the indecision and worry. Part one of making things right had just been handed to her.

On a satellite dish.

She parked down the block and checked her face in the passenger-side mirror. Meh. Not nearly camera ready; she slapped on some blush and lip gloss, and things improved slightly. Caught in an upswell of confidence, she grabbed the donuts and walked up to the house—sashayed really. As soon as the camera guys caught a glimpse of her, they swung into action.

"Madelyn!" everyone screamed at once and she turned and smiled at the cameras, making sure she was centered. That they all had a shot of her better side.

She recognized the reporters from her station, and from the competition, but there were also some cable guys she didn't know. Wild cards, maybe. But she just had to make it work.

"Whoa, everyone slow down." She smiled, making eye contact, turning on as much charm as she could. The local reporters smiled back at her, but the cable guys didn't respond at all. And then came the questions.

"What are you doing here?" one called.

"Is Billy suing the show?" another yelled.

And still another. "Are they Billy's kids?"

"Let me answer that last one first." She was quick. Decisive. "That is actually a terrible misunderstanding. I think maybe a young girl's idea of a joke. Billy is not suing the show. Billy's relationship with *AM Dallas* is the same." *Please please, let that one be true.* "And I'm simply a donut delivery girl."

"So who are the kids?" the man with ESPN on his microphone asked.

"Family. And that's all I'll say without Billy's permission. But rest assured, he's not the—"

"They're coming out!" a cameraman yelled, pointing to the far side of the house, past the bushes. Everyone ran to get a better angle, and once it was obvious that the only ones emerging were the kids, they lost all sense of private property laws and charged across the lawn.

Becky looked terrified, blinded by white lights. Charlie hid, crying into his sister's pants. But the journalists were unrelenting. Like piranhas with the scent of fresh blood, they blasted the kids with questions.

"Billy," Maddy screamed as she ran across the grass, getting in front of the kids, putting her hand out behind her, only to feel the children cowering against the back of her legs.

"Enough," she yelled at the journalists. "They're children. Back off."

Only the guy from her network seemed to be fazed—the others just kept yelling.

"Hey!" It was Billy, flying through the open front door. A bare-chested hockey berserker. "What the hell!" he shouted and shoved cameramen and journalists aside. One guy fell down to his knees, knocking another guy back. "Get off my lawn, assholes, or—"

"Or what, Billy?" the ESPN guy asked, looking slick

in a red tie, his white teeth glowing in the dark. "You'll put on a nice sweater? Get a haircut?"

In the startled silence someone swallowed a laugh, just before Billy spun back around and shoved the reporter onto his ass.

"What the hell, man?" the guy cried.

"Get up," Billy said. "And get the hell off my lawn."

Billy stepped in front of Madelyn and the kids, his face a screaming stop sign. And the camera guys and the reporters scattered like cockroaches, running back to the sidewalk, and their vans beyond that.

Billy led her and the kids through the lawn like he was splitting the Red Sea. All faith and fury. Madelyn hurried the kids after him like a band of Canaanites.

The donut box was crumpled in her arms.

Just inside the front door, there was a dining room chair—a blanket tossed over it—pushed against the wall, like a blockade. Beside it was a dirty ice cream bowl and three empty water bottles.

Once the door was shut behind them he turned on the kids.

"What the hell did you do? Sneak out the window?"

Becky was stone-faced, but Charlie nodded.

"We did! I jumped. Becky caught me and we fell down." He tried to shove his sister around to show the dirt and grass stains smeared across the back of her pants, but Becky wouldn't budge.

Billy ran a hand through his hair, all of it standing up around his head. Now he looked scary and crazy.

"That's the third time—" he muttered, and then yelled, "*third time!* I haven't slept all night, and I know you haven't either. I'm sitting in a crappy, uncomfortable chair, jumping at every noise, worried that you'll run away. And now you're climbing out the window?"

"It was a game." Charlie looked confused, like he

didn't understand how something so fun could be wrong.

"A game." Billy laughed without any joy. He looked right at Becky, both of them so tough. So fierce. So alike. So very alike. "It's not a game to me, Becky. I can't spend the rest of the day trying to keep you from running away."

Becky chewed already raw lips.

"A hundred bucks," she finally said.

"What?" Maddy asked.

"A hundred a day?" Billy totally ignored Maddy, so did Becky. But Charlie smiled up at her with his little Chiclet teeth, and she awkwardly patted his shoulder.

"A hundred a day and I won't run," Becky agreed and Maddy choked back a laugh. Then she suddenly realized that no one was joking. Billy was seriously agreeing to pay Becky to stay.

Oh Lord, Denise, she thought, *what were you thinking?*

Billy mumbled under his breath, opening a drawer in the small hall table with a key he pulled from a pocket in his sweatpants. Inside the drawer were his car keys, his wallet and a stack of cash. He opened the wallet, and took out a bunch of bills and threw them down on top of the small stack.

"Why don't you just give me the money?" Becky sighed.

"Because the next thing I know you'll be on a bus to who the hell knows where." And then he locked it all back up and put the key in his pocket. "I told you, Becky. You can't just leave."

"Yeah, and I told you, you can kiss my—"

"Donuts," Maddy said, lifting the crumpled box in her arms.

"There's donuts in there?" Charlie asked. Maddy looked down at his small voice, his brown hair, blue eyes. Pink cheeks. At his collar she could see that he wore a blue shirt, a red one beneath it, a yellow one under that.

All that color was spellbinding.

He stood on tiptoe, trying to look in through the plastic cutout of a donut on top of the box.

"Yeah." She laughed—who wouldn't? But then she looked at Becky and Billy, who were staring at her with narrowed, angry eyes. "I brought donuts."

"Why are you here?" Billy asked, cutting right to the chase.

Because I need to convince you to come back to my show. Because my career rests in your hands and I have no idea how to convince you to trust me again. Because these children are here and I feel like I should be, too.

"You need to eat, don't you?" she asked, saying none of what she needed to. She didn't give him a chance to argue, sweeping them all into action. "Come on, you two, let's get you some milk and some donuts in the kitchen." She hoped Billy had milk. Carefully, she ushered the two clearly exhausted children and the donuts away from Billy and the barricade he'd set up.

"Remember, Becky," he called after them. "I have the key to the sliding glass door."

Becky muttered something under her breath.

"That's a bad word," Charlie whispered up at his sister; Becky didn't respond, weariness obviously dogging her steps as she crossed the living room into the kitchen. Madelyn turned to follow them but Billy stopped her.

In the pre-dawn it was glaring how tired he was. Ravaged. As if he'd aged ten years since she last saw him.

"Did you know? About them? Did you plan to bring them on your show?" he asked, seeming somehow smaller. His bare chest and shoulders were caved in, all those smooth muscles collapsing in on one another.

"No, Billy. I swear. I was just as surprised as you. And

I'm sorry . . ." *Sorry for being a part of the show that did this to you. Sorry that I'm here to try and convince you to go back. Sorry that all I have are donuts.* "So sorry."

His face relaxed. It wasn't a smile, not quite, but the room got a little brighter and it didn't feel like she was about to be thrown out on her butt.

"Thanks for the donuts."

"Do you . . . believe me?"

"Are you telling me I shouldn't?"

"No, I'm not—"

"I believe you," he said.

He believed her, just like that.

Guilt churned in her stomach.

She escaped into the kitchen, where Becky had gotten Charlie a glass of milk before sitting down and resting her head on the table.

Madelyn slipped the box onto the counter and pulled out two chocolate cake donuts with sprinkles. They'd gotten banged up some in the run across the yard, but she doubted Charlie would care. The boy was practically bouncing in his seat.

She found some plates and put them down in front of the kids.

Charlie clapped, grabbed his donut, and dug right in. Becky didn't lift her head.

"Becky?" She put her hand on the girl's back, feeling every thin and fragile bone under the tight pull of her skin. Becky sat bolt upright, throwing aside Madelyn's hand.

Madelyn held it up. "Sorry."

"Whatever." The girl sighed and reached for her donut, plucking one pink sprinkle from the frosting and putting it in her mouth.

"Char, you're a mess," Becky said to her brother, who

had a ring of chocolate frosting around his nose and mouth.

Maddy dug through some cupboards until she found paper towels and she tore off two pieces to give to the kids.

"You guys okay?" Madelyn asked.

"No. We're prisoners." Despite being tired, Becky still had the energy to keep up the attitude.

Bravo, Maddy thought. Sometimes a little attitude is all a girl had to make it through.

"What's a prisoner?" Charlie asked.

"We are. Uncle Billy won't let us leave."

"I don't want to leave!" Charlie cried and Becky put her head down on the table.

Madelyn was so far out of her depth, she couldn't even see shore. She could handle kids on the show, when they'd been coached and their parents were around to keep them in line with snacks or threats.

Real kids? In real time? Particularly ones with the eyes of her childhood best friend? She was totally clueless.

"This place isn't so bad, is it?" she asked and Becky shot her a look of such scorching disdain that Madelyn felt like she had glasses and buck teeth again.

That kid's got powers, she thought, and then, because she was a coward, she grabbed a Boston cream, wrapped it in paper towel, and headed out to find Billy.

Billy, a lit bomb who could blow up in her face, was a safer bet than this angry, scared little girl.

She paused beside the table, thinking about due diligence and the barricade in front of the door. "You're not going to run away, are you?"

Becky didn't look up from the donut she was slowly de-sprinkling. "We won't run."

Relieved, Madelyn stepped into the living room. Billy was watching the big screen TV on the far wall—his back, muscled and smooth, was to her.

An ESPN anchor was talking while the picture of Billy after that fight in the play-offs loomed large over his shoulder.

"Things have not improved for Billy Wilkins since the Mavericks lost their chance to get in the play-offs," the anchor said. "The enforcer has tried to show his softer side by taking part in what has to be one of the most ridiculous makeover shows ever concocted."

There was a video clip of Tam measuring Billy's in-seam.

With his eyes glued to the screen, all the muscles in Billy's back pulsed and flexed. His fists dug into his hips, like he was bracing himself to take a punch. Or forcing himself to stand still.

He didn't glance away from the screen even when she came to stand beside him.

Part of her, the part that remembered comforting him, and had the will to do it again, wanted to put her arm around his waist, to let him know he wasn't alone.

It made her panic, how badly she wanted to be his friend right now. How badly she wanted to help him. His need, his loneliness was like quicksand and she'd been caught there once before.

It's not worth it, she thought, feeling like a deer in the headlights. *It's not worth my job to fall back into this situation with him.*

But it was. In so many ways it was. And as much as she needed him to come back on the show, it was obvious that he needed to do it, too. She just had to convince him of that.

And not end up his crutch again, lifting more than her share of his emotional weight.

The video clip ended and the anchor was back on, his grin wide. She'd always thought sports journalists were a little mean, especially the ESPN guys. Like the skinny nerds were finally getting their shot against the stronger, faster athletes, who'd probably bullied them growing up.

"Things took a turn for the worse yesterday morning when on the popular *AM Dallas* show the following accusations were made."

Now the clip was of her introducing Becky and Charlie. Maddy could only wince, her stomach erupting with acid and pain, while she watched her own clueless glance offstage. Her obvious confusion and then the hubbub behind the camera just before it spun around and found the two kids in the crowd.

"Hi, Daddy," Becky said, all bravado and fear. And that fear looked like it was directed at Billy. Like the little girl was scared of him. And that wasn't a good thing.

There were some camera misdirections and then finally the shot found Billy, staring at Madelyn with hate and violence in his eyes just before he kicked the chairs to the floor, shattered the coffee table.

The clip ended and the anchor was back.

"Daddy surprise? Kicking over chairs on television? Now, that would be enough to put Billy Wilkins at the top of our Athletes Behaving Badly list, but then he capped it off this morning with the following blowup."

Madelyn didn't have to watch to know what it would be. Billy shoving that guy on his front lawn.

"Billy?" she whispered.

"Don't talk," he said, without looking at her.

"Last night around midnight, Billy's agent released the following statement." The screen turned blue, with white words scrolling across the picture as the anchor read them.

"The children introduced on *AM Dallas* are Billy Wilkins' niece and nephew, whose mother died of a drug overdose seven months ago."

"Died?" she gasped and Billy only nodded.

Grief rolled through the room like smoke and for a moment she couldn't breathe. It wasn't a total surprise, but hearing how Denise died from the news gave it terrible power.

She thought of her friend, how badly Denise had wanted her life to be normal before she became the instrument of her own destruction and blinked back tears.

"As for the allegations made on *AM Dallas,* Billy can only presume the children were coached in an effort to secure higher ratings. Clearly, he finds these actions despicable and has severed his relationship with the show. Considering the amount of trauma these children have been through over the past seven months, Billy would ask that he be left alone to grieve for his sister and to help his family heal."

The blue screen vanished and the anchor was back, grinning widely. "I swear, we could not make this up. Do you think it's done? Well, it's not. Two more, that's right, I said it, *two more* women have stepped forward with claims that Billy is the father of their children."

Madelyn gasped, shocked. Horrified. Oh, she hadn't even thought of that, but of course the parasites would come out in droves once they smelled this kind of weakness.

"The Mavericks' front office has not made a comment as of yet, but I can't imagine Pat Hornsby, the gentleman coach of the NHL, is very proud of his bad boy defenseman. And that is why Billy Wilkins makes our Athletes Behaving Badly Hall of Fame."

The anchor switched stories and Billy hit the power button on the remote control, turning the screen black.

She stared at the donut in her hand, the chocolate frosting hard and cracked down the middle, the white cream peeking through.

Did she honestly think a donut would fix anything?

"When did you find out that Denise overdosed?" she whispered, so overloaded she was numb.

"Becky told me yesterday."

"I'm so sorry, Billy."

His laughter was dark and small and she knew the guilt he carried over his family, over the way they'd all turned out.

"Have you talked to Janice?" she asked and he shook his head.

"She won't even pick up her phone."

"What are you going to do?"

Violently, Billy rubbed his hands over his face, as if scrubbing away everything that was pulling him backward and down.

"She can't stand to be touched," he whispered. "She's thirteen and she's already been hurt."

"How do you know that?"

"I tried to help her out of the SUV the first time she attempted to run away." He glanced sideways at her. "She was trying to hot-wire my truck. Totally clueless. But when I put my hand on her to get her down, she . . ." His whole body stiffened, like he'd been electrocuted.

"What . . . what are you thinking, Billy? Their home is with Janice." *And you are a single man in a violent industry with a boatload of PR drama raining down on you.*

His gaze sliced right through her as if she'd totally disappointed him.

"You really don't remember what it was like," he said. She wanted to tell him that she remembered plenty. That she'd been by his side. But that would start a fight and she wasn't here for that.

"What about their father?"

"Fathers. Plural. Becky doesn't know who her dad is and Charlie's is in jail."

It was like a rabbit hole of tragedy. They had to climb out quick or they'd be lost forever.

"What can I do to make this better?" she asked.

"Which part?" he asked, his sarcasm vicious. "My niece and nephew in the kitchen? My dead sister? The part where your show sabotaged me? The part where reporters and camera crews are camped out on my lawn? Women I don't know are claiming they have my babies? Tell me, what part of my life are you and your stupid fucking donuts supposed to make better!"

He grabbed the donut from her hand and heaved her sad little peace offering across the room, where it splattered violently against the black TV screen.

She jumped, startled, painfully, hideously on edge. The whole house was electric with tension—the kids in the kitchen, Billy in here. It was amazing the foundation was still intact.

Billy was barely keeping it together. His eyes were wild in a way that was all too familiar.

A million years ago, when they were young and kind and thought the best of each other, she would have told him to go for a run, or find some ice. She would have taken him to bed just to give his body a chance to process the emotions he couldn't get a handle on.

"Look, Billy, you're mad and you've got a right to be. But we need to figure out how to get you out of this mess. I'm here trying to help. And you can stand there—exhausted, two kids in your kitchen, ESPN on your lawn—and throw donuts against the wall or we can do something to try and fix this."

"Weren't you watching?"

"It's bad, Billy. It's really bad. But maybe . . . maybe if you came back on the show . . ."

He shook his head, his hands in fists like he was working really hard at not strangling her. And he probably was.

"I can guarantee that I will not step foot on your show again."

No. No. He was digging himself in, soon to be immoveable.

"Phil's been fired."

"Doesn't matter, Maddy. Your show used me. Used those kids." His throat bobbed as if he was swallowing back tears. "I won't go back."

She opened her mouth to argue, but didn't. How could she possibly convince him?

"And frankly, I can't believe *you're* going back. They sabotaged you, too!"

"That show is my job, Billy. My life—" She stopped, suddenly remembering so clearly that first day he came on the show, when she'd said, *Hockey is all you have left, isn't it?*

The show is all I have left.

Suddenly there was a furious pounding on the front door and she jumped, startled.

Billy quickly moved to the door, pushing aside the curtains at the window before opening it.

"Good Christ, Billy." Billy's agent stepped inside. Over his shoulder she could see that the vans were still outside and reporters were still standing sentinel on the sidewalk out front. "You've really stepped in it this time."

"I'm no kid's father," Billy said. "Those women are lying—"

Victor held up his hand. "I know. Everyone knows. But we've got bigger problems."

"Bigger?" Billy laughed, but then sobered as Victor nodded.

chapter 19

Billy collapsed backward onto the couch, the fight that had been keeping him upright left his body so quickly he was light-headed.

"No one?" he asked.

"No one wants you. Management made it real clear that no one in the league would negotiate a trade, not even with cash attached."

"What about Hornsby?"

"His hands are tied, though I don't think he fought too hard."

"So he couldn't even pay someone to take me."

He was going to throw up. Quickly, he leaned forward, resting his head in his hands, waiting for the dizziness to pass. But it didn't. The sickness in his stomach got worse. He swallowed the bile in his throat.

"They gonna buy me out? Set me free?"

Victor was silent and Billy looked up at him. His agent was decidedly green. Oh God. This wasn't going to be good.

"They're sending you down to play in the minors. Management's trying to teach you a lesson."

The silence boomed through his chest. Embarrassment crawled over his skin.

"Oh, Billy," Maddy sighed and it was just an extra special layer of hell that she was here to witness this.

"Like Sean Avery?" He laughed, though it wasn't funny. None of it was funny.

"If you play well, keep your nose clean, maybe you'll suit back up for the Mavericks."

Billy stood, unable to just sit there and gag on the sour taste his life was leaving in his mouth. Pacing helped, so he walked toward the big screen where that donut still stuck, mangled on the television console.

His career was looking a lot like that donut.

Disappointment wasn't something that sat well with him; he wasn't used to it. Had, in fact, gotten rid of that useless feeling after his divorce. Disappointment only came after contemplation, after thinking about how badly he'd fucked up, and he didn't do that shit anymore.

"Fuck 'em," he said.

"No." He could hear Victor getting to his feet, crossing the room to put a conciliatory hand on his shoulder, but Billy wasn't having that. "Look, maybe you can go in and talk to Hornsby. Throw yourself on his mercy. Apologize."

He spun around and paced over to the window. "I won't do it."

Victor stared at him long and hard, his disappointment all too obvious. "Then you're on your own."

"You're dropping me? After all these years?"

"You're not giving me a choice! I'm an agent for athletes. If you don't play hockey . . ."

Then who am I? It was as if he'd screamed it. The roof shook with the force of everything he wasn't saying.

"I'll just check on the kids," Maddy said, slipping back toward the kitchen just as his life was exploding around him, giant chunks of turf and cement falling down around his head.

Two kids.

No agent.

No hockey.

Oh God, he was going to twitch right out of his skin. Right out of his mind. He had to do something or he'd start throwing punches, and as mad as he was, as blind angry, he knew that wasn't the right choice. There was no one here he could hit.

"I'm going to go work out," he said.

Victor threw his hands up. "I can't help you if you won't at least try."

Try? Billy stormed down the hallway. Try what? Everything he'd ever tried was coming down around his ears.

Maddy had no idea what she was supposed to do. Handling a PR nightmare like paternity accusations, that seemed do-able, oddly enough. Like a problem that could be taken apart piece by piece and made right.

Billy playing in the minors? Walking away from his career?

Too much. It was asking too much of her to help him through that. And maybe it meant she was a coward—she could live with that. But it was clearly time for her to leave, to retreat and formulate a new plan.

She crept into the kitchen, only to find both kids asleep where they sat, heads resting on their curled-up arms. Charlie's face was covered in powdered sugar and icing. Becky's donut had half the sprinkles picked off, but was otherwise intact.

"Becky?" she whispered; the girl didn't stir.

Remembering what Billy had said, she carefully nudged Becky's elbow, which didn't even cause her to twitch.

But when Maddy laid her hand on Becky's shoulder, the girl leapt up.

"What!" she cried, all wild-eyed panic. "Where's Charlie?"

"Shh. Shh, Becky, Charlie is right here. You're okay. Everyone is okay."

Slowly the girl seemed to get her bearings, staring at her brother where he slept. "He's out cold."

"You were, too. Why don't you go back to your bedroom? Get some real sleep."

Becky's yawn could have cracked her jaw.

"Yeah," she said and slowly stood up from her seat. "Come on, Char."

The young girl moved to pick up Charlie, but Maddy stepped in. "Honey, you're about to fall over. Let me carry Charlie."

It was obviously a big deal to Becky, letting someone else take care of her little brother, and Maddy was reminded so much of Billy and Denise. The way he'd carried that girl under his wing for so long. Her and Janice, really.

"Okay," Becky whispered and then watched as Madelyn lifted Charlie, his dead weight awkward and heavy.

"Oh my gosh, girl, how do you do this?"

Becky didn't even laugh. "Careful with him."

"Of course." Maddy sobered. Becky apparently wasn't in the mood for jokes. "Lead the way."

Once they reached the guest bedroom, Madelyn put Charlie down on the bed, pulling the comforter up over his shoulders. Becky crawled in next to him, lying on her back, staring up at the ceiling.

Becky glanced over at Charlie, as if she was making sure he was there, and then went back to studying the ceiling.

There were twenty different things Maddy wanted to say to Becky. About her mom. Her uncle Billy. How no one was going to hurt her. Maddy wanted to know if the girl had been hurt. And how. And then she wanted to unleash Billy on that person.

"What?" Becky asked, finally glaring in her direction.

"I'm sorry about your mom."

Becky's shrug wasn't fooling anyone.

"I . . . I knew her, a long time ago. We were friends."

I'll braid your hair, she remembered saying that night, to try and get her to stop crying.

Becky licked chapped lips and Madelyn wanted to tell her to stop. They were going to bleed soon. She made a note to leave the girl the ChapStick she had in her purse.

"When you were kids," Becky said. "I know."

Becky wiped her nose with the sleeve of her sweatshirt. "She told me about you when she was pregnant with Charlie, she told me some friend of hers had gotten rich and sent us some money. Aunt Janice said it was you, before we came down here. She showed me a bunch of pictures of you when you were a kid."

Oh. As far as ties went, it seemed weak. Terrible.

"You really grew up on the Hill?" Becky asked.

"Around the corner from your mom and Billy."

Becky laughed a little, like she just couldn't believe it. "How'd you end up here?"

"I worked really hard."

"Yeah. And got your teeth fixed."

Maddy jerked at the accusatory tone of Becky's voice, but then somehow, with the hungry sixth sense that came from being raised in that neighborhood, she realized Becky was trying to make her own associations. Trying to connect every dot from where Madelyn stood to where she'd come from. Because it wasn't something that happened all that often, and the map, at least from where Becky sat, was a mystery.

She remembered, all too well, how that felt.

"I had pretty bad teeth."

"Marrying Uncle Billy must've helped."

She nodded. "It didn't hurt."

"And you probably had like straight A's. You must've been smart. Like for real."

"You know, Becky . . ." She ran a hand over the comforter tucked up high around Charlie's ears. He sighed and rolled over, flinging out an arm. His hand was so small and pink. She resisted the urge to touch a finger, just a finger. "Not really. Not any smarter than you probably are. I really wanted out of that neighborhood."

Becky's eyes filled with tears and Madelyn forced herself to pretend she didn't notice them. She took great care to tuck Charlie's hand back under the blanket.

Becky turned her face to stare at the ceiling and the tears ran from the corner of her eyes to soak into her hairline.

Madelyn didn't know what to do or say. She wasn't even sure if the girl was scared or sad or homesick.

"No one is going to hurt you," she said, taking a shot at scared.

"Tell that to Uncle Billy."

"He's . . . he's scary, but I swear to you, he won't hurt you. He won't lay a finger on you."

Becky stared at the ceiling so hard, as if she were the only thing keeping it from falling and crushing them.

"Get some sleep, Becky," she said. Becky sat up and grabbed Maddy, her sweaty fingers a handcuff around her wrist.

"Are you leaving?" she asked. The girl's attempts at bravery, at cool indifference, were gone. She was white with fear, wide-eyed with worry.

"No," Maddy said, her plans changing on a dime. "I'll be right outside."

Becky lay back down, collecting herself as if she was painfully aware of how young she'd sounded. How panicked. "It's okay," she said, too late to take back what she'd revealed. "Do whatever you want."

"I'll be right outside when you wake up."

Becky turned her face away, curled up on her side, the

small bones of her spine pressing against the thin sweatshirt she wore.

Maddy took the hint and shut the door behind her before resting her hand against the wood for a second, as if she could send her unvoiced, unsure hope for healing through that wood.

Billy was right—she had forgotten. She'd forced herself to forget what it had been like to grow up in that neighborhood, with the Wilkins family, because the burden was too heavy to carry.

Behind her was the whir and thump of a treadmill and she followed the sound to a back bedroom. The door wasn't completely shut and she stood in the shadows of the hallway watching Billy through the crack.

He ran at a relentless, punishing sprint. Sweat ran down every clenched and rigid muscle, dripped off his nose, from the stubborn thrust of his chin. And despite looking like the epitome of health, she knew he was wounded.

Bleeding out in front of her eyes.

The white wires of his MP3 player bounced against his shirtless chest and she realized, with a sudden pang of affection, that he'd put on the iPod so he wouldn't disturb the kids.

She had no idea why it comforted her, but it did. A small sign that things might be all right. If he could just hold on to his compassion and his reason, he would be okay. He'd see himself out from under this mess.

"Goddamn it!" Billy yelled, and smacked the face of the treadmill with the flat of his hand. Again. And again. Until the treadmill readout cracked.

Or, she thought, ducking back into the shadows, away from the eruption of Billy, he'd screw this situation up worse with his blind anger.

One just never knew which way Billy would go.

* * *

Maddy's eyes blinked open and she was lost. She was on a couch. Brown leather, so not hers. The gray blanket thrown over her was fleece. Definitely not hers.

"Why in the world is she here?" A woman's voice said, muffled by walls and distance.

The smell of garlic in butter filled the air and her stomach roared, waking her all the way up.

She was on Billy's couch. After cleaning up the donuts she'd sat down on the couch and must have fallen asleep. Judging by the sun falling in great sheets through the windows, she'd been asleep for a few hours.

"Billy," the woman's voice said and Maddy lifted her head, realizing it was coming from the kitchen. Tara Jean. That steely southern magnolia tone was unmistakable. "It's her show. She took advantage of you. You can't tell me she wasn't planning that shit all along."

There was a clatter and clang of dishes, a sizzle and the smell of searing meat.

"She told me she had nothing to do with it," Billy said. "And I believe her."

"I'll tell you what I believe—"

"Tara," another voice chimed in, deep and resonant. "You've been telling us for the last half hour what you believe."

"Fine," she snapped after a moment. "But I don't want Billy to be hurt."

"Maddy won't hurt me."

Internally, Maddy flinched, his faith painful. *No,* she thought, *don't believe in me.*

"I swear," Tara Jean murmured and Maddy imagined the woman hugging Billy, her thin arms around his thick neck, her mouth against his cheek, and jealousy—irrational and sudden—stabbed her. "When she wakes up I'm going to tell her what I think of her."

Great. Maddy sighed and sat up, only to find Becky sitting at her feet, Charlie wrapped in her arms.

"That woman does not like you," Becky whispered, her eyes bright. Maddy wasn't sure if it was because the girl was laughing at her or because she'd finally gotten some sleep.

"Yeah," she muttered. "I got that sense. How long have you been sitting there?"

"Not long. Charlie just woke up."

And they sat here with me, instead of going into the kitchen. Maddy was uncomfortable with that trust, too.

"I'm hungry," Charlie cried and all noise in the kitchen went silent.

Becky winced. "Uh-oh."

Yeah, uh-oh. Maddy threw off the blanket and got to her feet, smoothing down her hair in a lame attempt to be ready for Tara Jean when she came around the corner.

But it was Billy. In blue jeans and a faded blue Mavericks T-shirt. His feet were bare and he looked like every Sunday afternoon they had ever shared.

"You're awake." His eyes ran over the kids, as if checking for wounds or stolen silverware. "All of you."

"Sorry," Maddy said. "I didn't mean—"

He waved her off. "It's all right. Everyone needed some sleep. Are you guys hungry?"

"Starved," Charlie said, jumping around the floor for no reason.

"Becky?"

She shrugged, which seemed to be the most fluent of Becky's languages. "Okay, we've got lunch coming in a little bit. My friend Luc is making meatball subs."

"Meatballs!" Charlie yelled—the kid couldn't have been more excited if Billy had announced that a circus had moved into the kitchen. Billy seemed taken aback by his sudden enthusiasm.

"Calm down, Charlie," Becky admonished, reading Billy's unsure surprise. The girl was incredibly adept at gauging a room and calculating moods, Maddy thought.

Survival skills.

"No, it's fine. I feel the same way about meatballs," Billy said, smiling down at the boy. "Luc could probably use some help."

Charlie charged off before Becky could stop him, and without him by her side, she seemed suddenly lost. Suddenly very young. Her hair was coming out of her ponytail in a frizzy little halo around her head, and she still had a wrinkle from the bed across her cheek.

"So that's what he's like when he's had some sleep," Billy said, with a small smile at Becky. Maddy had to look away, emotion swelling high in her throat. He was trying, he was trying so hard.

Becky ignored his attempt to build a bridge between them and tucked her hands into the sleeves of her sweatshirt. "Have you heard from Janice?" she asked.

Billy shook his head. "She won't answer my calls or call me back."

"You gonna put us on a plane?"

"Not until I talk to her," he said.

"She may never answer her phone. It's probably been turned off."

Billy stretched out his neck, as if an invisible collar were getting a whole lot tighter. "Well, we'll figure that out later. Right now, let's have some lunch."

"Becky!" Charlie yelled and Becky took a deep breath.

"I need to use some of that money you gave me," she said.

Billy's eyes narrowed. "Why?"

"We need more diapers. And some cream for Charlie's butt. And vitamins, and he can't use adult toothpaste, and—"

Billy held up his hand. "Got it. We'll go shopping after lunch."

Becky nodded, her shoulders relaxing around her ears.

"Hey, you guys coming?" Tara Jean stood in the doorway to the kitchen, glaring at Maddy. It was obvious her words were for everyone else.

"Yeah." Billy turned sideways, lifting his arm as if to touch Becky's shoulder to usher her into the kitchen, but he stopped himself when the girl flinched away.

Billy wasn't ushering Maddy anywhere. In fact it was very obvious that it was time for her to leave. Past time.

"I'm . . . I'm going to head home," Maddy said.

"What?" Becky asked, panic all over her face. And she wanted to tell the girl that she'd bet on the wrong horse. Tara Jean, who looked like she would draw knives on the girl's behalf, would take better care of her. Maddy didn't have anything maternal inside her. She'd forgotten how to give of herself. "You said you would stay."

"I . . . can't—"

"She has to go back to her show," Tara Jean said, her eyes narrowed like every playground bully Maddy had ever known. "She's got some more lives to ruin."

"TJ—" Billy said, trying to step in, but it was too late. Maddy could fight her own battles.

"I didn't know," Maddy told Tara Jean. "And I'm doing everything I can to make it right."

"I saw the donuts. Very generous."

"You think you know me? You think because you watched that clip you have any idea how bad I feel? Denise was my friend, my very first friend, and Billy was my—" Her voice cracked. *My life. For so long.*

She took a deep breath, reining herself in. No wonder her ideas about friendship were such a mess.

"Billy was my best friend," she finally said, careful not to look at him. "And I just wanted to help."

And save my career.

How did this all get so complicated? Nearly blind with tears that she wasn't about to shed here, she found her boots by the door and shoved her feet inside.

When she glanced up she saw Becky, stone-still with fear.

"You'll be all right," Maddy said, hoping she wasn't lying. "I told you, Billy's a good guy."

"But—"

"Here." Maddy pulled out a business card from her big purse and a pen and wrote her cell phone number on the back. "You can call me anytime."

Becky took the card, holding it with both hands as if someone might take it away from her.

"I mean it," Maddy said. "Anytime."

"Tomorrow?"

"Yes." She would stand by it. Sometimes doing the right thing didn't give you much of a choice.

"Becky, come here!" Charlie yelled from the kitchen.

"Okay," Becky called back, tucking the card into the pocket of her jeans. She walked away and Tara Jean followed, leaving Maddy alone with Billy.

He must have run off the worst of the frantic energy, because he seemed much calmer. Subdued almost.

Was it just a week ago he'd given her that ride home from the charity function? Just a few days ago he'd kissed her body as if she were precious. Special.

"You don't have to leave," he said.

"Tell Tara Jean that."

"It would be close, but I think you could take her."

Maddy laughed. "My girl fighting days are behind me, Billy."

"What are you going to do?" he asked.

She blinked, surprised by the question. "What do you mean?"

"You going to quit?"

"My job? No."

"You're going to go back to the job that just ambushed you."

"The job didn't ambush me. Phil did. And, yeah, I'm going back to the job that I love, to try and make things right. I don't want this to be the only thing people remember me for. I would think you'd understand."

He stiffened, crossing his arms over his chest. The thin blue sleeves of his shirt stretched across his biceps.

"What are you going to do, Billy?"

"You heard Victor, what can I do?"

Maddy swung her purse over her shoulder. "I never thought I'd see the day Billy Wilkins would go down without a fight."

"Hornsby doesn't want me to fight. He wants me to grovel."

"Isn't it worth groveling, or doing whatever it is he wants, so you can end your career with some pride?"

"I've got pride!" he nearly yelled. "That's why I'm walking away."

"Oh, Billy," she sighed, and though she wasn't sure what her reception would be, she couldn't stop herself from reaching for him, curling her hand around his wrist, feeling the bones, the muscles and tendons under his skin. And for a moment, brief and wonderful, she was restored by the reality of him. Recharged. A thin reminder of what it was like to be on his side. "I don't think that's pride."

"Why does it seem like you're calling me a coward?"

"Because I am. You are the bravest fiercest coward I know. You are the only person I know for whom fighting is the easy way out."

"You think fights—"

"Stop." She squeezed his hand. "Stop right there. For you fighting is the easier choice. It's easier to not think, to not put anything but your body on the line. You act stupid better than anyone I know."

She could tell he wanted to argue, but no one knew him like she did. A truth neither of them could deny, much as she might want to.

"You know why everyone liked you on my show? Because you weren't fighting. You were vulnerable and uncomfortable. You were honest. It was like seeing you when we were young, before hockey got to you. Got to us."

He grabbed her hand like a lifeline in rough seas and pulled her closer. She knew it was a mistake even as she did it, but she let him pull her into his arms.

They hugged, that was all, just their arms around each other for comfort. Comfort they both needed.

"Stay," he whispered against her hair.

She pushed back, tried to smile, tried to pretend she wasn't rattled and shaken all the way down to her bones. "I think you have a full house."

"I'll ask Tara and Luc to leave." His eyes were dead serious. *I choose you*, he was saying all over again. *Over everyone else in my life, I choose you.* "You were my best friend, too."

"It's not that easy, Billy."

"It is for me. It always has been."

She had no answer for that.

"Now who's the coward?" he whispered.

Oh, what a weak word for all the fear she felt. She was afraid of him, of her, of how inadequate all the problems in this house made her feel.

She was terrified of the millions and millions of gossamer thin threads that connected them. Past and present. She was scared of being the girl who would give up anything to share what he had.

"I'll talk to you tomorrow, Billy," she said, proud that

her voice was clear and strong when the rest of her felt paper thin and torn.

And it was so hard walking away.

The front door closed behind her and she leaned backward, suddenly so weak. She pressed her hands to her face and tried to find her footing.

Remember, she told herself, trying to pull back from the allure of the past. The allure of Billy. *Remember who you are. Remember how hard you worked to put your past behind you. The woman on television every morning had no memory of the kind of hunger Becky had in her eyes. Not for food, affection, respect, but for a* choice. *A choice that didn't suck.*

Remember how hard you worked to put yourself back together after Billy broke you into a thousand pieces.

She dropped her hands, stared straight into the sun.

Truthfully, and she was too worn down to lie; truthfully, she couldn't stand on Billy's front porch and tell herself that he was the same man he'd been.

Billy was different. And that was the problem. This man he'd turned into was infinitely more generous and kind and appealing than the boy he'd been. And she didn't know what to do with that. How to resist that terrible, beautiful temptation.

The last reporter lingering outside Billy's house started to approach, and Maddy walked to her car, ignoring his questions as she slipped her sunglasses on.

If Billy didn't go back on the show there was a good chance she would lose everything she'd worked for in her career. But getting him to do it would require her to embrace everything she'd given up in order to be Madeyln Cornish.

And right now, this moment, hounded by a reporter, she couldn't say which was worse.

chapter 20

Twenty-one years ago

"Oh my God," Fiona whispered. "There he is."

There could only be one "he" that would make Fiona talk like that. Maddy looked up and there, pausing at the end of the cafeteria food line, a tray in his hands, his eyes searching the crowd, was Billy Wilkins.

His eyes landed on her and he grinned, his face lifting, the scar twisting.

Nervous heat prickled all over her skin, like she'd been caught doing something bad. Not sure if she was going to laugh or cry or vomit, she had to look away.

The faded blue jeans and red shirt he was wearing were nothing special, but he was still so hot.

He usually ate out in the parking lot with the rest of the jocks, but for the last week, he'd been coming into the cafeteria to sit with her and the theater nerds.

It was the strangest thing that had ever happened to her.

After that slumber party, after he'd gotten out of the hospital, she would see him at his house sometimes when she went over to hang out with Denise. But he'd thrown himself into hockey, working harder than anyone had ever dreamed he could. And she went to high school, drifted away from Denise, who was getting into drugs and trouble, and never saw Billy anymore.

It was like they lived down the street from each other on different planets.

But this summer she'd seen him at the pool and it had been . . . different. She'd gotten boobs and this stupid butt and her red swimsuit was too tight and all the boys said stuff about her.

But not him. He'd just smiled, that sweet twisted smile, and her whole body freaked out.

Maddy reached up to her hair, trying to push away the curls that had gone frizzy halfway through second period. Stupid hair.

"What is he doing?" Fiona whispered and Maddy dropped her hand, feeling foolish for caring when he probably wasn't really here for her. Maybe he wanted tutoring and didn't know how to ask?

"I don't know," she whispered back. "Stop talking."

"He's coming over here. Again!"

"I know. Shut up, Fi!" She could hear his boots on the cafeteria floor, and she knew in her gut she would recognize his footsteps anywhere. She could be blind and she would know when Billy Wilkins was coming toward her.

Oh God. Her heart was going to pound right out of her chest, the hamburger on her plate blurring.

"Hey, Maddy."

Fiona giggled and Maddy kicked her under the table.

"Hi, Billy," she managed to say. Billy was the biggest kid at Schelany High School. Bigger than even the seniors on the football team. Denise had told her that all he'd done last summer was lift weights and work out, trying to get bigger so he'd be invited to try out for the National Junior Team.

It had worked. Billy was huge. Nothing but muscle. And word was that he'd been asked to try out for the team last week.

Looking at him made her nervous and happy at the

same time. It was like she could feel her skin from the inside. And all of it felt good.

Denise had said he'd gotten a girlfriend over the summer. Some older girl who gave him blow jobs in her car. And the thought of it, of him . . . like that . . . made her heart race. And hurt a little, too.

The sun came in through the high windows and turned his brown hair to caramel. His eyes were the color of chocolate.

She wasn't totally sure what a blow job was, but if it meant putting her mouth on Billy Wilkins—getting to taste him, even just a little bit—it seemed like a great idea.

"Can I sit with you?" he asked, like it was normal. Like he wanted to sit with Maddy and her overbite and Fiona, who couldn't stop staring, and the theater nerds, who were doing their homework at the table.

She could feel the eyes of every single person in the cafeteria on them.

Why? she wanted to ask. *Is this a joke? Some kind of prank you're pulling with the rest of the jocks?*

"Sure," she said.

The chair he pulled out scraped across the floor and the guys with their homework looked up at him, furious.

"Sorry." He winced.

Billy sat down, his long body curling and uncurling into a chair. Under the table, his feet touched hers and even through their shoes she felt a zing shiver up her legs to rest low in her belly.

Go, she mouthed to Fiona and her friend rolled her eyes but moved over two chairs, closer to the boys, giving Maddy and Billy a bubble of privacy.

"How are you?" Billy focused on her like they were alone in the cafeteria. It was crazy how he could do that. How he could make everyone and everything disappear.

"Good." She couldn't look at him for too long. It was

like staring up at the sun, if she did it for too long she'd see spots. Or go blind.

"Hey, guys, mind if I join you?" Kevin Dockrill, with his pockmarked face and tiny little eyes, pulled out the chair Fiona had been sitting in and sat down, his tray of French fries clattering on the table.

Maddy stiffened, every muscle in her body turning to concrete. Kevin was a jerk. Always had been, since they were little kids growing up in the same neighborhood. And when the word spread that Billy was going to try out for nationals, Kevin had started riding Billy like crazy.

"What are you doing, Kevin?" Billy asked, not even pretending to be nice.

"A guy can't talk some hockey with an old friend?"

Billy said nothing, his eyes focused on the edge of the table.

"What, you're such a big shot you can't even talk?"

The whole room was silent, pulsing with dangerous energy Maddy didn't quite understand. But Kevin was staring holes into Billy's head and Billy was looking away.

"I heard this rumor that you were scared about try-outs. You were crying in the locker room."

"That's a lie," she said, the words erupting from her mouth like they had a mind of their own. "He's not scared, everyone knows he's going to make it!"

"Oh, hey, man." Kevin sat back, his jean jacket falling open over his faded KISS concert T-shirt. "You got yourself a cheerleader."

"Leave her alone," Billy muttered.

"I will," Kevin said, "when you look me in the eyes like a man."

Billy looked him in the eye, bigger and stronger than ever before. "I'm not fighting you, Kevin. Say what you want. Do what you want."

" 'Cause you're chickenshit?"

" 'Cause you're not worth losing my tryout over."

Suddenly, Maddy realized what was really happening. Kevin wanted Billy to fight because if Billy got suspended from school, he'd couldn't try out.

She stood up. "Let's go."

"Go?" Kevin asked. "Where you gonna go?" He opened his beady little eyes real wide like something had just occurred to him. "I heard Billy had some girl giving him head in his car, is that you?"

Billy stood abruptly, his chair screeching across the floor, and now everyone really was looking. People on the other end of the cafeteria were standing up to get a better angle.

"Shut your mouth, Kevin."

"You want to fight over this girl?" Kevin said. "She must be really good. Hey," he touched her hand and she snapped it away, "maybe you want to come out into the parking lot with me?"

Billy shoved the whole table aside, and Fiona and the guys stared openmouthed as their lunches fell to the floor. Billy took one big threatening step toward Kevin, who jumped to his feet, his hands in fists.

Maddy had no idea she was going to do what she did until she was doing it.

But suddenly she was in between Billy and Kevin. "Get out of here, Kevin," she said.

"Maddy . . ." Billy tried to push her behind him, but she wouldn't be budged.

"You need a girl to fight for you?" Kevin laughed and other kids started to join in.

"No, he doesn't," she said, feeling anger churn through her. Anger for Billy, for herself, for the way they grew up, for the choices they had to make and the assholes like this guy, who wanted to make fun of them for trying. "He could take you with one arm behind his back. But he's too smart to do it."

"I don't think Billy has ever been called smart," he sneered.

Oh that made her mad. "Yeah, well, neither have you. Now go, before you get us all in trouble."

"No." Kevin folded his arms over his chest. Suddenly, Maddy remembered her dad dealing with a drunk man at the arena one time. A belligerent dad who wouldn't shut up and wouldn't walk away—just like Kevin.

And so, just like her father had done, Maddy reached out and smacked him, openhanded, across the face. More insulting than painful.

The entire cafeteria gasped and Maddy's hand stung and her heart stopped.

"Oh shit," Billy muttered and finally pulled her behind him, just as the cafeteria erupted. Kevin charged Billy, trying to get at Maddy. Billy held him off with one hand, but another fight broke out behind them and someone caught her in the eye with their elbow.

She was stunned. Reeling. Holding on to the back of Billy's shirt like her life depended on it.

Suddenly, there was a whistle and Coach Roames was standing on a table, bellowing.

"Who started this?"

Everyone slowly turned and pointed their finger at her.

"Oh shit," Billy muttered again.

Ten minutes later Maddy was sitting outside the principal's office with an ice pack pressed to her eye. She'd never been in trouble before and was pretty sure she was going to throw up all over herself.

The door to the main office opened and Billy slipped in, carrying her book bag. Her heart dropped into her stomach and she didn't know if she was happy or embarrassed. He sat beside her and she tried to pull her body, her skin, as far from him as she could.

"You all right?" he asked.

"My eye hurts."

His fingers touched her chin, turning her face toward him, and she burned at the touch. From her hair to her toes, she burned.

"Let me see," he whispered, and he lifted the cold pack. He whistled, long and low.

"It's bad?" she asked.

"It'll be a shiner."

"My dad is going to kill me."

She leaned back, staring up at the ceiling.

Billy shifted and cleared his throat.

"You don't have to sit here," she muttered.

"You think I would leave? After what you did?"

Oh God, she felt stupid and small.

"I'll explain to Mr. Pursator," he said. "And your dad."

"You'll explain that I slapped Kevin Dockrill?" Saying it sounded ridiculous, like it had to be someone else who'd slapped him. Someone else that dumb.

"I'll explain that he was saying shitty things about you and you stood up for yourself and you . . . you know . . . you stood up for me."

The silence pulsed around them. When he put it that way, she didn't feel quite so bad. In fact, she felt kind of . . . right.

"You think that will work?"

"Yep." He nodded, like the case was closed. No problem.

When she smiled it hurt her eye, but that didn't stop her. "Thanks."

His fingers touched hers, the knuckle, the palm of her

hand, where she could still feel that slap. "Thank you," he whispered. "No one has ever done that for me."

"Slapped a guy?"

"Stood up for me."

She got lost for a second in his eyes. They were so pretty and she could see so much in them. "You're not stupid," she said.

"I know." But he didn't, she could see that in his eyes, too.

They sat there quietly, waiting for the principal to open the door. Listening to the buzz in the main office, the clock in the hall count off the seconds.

It was weird sitting there with a black eye and Billy Wilkins. But there was nowhere she'd rather be.

And when she looked into his chocolate eyes, she got the idea that he didn't want to be anywhere else either.

chapter 21

After meatball subs, Tara Jean suggested a trip to Target. Charlie jumped up and down, which Billy was beginning to realize was the kid's normal state. He must have been truly scared, truly exhausted before, to have subdued all this ceaseless joy.

Surprisingly, despite her sullen stillness and silence, Becky lit right up, too. For the first time she actually looked like a thirteen-year-old girl.

The sight was sort of breathtaking.

"I need the money." She held out her hand. "The hundred in the front hall drawer."

"I think I can afford some stuff from Target," he said, pushing himself to his feet.

"We can pay our way." *We don't need charity,* that's what she was really saying. He knew that tone of voice. Remembered using it with all those rec league coaches who talked about fund-raising and scholarship programs for a kid who had to work so hard just to buy skates, much less pay his fees.

"Becky." He felt every minute of his years, every ache in the bones of his body. "How many of your birthdays have I missed?"

"All of them."

"Charlie's?"

"All of them."

"Right. Consider this payback."

She didn't even hesitate. Charity was one thing, overdue presents, quite another. "Fine."

"I'll drive." He turned for the living room and the foyer with his shoes and keys, but Tara Jean stopped him.

"If you go, every person in the store will be snapping pictures of you on their cell phones."

God, he was exhausted. He rubbed his face, his eyes, ran a hand through his hair, getting himself ready to practice his indifference. To summon his patience.

"I got this, Billy."

Oh Lord, really? He couldn't even pretend not to be totally grateful. Honestly, at this point, he would take a bullet for Tara Jean Sweet.

"You sure?"

TJ shrugged. "How hard can it be?"

Luc, still sitting at the round table, the daylight haloing his face, laughed.

"I can do it!" Tara Jean protested.

"I have no doubt that you can." Luc grinned at his girlfriend, his faith in her palpable. "You can do anything." Their happiness was bittersweet to watch and Billy looked down at his feet.

He'd begged Maddy to stay and she had left. Part of him understood that—hell, he'd leave if he could. But he'd been floored by how badly he'd wanted her here. It was one thing to love her, but the need kind of surprised him.

"Saddle up, kids," Tara Jean said, herding them out the kitchen door. As they passed Billy, she held out her hand and he shoved all the money he had at her.

"A car seat," he said. "And some kid crap. Movies and things."

"Got it."

Without looking at or counting the money, she just tucked it into her pocket. He knew if he was short, she would fill in the gaps and never say a word. That was friendship.

After they left, the house was silent in a way it had never been before. There was silence and then there was the absence of noise. Of people.

Billy dropped into a dining room chair as if all his bones had broken at once.

"You all right?" Luc asked, sitting beside him.

"Thanks to you guys." Billy was at a loss, it had been years since he'd been in such debt to another person. After the divorce, he'd developed a steady pattern of pushing people off to a comfortable distance.

Nothing like an emergency to shrink that comfortable distance down to nothing.

"Our pleasure, man. I wish we didn't have to fly to Toronto tomorrow."

"No, don't worry. Honestly." Billy had regretted asking them to stay the night nearly the second he'd done it. A knee-jerk desperate response to being all alone with two kids. To being so exhausted he couldn't see straight.

It was almost better that Luc and TJ couldn't stay; he was uncomfortable enough with all this help. All these well-meaning witnesses to his floundering at rock bottom. "I'll be all right."

Luc stretched his legs out in front of him. "What are you going to do?"

"About the kids? I feel like I can't do anything until I talk to Janice."

"What about Maddy?"

Billy dropped his head back, his laugh strangled. "I have no clue. No. Fucking. Clue."

"Then let's talk about hockey."

Luc watched Billy as if he was waiting for him to say something. Billy finally shrugged, tired of feeling so damn clueless.

"If you have something you want to say, spit it out, Luc. I'm too damn tired to read your mind."

"Hornsby was trying to save your hide, Billy. You're the one who didn't help. And this whole thing with Maddy and the kids, you know that's not what he's really upset about."

"So now you're an expert on my coach?"

Billy tried to make a joke to kill the tension that was coating the room like a thin layer of ice, but Luc just gave him that level cut-the-crap stare.

Billy got to his feet and walked toward the fridge even though he wasn't hungry. Between the exhaustion and the emotional upheaval of the last few days he felt raw. As if every breeze was a hurricane force wind and he couldn't keep himself on his feet.

"I've been playing professional hockey for sixteen years, Luc. I am the kind of player teams need, not to be a leader but to get shit done. To stir the pot." He pulled a glass out and filled it with water he didn't really plan on drinking. "I don't make speeches, or score points. I get in the other team's head. I take the hits, I make the hits—all so guys like you can do your jobs."

The black edge of resentment in his voice surprised him. Shook the corners of the room. Shook his corners. But Luc just nodded, as if he'd known all along.

"You know, buddy, I've never said this before, and I'll never say it again, but the day we started playing on the same team was the same day you stopped being the player you could have been."

The glass hit the counter with a crack. "What the hell are you talking about?"

"You weren't an enforcer until you and I were in Toronto." Billy started to tell him that he was crazy, but Luc lifted his hand. "No, you weren't a finesse player, and yes, you were rough and aggressive. You've played with a chip on your shoulder your whole damn career, but you scored points back then. You led by example, you showed all of us what it meant to play hockey with nothing held back. But the more we were on the ice together, the more you let me shine and took the hits and handed out the retribution."

Billy rolled his eyes.

"No, listen. For once, just listen without fighting. I started to hit my stride and you and I fell into a rhythm. And it was good for all of us. But I think you let go of the player you could have been."

"I'm pretty damn happy with the player I am."

"Really? Because they're sending that player down to the minors."

"That doesn't have anything to do with the way I play!"

"That's right. Because you didn't play the last half of the season! Is this really the way you want to go out, Billy?"

They were standing. Yelling at each other. Billy had his hands wrapped around his glass like he was going to throw it at his best friend. His only friend.

"I'm sorry," Luc said.

"Don't be sorry." Billy sighed. "You're right."

Luc blinked.

"And I won't ever say that again, so we're even."

Luc laughed and the tension in the room vanished. Billy wasn't a guy who had heart-to-hearts and Luc knew that, so he dropped the subject.

"You look like you could fall asleep," Luc said. "Let's go see if there's anything good on TV."

"I'm sure you've got other things to do besides hang out with me."

"Nope," Luc answered definitively and walked to the living room, talking about how he wanted to see Billy's epic movie collection.

"Grab that candy Tara Jean brought," he called and

Billy, on autopilot, pulled the licorice from the cupboard under the counter.

Somewhere in the parts of his brain that cataloged things like loss and grief, he realized Luc was right. Coming up in the league, he'd been a powerful defenseman, capable of scoring points, of quarterbacking the power play. But he'd been an angry player—ready to fight all the time.

And everyone had wanted a piece of that anger. Wanted to capitalize on his willingness to fight. Wanted to use him like a weapon, and he'd been all right with that. He'd had more than his share of hate for the world. But somehow, over the years he'd been sharpened so much, so effectively that there was nothing left but that black, black anger.

Was this how he wanted to go out?

No. What a stupid question. Who wants to go out in the minors, without playing most of his last year of NHL hockey? No one.

And he could be stubborn and stupid and fight this some more, but what was the point?

Swearing under his breath he grabbed his phone and texted Hornsby:

I'm sorry. Is there a time when we can meet?

Almost immediately the answer came back:

Monday morning 9 a.m., my office.

"Look!" Charlie, sitting in a puddle of early morning light next to the couch, held up a LEGO blob.

"A dog?" Becky asked, taking a sip from her Coke can. Icy cold and sweet, the drink woke up her mouth. Her whole body.

"Robot."

"That doesn't look anything like a robot."

"Yes it does." Charlie made the blob walk and in his best robot voice said, "I am a robot."

She laughed. "I see it now. Good one." She smiled at him as he started to build another one.

Charlie had never had so many toys. Yesterday, Tara Jean had kept putting toys and clothes and food in the shopping cart, like it was all free or something.

It got to the point where Becky couldn't even protest without Charlie throwing himself a monster fit. More and more things just ended up in that cart. So now he was sitting in the warm sunshine in brand-new, fuzzy Thomas the Train pajamas, playing with brand-new LEGOs while she drank icy cold Coke. And there were eleven more cans in the fridge. Along with more fruit and vegetables than Charlie had ever seen in his life.

For the moment, at least, it didn't seem like she'd totally screwed up.

"Do you like it here?" Becky asked her brother.

"Yep."

In the quiet of early morning, without any screaming or the smell of Aunt Janice's cigarettes, she let herself smile.

"Hey."

She flinched at the sound of Uncle Billy's voice.

"Look!" Charlie yelled and held up his gray LEGO blob.

"Great robot, buddy," Uncle Billy said and came to stand beside them. "You guys are up early."

"It's eight."

"That's not early?" He yawned and stretched, his big muscles pulling and pushing against the T-shirt he wore. "Feels early."

She wished she could hold on to this morning a little longer. If he'd just stayed asleep and let her keep pretending, it would have been like a vacation or something. A dream.

But he was here and if this was a dream, they had to wake up sooner or later.

"Have you heard from Janice?" she asked and Uncle Billy shook his head.

Becky tipped a blue LEGO piece right side up and then another, creating a tiny wall that wouldn't hold back a thing.

"Is there . . . is there someone else we should call?" Uncle Billy said. "Someone who would be worried about you? Your school?"

She started to add a second story to her wall. "I didn't go to school all that much."

"What? Why?"

She shrugged. "Didn't like it."

"I don't believe you."

"Why?"

"Because thirteen-year-old girls love school. It's where all the boys are."

Boys were stupid. All they did was get girls pregnant and sweat. Honestly, she didn't see the appeal.

Uncle Billy sat down on the floor beside Charlie and Becky jerked her legs closer to her body.

"Help?" Charlie shoved a bunch of LEGOs toward Uncle Billy, bouncing with happiness.

"Sure, buddy," Uncle Billy said with a smile and started to put together his own robot. "Why didn't you go to school?" he asked Becky again.

"Someone had to take care of Charlie." She was on to the third story of her wall, stealing blocks from Charlie, who didn't seem to notice.

"Denise didn't do that?"

"She was a junkie."

She knew he was looking at her, but she just focused on her wall.

"So you couldn't go to school?" Something about the

tone of his voice made her angry. Like he didn't believe her. Like she was just lazy or something. Stupid.

"You don't know anything about my life."

"So tell me."

Once the social worker lady from the state had come to their house and Becky had managed to keep her mom sober for long enough to meet with her. They'd told the woman that Becky was being homeschooled. But there had been a moment in the middle of all those lies when Becky had imagined telling the truth. Opening her mouth and letting it all spill out, because she was just a kid and Charlie was a baby and she didn't know what the hell she was doing. And she wanted to tell the truth. Because she was pretty sure what was happening wasn't the best for anyone.

But then the social worker had given Mom a bunch of tests that Becky had to do to prove she was being homeschooled. And the moment was over. The DCFS woman left. Mom got high. Becky put Charlie down for a nap and did the tests.

And the moment to tell the truth never came again.

Until right now.

"She was clean when she was pregnant, but like three months after Charlie was born she started using again." Uncle Billy wasn't playing robots anymore, he was watching her. No judgment on his face as far as she could tell, and she'd seen a lot of judgment. "One day I came home from school and Mom was passed out on the couch, the needle in her arm, and Charlie was screaming his head off in his crib, still in the filthy diaper he'd worn all night. She hadn't even fed him."

"Oh my God, Becky."

"How was I supposed to care about school or boys when all I could think about was Mom starting a fire with a cigarette and being too high to get Charlie out of the house?"

"No one helped you?"

"Who was going to help?" *You,* she thought. *You were supposed to help.* She knew better than to say it, but the words were there all the same—a terrible, terrible scream that wanted to get out.

For months after Mom died she'd thought about her rich, famous uncle Billy showing up in a limo to take her and Charlie away to a house where no one smoked and no one smacked and everything was safe and clean.

"What about Janice?" he asked.

Aunt Janice was a question she didn't know how to answer. Yeah, she'd taken them in, but it was so bad Becky had wondered if they'd be better off at the church shelter.

She rubbed her wrist, where she could almost still feel Aunt Janice's tight grip from the last time she got mad. Right before Becky bought those plane tickets.

"She's my sister," Uncle Billy whispered. "I know what she's like."

"Then why'd you leave us with her?" she asked, knocking over the wall she'd built, the words flying around the room like mean birds. "Never mind." She jumped to her feet, wishing she was eighteen. Wishing she could at least drive. Wishing she could just *leave.* Just leave. That's all she'd ever wanted.

"Please, Becky," he said, looking at the pieces of LEGO instead of at her. "Sit down."

This whole morning was ruined. Charlie wasn't making LEGO blobs anymore, he was watching the two of them, worry all over his face, his thumb creeping toward his mouth.

"Don't do that, Charlie," she said, pulling his hand down, holding his fingers. Keeping her eyes off of Uncle Billy.

"Forget what I said," she told Uncle Billy's knee. "It's wonderful where we are. I go to school and I'm on the honor roll and Charlie goes to a great day care where no one smokes and they teach him stupid songs about wheels and buses!"

She felt the tears coming, tears that wouldn't make anything right. She blinked them away, staring up at the ceiling.

"Becky," Charlie whispered, patting her leg. "Becky, don't cry."

"It's okay, Char," she whispered back, sitting down on the couch so he could climb into her lap. She put her head in his neck, breathing in the smell of him. Banana and new pajamas.

"I wish I could say that I hadn't known about you. But I did," Uncle Billy said and she couldn't breathe. "And I just . . . it was easier."

"Easier?"

"To pretend that I didn't know about you. What your life must have been like. I'm sorry, Becky."

"Sorry doesn't always cut it," Charlie said, turning on Uncle Billy, her little defender. For about the hundredth time she regretted saying that to Charlie once when he'd spilled hot soup all over her.

Although this time "sorry doesn't always cut it" sure seemed to fit.

"I know," Uncle Billy told Charlie sadly. "But listen, I have to know about Janice."

"Why?"

Uncle Billy had that same look on his face that Mrs. Jordal always had. That I-can-be-patient-while-you-figure-it-out look.

"She's mean," Becky finally said. "I was scared to leave Charlie alone with her all day."

"Did she hit him?"

"No. But she hit me plenty, so I figured it was only a matter of time."

Uncle Billy swore under his breath.

"Bad word!" Charlie the word-police pointed his finger at Uncle Billy.

"You want a Coke?" Becky stood and put Charlie back on the floor, uncomfortable with the broken walls and mean birds. The details of her life that were so ugly.

"For breakfast?"

"You drink coffee, don't you?"

"I didn't when I was thirteen."

"Well, good for you."

In the kitchen she opened the fridge and grabbed another can, and then swiped a banana from the counter for Charlie. But she couldn't make herself go back into the living room. Charlie was talking to Uncle Billy, his voice excited, and Becky just stood there, the Coke in one hand and the banana in the other.

Her stomach felt queasy, like she'd already had too much pop.

So, she thought, staring at the perfect yellow of the banana. Not at all like the brown ones she bought on the half-off rack at the Giant Eagle. *I did it. I said all those things.*

"Becky?" It was Uncle Billy, behind her, and she closed her eyes for one minute, praying, even though she'd stopped doing that like a million years ago.

Let us stay. Say you're going to let us stay.

"Yeah?" she asked and turned to face him, trying not to let all her hope show.

Becky, she imagined him saying. *I'm not sending you back. I'm going to keep you here in this clean house. And you can go to school and Charlie will have a nanny and you'll have a normal life.*

"I have to make a few calls today, but maybe . . . maybe after that we can go have some fun."

Her heart punched her stomach, disappointment making her sick. "Fun?"

"Yeah, it's probably been a while for you, but there's this water park down the road . . ."

A water park? Was he nuts?

Her can hit the counter with a thunk, causing a little pop to slosh up over her fingers.

"We don't have swimsuits."

"We can get some."

"Charlie doesn't know how to swim."

"Do you?"

She blinked, wondering why he was doing this. Was he thinking that he wouldn't have to worry about them if they drowned?

"Man," he laughed. "I can practically hear your suspicious thoughts. I just thought it would be fun."

"Isn't your career ending or something?" She was being mean. Trying to get him to say "Forget it," because what if they went? What if they did have fun? And then what would happen when Aunt Janice called and it was time for them to go back?

"Yep. It's in the toilet. And instead of sitting here thinking about it all day on a Sunday when I can't do anything about it, I thought a water slide, or a hundred, might help me forget."

Like it will make me forget where I come from? Everything I just told you? I tell you my aunt beats the shit out of me and you want to take me to a water park?

"No." She shook her head and took a giant sip, trying to rinse the taste of stupid wishes out of her mouth.

"No?"

"That's what I said."

He looked confused and angry. "Then what do you want to do?"

They were in a total stare down and maybe Maddy was right, Billy wouldn't hurt them. Not on purpose. Not with his fists. But showing her and Charlie a little of what life could be like and then sending them back to Pittsburgh? He might as well punch her in the face.

Thinking of Maddy gave her an idea, a possible Plan C.

"I want to go to Maddy's."

His eyebrows went way up on his head, but he was smiling and she knew he wouldn't say no—she'd seen the way they looked at each other.

"Give her a call. See what she says."

She pulled the card from her pocket and hoped that Plan C went better than Plans A and B.

chapter 22

Janice hit Becky.

The words kept repeating themselves in an awful loop in his head.

There was no way the kids were going back.

The decision came with a thousand worries, but none of them as great as the doubt he'd been living under for the last two days. Making the decision felt good. He could breathe again.

He was going to keep the kids.

Keep the kids. It was so simple. He turned and started to make coffee.

"Maddy said we could go over," Becky said, coming back into the room ten minutes after she'd left to make her call in private.

The scoop hit the edge of the coffee machine, scattering grounds across the counter. He swept them away. Waiting to turn around until he got the smile on his face under control.

"That's great," he said. Still smiling, but now down at the coffeepot. He hit the on switch.

"She told us to bring swimming suits. Her condo has a pool."

"Are you kidding—" he started to say, turning. But she was gone.

That girl was working on something.

But then, so was he.

For the next few minutes, Billy did the best he could, laughing and joking with Charlie, trying hard to get Becky to smile—all while getting a diaper bag packed.

"I gotta make a phone call, guys," he said and nearly ran to his bedroom.

It was still shadowed and dark in there, a cocoon with the shades pulled down. His purple duvet looked black.

He shook out the tight and tingling muscles in his arms before dialing. Not expecting an answer, he nearly dropped the phone when his sister said: "Hello?"

"Janice?"

"Well, well, if it isn't the hockey star." He heard the snick of a lighter, the quick inhale of her breath. He could imagine her so clearly—her face familiar but terribly older. Meaner.

God, he thought, closing his eyes against the sharp stab of pain. How had it all gone so wrong?

"Tell me, how is your day going?" Her voice was snidely amused. She'd sent those kids down, alone and scared, to fuck with him.

"This is a shit move, Janice. Even for you, sending those kids."

"Oh, I didn't send them. That was all Becky's idea."

"You didn't pay—"

"Fuck you, Billy, like I got that money."

He put the phone down, rested it against his leg. Becky was one tough kid. He was proud of her, he really was.

"Billy!" Janice yelled and he lifted the phone up.

"Yeah."

"Are you mad because we ruined your makeover?" Her laugh, which disintegrated into a hacking cough, set his teeth on edge.

"It's not funny. They're kids, Janice." *Are you such a monster?* he wanted to ask. *Has every bit of decency just abandoned your body?*

"Yeah, Denise's kids, and I been taking care of them

and Denise for years. Dressing 'em. Schooling 'em. Paying for shit. All while you've been making millions! You try raising them."

Most people didn't realize that fighting during a hockey game wasn't just about a guy losing his temper and going after another guy, though there was plenty of that. Cheap shots and ugly checks into the boards. But for a fight—a real, center of the ice, two-guys-going-at-it kind of throw down—there was a protocol.

If a guy dropped his gloves, he'd wait until the other one dropped his gloves, signaling he was ready to go, before taking a swing.

Janice had just dropped her gloves.

And he could drop his and they could scrap like dogs over a bone. It's what she wanted, she'd wanted it for years. To start a huge fight. To play out some petty vengeance. Not because he was rich, though that had to sting.

But because he got out.

And she was sleeping up in Mom's bed on 12 Spruce.

"Fine."

"What?"

"I'll take it from here, Janice. You'll never—ever—touch Becky again."

"Oh, you think it's easy? Charlie's three and still wears diapers and that girl's got a mouth on her. She can find a way to ruin anything. They're fucked up—"

"Then you'll have no problem giving me custody."

There was a long pause, the sound of her sucking on the end of a cigarette, and he worried, he really did, that she would dig in her heels for no good reason. To do nothing but cause him trouble.

"Oh fine, big shot, you think you can do better? Go right ahead. You'll be sending them back in two months."

"No, I won't. You'll be hearing from my lawyer."

He hung up. Every muscle clenched and the phone in his hand felt like a missile he could fire into space. Fire a thousand miles right into his sister's face.

Part of him wanted to charge right back out into that living room and tell Becky that she was never going back to Janice's house, that she was safe. But he was working hard on doing the right thing. And the right thing was almost always more complicated than he thought.

So he called his lawyer.

"Jesus Christ, Billy," Ted said when he answered. "It's Sunday morning."

"What? I don't pay you enough? It's an emergency."

Ted sighed. "It always is with you. What's up?"

"I need to get custody of these kids."

"Wow. You don't fool around."

"My sister hits her, Ted. I can't . . . I can't just leave her there." Again, he thought. He yanked open the shades, blinded by sunlight. "Janice said she'd give up custody."

"What about the father? *Fathers*."

"They're not in the picture."

"I bet they will be once they hear you want the kids."

"Fine. I got money."

"It's not that easy, Billy. Getting your sister to give up custody is only part of it. You have to be approved as a foster parent before you can take them."

"Well, how hard can that be? Janice did it."

"Not that hard if you haven't been all over the news hitting reporters, breaking chairs, being accused of fathering children you've abandoned—"

"Okay, okay, I get it." He closed the shades again. "What do I do?"

"We'll start the paperwork tomorrow. Try to keep your nose clean, if you can. And Billy, you gotta fix this nightmare you're in. Set some facts straight."

"I'm working on it."

"I'm not kidding."

"Do you think I am?" He slammed the heel of his hand against the wall.

"Okay. I'll get started on the paperwork, and send it to you tomorrow to sign."

"Can I tell them?" he asked, closing his eyes, resting his head against the fist on the wall, and knowing the answer even as the question left his mouth.

"You might not get approved, and if she decides to still give up custody anyway, those kids . . . they might end up in separate foster homes."

He thought of Becky losing Charlie. Thought of her face, the scream. The way she'd fight everyone trying to hold her back from her brother.

That couldn't happen. Couldn't.

"When will I know if I'm approved?"

"We'll push as hard as we can. Your money will help, but you still . . ."

Still have to get approved.

"Okay, thanks Ted."

Kids. Kids were coming to her condo. Madelyn might have gone overboard with the juice boxes. The value pack of twenty-five, which took up one whole shelf in her fridge, was probably overkill.

Calm down, she told herself as she threw cheese sticks and apples onto the other shelves. *They're just kids.*

And Billy.

Maybe she'd have a better chance of convincing him to do the show while they were on her turf.

Maybe you'll have a better chance of convincing him to do the show if you grow bunny ears and hop around the place.

But God, kids. And cupcakes. In her house.

It made her feel . . . unsafe. Unbalanced. Like the house might come down around her if someone else was in here.

Having Billy here that morning had been one thing, he'd barely even seen the place. But this, juice boxes and cheese sticks and swimming parties—this was something else entirely.

Her buzzer rang and she jumped, her heart pounding.

She leaned over and pushed the button to the doorman.

"You have a very excited boy down here, wearing goggles, Miss Cornish. He says he's going to go swimming."

She laughed, imagining the scene. "Send them up, Lou."

In the minutes before their knock she turned and did a last check of her condo. It matched so perfectly the idea she'd had of a self-made woman's house. A woman with taste and refinement, who could handle anything. Who'd pulled herself up out of the mud.

It will be okay, she told herself. *They're just kids. It's just Billy.* But it felt like so much more. It felt like danger right around the corner.

There was a furious pounding at the door, like cops on a raid.

"Maddy!" Charlie yelled. "Let's go swimming!"

She opened the door and there was Charlie, with goggles and water wings and a giant grin on his face.

Irresistible. The boy was literally irresistible. She would have reached down to hug him if Becky hadn't ushered him in.

"I told him he had to be quiet," Becky said, wearing a pink hoodie, her hair pulled back in a super-tight ponytail. It looked like it was giving her a headache.

"It's all right," she said. "There are lots of kids who live here. Everyone is used to a little noise."

"When can we go swimming?" Charlie asked, doing a

dance in her front hallway that involved a lot of butt shaking.

"Yeah." Billy, wearing a pair of board shorts and a T-shirt with the sleeves torn off, stepped into the condo, mimicking Charlie's dance. Billy's moves delighted the boy to no end so he started dancing more and the butt shaking got super-sonic.

"Becky?" Billy asked, clearly inviting her into the dance routine. He bumped Becky with his hips and the girl rolled her eyes, stepping sideways to lean against Maddy's pink table.

"You guys are stupid," Becky sighed and Billy stopped dancing.

"You are a killjoy," he said and stuck out his tongue at her.

Maddy laughed before she could help it. Becky glared at her and she clapped a hand over her mouth.

Of course Billy would be good at this. He was a giant kid. He'd probably been just waiting for two kids to arrive on his doorstep so he could go swimming. So he would have an excuse to shake his butt.

"Well," Maddy said, "you can go swimming right now. The pool is on the top of the building."

"The top of the building?" Charlie asked, his eyes round as quarters under his little steamed-up goggles.

"Can you believe it?" she asked, opening her eyes as wide as she could.

Charlie charged back out to the hallway and Billy just barely caught him by the edge of a wing.

"You guys coming?" Billy asked. "I can't hold him back much longer."

"I need to change," Becky said, staring down at her feet. She nudged Maddy's pink and white running shoes with the toe of her beat-up Keds knockoff.

"Go on up." Maddy handed him the pass card to get into the pool. "Becky and I will be there in a little bit."

The boys cleared out, the door shutting behind them with a heavy click.

"You, ah, you have your suit?"

Becky lifted a Target bag, but made no move to find a place to change.

"You want to get ready?" Maddy asked, but Becky was looking around the apartment like she was sightseeing.

"I like your house," she said. "I've never seen white carpets before."

She'd gotten white because it seemed so modern. So clean. So unlike her past. She'd made the decision as the thirteen-year-old girl she'd been. Funny, she'd never really seen that before.

"Nice view," Becky said, standing in front of the windows.

"It's why I got this unit," Maddy said. "It's pretty at night."

Becky humphed a little laugh. "Your job must pay pretty good."

"I guess." Maddy suppressed a smile. She knew when her place was getting cased. "You want a juice box or something? While you go through my stuff?"

"Juice box? You think I'm ten?"

"I think you might be thirsty."

"I'm not going to steal anything."

"I know, Becky. It was a joke." Maddy ducked into the kitchen and grabbed a juice box and cheese stick just to be sure. When she came back out Becky was looking at her bookshelves.

"You like to read?" she asked.

Becky shrugged.

"I remember what it's like, you know? But pretending to be stupid doesn't get you very far."

Becky smiled, really fast, and that smile was beautiful. It made Maddy wonder what the girl would look like with some color in her cheeks. The dark circles out from under her eyes. A good haircut.

"Did you have Mrs. Jordal in school?" Becky asked.

"No. Why?"

"That's something she said to me once. I like to read. A lot."

"You can borrow any of the books. If you want." She pointed to the top corner where she kept some of her favorites from high school: *Lord of the Flies, To Kill a Mockingbird, Flowers for Algernon.* "Those are good."

"I've read those."

"Well," she laughed, "look at you."

"Just because I don't go to school doesn't mean I can't read."

"You don't go to school?"

Becky shook her head, backing away from the bookshelf. Turning to look at the photographs of different guests that had been on *AM Dallas*. Most people had pictures of family, she had pictures of acquaintances. It had never seemed ridiculous before now.

"Why?"

"Someone's got to take care of Charlie."

"Denise couldn't do that?" It wasn't an accusation. Wasn't even really a question.

Becky shook her head.

"Your mom wasn't always like that."

Becky got still, like a mouse startled by a sound waiting for something to swoop out of the shadows and snatch it.

"I don't remember," Becky whispered.

"She was fun," Maddy said, pulling up dim memories, trying to make them bright for the girl. "Loved playing practical jokes. Especially on Billy. She'd hide his stuff. Fill his shoes with shaving cream."

Becky smiled.

"She loved to read, too."

And just like that the smile was gone. "I'm nothing like her."

"It wasn't all bad, honey."

"It was for me."

Side by side and silent, they both looked out the window and Maddy felt like she often did with Billy when they were younger, like there was nothing she could say, not one thing. But by not leaving she had already been better than most people in the girl's life.

"Can we stay with you?" Becky asked.

If all the glass shattered at once she couldn't have been more alarmed. "Here?"

"It's where you live."

"What about Billy?"

"He . . . he doesn't want us."

"Becky . . ." She sighed. She didn't know what to say. There were no words.

The girl's blue eyes bored right into her. "We'll be good. I promise. I mean, Charlie's pretty easy. He's almost potty-trained. And he's . . . he's sweet, you know. Quiet. Sometimes he has nightmares, but if I sleep with him he's okay. And I can stay home with him so you don't have to pay for a nanny—"

"No. No, please, honey, stop."

Becky closed her mouth so hard her teeth clicked and Maddy didn't know what to do. What to say. How to manage this girl's pain.

It was a mistake to have them here.

She had to suppress that part of her, the small, bitter part who liked her house clean and her life devoid of anything as uncomfortable as love, as painful as this girl's hope. She'd spent years creating this place where emotion didn't touch her, and in five minutes Becky had smashed it to pieces.

She swallowed those terrible petty instincts. She swept that small woman aside and let herself do the right thing. As right as she was able—it was meager and pitiable, but it was all she had.

"Becky, don't you want more?"

"More than having Charlie safe? More than a nice, clean house with a pool on the roof?" It was like she couldn't imagine anything else, anything better for herself. And it devastated Maddy.

"You deserve more. You deserve to go to school. College, even. You deserve to have a chance at your own nice, clean house."

Becky shrugged, but it wasn't as fluent as her other ones. It was broken. She was broken. The girl knew "no" when she heard it. "I would like to go to school."

"You will." There couldn't be any other way—and frankly, just saying the words, just committing to another person, washed Maddy with light. With sudden purpose, the warmth of feeling that comes from trying to help someone else. "Whatever happens, I'll . . . I'll make sure you go to school."

"We can stay?" Becky's eyes lit up, and she looked so much like her mother in that moment that Maddy gasped.

"I can't . . ."—and the hope died—". . . I can't take you away from Billy."

"You're not taking us away. You're not. He doesn't want us."

"Are you sure about that?"

Becky shot her a look that spoke volumes. This girl had never felt wanted in her life. She wouldn't know the feeling if it took her out at the knees.

"It's complicated," Maddy whispered, the words so lame.

"Whatever." And just like that, all the sweetness and kindness, those thin fragile bonds, were gone. "We better go. Charlie doesn't know how to swim."

"You want to go to the bathroom, put on your suit?"

"I'm wearing it," Becky said and walked right past her with the Target bag, which must be empty.

She'd been planning this thing all along.

Maddy followed, wondering how she and Billy were going to handle this new development.

And she wanted to resist the idea of her and Billy handling *anything* together. She wanted to reject it as fast and as hard as she could, but her conscience wouldn't let her. The dejected slope of Becky's shoulders as she marched down the hall ahead of her, the tender pale skin at the nape of her neck, all that vulnerability she worked so hard to hide—none of those things would let Maddy walk away from these kids.

Somehow the past had resurfaced and tied her and Billy together again.

chapter 23

Billy and Charlie were in the shallow end of the pool. Charlie stood on the first of the wide steps, the water lapping his ankles. Billy sat on the third step, his lower body in the water. Overhead there was nothing but glass and blue skies. White fluffy clouds.

"Char," Billy said, "it's not really swimming, what you're doing. It's wading."

"I'm scared."

Billy put his hand on the boy's shoulder, felt the small bones, the twitching muscles. The shivering skin. "I'm here. I won't let anything happen to you."

Charlie, so serious beneath the goggles and yellow water wings, took a deep breath and jumped down to the second step.

"Hey!" Billy cheered and Charlie clapped, but then lost his balance and grabbed on to Billy's shoulders, climbing into his lap like the water was rising fast.

It was strange having a little kid in his lap, especially since the little kid's knee seemed to have unerring aim for Billy's testicles. But it was nice—great, actually. Having a kid wrap his trusting little arms around Billy's neck had been a sensation his life had been missing up until now.

"Billy?" Maddy crouched down beside them. She wore a red swimsuit. Conservative by most standards.

He couldn't see her boobs or her belly button or any of her butt—but the color itself was x-rated.

When he was fifteen, she'd had a red suit and he'd gone to the pool every day to watch the fabric of that bikini cling to her boobs and hips.

She'd been a dream in that red one-piece.

This one wasn't any different.

"Hey," he said. "You didn't ring the bell to be let in."

"I have another pass card."

"We're swimming!" Charlie yelled, waving over Billy's shoulder, toward the hot tub. "Becky. Look."

"Why don't you go sit with your sister for a second," Maddy asked Charlie and the boy didn't have to be asked twice. He was up, dripping and running across the tiles toward his sister, who sat hunched and small among the bubbles of the hot tub.

"Are kids supposed to sit in hot tubs?" Billy asked.

"The temperature's super low, it's like a bath."

"Well, that's good. The kid could probably use one." Billy pushed off the steps, drifting out into the pool. Like it was twenty years ago, he grinned at the woman in the red swimsuit who made him crazy and happy in equal parts.

"Come on in," he said.

"We need to talk."

"If it's about the show—"

She glanced over at the kids. "It's about Becky."

He swam back to the step. "What happened?"

"She asked if she could stay. With me."

"Oh Christ." He had this sudden memory of Denise getting her period for the first time. Janice had been gone. Mom had been passed-out drunk. It had just been him and the mysteries of womanhood and a crying twelve-year-old girl.

He'd felt utterly inadequate to the task.

This moment felt that way.

"What are you going to do about the kids?"

"I talked to Janice this morning and she said she'll give up custody."

"You're trying for custody?" She didn't look horrified, or like she thought he might be joking. She seemed proud. And he didn't want to need her approval quite like he did, but he couldn't lie—it felt good.

"It's not that easy, but I can't send them back to Janice. She . . . she hits Becky."

He saw the anger brew on Maddy's face. She wasn't a fan of bullies and Janice was nothing but a chain-smoking bully. She always had been.

"So what do we do?"

We? he thought, the word like a neon sign in the dark. "We?"

"Don't get ahead of yourself, Billy. I just want to help. What can I do?"

"Well, I'd probably have a better chance at being approved as a foster parent if I wasn't a single man . . ."

She couldn't quite fight the smile. "I was thinking more along the lines of a letter of reference."

"I suppose that would be good, too."

"So have you told Becky you're not sending her back?"

"My lawyer advised me against it. Said if Janice gave up custody and I didn't get approved as a foster parent, the kids could be split up, sent to separate foster homes."

Maddy glanced over Billy's head and he turned to see Becky and Charlie sitting on the edge of the hot tub, corralling bubbles with their hands.

"They can't get split up," Maddy sighed.

"I'm doing the best I can."

In her eyes he could see his reflection, the scars and muscles, the tools he used to terrorize men on the ice. But he always looked like so much more in her eyes, too.

Funny how he was finally starting to believe it.

"If word got out about what a good guy you are, your reputation would be ruined," she murmured.

Ah, man, first the red swimsuit and then the "we" stuff and now she thought he was a good man. He sat back down in the cold water before he got ahead of himself.

"Hey!" Charlie came running back across the tiles, water splashing and sloshing out of his cupped hands. "Look at the bubbles!" When the boy slid to a stop beside them, his hands were empty.

Billy laughed at Charlie's crestfallen expression. Two days these children had been in his life. Two days. And yet he could tell nothing would be the same again.

Becky sat shivering in the hot tub. Uncle Billy had convinced Charlie to try to put his face in the water, so Charlie stood on the middle step in the shallow end, bending over at the waist, trying to lower his face into the water.

Uncle Billy and Maddy were cheering him on, but at the last minute Charlie pulled back up, jumping and dancing, nervous and excited.

The grown-ups both groaned.

Becky bit her lip hard, and when the skin tore a bit, she yanked at it, pulling off a big sliver. She tasted blood but she kept on licking the spot even though it stung like crazy. She couldn't stop. She just kept on licking, stinging, and bleeding, and watching Uncle Billy and Charlie and Maddy.

A little family. That's what they were.

If Becky walked over, there wouldn't be any more happy family. Uncle Billy would yell at Becky, or Becky would yell at him, and the whole scene would be ruined.

And that, she told herself—mean as she could be, as awful as Janice and Mom dying—*is why no one wants you. No one.*

Funny, she'd thought she left everything bad behind in Pittsburgh. But the bad was in her.

Charlie was happy and that was the only thing that mattered. Uncle Billy seemed to like him. Way more than he liked her. What with all that hugging.

Yeah, and whose fault was that? she wondered, a little embarrassed by the way she'd been acting all day.

Why do I do that? she wondered. Maybe Janice was right about that, too—Becky just wanted to make life harder. It's not like she woke up every morning thinking "How can I be a total bitch?" It just happened. Someone tried to be kind or give her a hand and it always seemed fake to her.

Charlie hugged Uncle Billy, his arms around the guy's big neck, and Uncle Billy patted her brother's back. He didn't force him to go underwater, or make fun of him for being scared.

Uncle Billy took such good care of Charlie. Which was awesome. Strange and totally unexpected, but awesome.

So awesome, in fact, that it gave her a new idea. Finally, days after Plan A fell to pieces, Plan B was ruined because she couldn't hot wire a car, and Maddy shot down Plan C, Plan D came to her.

She would just leave. By herself.

Uncle Billy had money, he could pay for two nannies to take care of Charlie. And those women would teach Charlie to use the bathroom, because he never would for Becky, and they would walk him to school on the first day of kindergarten. And take him to soccer. Teach him to read.

Her raw and bloody lips burned as tears ran into her mouth.

And running away without him would be so much better for her. She wouldn't have to worry about diapers, or where he would sleep, or if he was clean. Or scared. Or getting hurt.

Away from her, with Uncle Billy, he'd be safe and happy and wearing new clothes and playing with toys and she could just worry about herself.

Just herself. Alone.

She glanced behind her at the big windows, the sunshine and the blue, blue sky.

It would be easy to walk out of here. Really easy. Her clothes were in a locker in the changing room, and she had the key around her wrist. She could change and be gone before Uncle Billy and Maddy even realized she wasn't in the pool.

She'd taken sixty bucks out of Uncle Billy's wallet. It wasn't as much as what he owed her, but it was something. She could make it last.

Charlie's scream—a happy one—made her heart stop, and out of habit she turned to look for him. There'd been more of those happy screams in the last two days than she'd heard since Mom died. And that made Becky happy—it did, but it also made her heart hurt.

She had kept him safe and clean, but she hadn't managed to make him happy.

I won't be able to say good-bye.

She tilted her head back, trying to get a breath, because suddenly there was no air.

Charlie was little, a baby practically—he'd cry for a few days, but he'd probably forget her. In a few years he wouldn't remember her at all, it's not like there were any pictures of her. Or any of him that she could take with her.

Another strip came off her lip.

"Becky?" She whirled and found Maddy standing behind her. "You okay?"

Becky lifted her wrists to wipe away her stupid tears

with her sleeves, then remembered she was wearing a swimsuit.

"Charlie needs a nap," Becky said. She had the same trapped feeling that she'd had when she and Charlie packed their stuff to move into Janice's house. There was nothing, nothing she could do to change things. It was like the whole world was sitting on her chest and her brain was crazy from trying to think of different ways they could get out of the situation. But in the end she was only thirteen, just a kid. "Charlie takes a nap every day. Every day at one. If he goes to sleep later than that he stays up all night."

"Oh . . ." Maddy looked over at the pool, where Charlie was holding on to Uncle Billy's neck and Uncle Billy was carefully swimming so that Charlie's head never went underwater. "We can take him down for a nap. Do you want lunch—"

"He's allergic to strawberries." Becky couldn't look at Maddy or she'd cry worse.

"I didn't buy any strawberries."

"He doesn't like eggs. Or fish sticks. Fish sticks make him throw up."

"I have ham. Can he eat ham?"

Becky nodded, swallowing back the puke in her throat. "But not in a sandwich. He likes it if you roll it up and put it in his hand."

"Becky, are you okay?" Maddy's hand touched her shoulder and Becky jumped up and away, out of the water. She felt naked in her swimsuit. The bruises were gone from the last time Aunt Janice got mad at her, but she felt like they were still there. Like everyone could see them. Would always be able to see them—and no one, no one, would ever want her.

"I'm fine. Totally fine."

* * *

Becky was right, Charlie needed a nap, he was practically asleep in Billy's arms as the four of them took the elevator back down to Maddy's apartment.

Today was an anomaly. A surreal departure, and so, because surreal departures didn't matter, Maddy let herself look at Billy with that kid in his arms and she let herself be happy. Very, very happy.

She forgave herself for being weak—what woman wouldn't be at the sight of such tenderness from the scary hockey player, and the trust from the young boy whose life had been turned upside down.

If she took his picture and created a poster out of it, she'd make a fortune. *THIS IS BILLY WILKINS*, she'd print in big bold letters on the bottom of the poster. The real Billy Wilkins.

The one no one saw but her.

The elevator doors binged open and Maddy led them out.

"I forgot my towel," Becky said, putting her hand against the doors, her feet still in the elevator.

"Oh . . ." Maddy glanced at Billy. "We'll come with you."

"I'll go," Becky said. "You don't have to come. Put Charlie down. I'll be right back."

"Okay." Maddy handed her the key card and Becky disappeared behind the elevator doors.

"Come on," Billy said. "This kid isn't as light as he looks."

Inside the condo, Billy put Charlie to bed in her spare room and Maddy closed the shades, making the room dark. Maddy and Billy stared at each other over the bed and Charlie's sleeping body.

"She wouldn't run away without Charlie, would she?" she asked.

"I don't trust her. I'm going up there."

"Okay I'll . . . I'll stay here."

Then Billy was gone and Maddy worried maybe they were being ridiculous, but the girl's behavior in the hot tub had been really strange. And if she balked at having Billy follow her every move, then maybe she shouldn't act so strangely.

Maddy heard the front door shut and leaned over the bed to carefully tug the goggles off Charlie's damp head and the water wings from his little arms.

The plastic squeaked and pulled and she winced, hoping she wouldn't wake the boy. In the end, she had to lift his arm all the way off the bed to get the wing off.

Holding her breath, she waited for him to scream, but he just sighed, rolling over in his sleep, leaving a wet spot on the quilt from his trunks. She went back into the living room, where Billy had left his duffel bag, and she found Charlie a pull-up and a pair of thin sweatpants that looked comfortable to sleep in.

Back in the shadowed room she weighed her options and decided quicker was better. Just strip him as fast as she could, get him redressed, and hope he was tired enough to sleep through it.

Luckily, he was—until the very end, when she pulled the quilt over his thin, pale, baby bird chest.

"Becky?" He sighed, his eyes opening halfway.

"She'll be right back," Maddy said and really really hoped that the cold knot of worry in her stomach was wrong.

"Cuddles," he said and scooched over until his head was at her knee and his arm was thrown over her waist.

Cuddles, she thought. Cuddles sounded very good. She slipped down in the bed and pulled his cool body to her side, waiting for Billy to come back.

The bathrooms near the pool were empty. The pool was empty.

She'd run away.

Billy hurried back into the elevator and jabbed the button for the main floor—and when the doors took too long to close, he jabbed that button, too.

He couldn't think, he couldn't formulate a plan past the swearing in his head. It was one long line of very freaked-out and scared *fuck*s, ricocheting around his brain.

The doors binged open and he sprang out across the lobby, his flip-flops squeaking against the polished floor.

Lou at the front desk looked up.

"The girl I came in with," Billy said. "The girl in the pink hoodie, did she come back through here?"

Lou nodded and pointed toward the door, the wide world outside. "About five minutes ago."

"Which way did she go?" he asked, pushing open the doors, letting in the heat, the sunlight, the sounds of cars and a thousand other things that could hurt a girl on her own.

"North," Lou said. "Toward the street lights."

Billy checked both ways anyway but headed north, sprinting past women pushing baby strollers, couples walking hand in hand—all of them so blissfully unaware of the fear in his heart. Billy's stomach was spewing acid. He was never going to be the same after this.

He checked every face he could, glanced across the street, looked behind him, but he couldn't find her and the freak-out in his chest escalated.

"Have you seen a girl in a pink hoodie?" he started asking strangers. Most of them just shook their heads. No help. No help at all. Should he call the cops? Should he call Maddy?

"Christ!" he muttered, and then, at the corner, stymied by a red light, he yelled it. Scaring away birds and people in equal measure. He fisted his hands in his hair and looked both ways down the side street.

And there, a half block ahead, was a young girl in a pink hoodie.

Relief flooded him so furiously that for a minute he saw spots. He didn't wait for the light to turn before running across the street, dodging cars slamming on their breaks.

"Holy shit, buddy!" someone yelled and Billy ignored him, jumping over the curb, running down the city block in his flip-flops.

"Becky!" he yelled. "Becky!"

When she finally heard him, she turned, took one look at his face, and jabbed her thumb out at the traffic driving by.

"Oh, no, you don't," he yelled and pulled her hand down. Hitchhiking? Didn't she watch movies? Didn't she know what happened to thirteen-year-old girls who hitchhike?

"Don't touch me!" she yelled. Her lips were bleeding and raw and it was obvious she'd been crying. And he didn't know what to do about that. What to do about any of this except fight his way through. Bully and push until he got her back to the house, where he would then lock every door and pay her a million dollars a year to never scare him like this again.

"What are you doing?" he asked, and as far as stupid questions went, it was about the best he'd ever asked.

"Leaving. I thought you'd be happy."

"Happy? Are you crazy?" He knew in the dark corners of his mind that he wasn't doing this very well.

"Yes!" she said. "I'm crazy and stupid. And poor white trash. And nothing but trouble for everyone. So why don't you let me go?"

"What about Charlie?" he asked. "You were just going to leave him?"

Her face got that terrible broken look that women's faces got when they were trying not to cry. But the tears leaked out the sides of her eyes anyway. He was stupid in the face of that look. Useless.

"You like him. You won't send him back." She had to yell over the sound of traffic. "You'll take care of him, right?"

The clouds of his fury parted for just a second and he got a glimpse of what was really happening.

"I know you paid to come down here, Becky."

"So?"

"I know you want to be here."

"Fuck you."

Oh, she was trying so hard to be grown-up, and the words, so ugly and raw, just proved how young she was.

"Will you please come back?" he asked, feeling himself break and crack, splinter apart.

She shook her head.

"Becky, I can't talk about this on a busy street."

"And I can't go back to Aunt Janice." Her voice was lost in the wind and the dust, but her heartache filled the landscape, pushing him onto his heels.

"I know," he said, he reached for her, forgetting for a moment the scars she carried, and she flinched back so hard, so fast, she tripped over a rock, falling on her butt in the dirt. "Don't. Oh God, Becky." He stood there, helpless, and watched her pick herself up, get back on her feet. His entire body ached to touch her, to pick her up and carry her out of danger.

But she wasn't going to let him.

No one took care of Becky.

Tears ached behind his eyes.

"Trust me, Becky." He held out his hand, knowing she

wouldn't take it, but he had nothing else to offer her. "I will do everything I can so that you don't have to go back to Janice."

Her eyes were wet, her lips cracked and red, and he'd never seen a person more lost. "Trust me," he whispered.

chapter 24

After a long moment, shoulders hunched against the wind, she walked by him and started back toward Maddy's condo.

He followed a few feet behind her, trying to figure out what he was supposed to say. How he was supposed to make this right.

A semi went by and he felt himself blown apart by the wind, pieces of him lost into the sky, to the horizon.

Over the last fourteen years, so much of his life had slipped by without a fight. If it wasn't hockey, he didn't try all that hard, the effort not worth the pain of failure.

Losing Maddy had taught him that.

And now he stood on the precipice of a fight he'd never once contemplated. And he had no idea how to win.

Once they got in the foyer of the condo, Lou scrambled to his feet. "You found her," he said, obviously relieved.

"I found her," Billy said, trying to make it sound like it was no big deal. He even managed to smile, but once they got in the elevator he slumped against the walls.

"You took about a million years off my life, Becky."

She didn't say anything, just watched the illuminated numbers as they climbed. The doors binged open and Maddy was standing at the end of the hallway, half inside her condo, half out.

"Oh, thank God. I was beginning to get nervous," she said.

"She was halfway down the street," he told her, once they were closer.

"Are you okay, Becky?" Maddy asked, but Becky walked right on by without answering.

"Is she okay?" Maddy whispered to him.

"I have no clue," Billy answered, feeling about as shitty and out of his depth as he ever had. It was like the end of their marriage all over again, not the *end* end, but the stuff before, when everything he said was wrong and everything he did only made it worse.

"Are you okay?" she asked, her hand curling around his arm, firm and warm and competent.

Her touch brought him back to himself. She gathered him, collected him. Centered him.

I need you, he thought, fighting the instinct to grab her, to cling to her. *I need you to do this with me. I can't do it alone, and don't want to think of doing it without you.*

But he knew that was her great fear. That she'd get sucked into his life and lose herself in the process. If she was going to help him, she needed to be there by choice.

"I'm okay," he lied.

"What a liar," she whispered, knowing him so well. "Just tell her, Billy. Your lawyer be damned, she needs to know she's not alone."

"Yeah?" That's what his gut was saying, too. But his gut could get things wrong.

"Yeah." She touched his face, just once on his cheek, and he turned his whole focus to her. Such was her magic. "You're not alone, either."

It was everything he'd ever wanted, all over again. But better somehow. As if the years had rubbed off the excess, leaving only exactly what they needed of each other. His strength and commitment, her brain and fierce heart.

Maddy, back by his side, on his side. He felt stronger with her there.

"Thank you," he said.

The door opened and shut behind her and Becky tried not to flinch. She stared out at that view and tried to imagine she was a bird, or a fox or something. Something fast. Something no one could catch.

"Becky," Uncle Billy said and she could see his reflection in the glass, beside her—shadowy and incomplete, but there he was. Maddy was on the other side of her. She'd pulled a yellow T-shirt and black yoga pants over her swimsuit, her hair was clumping and weird, but she was still the prettiest woman Becky had ever seen.

And, there in the middle, was her. Too young, too stupid, too slow. Her hair was a crazy mess from the wind outside.

With as little motion as possible, because it felt like every bone in her body was broken, like every muscle had been bruised, she pushed her hair away from her eyes.

Trust me, he'd said and she had and she hated it.

I think I'm going to be sick.

Maddy touched her back so gently Becky didn't even feel it, wouldn't even have noticed if she hadn't seen it in the glass.

Because you're a freak, she told herself.

"Becky," Uncle Billy said, "I need you to look at me."

She shook her head, there were some things she couldn't do. Uncle Billy walked in front of her, and she could see his feet. His flip-flops were gross, dirty from running down the street.

And then he was crouching down in front of her.

She reeled back, only to trip and fall onto the couch. The white couch, which she was going to get dirty from the crap on her pants from the street.

She tried to stand but Maddy sat beside her, fencing her in, keeping her in place.

"I'm going to do everything I can," he said, his brown eyes never leaving hers, "*everything,* to make sure you never go back to Pittsburgh or Janice."

"Where will you send us?"

"Nowhere. You'll stay here."

There was a thunderclap of happiness in her chest. But Uncle Billy kept talking. "I decided this morning," he said. "After you told me what it was like living with Janice. I thought it would be easy, I have money and I've never hit a kid in my life, but my lawyer said it might be difficult."

"Why?" she whispered, that happiness draining right out of her. God, she was tired. She was so damn tired. Tired of hope and anger and disappointment. Why couldn't good things just happen?

Uncle Billy glanced at Maddy. "I've got a temper," he said. "And I've done some things publically over the last few weeks that don't make me look so good."

"You're better than Aunt Janice," she said.

"I'm glad you think so. And that's what I'm banking on." He smiled at her, but it didn't make her feel any better. She knew an empty smile when she saw one. He had no clue if he'd be able to keep her and Charlie.

"You're going to stay, Becky," he said anyway, like just saying something could make it true. "I'll do whatever it takes."

"And I'm going to help," Maddy said. "The two of us are on your side."

On my side?

She should feel something, right? Besides small and black and poisonous.

"Becky?" Maddy asked. She and Uncle Billy were looking at each other like she was something they didn't understand. "Do you want to stay?"

I want you to want me to stay. And I want you to promise it will be forever. And I want to know right now. I want to stop being scared.

She could say that, and watch Uncle Billy lie to make her feel better, and that would be awful, so instead she shrugged.

Uncle Billy sighed and she realized how stupid she was being. This was the new chance she'd wanted. What did she care why he was doing it. Didn't she tell him about Aunt Janice and all that shit this morning so he'd feel bad enough to take them in?

He was trying and she had to give him some credit.

"You'll send Charlie to day care?" she asked. "A good one? He needs to hang out with other kids."

"Of course," he said, watching her solemnly. "And you'll go to school. The best one we can find. Whatever you want."

She wiped at her nose with the sleeve of her hoodie.

"What's wrong?" Maddy asked and Becky finally stood, feeling crowded, like she wanted to jump right out of her skin. She stepped past Uncle Billy, who sat down on his butt to look at her.

"Nothing." She tried to smile, but it felt stupid. "It's great."

"You're not really selling us on that," Maddy said, but Becky didn't know what that meant.

"Where's Charlie?" she asked, needing to see him. Needing to hug him. Tell him she was sorry for even thinking about leaving him. Not that he'd known, but still.

"He's asleep in the spare bedroom."

Uncle Billy stood, curling up from the ground in one smooth move. He could have hit her, Becky realized.

Aunt Janice would have. Mom would have too for this stunt. But Uncle Billy hadn't.

That counted for something.

"I'll get him," Uncle Billy said, "And we'll head home."

"No." Maddy caught his arm and Uncle Billy stopped. Just stopped. Like he was a machine and she'd pressed the off button. "It's all right. Becky, if you want to lie down, go ahead. But stay. I have twenty-four juice boxes and a bunch of cupcakes I need you to eat."

Becky looked at Uncle Billy, who looked right back at her. "You want to stay?" he asked. It was cool that he was letting her make the decision, when it was obvious he wanted to stay. It was obvious he wanted Maddy.

Sucker.

She shrugged like she didn't care, but her mind was already on that bookshelf. Uncle Billy didn't have a whole lot of books at his house.

"I'll take that as a resounding yes."

"Can I . . . ?" She took a half step toward the bookshelf.

"Go ahead," Maddy said and then came over to stand beside her, pulling down a whole bunch of books. "Have you read *The Hunger Games*?" she asked and Becky shook her head.

"Oh my God, you're going to love it." Maddy pulled down two more books, big expensive ones. "I have the first Twilight, but stopped after that—"

Twilight had that hot vampire dude. "Okay."

Maddy's eyes twinkled like they shared a secret and it made Becky's skin burn. But not in a bad way. "That should keep you busy," Maddy said, adding the vampire book to the pile in her arms. "And if Charlie wakes up and you want to keep reading, send him out. We can keep him busy."

"Really?" she asked before she could swallow it back.

It felt like she hadn't had time to herself since Charlie was born.

Maddy had that look in her eye that Mrs. Jordal used to get sometimes, like she wanted to hug her. Becky stepped back out of reach, clutching the books to her chest.

"Thanks," she whispered, because that's all she knew how to say but it felt sort of small in the face of all these books.

Becky went into the dark room with the soft bed and softer sheets, where her brother was sleeping so hard he was sweating, and she picked the first book off the pile.

The vampire book. The cover was shiny and pretty. The book smelled good. Not like cigarettes.

It made her want to cry.

Don't get used to this, she told herself, desperately. *This kind of stuff never lasts. It's never for you.*

Then she was going to have to read fast.

The sun blazing through the windows cast Billy in golds and purples and reds.

Beautiful, Maddy thought. *He's so beautiful.*

I love you. The thought was a bell ringing. Clear and loud and undeniable.

He collapsed backward onto her white couch, his ivory skin looking almost dark against the stark white. His torn T-shirt was deliciously, outrageously masculine against the sleek femininity of her house.

I love you. She wouldn't tell him, couldn't. It would be like asking to be hurt. It would be like picking the knife up herself.

"Tell me you have a beer," he whispered, staring at the ceiling.

She actually did. She'd bought a sixpack at the grocery store when she picked up the snacks for the kids.

So she could get him one. She could hand him a beer—hell, she could have one too, and they could talk about what had just happened. They could talk about Billy starting a family and filing for custody and taking on his sister.

But she didn't want to talk.

Her body shook with her desire, with all the things she could say. *I'm proud of you. Of the man you've become, of the way you've stood up. I'm proud of how gentle you are with Charlie and how careful you are with Becky and how when you're with them I can see the man you were meant to be.*

"Maddy?"

Hit by sunlight, his eyes glowed. His face was hard, the muscles in his arms stood out in relief, and she felt the moment he stopped caring about the beer.

Without words, because whatever she might say was inadequate and terrifying, she walked over to him until her knees touched his. Small electric shocks lit up the air between them, landing on the skin of her arms, her chest and neck, bringing her to tingling life.

He didn't reach for her. This was on her, she understood that. But there was no hiding his desire for her, there never had been. It was in his eyes, the tightly wound nature of his body, the way he sat, waiting for her touch to relieve him.

She put her knee down on the couch beside his hip, her other hand bracing herself against his shoulder, the skin warm. She brought her other knee up to the other side of his body, her eyes never drifting from his.

I know you, she thought, but at the same time in a delicious, exciting paradox she also thought, *This man you are right now is a stranger to me.*

And it couldn't be any hotter. The air she breathed was bathed in fire and her body smoldered with every breath.

Carefully, slowly, she sat down on him, against him, pressing herself to him until they both gasped. His hands, large and rough and familiar, slipped around her waist and over her back

Don't say anything, she thought, and he must have understood, because he closed his mouth. His lovely chocolate eyes looked into hers, and she wondered what he saw.

The sunlight danced with dust motes and she leaned through the glitter and light from one shadow to the next to press her lips to his.

A kiss.

After all she'd denied.

He gasped as if surprised, as if touched by a cold hand, but then, like he always did, he melted into her.

It was tender, this kiss—careful, brand new. As if she was learning his taste all over again. Or perhaps learning his new taste.

It was bitter and sweet.

The tide that lived between them, hidden but dark and deep, began to surge, beating against both their bodies, leeching the innocence out of the kiss.

His hands found her face, his fingers cupping the back of her neck. She opened her lips, letting him in, and his tongue stroked hers, licked it. Close. Closer. The heat of his body beneath his shirt was transcendent. Burning. Warming her down to her soul.

Under her fingers the skin of his neck and shoulders felt like silk. Lust coiled and grew in her belly, snaking out to her limbs, and she shook, trembled with her desire for Billy.

Unable to stand it, his strength, her weakness, she gripped his hair in her fingers, pulling hard enough that he gasped and arched against her, curling over her. A beast, strong and violent and at her command.

One kiss turned into another, a thousand. Endless and

consuming. Every kiss she'd denied him, every kiss they'd lost in the years they were apart.

I can do this, she thought, feeling brave and wanton. Whatever this was between them, she could do it. And as if he could taste the acquiescence on her lips, he surged to his feet, holding her so her feet dangled just over the floor and he walked, still kissing her, down the hallway, past the door of the kids' room.

She felt him falter and she wrapped her arms around his neck and kissed him along that scar, to his ear. She pulled his earlobe between her teeth, bringing him back to her with just a little pain.

You're doing the right thing, she told him with her lips. Her arms, her heart pounding against his. You are amazing. *You are strong and smart and more than enough to raise those children.*

I love you.

He leaned away from her. Opened his mouth: "I love—"

No. No. Words were dangerous, particularly those.

She kissed him again, to stop him from saying something he couldn't take back. He seemed to understand and threw himself into it. In the shadows of her bedroom, their clothes fell off with barely a touch. Their skin—at their hips, their thighs, their arms—brushed and set off sparks that flew into the air and the room was lit with their own light.

Against the bed, they fell. He was over her. A living blanket, warm and smooth, comforting and exciting all at the same time. He was everything to her, as he'd always been.

Her fingertips skated over the ridges and hills of the muscles along his back, his ribs, and down over his ass. He twitched, arching against her, his breath catching hard in his chest.

He turned sideways, taking her with him, and his

hand slipped into the dark shadows between them. He rubbed the aching tips of her breasts with his knuckles before bending to kiss his way across her chest to take a nipple in his mouth, the sensation rippling through her body. She gasped and clutched him closer, slipping a leg higher over his hips so that the hard edge of his erection teased the electrified center of her body.

He groaned, arching against her, his erection slipping through her curls and heat and wet to brush the pebble of her clit. She jerked away, too sensitive, but the next second went back for more. His lips still on her nipple, he ran his fingers on a long, slow meandering path down her body to where their bodies touched so intimately.

So knowing, so sure, his fingers played her favorite rhythm over and in her, and she felt herself lift away from the bed. Away from all the things in the world that weren't him. That weren't this pleasure.

That weren't them.

The orgasm rolled through her and she shook, her nails digging into the muscles of his arms.

As it passed, she sighed, all her sharp edges lost, all her boundaries blurred.

She made the terrible mistake of looking at him. His eyes were so full of love for her that she flinched, too raw to accept it with grace.

Quickly, she slipped away from him, down the mattress. He rolled over on his back and she crouched over him, the hair on his legs tickling the sensitive skin of her inner thighs.

It was all so familiar: taking him in her mouth, the way he sighed and slipped his hand down her back, to cup her elbow for a moment and then slip down to hold her hand.

That familiarity was razor sharp, and she couldn't bear it. The desperation came back a thousandfold and she pulled away from him.

"There are condoms in the bedside table," she murmured, the words so loud in the silence they'd created.

He twisted sideways to dig through her bedside table, every muscle in his stomach and along his back rippling and contracting. She ran her hands over each one, fascinated all over again by his body.

After rolling on the condom he shifted back toward her, lifting her, arranging her like she weighed nothing, and it was exciting. So exciting to be positioned for someone's pleasure.

His chest against her back, he curled up behind her.

Yes, she thought, *like this. Just like this.*

They shifted and moved and then, with ease and power, he slid inside her. This position reminded her of sweet, sleepy morning sex. Her heart squeezed in her chest as her body welcomed him.

His hand slipped beneath her to cup her breast and she leaned forward, finding that spot of friction that made her crazy.

"Baby," he groaned, his fingers clutching her hips as he sped up the rhythm. It was quiet in the room. No squeaking mattresses. No banging headboards. Just tortured, silent sex.

She gasped, ducking her head, feeling the pleasure start again. They curled and uncurled, slow and hard until they couldn't stand it anymore. He tipped her forward so she lay on her stomach. He lifted her hips, coming to his knees behind her and she pushed up on her arms.

His hand ran up her spine, from the top of her ass to her neck, where he held her.

"Come on," he groaned and eased all the way out of her and then pushed back in, hard. So hard she shook with it. Her toes and fingers curled and she pushed when he pulled and the dance between them was remembered and perfect.

Three strokes, four, and she splintered, exploded. He moved faster, quiet, always quiet, he slammed against her and then he was shaking, his fingers curled in her hair, his other hand gripping her hips so hard there would be bruises.

"Baby," he moaned. "Oh God, Maddy . . ."

She collapsed on the bed and he fell beside her.

Don't she said to the recriminations circling her. *Stay away for just a few more minutes,* she told the regrets that were looking for a way in.

He reached between them and held her hand, twining his fingers with hers. Still silent, as if he had his own ghosts to persuade away.

From the other bedroom came the sound of Charlie's muffled cry, and Billy and Maddy burst into action, throwing their clothes on. But then it was silent again and they stood like deer in her dark room, half-dressed.

He chuckled and then she did too and then they were laughing.

"How come we're always sneaking around?" she asked.

He stepped over to her, cupping her face in his hands, her hair pressed against her head. There were a thousand things he could say, none of which she knew how to deal with. As if he knew, as if he could read her mind—and he probably could—he was silent.

He kissed her. Once. Again.

"Billy—" she sighed, but he shook his head.

"You're thinking too much. This . . . this is simple."

She sputtered with laughter. Nothing between them was simple. Ever.

"It is. You just make it complicated. For today, let's just be simple."

A coward at heart, she nodded. "Simple."

"So do you or do you not have any beer?" he asked.

"I do," she whispered and they walked into her living room, bathed in bright daylight.

But the brightest light brought out the darkest shadows and she was reminded with terrible piercing clarity that love had never been the problem for them.

It was the stuff that came with it.

chapter 25

"*Oh my God!*" Billy breathed and rolled down the windows in the backseat of his car. He was fighting traffic into the city on Monday morning, but there was no way of fighting the smell in the backseat.

"See," Becky said. "We shouldn't have gone swimming yesterday."

"It was your idea!" he cried. Becky had woken up this morning looking for blood, his. And he didn't know how to manage going into Hornsby's office to beg for his job back and a thirteen-year-old girl's grudge match at the same time.

But fighting with her did keep his mind off the groveling, so it had a hidden benefit.

"I think it was the fruit you were force-feeding him this morning."

"Charlie likes cantaloupe."

"My tummy hurts," Charlie moaned.

"I told you to go easy with the fruit for the first few days since your systems aren't used to it." He flashed his lights at the semi that was traveling at a snail's pace in the fast lane.

"Don't worry about our systems," she snapped.

"Well, it's hard not to when Charlie's is polluting the air." The semi was slowing down. Honest to God, the world was working against him.

"You are so crabby this morning."

"*I'm* crabby?" He passed a semi on the right. "*Me?* You're the one who's acting like I'm the bad guy."

"You should have just left us at your house."

"Yeah. Right." Billy looked at the girl in his rearview mirror. "Like you'd be there when I got home." Whatever no-running-away agreement they'd established felt wafer-thin this morning. He thought they'd made progress at Maddy's, but apparently not.

Women were such a freaking mystery, at any age.

Billy rolled down his own window because under his dress shirt he was starting to sweat. How ridiculous was it that he'd dressed up for his meeting with Hornsby?

And bringing the kids?

What the hell am I thinking? Becky was a bad-spirited, stubborn foul-mouthed loose cannon. And Charlie smelled like crap.

But it wasn't like he had a choice. Even if Becky kept her promise about not running away, it just felt wrong to leave the kids alone. They'd been left alone too much already.

And there wasn't anyone he could call. Tara Jean and Luc were away. Maddy had her job.

He was solo with two kids.

Welcome to the rest of your life, he thought.

He'd briefly thought about calling Vince for some backup with Hornsby. But this minor league situation, and needing to clear up the mess he'd made in order to get okayed as a foster parent—it all felt personal.

Having Vince there would only muddy the waters.

Besides, he didn't need any more witnesses to the humiliation fun house of swallowing his pride and begging for another chance.

A few gag-filled minutes later, he pulled to a stop in the players' parking lot and turned off the car, just as Charlie let another one rip.

"You need to go to the bathroom?" Becky asked her

brother and Billy turned to look at them. Somehow in the twenty-minute drive from his house to the office, the kid had gotten dirty. His face was smeared with something green.

"What—"

"Marker," Becky said. "He had it in his pocket."

"Great." He sighed. Outside of the green on Charlie's face, the kids looked good. The trip to Target had resulted in some new duds. Charlie was proudly wearing a Yoda T-shirt. And Becky had on another hoodie, this one purple, the zipper covered in rhinestones.

"We can wait in the car," she said, all sneer.

Billy snorted, climbed out of the driver's seat, and opened the back door, looking at Becky. She had a Target bag at her feet, full of diapers and spare clothes for Charlie. Some toys and snacks.

Thirteen years old and the girl knew how to pack a diaper bag. Guilt squeezed his chest down to nothing. One more negative emotion on top of the volcano he was already feeling.

"Look, this is a big deal for me, this meeting," he said and Becky rolled her eyes. Ever since he'd told her he wasn't going to send her back to Pittsburgh she'd been pushing him. He was no stranger to that type of behavior, having perfected it himself when he was a kid, but it didn't make it any easier to deal with.

"No. I'm serious. This is my career on the line. Right now."

"Okay, fine. What do you want from me?"

"For you to be good. To not touch anything. To make sure Charlie doesn't touch anything. Try to make sure he doesn't gas the receptionist."

"I can't control Charlie's farts." Oh man, that attitude. It was so familiar. And so infuriating. He suddenly had a lot more sympathy for every teacher he'd ever had who had reached out a helping hand only to have him snap it off at the bone.

Billy growled and walked around the car to lift Charlie out of his seat. If he were a cartoon, the boy would have green fumes rising up from his diaper.

"Charlie." Charlie smiled up at Billy as he held the boy in his outstretched arms. Becky may have had some terrible change of heart toward him, but Charlie had nothing but love for Billy. Which was strange and slightly uncomfortable, but he would take support where he could find it. He checked Charlie's diaper—no poo. "Can you hold it in for just a few minutes? Until Becky takes you to the bathroom."

"Yes, Uncle Billy."

"Good boy."

"Whatever," Becky sighed, and Billy was beginning to think that word was her personal motto or something. But he let it slide, unable to fight every battle.

They walked in the players' entrance to the arena and then took an elevator up to the office level.

"What are you going to do in there," Becky asked, "that's so important?"

Billy watched the numbers climb on the readout above the door. *Swallow my pride. Grovel. Throw myself on Hornsby's turtlenecked mercy.*

"Ask for my job back."

"You got fired?" Becky asked, her voice scandalized. He glanced down and realized she wasn't scandalized, she was worried. Scared, even.

"Sort of," he muttered and looked back up at the numbers.

"I thought you were just in trouble."

"It's a little worse than that."

"Because of us?" she asked. "Because of what I said on the show?"

"No." He waved her off. The numbers stopped and

the doors opened with a bing and he took a step out. But Becky didn't follow, and when he glanced back at her, she looked stricken. White. Her eyes round.

Oh.

"Becky, I'm in trouble because I'm kind of a jerk. It doesn't have anything to do with you."

"You sure?" she whispered.

"That I'm a jerk? Yes." She didn't even break a smile. "It has nothing to do with you," he said. "I swear."

She tucked all that anxiety away, her face closed off again, and she took Charlie by the hand and led him out of the elevator. If Billy had more room in his body, he might try hard to assuage whatever guilt she felt, but he was besieged by his own demons at the moment.

"Wow!" Charlie cried as they turned the corner into the reception area of the Mavericks' front office. "Fish!" He ran toward the giant fish tank built into the wall, smacking his hands and pressing his face against the glass.

"Excuse me—" Heather, the receptionist, stood up behind her desk, sending out all kinds of disapproving vibes, which only got worse when she saw Billy. "You're nearly fifteen minutes late, Billy."

"I am?" he said, while Becky tried to pull Charlie away from the glass. "I'm sorry, it's surprisingly difficult to get a three-year-old out the door."

"Well, Coach Hornsby is very busy today." Heather raised a skeptical eyebrow. Despite her young age she was ironclad. Nothing happened on Heather's watch that she didn't expressly okay.

He thought of Charlie's gas and smiled. "I understand, if you could just let him know that I'm here?"

"What . . ." She glanced over his shoulder. "What are you going to do with them?"

"You can't watch them?"

She literally gasped in horror.

"I'm kidding, Heather. They'll be fine."

Just as the words left his mouth there was a wild ripping sound and a foul, foul odor filled the air.

"Charlie!" Becky cried.

"My tummy doesn't hurt anymore."

"Did he just . . ." Heather's lips didn't move, her face was frozen.

"Poop? In your office? I think so."

"Oh. My. God." Heather's lips still hadn't moved.

Hornsby's door opened and the man himself stood there, backlit by the sunlight beaming in through the windows of his office. Like he was God come down to earth.

"Billy?" he asked. "What's going on? You're late."

Charlie shrieked and Billy, his heart pounding in his chest, turned around, expecting fecal disaster, but it was only Becky trying to catch her brother, and Charlie running away.

"Can you just give me a second?" Billy said, distracted by the kids. The smell. Heather's panic. Hornsby's judgment.

Hornsby made an expansive, go-right-ahead gesture.

Billy cornered the kids near the fish.

"You need to go change his diaper."

"You think?" Becky whispered. "Tell him that."

"Charlie, let Becky change your diaper. Why the hell does he still wear those things anyway?"

Becky turned wide eyes on him. Right. Not the best time to discuss toilet training. He crouched, getting eye to eye with Charlie, who stank more than rotting garbage.

"Charlie, I will give you anything you want if you just let Becky change your diaper."

"Fish?" he asked, pointing at the aquarium.

"Anything."

"Chuck E. Cheese?"

"God, no."

"Billy?" Hornsby looked at his watch. "I have a schedule to keep."

Billy looked from Hornsby to Charlie. "Yes. Okay. Chuck E. Cheese." He turned toward Becky. "I will pay you fifty dollars if you can get him to behave himself."

"On top of the hundred for not running away?" she asked.

"Yes."

"And Chuck E. Cheese?"

And here he'd foolishly thought that his life could not get any worse.

"Yes."

"Deal." Becky held out her hand and they shook on it.

"Here." He pulled out his phone and tapped the Angry Birds app on the screen. "This should keep him busy."

He passed Heather's desk. "Coach Hornsby has an appointment in ten minutes," she said pointedly.

"I'll only take twenty."

She scowled at him and he grinned.

But the grin faded when he stepped into Hornsby's office and his coach shut the door behind him. Suddenly all of his failures, large and small, filled the corners of the large office, each waiting for their due.

He had no clue what to say, where to begin.

"Those are the kids from the show," Hornsby said, walking past Billy, toward his desk.

"My niece and nephew."

"Not your children."

Billy swallowed the words that wanted to escape—the swearing, ranting protestation that came to his lips. "I don't have any kids. Those women—"

Hornsby waved his hand as he sat in his chair. "I know, Billy. It was a joke."

"Oh." Billy managed a very strangled laugh. Hornsby was not funny. At all.

Unable to sit, Billy stood behind one of the chairs, his hands braced against the back. Nervous, unsure of what to do with his sweaty, panicky body, he nearly tipped the whole thing over.

"Sorry."

"I'd rather you sat in my furniture, instead of breaking it."

Now he had no choice but to sit down, and the second he did, he started bouncing his legs, his skin twitching. His mind racing, careening off the walls and windows. If they could just have this conversation on the ice, he might do okay. But sitting in an office, wearing a tie—he had no chance at winning.

"How old are the kids?"

"Three and thirteen."

"Thirteen is tough. My daughter got arrested for shoplifting around that age."

"Really?" Billy tried not to sound slightly delighted, but Christ, that was good news. Maybe Becky wasn't such a nightmare after all.

"She did it on a dare, but . . ." Hornsby trailed off.

"Becky tried to hot-wire my car three nights ago."

"You're joking."

"I wish. They spent the whole night trying to run away. They even jumped out a bedroom window at dawn. They probably would have gotten away if it hadn't been for the news crews on my lawn."

"Ahh. Is that when you shoved the reporter?"

"He was on my property. Scaring the kids. Am I the only one who thinks that kind of behavior deserves a shove?"

"No, you're not. It's one of the few times I can say you were right to shove someone."

The guy was saying Billy was right, but his whole vibe was unforgiving.

This was exactly like the night he and Maddy had gone to tell her parents they were getting married. He'd sat in that dining room, with the fancy centerpiece and all the china, and gotten bitch-slapped by their silent condemnation. They'd talked about hockey and Maddy going to college, but the only thing he'd heard, the only thing he'd felt, was *you're not good enough.*

"Why are you here, Billy? We can talk about parenting pre-teen girls all day long. But your career is in the shitter and I thought that's why you called."

"It is." Billy stood because he couldn't rip out his heart and throw it on the desk while he was sitting. "I'm sorry I didn't answer your calls and I'm sorry I've been such an asshole this year." Billy laughed, watching the traffic outside the windows. "I mean, I'm always an asshole, but I really took it to new heights this year. And you're right, I don't want to go out this way. I'm better than this."

And he was. He knew that in his heart. Without Maddy having to tell him, he knew he was better than the way he'd been acting.

Despite the flop sweat and the panic and the pride-swallowing, the thought made him smile. Gave him a small measure of peace.

He exhaled, letting go of as much of his anxiety as he could.

"I might be too late." Billy turned to face Hornsby, who sat back in his chair as if he'd been blown there. "I fully appreciate that, Coach. You tried harder than just about anyone in my life and I'm sorry to have failed you."

"You didn't just fail me."

"I know. Blake, the guys, I failed all of them. And maybe worse, I failed myself. I've gotten so good at that,

I don't even see it anymore. But I'd like the chance to be . . ." God, it sounded so stupid. "To be a better teammate and leader. I'd like to be the kind of player you need me to be."

Hornsby stared at him, the silence tense. "Wow," he finally said.

Billy laughed.

"You been working on that awhile?"

"All night." Billy smiled.

"Christ, Billy, if you'd just called me back on Friday I'd have a fighting chance to change the GM's mind, but you've tied my hands."

Billy blew out a long breath. That was the answer he'd been afraid of. "Is there anything I can do?"

"Well . . . Nothing is guaranteed, you get that? Even if you do everything I tell you to do, you still might be sent down."

"I know."

"Okay, the first thing you need to do is go back on *AM Dallas* and tell your side of the story."

"Done." It rubbed him raw to agree, but he would do anything.

Hornsby blinked. "You're going to need something national, too."

"I'll call Dominick Murphy today. He's been bugging me to do a story."

"Dom is an excellent choice."

"Is it enough?"

"To salvage your career?"

"To . . . to go out the way I should."

Hornsby stared at him for so long, Billy started to feel like a bug under glass.

"What makes you happy, Billy?"

Oh Jesus, just when he thought they were making progress, Coach was bringing out the Oprah shit again.

But instead of storming out of the office, he decided to answer.

"Hockey."

Coach nodded. "Anything else?"

Maddy, he thought, but didn't say. Coach hummed in his throat like he knew it anyway. "This sport gives a lot to its players. But there are some guys it only takes away from."

Billy couldn't blame hockey for his lack of a family. For Maddy. It wasn't hockey that had ruined their marriage, or even him, it was them. Their youth. Their inexperience.

He didn't see all that Maddy had been giving him, had no way of knowing how she'd been eroding away. Even at this moment, years later, he wasn't sure how he could have stopped that.

"My mistakes have been my own," he said.

A buzz, then Heather's voice over the intercom. "Your nine-thirty is here," she said.

Hornsby pushed a button on his phone as he stood. "Thanks, Heather."

Hornsby walked Billy to the door.

"I'm glad you came in today," Hornsby said.

"Me too," Billy said. "If nothing else, I'm glad I got to apologize. You didn't deserve the way I treated you."

Hornsby opened the door and the two kids were standing in front of the fish tank, their faces illuminated by the light. A yellow fish swam by Charlie's wide eyes.

"What are you going to do about them?"

"I'm trying to get custody. But I have to be accepted as a foster parent first, which might not be so easy."

Hornsby's eyebrows lifted up to his hairline.

"You can tone down the horror," Billy muttered.

"I'm not horrified. I'm surprised and . . . proud of you. If there's anything I can do to help, please let me know."

"Really? Because I'm going to need some serious character references . . . though you'll probably have to lie." He tried to make it a joke but Coach didn't laugh. He clapped Billy on the back so hard, things were shaken lose inside his chest. All the resentment and bitterness toward those men in his life—all those well-meaning coaches and trainers, even Maddy's dad—who would have been a father figure for him, all of it got pulled down. And instead of feeling claustrophobic he just felt grateful.

"No," Coach said. "I won't have to lie at all."

Madelyn flopped back in the chair in front of her makeup table just as Ruth sat down in her customary seat in the corner. She'd practically run off the set after the cameras went dark. The applause had been empty, the grumbles behind the clapping loud and clear.

"That was terrible," Maddy said.

"Awful."

"Dogs that juggle?"

"It was all we could get on such short notice."

Maddy's BlackBerry buzzed on the corner of her desk and she picked it up.

She had to read the message twice before she could believe it.

"He's coming in," she said.

"Who?"

"Billy. He's coming in to talk about doing the show. He'll be here in an hour."

They stared at each other for a moment, and then suddenly they were hugging. Laughing and hugging.

"You did it," Ruth said.

The sex did it, she thought and felt awful. Felt truly squeamish. It hadn't been her intention, but the result was the same.

She'd slept with him and now he was coming in to talk about the show.

"It will be the perfect launch for our new format," Ruth said and she was so right that it made Maddy feel sick. "We've got some work to do before he gets here. Go ahead and get changed, and then meet me in the conference room in ten minutes."

"Great," she agreed and Ruth left, leaving Maddy with the sharp edges of her doubt. Not about the show, but about Billy. She shouldn't have slept with him again. That was so obvious. All the warmth that had been generated from yesterday, that sense that they were in this together, it wilted.

She felt mercenary.

The phone on her desk buzzed and the receptionist from the front office got on the intercom. "Maddy, I have a call for you on line one. A reporter who wants to ask you some questions."

Maddy reached over to the phone and pressed line one, and lifted the receiver.

"Maddy Cornish," she said and then winced. "Madelyn," she amended very quickly.

"Hi, Maddy, it's Dominick Murphy, I met you at the New School fund-raiser—"

"Of course." She smiled, thinking of the grizzled writer with the seasoned hair. "What can I do for you, Dom?"

"Well, Billy has finally agreed to let me do a story on him and I was hoping to ask you a few questions."

"About the show?" she asked, unzipping her too tight boots. She got the first one off.

"No." He cleared his throat. "About your marriage."

The other boot fell.

Her heartbeat echoed in her ears.

"How . . . how did you find out?"

"I'm a reporter, Madelyn. It's what I do. So, can we meet?"

Meet? she thought. How innocent. How utterly clueless he seemed to be about the pain of being Billy Wilkins' wife. Like she would just talk about it. Like she had sweet, clever stories about their years together.

With icy white clarity she saw the real mistake of Sunday. In kissing him, letting him into her bed, her fucking house. In falling right back in love with him, she'd opened herself up to that pain all over again.

She'd opened up her life all over again.

The thought shut her down. Closed every door that Billy had managed to open in their time together.

This wasn't about her identity. It was about survival. And she couldn't survive that kind of pain again.

She had to stop this now. Because if she continued, thinking she could handle him, handle her emotions, there'd be no keeping Billy out. He'd be her past and her present, and how long would it be until she just handed over her future? How long until they were saying things like *Let's try again*?

And how would they hurt each other this time? How would they fail each other? No. No, she wouldn't do it. Couldn't risk it.

She liked her life. Cold and sterile, counting calories and relying on the products on infomercials to make her house a home, to make her life look like someone was actually living it.

"I don't talk about my relationship with Billy."

"Madelyn—"

"Good-bye, Dom." She hung up. Stared at the phone.

Her life might not be happy, but at least it didn't hurt.

chapter 26

Billy walked back into the studio of *AM Dallas* with a headache, and a foulmouthed entourage.

"What about Chuck E. Cheese?" Charlie whined.

"I just have to do this first," Billy said with fraying patience.

"This is bullshit," Becky muttered just loud enough for Billy to hear.

He stopped and Charlie ran into the back of his legs. "Say it one more time, Becky," he warned, staring up at the ceiling, "*one more time,* and I swear I'm going to take twenty bucks from the money I've given you."

"Bullshit, bullshit, bullshit."

Billy turned, murder in his heart. Charlie stepped backward and tried tugging Becky with him. But Becky didn't go—nope, she put her chin up and faced him head-on.

If all that murder weren't in his heart, he might laugh.

"What is with you?" he asked. "I thought . . . I thought we had a good day on Sunday. Why are you so mad?"

"Why are you so mad?"

He rolled his eyes as he turned, only to come face-to-face with Maddy. Who looked about as warm and welcoming as Becky.

Great. Just great.

"Hi, guys," Maddy said, giving the kids one of her smiles, which seemed to dry up when she looked at him.

"I had to bring them," he said, wondering if she was mad because of the kids.

"Of course. You guys can hang out in my office while we meet in the conference room. Ruth is waiting for you in there, Billy."

"Sounds like a blast," Becky muttered and stormed past him.

Maddy shot him a *what the hell?* look and all he could do was shrug, which for some mysterious feminine reason made her shake her head like she should have known. And then she was gone, catching up with Becky. He watched as Maddy lifted her hand as if to touch Becky's back and then dropped it when she remembered. No one touched Becky.

Maddy didn't look particularly touchable either. Not at all like the woman from yesterday. She'd had half a beer and she'd told him about living in Miami, how her mom had lost a hundred pounds doing aqua aerobics and drinking tomato juice. He'd told her about meeting Luc in Toronto and how Luc had had an even more messed-up childhood than his own, which had gotten Billy seriously thinking about his New School idea. They both wondered if Becky would benefit from a program like that.

And there hadn't been a moment in the last fourteen years when he'd been half as happy.

But as he watched Becky and Maddy walk off down the hallway, he felt a long way from yesterday. Years and miles.

Thank God he still had Charlie. "What have I done wrong?" he asked the three-year-old.

"Maybe she wants to go to Chuck E. Cheese."

"That's your solution to everything," Billy muttered. Taking Charlie's hand he followed the two most frustrating women in his life. At the corner, he sent Charlie on his way to Maddy's office.

"Can I have your phone?" Charlie asked. "I want to play the bird game."

"I've created a monster," Billy said, before handing it to a kid who still crapped his pants.

What has the world come to? he wondered, watching Charlie run down the hallway, zigging and zagging around the knees of the people walking by him like he was cutting up the ice.

As frustrated as Billy was, as confused and strange as everything had become, he couldn't help but smile.

That kid was funny.

Charlie came barging into her office and quickly made himself at home in her chair. He had Billy's phone and she recognized the music from Angry Birds.

The boy was three and he knew how to play that game—she didn't know if she should be proud or worried.

"So?" Becky asked. "What are we supposed to do? Just sit here?"

Becky's brown hair, pulled back in the same ponytail she'd been wearing since last Friday, was thick and shiny with a slight curl at the ends. When she wasn't squinting or sneering or trying to look above it all, like when she'd been looking at Maddy's bookshelf, her blue eyes were big and clear as ice, and in a few years when she realized the importance of mascara, they'd be stunning.

"Well," she said, "I thought you might like to meet a friend of mine."

"What kind of friend?"

"The kind who does my hair and makeup every day."

Interest flashed before the girl quickly returned to looking bored. "Whatever."

"It'll be fun."

"You guys are, like, obsessed with that."

"Fun?"

Becky nodded, looking at her chewed-up fingernails.

"You're thirteen, you should be obsessed with fun."

Becky went back to work on her ravaged lips, delicately pulling off the skin that remained.

Well, so much for that conversation.

Maddy had to hope Gina's bag of tricks would work better than her rooftop pool had.

She used her phone to page Gina, and a few minutes later her hair and makeup guru was poking her head around the door.

"You rang?" she asked.

"I did. We did actually." Madelyn stepped aside, putting her hand on the back of Becky's chair. "You got time for a little hair and makeup?"

Gina, bless her heart, acted like she couldn't think of anything better. And maybe she couldn't.

"I'll be right back," she said and a moment later returned with her tackle box of makeup and her scissors case.

"What's that?" Becky asked, sitting up straighter.

"Magic, sweetie. Magic in a box. Now, let's get a look at you." Gina pulled Becky's ponytail out and fanned her hair over her shoulders. "Hmm . . . I think maybe some layers, make these curls bounce a little more. You've got some split ends, so we'll get rid of those. And maybe some bangs? What do you think?"

"Are you asking me?" Becky asked.

"Well, of course I'm asking you." Gina laughed and Becky smiled. Radiantly. Beautifully.

But she pulled away, last minute. "Charlie needs a cut, though."

Gina glanced back at the boy, who didn't look up from the Angry Birds game. "Please, that's three seconds. Let's start with you. What do you want?"

It took Becky a second, but then the smile was back.

"Bangs," she said, a thirteen-year-old girl with nothing but a new haircut on her mind. "Totally bangs."

And my work here is done.

"I'll be back in a bit," Maddy said.

"Take your time," Gina sang. She went to the closet and pulled out the cape she used when trimming Maddy's hair.

On those TV shows where ugly women got haircuts and put on some mascara, they looked so different afterward. That's what Becky was counting on right now.

Looking really different.

"So, you're thirteen?" Gina asked, brushing out Becky's hair, running right over the snarls like they were speed bumps. "What's that? Ninth Grade?"

"Eighth." Ouch. She winced.

"You like school?"

"It's all right."

Gina got out a spray bottle and started spraying Becky's head. "You got a favorite subject? Boys? Recess?"

"I like English. And science."

"Those are not fooling-around subjects."

"Well, I don't go all that often."

"Oh no," Gina whisked her comb through Becky's hair, sending droplets of water flying. "Don't tell me you skip school."

"It's just hard to get there sometimes."

"Right, that's what my niece says. But I think really she's too busy smoking cigarettes behind the school to actually get to her classes. Is that what you're doing?"

"No. I'm not smoking at school. I'm babysitting my brother."

"Well." Gina got out all these clips and started putting big sections of her hair up on her head. In the mirror

Becky made a face, just to make sure it was her. "My sister is sending my niece to that boarding school outside of Ft. Worth."

"What's a boarding school?" Becky asked.

"School where parents send kids to live when they can't stand them anymore." Gina laughed.

"Really? They live at the school?" Becky asked. "Like forever?"

"No. They go home for holidays and over the summer, but they stay at the school most of the time."

Gina got out a pair of silver scissors.

"You ready for a big change?" she asked Becky, holding up the section of hair right in front of her face that she was going to cut into bangs.

"I am," Becky said, hugging herself tight against all the excitement in her body.

In one long snip Gina sliced off the hair and Becky let out a sound that was part sob and part sigh. The actual sound of big change happening.

Plan E was coming right up.

The first hockey practice after the first time Billy and Maddy had sex, Billy was alone in the guys' locker room at the arena with Maddy's dad, Dougie. Billy was sure the old man knew what Billy had done to his daughter after prom. He was certain the man could smell it on him.

While Billy changed his clothes, Dougie swept with his big push broom, picking up water bottles and tape, sweeping it all into the corner where Billy had his stuff.

The silence was excruciating. And then Dougie started whistling and Billy nearly pissed his pants.

"Maddy said you two had a good time," he finally said and Billy was sure that was code for something, so he barely managed to nod.

"That's good," Dougie said and swept his pile of garbage right out of the room.

Billy exploded with relief. Literally fell down on the bench, thanking God.

Sitting with Ruth in the conference room sort of felt like that. Except Billy was Dougie. And Ruth was him, and she was so totally uncomfortable, he almost started whistling.

"I didn't know about the kids," Ruth finally blurted. "I mean, not until that morning."

"Well, you knew before I did, so you don't get any points."

"Phil's been fired."

"I heard."

Oh, the silence was amazing. So thick he could practically scoop it up in his hands.

"I'm sorry."

"It's all right," he said, running his hands along the surface of the table as if wiping it all clean. "It's actually worked out for the best."

Ruth's eyes went wide behind her black glasses. "It has?"

Billy explained that he was trying to get custody and Ruth didn't seem nearly as horrified as he'd expected her to be, so he decided she wasn't that bad.

"Well, coming on *AM Dallas* should help you clear the air. Hopefully it will also help you in your case."

"That's why I'm here."

Maddy walked in at that moment, sliding into the conference room on a current of arctic air.

Déjà vu, he thought.

"Billy, we're glad you agreed to come in," she said, sitting down on the other side of the table, next to Ruth. She didn't look at him. Not at all. They were back to being strangers.

What the fuck?

"Has Ruth filled you in on some of the changes at the show?"

"Ah . . ." He looked at Ruth. "I know Phil's been fired."

"We're making some drastic changes and we're excited to have you as a part of our launch week. Our launch episode." Maddy started talking about an hour-long conversation/issue show.

"You want me to talk for an hour?" he asked.

"Well, not a whole hour." Her tight-lipped smile told him he was being stupid and he reeled back for a moment. Was this about the sex? Was she worried about Ruth knowing? Was she treating him like this so Ruth wouldn't expect that the ice queen had gone slumming with the hockey thug? Again?

He didn't know whether to try and set her mind at ease or be insulted. He was leaning toward insulted.

First the no-kissing thing and now this? He couldn't believe she was pulling this nonsense after everything they'd been through, not just in their lives, but yesterday in particular.

They weren't teenagers anymore.

"We just need to get the framework of the show," Ruth said. "So we can put together some package ideas and questions and considering your . . . ah . . . past with the show, we thought you might want some input."

"Yeah. Fine," he snapped, jerking his suit jacket out of the way. Ruth cleared her throat and consulted the list in front of her.

"All right, do you want the kids to be a part of the interview?"

"On air?" he asked, looking at Maddy. "No. Come on!"

"Fair enough." Ruth put her hands up like she was going to back away slowly. "I imagine we'll start with your past? Your childhood?"

"Sure," Billy said. "I suppose I need to explain a little bit . . . about the kids."

"That seems reasonable." Ruth nodded and then glanced sideways at Maddy. "What about your marriage?"

"No." Maddy said. Billy flinched, surprised by her vehemence. "Our shared past is off-limits."

Ah. Here they were. Again. Staring at each other over a conference table, their marriage the big fat elephant in the room she wanted to pretend wasn't there.

"I think we should talk about it," he said.

"There's no point."

He shook his head, befuddled and sad and angry all at the same time. "What's going on?" he asked. "Can we stop the bullshit and just talk?"

Maddy cleared her throat before turning to Ruth. "Could you give us a second?"

Ruth was already on her feet and halfway to the door. "Text me when you're ready," she said before slipping into the hallway.

Billy stared at his ex-wife across the table.

"Dom called," she said. "He wanted to ask me a few questions about you. About our marriage."

He blinked at her, wondering why that made her mad at *him.*

"I didn't tell him, if that's what's got you so pissed. The guy's a reporter. He's just doing his job."

"I don't want you to talk about me. I don't want my life, everything I've worked for to get eclipsed by you. Again."

He pushed away from the table, suddenly remembering how it had felt years ago coming home from practice knowing he was going to be ambushed by his wife. Knowing in his guts that he was walking in on the end of his marriage.

She's going to do it again. End it. Right now.

"You're a bigger celebrity in this town than me,

Maddy. It will be a big deal for about ten minutes and then it will be over."

"And then everyone in town will look at me and think of you. I'll be Mrs. Billy Wilkins again."

"And they'll look at me and think of you. And you know something?" He stood, the chair zinging across the floor to collide with a box of magazines. "I'm proud of that. Proud." He waited for her to crack, could see her shaking. But she kept her mouth shut. "You know, I thought we had something."

"What? Sex in my dressing room? I wouldn't let you kiss me."

"You let me kiss you yesterday."

She blinked up at him, not giving an inch. Not a single inch. It was as if she'd erased that time in her bedroom from her mind.

"What about the kids?"

"They're not ours. We are not a family."

It was like she'd stabbed him and twisted the knife deep in his gut. "Man, I keep getting that confused."

"What did you think was going to happen between us, really?"

"I love you." She flinched when he said it. "Don't act surprised. You knew. You always knew. And I saw you yesterday, Maddy. I saw your eyes. You love me, too. You can't deny it. And the rest of this garbage, it's all bullshit, isn't it? Being worried about people looking at you and seeing me. Being worried about your life getting sucked up by mine. It's not the real reason you're freaked out and playing the ice queen, is it?"

"You're right. I can't deny it. I do love you. I have always loved you, even when I hated you I still loved you. But you know something, love was never our problem, Billy. It's the rest of the shit we can't do."

"It's been fourteen years. I'm not the boy I was,

Maddy." He could say it with certainty. It was an absolute. He wasn't that kid.

"I know."

He could see the doubt in her, how she wavered when she didn't want to. He stepped around the edge of the table to touch her, to press his advantage, but she stepped back, suddenly fully resolved.

"And you're not the girl, can't you see that? You won't get lost again. Not you." He couldn't tell if she believed him. Couldn't see anything in her ice cold eyes.

"I can't do it Billy, I can't. I can't go through that pain again."

"Maybe there won't be any," he said, and continued to approach as she retreated, until finally she was against the wall. "Maybe we'll get it right this time. Have some faith, baby."

"In us?" She laughed, and it stung like a thousand needles, forcing him to back up a step. "Please. The only thing I have faith in anymore is me. Everything else hurts."

"It wasn't just pain," he said. "There were good times, too." But she was shaking her head, denying him. Denying everything between them that wasn't heartache.

It killed him that she was doing this, that she was rewriting their history, painting it all with a black brush.

"You know, I came on this show feeling like I needed to atone for the things I'd done to you. I came here believing that the worst of what happened between us was my fault, and I'm not saying it's not. But you weren't innocent either."

"I know." Her admission did nothing to ease his mind. It only made him feel worse.

"I carried around my anger for a lot of years. I pushed people away and I let it define me. And I think . . . I think you've let your anger define you, too. Where are all those friends you were going to get? All that love I wasn't giving you? You live in a modern ivory tower and on your show you pretend to be half the woman you really are. Just so no one gets too close. So no one can really see you."

"You think that was an accident? You think I don't know that? I made those decisions so that I wouldn't get hurt by anyone the way you hurt me. So that I wouldn't get lost. So that I wouldn't find myself all alone with nothing, not ever again."

"And are you happy with those decisions? Are you happy being scared and angry and alone?"

"I'm on the top-rated morning show in Dallas! I'm a celebrity."

"That doesn't make anyone happy. We both know that."

She clamped her mouth shut, not engaging. There was nothing left but total honesty. Nothing but raw truth.

"I'm not happy, Maddy. I should be. I've got a career I've practically killed myself for, a house, a boat. Friends. But somehow none of it makes me happy. Because you're not in my life to share it." His heart was still in his chest, a dead weight as he waited for her response. "And now these kids are here."

"Right. The kids are here and you need me again. You need me to be their mom, to be your partner. Right?"

He blinked, unable to deny it. "That's what I want. Why is that wrong?"

"What about what I need? All I've ever done my whole life with you is be what you've needed. I can't sacrifice myself again."

"Fine. Let me sacrifice. What do you want? You want me to give up hockey? I'll do it. You keep the show, I'll stay at home. Whatever it takes."

"Stop!" she cried. "Stop, Billy. Listen to you. Love isn't supposed to be that way, is it? One person gets diminished for the other?"

"I don't know, Maddy. All I know is that I'm better when you're in my life. And I want to give you that feeling. I want to make you better. Make you the most you can be."

There it was, his heart, shivering and cold on the table between them. And for a minute he thought she would do it. He thought she was brave enough to meet him halfway.

But then she shook her head.

"I can't, Billy."

"You won't."

"Semantics."

The Maddy he knew, the Maddy he loved, was gone. And this stranger in front of him was empty. Empty of her fire and her passion and her loyalty, and he couldn't . . . he just couldn't believe that she was happy like this.

"All this time, in my head, you were a fighter. You fought for me, fought to get out of that neighborhood. Fought to be who you are. You're going to give up now?"

"I can't be the person you need me to be just because that's the picture you have in your head. And I can't talk about our past and have you here in my present without thinking about the future. And there's no future with you."

He stepped back. Again. Another step. There were no windows in this room. It felt like a coffin. On the far wall there was a poster of Maddy in a blue dress that looked sort of familiar. She was smiling.

Mocking him.

"I'll tell Dom I won't talk about our marriage."

"Thank you."

"But I'm not doing this show."

"What?"

"Sit for an hour and talk to you about my family? Tell

you about where I grew up like you don't know? What do you want from me, Maddy? I love you. I won't edit you out of my past like you've done to me. I won't."

"Billy, if you don't do the show, I'm fired."

Her words echoed in the coffin and there was no way he heard her right. No way.

"What?"

"If you don't do the show, I'll lose my job."

"If you don't do the show, I'll lose my job."

She heard the hitch in his breath when it sank in.

"Is that . . . Oh my god." His laughter was razor sharp and both of them were sliced. "Is that why you slept with me?"

"No." That was emphatic. Making love with him had nothing to do with the show and everything to do with what was between them.

He stepped back, tripping into a chair.

She waited, braced herself for his rage. But he stared at her. Just stared. Until she couldn't take it anymore. Couldn't meet his eyes.

"You started this, Billy," she said, guilt making her angry. "You forced your way onto my show, and just because you got mad you think you have the right to walk away. The world doesn't work that way! You owe me!"

"Okay."

"What?" she asked.

"Okay. I'll do the show."

He was forcing himself to stay calm, she could see it in his body, the way she'd seen it when they were kids and he resisted putting his fist in the face of every kid or adult who called him stupid.

I just keep hurting you, she thought.

"I love you," he said, the words a curse, an epitaph.

And even though she knew it, hearing him say it like that was shocking, painful, pricking her self-righteousness until it vanished. She couldn't help flinching every time he said those words. "Do you get that, Maddy? *I love you.*"

"I'm sorry, Billy. I'm so sorry."

His sigh turned to laughter, shallow and sad. "I know. And I'm sorry too, but I'm learning how to be honest with myself," he said. "For the first time in my life, I'm fighting for what's really important. You should try it."

He walked to the door, leaving her there, wasted.

"Have your people call my people, or however the hell it works for you now."

"Billy—"

"And then let's just leave each other alone, okay? You're right. It hurts too much."

chapter
27

Twenty-four years ago

Billy ducked into his sisters' bedroom. Even though his older sister, Janice, liked to pretend that she wasn't bothered by the screaming downstairs, his younger sister, Denise, still got scared.

And so did he. He wouldn't say that out loud—he was twelve, for crying out loud—but the second he heard his dad's voice, his whole body went cold and then hot and he started looking for a place to hide.

And if things really went to shit downstairs, his sisters' room had the window over the porch, so they could get out.

"Hey—" He stopped, the door at his back, stunned to see that his sisters weren't alone. "What's she doing here?" he asked, pointing to the dark-haired girl sitting with Denise on her bed, looking like she was about to wet her pants and the faded pink quilt underneath her.

Mom and Dad going at it in the kitchen had that effect on people.

"Maddy's here for a sleepover." Denise said it like sleepovers were something that happened all the time at the Wilkins' house.

"Did Mom say it was okay?" He asked Janice. Denise would just lie.

"She made cupcakes," Janice said, exhaling toward

the open window because Mom would kill her if she ever smelled smoke in the house. But ever since Janice had turned fifteen she acted like no one could touch her. She'd gotten hard around the edges and scary.

"It's the last Friday of the month," he said, but Janice only shrugged. His dad's disability check came in on the last Friday of every month and he crawled out of whatever hole he'd been drinking in to come home and get it. Which always resulted in a screaming match. Sometimes his mom and dad smacked each other around and sometimes Billy had to call the cops.

Once he had to call the ambulance.

All of those things would ruin a slumber party.

"You want to go home?" he asked the girl, whom he suddenly recognized as Dougie's daughter. Dougie was the janitor at the hockey arena and Billy thought he was too smart to have let his daughter spend the night over here. But his wife was one of those women who wanted to believe the best of people. She'd probably been the one to okay this stupid sleepover idea.

"No, Maddy doesn't want to go home!" Denise cried, clamping her hand down on Maddy's leg, like a little kid claw. "We're having fun!"

Something shattered downstairs. They were throwing dishes. The sound of fun.

"I was asking her."

"Don't go," Denise said to Maddy, who was so scared she was white-faced.

"Yeah." Janice was only sarcastic these days. Only mean. "Join the party."

"Should someone call the police?" Maddy asked him. Her eyes were pretty. Golden.

"No." He sat down on Janice's bed, on the faded yellow flowers on the sheets. "That only makes them mad at us."

"What are they fighting about?" Maddy asked.

Billy shrugged. "Everything. Money mostly."

There was a fleshy thud, a scream and the sound of something else breaking. Janice lit another cigarette and Denise started to cry.

"They're ruining my slumber party," she whispered, tears plopping onto her hand-me-down Hello Kitty T-shirt.

Billy didn't know the first thing about saving slumber parties, so he hooked his thumb in the hole at the knee of his jeans. His mom would kill him for making it bigger, but she'd be busy for the next little while nursing whatever injuries his dad was currently creating down there.

"I'll braid your hair," Maddy said and Denise's tears dried right up. Apparently Maddy knew how to save a slumber party.

Janice laughed from her perch in the windowsill.

"I could braid yours, too," Maddy said. God, she was out of place here. Like a bright new penny sitting in the mud. He had to give the girl credit—she was scared, but she was still here. Tough. Foolish, maybe, but there was something cool about that.

"No thanks," Janice sneered.

"How about mine?" Billy said, running his hand over the crew cut his mother had given him a few days ago. Trying to make a joke.

There weren't enough jokes in the world to hide how gross his family was. How ugly. But he was glad when she played along.

"Sure," she said with a nervous smile. For a minute the fear lifted right up out of the room, and he could almost forget what was happening downstairs.

But then the most terrifying sound in the world echoed through 12 Spruce.

The sound of his dad's work boots on the bottom step of the stairs.

"Oh Jesus," Janice said and put out her smoke before lifting the window all the way up.

"What's going on?" Maddy asked, her fingers still wrapped in Denise's long hair.

Scrambling to his feet, Billy walked over to Denise's bed. Janice was already halfway out the window and onto the roof of the porch. From there, she would climb down the rusty rain gutter.

"Listen," he said to Maddy as he pulled Denise off the bed. "You have to climb out the window."

"I don't want to, Billy," Denise said. "It's scary."

"Yeah, well, so is Dad."

"He's coming up here?" Maddy leapt off the bed.

"Yeah, and if we just get out, it's no big deal." He hoped his big fake smile was enough to convince her. Denise was whimpering and crying as she climbed through the window, which didn't help.

"Trust me." He squeezed Maddy's hand, surprised when she squeezed back. "Everything is going to be okay."

"You sure?"

"Absolutely," he lied.

His father's footsteps were getting louder and Billy started to rush her, pushing Maddy over the splintered windowsill. Luckily it was summer and both of the girls had their shoes on. The sky was clear, the moon bright, practically lighting their way. Everything would be fine.

"Billy!" his father cried, his voice clear now that he was on the steps. "Where's your hockey money?"

Billy froze. One foot out the window. No. No way. Not his hockey fees. He'd just made the rep league and there was no way his dad was taking that money. He'd been working all spring and summer cleaning gutters and mowing lawns. Walking Mrs. Monroe's stupid dog.

He climbed back into the room.

"What are you doing?" Maddy grabbed onto his T-shirt.

"He'll go through my room," he said. "He'll find my money."

"But . . ." She was so scared and he felt bad, he did, but he couldn't lose that money. "He'll hurt you."

Probably. "It's okay. Honestly. Climb down the rain spout and go on home. Don't come back over here for anymore sleepovers."

He yanked himself away from the girl and jerked open the door just in time to see his dad opening the door to his room.

"Hiding with your sisters?" His dad asked. He was drunk, but that wasn't unusual. He had a cut on his forehead that was dripping blood down the side of his face. His mom must have got him with a plate.

"Where's Mom?"

"Minding her own goddamn business!" he yelled backward down the stairs. "I need some money, Billy."

"I don't have any."

"Bullshit." He smiled, which was always more terrifying than when he yelled. Everyone said Billy looked just like his dad. Big, tall, thick brown hair, and dark brown eyes. A chip off the old block. A charmer, just like his father had been.

Nothing charming about his dad right now.

"Everyone in the neighborhood knows you've been saving money for the rep league."

"I already gave the money to Coach."

That made his father pause. But then he stepped into Billy's room anyway.

"What are you doing?" Billy asked. "I told you there's no money!"

"What about this shit, though?" His dad grabbed Billy's hockey bag and tore open the zipper. "This equipment costs money, it's probably worth something."

Hurt and rage and his own fucking uselessness bubbled up and he knew better, he really did, he'd been taught at a pretty young age to just stay out of his dad's way when he was like this, but he couldn't let anything happen to his hockey gear.

It was his. All his. The only thing in his life that meant anything.

"Don't touch that!" he cried and jerked his bag sideways. His sticks clattered down from where they'd been propped against the wall and hit his father in the head.

The smile vanished from his dad's face, and quick like a rattlesnake he reached out and cuffed Billy hard on the side of his head. It hit against the door frame, but Billy didn't let go of the bag.

Which didn't stop his father from ripping open the zipper the rest of the way and taking out Billy's skates.

"What are these worth?" he asked. "Christ, this stuff stinks."

"Don't—" He grabbed the skates by the blades but his dad jerked them away, slicing open Billy's hands. He'd just had the blades sharpened and they were like knives.

Billy reached for them again, but his father smacked him backward, holding the skates in front of Billy's face like a switchblade.

"Listen, you little shit, my money bought this stuff—"

"No, it didn't. I bought those skates. They're mine!"

His dad leaned in closer, the cool metal of the blade touching Billy's face, the corner of his lip. Fear prickled all along his back, his hairline. Billy tried to back up, but he was pressed tight against the door frame.

"You think you're a big man, huh?" He pressed the skate against Billy's mouth until the metal touched his teeth. Billy forced himself not to wet his pants. "Some kind of hockey star? Well, let me tell you, son, you're a Wilkins. Which means you ain't shit."

"Leave him alone!"

Out of nowhere, his mom cannonballed into her husband, shoving him sideways, just as Billy jerked his head.

For a moment he felt nothing. His father just stared at him, his face white with horror. And then he dropped the skate and ran.

His mother started screaming.

Pain exploded across his face. It hurt, his mouth, his face, it hurt so much he wanted to climb out of his skin. He wanted to die.

"Mom!" he tried to scream, but his mouth didn't work and blood sprayed the white wall.

Holy shit, he thought as he slipped down the door frame.

There was a thud. Someone screaming.

The world throbbed in time to the pain. And he curled into a ball on the floor. In his blood. He was all alone.

Oh shit. Oh God. Please. He wasn't sure what was going on, but it was bad. He needed to call an ambulance. He tried to brace himself to stand, to go find the phone, but he slipped in the blood, his head light.

"I called the police," a voice said, high and thready and panicked.

He looked sideways and saw Maddy.

Maddy.

Those copper eyes were wide with panic and fear but she was there.

"It's . . . it's okay." She stepped closer. Crouched down.

"I'm sorry," he tried to say. The black edges of the world were creeping in and he lost himself, but then he felt her hand, warm and real.

And he grabbed on tight.

Don't let go, was his very last thought before he passed out.

chapter 28

Billy didn't remember the drive home—they could have ended up on the moon, for all the attention he paid to the road. Luckily his subconscious remembered where he lived.

Charlie fell asleep in the car, which Becky seemed to think was a sign of the end of the world.

"He won't sleep tonight," she muttered as Billy carried the sleeping boy into the guest room of his house.

Billy put Charlie down on the bed and stood up, facing Becky.

"I swear . . ." he whispered, smiling a little because she looked so . . . new. So pretty. Her hair had dried into big pretty curls around her face. She looked somehow older and younger at the same time. Wise and vulnerable. A girl walking into womanhood. It made his throat feel tight with a certain nostalgia and affection. ". . . I don't even recognize you."

She frowned at him, her scowl utterly familiar. What was it about him that made the women in his life so angry? So furious with him?

"Ah," he said, trying to make a joke of it all, when there was nothing funny about a single thing in his life. "There's the angry girl I know."

He walked past her and curbed the instinct to put his hand on her head. Never so keenly had he felt the lack of touch in his life.

He collapsed onto his couch, his head back on the headrest. He felt empty. Like if they drove back to the studio, there would be a trail of his blood and guts along the roads and highway. His still-beating heart in Maddy's hand.

What do I do now? he thought. How do I get over this? He wished the season wasn't so far away. He'd even be happy to play in the minor leagues, if it would start right at this moment.

He didn't want to fight. For the first time in his life, he was mad and angry and he didn't want to put his fist through a wall.

Maybe he'd take the kids on a fishing trip. The thought lifted some of the pressure in his chest.

"Hey?"

He looked up to see Becky in the doorway, her sleeves pulled down over her hands. Her lips totally ravaged, which was usually a precursor to her running away or doing something equally drastic.

He sat up, marshaling himself to focus on Becky.

"What's up?" he asked, hoping whatever she was planning would be a good distraction but wouldn't get anyone hurt.

"I . . . I had an idea."

"Does it involve stealing my car?"

"No."

"Then shoot."

"Gina—the lady that cut my hair—was saying there's this boarding school right outside of Dallas. Her niece or something goes there."

His whole body went still, like those moments before sliding into the boards, both braced and relaxed, waiting for the hit.

"Boarding school," he said, just to be clear.

"Yeah, you know, where kids live at the school they go to. Maybe . . . maybe you could send me there."

It wasn't personal, he wasn't stupid enough to believe that. She was scared and alone, but right now, beaten and battered, it still hurt. It still felt like rejection.

"Do you want to go there?"

"Sure."

"Why?"

"I . . . I don't want to feel shitty every day for being here. For being a problem."

"You're not a problem!"

She turned sideways, touching her fist against the wall, the oak wainscoting. "You don't have to lie," she whispered.

Billy rubbed his scar, looked out on his backyard, shining and sparkly from the recent rain. "We're family," he said.

"So?"

He cleared his throat and decided this was just his day for letting it all out. The words he didn't want to spill, the vulnerability he didn't want to show—he couldn't hide it anymore.

Maybe being a family meant not pretending. If that was the case, if it would help, he'd show this girl his heart.

"Maddy had a great family growing up. A mom who made dinner and made sure Maddy did her homework, and a dad who worked really hard to make sure they had food on the table and they could go to Dairy Queen every Sunday night. I used to be so jealous of that."

She was silent, tracing a circle in the wood.

"My mom tried, but she was a mess. My dad was never around, and when he was . . ." He got caught for a moment in the memory of the pain and the blood, the screaming, the escape route over the porch. Maybe he'd tell her that story later, when she was older. "Well, let's just say there weren't any trips to Dairy Queen. Janice and Denise . . . I'm not sure they cared. Not like I did.

Maybe when we were all young we wanted to be a family, but after a while they seemed to think how we were, how awful our house was, was normal. But I still wanted it. I still wanted a family." He waited for her to look at him. Outside, birds flew, clouds broke apart and scattered to mist. Finally, quickly, she glanced sideways, her eyes meeting his and then sliding away.

He recognized that look so well. Like a kicked dog, searching for a little kindness.

"And I still do. I want a family. It's all I've ever wanted." She stared at a spot on the carpet, three inches from the front of his feet. Closer, but not close enough. He could feel her yearning, as painful and unbelievable as his. "Please, Becky . . . please just look at me."

Finally, she did. Her blue eyes swimming with tears, huge and liquid. "If you really want to go to boarding school, we'll do it. I'll send you wherever you want to go, Lord knows you've earned a shot at being happy. And I have enough money for you to do whatever you want. But I am really hoping you might be happy here. With me."

She sniffed. Lifted one wrist to rub at her eye.

And suddenly they were in one of those moments that could change everything. For him. For her. It was a line in the sand and someone had to be brave enough to cross it.

Despite being gutted by the woman he loved, he was suddenly that someone. Brave enough for the two of them.

He climbed to his feet, taking his time crossing the carpet, feeling like he was a hundred years old, hurt and wounded but somehow hopeful all the same.

His arms were loose by his sides and she had plenty of time to run, to dodge him, but she stood there, shaking. Tears dropping off her nose onto her sweatshirt. Careful, aware of how fragile she was, how fragile the moment was, he touched her back. She flinched but didn't run, and he rode it out. Waited patiently for her to relax into the contact. Just his hand gently resting there.

And when that seemed okay, he carefully, slowly, pulled her sideways into his chest. Her shoulder at his sternum, his hand at her elbow.

"I want you to stay," he said, and he felt her drawn so tight he was worried she might snap. Might break into a thousand pieces at his feet.

She coughed. Or something. And then another. Her head bent over, her hands clenched into fists at her stomach, and he realized she wasn't coughing, she was sobbing. Nearly bent double, she was crying her heart out.

"I want you to stay," he said again and she turned sideways, putting her arms around his waist. Sobbing against his shirt.

Yeah, he thought, patting her back, holding her close, letting her cry—probably all things that hadn't happened to her in years.

This is right.

The only thing that might make it more right was having Charlie awake. And Maddy here. A real family. The only family he would ever dream of wanting.

But some things just weren't meant to be.

Maddy closed the door to her condo behind her and in the darkness she shrank back against the wood. For three years this place had been her sanctuary. Three years.

Ivory tower. Fine. Yes. He was right about that.

But why was it wrong? Why was it wrong to be safe? To create a place for herself that was hers and hers alone. Why was that intrinsically bad?

Just who the fuck was he to judge her?

And the fact that she felt lonely? The fact that she

stood here, in the dark and shadows of her own life, and felt like a sliver of a person, a quarter of who she'd been, as if the last few years had sucked something vital and real and important out of her. Maybe that was just growing up. Maybe that was divorce.

She felt righteous about that for a few moments, righteous enough to kick off her shoes and turn on the lights.

But it was somehow worse in the light. As if the starkness of her condo was reflective of how stark her life was. Pictures of guests on her wall? That didn't seem right. No matter how famous, or how great the picture. Because it wasn't love.

"Stop it," she cried. "Stop it." She yanked off her earrings and tossed them in the bowl on the pink table in her hallway. She'd work out. That's what she needed. It had been a few days, what with the drama of the kids and Billy, and she was simply missing the endorphins of a good sweaty workout.

But in her bedroom the recumbent bike looked like a torture device.

A run?

Rain pounded against the windows.

No. No. Not this.

The dark edges of depression crept in. That crippling melancholy that had kept her in bed for weeks after she and Billy had broken up the first time was coming back tenfold. Darker. Thicker.

She rejected the depression. The idea of it. He wasn't going to have that power over her anymore. Never again.

Knowing a surefire way of reminding herself that editing Billy from her life was the right thing to do, she picked up her phone and called her mother.

"Honey!" her mom cried upon answering and Maddy fell backward onto her bed. "How are you?"

Surprisingly, Maddy found herself swallowing back tears, waiting until the pain in her throat and behind her eyes passed so she could talk.

"I'm good, Mom," she said, happy for all that voice training that allowed her to sound normal. "How are you?"

"Good. I'm good. Well, Paige and I lost at bridge today, but you can't win them all, can you?"

"I guess not."

"You don't sound okay, do you have a cold?"

I'm so bad, Mom. I'm so scared and so in love and . . . unhappy. Deeply, terribly unhappy, and I can't pretend I'm not anymore. I can't pretend that being Maddy Cornish is satisfying. I can't keep living like this.

The words were a scream in her throat. The same scream she'd been holding in for fourteen years. But letting it out . . . oh, she couldn't imagine the power of that scream. How it would change her life. How she'd never be able to look at herself in the mirror again if she released it.

It had been bad enough telling Billy she loved him. Close enough to hitting some terrible dark spot of no return.

She opened her mouth to tell her mother that Billy had been on the show. That he was back in Maddy's life, but suddenly she couldn't do it. She didn't want to listen to her mother's old poison about him. And she really didn't want to think about what that meant.

"Are you happy, Mom?" she asked, instead, rolling onto her side and pulling the duvet up over her body.

"Sure. I mean, I wish you were closer. I wish your father were still alive, but yeah, I'm happy."

How does that feel? she wondered.

"I'm glad, Mom," she said.

Tears leaking silently from the corners of her eyes, she made the right noises about weather and bridge games and taking a trip down there in the winter. Maybe for a week this time, she was owed some vacation.

"Honey," Mom said. "You really don't sound like you're okay."

"I'm fine," she lied, the words, like so much of her life, a candy coating over something very, very rotten.

Having pulled herself back from the brink, Maddy decided that if her life was unhappy, it was her own damn fault, and she threw herself into the revamp of the show.

Who the hell was Billy to tell her what mattered? She'd show him a fight.

Every day for a week she woke up thinking it would get better, that the thoughts of Billy and the kids would fade and the pain would ease. But every day it was there, like glass just under her skin.

And every day she tried to get past that pain with work. It had been the right medicine once, but it wasn't working anymore.

Empty, she thought, as she lined up guests and story ideas.

I don't give a shit, she thought as she listened to theme music options and discussed brand marketing.

Ruth slapped her notebook against the conference room table and everyone jumped. "Clear out," she said to Sabine and the rest of the crew, who were all in there working on the last of the presentation they were going to give to Richard the next day.

Maddy pulled together her stuff and started to stand.

"Not you, Madelyn," Ruth said and Maddy sat back down and waited for everyone else to clear out.

"What the hell is going on with you, Maddy?"

"Nothing."

Ruth leaned back in her chair. She was wearing a red sweater today, her black-on-black theme seemed to have been derailed over the past week. Color looked good on her.

"You're a liar, Maddy. And up until now you've been pretty convincing. But today, I can see right through you."

"I'm not a liar!" she cried, appalled at the notion.

"Please, we both are. In fact, I'll reveal a lie I've been telling for three years." She threw her arms out, as if throwing something away. "I don't want to move to New York. I don't want a network job."

So that explained the red sweater. "Really?"

"Really. I like it here. And now that we're working on the new format, I have no desire to go anywhere. Here's another piece of honesty for you." She leaned across the table, suddenly razor sharp, suddenly more present than Maddy had ever seen her. She was sparkling with purpose. Confronted with all that energy, Maddy felt like a burnt-out lightbulb. "If you don't get your head out of your ass, this show is going to flop. And flop hard. You want to host a show like this, then you need to *connect,* Maddy."

"I connect." Her protest sounded stupid. Weak.

"Bullshit, and you know it. We need you to really connect, and the person you are right now, this shell, I don't think she can do it."

Maddy wished she could deny it. Wished she could be outraged. But part of her knew Ruth was right.

"I'm not saying you can't do it; you can. You could be great on this show. But not like you've been the past week. You need to think about that before the pitch meeting." She pulled her papers into a stack and slapped it against the table, lining up all the edges with one sharp bang. Maddy flinched. "Now, let's go get a drink."

"I think . . . I think you just insulted me, Ruth. I'm not sure I want to get a drink with you."

"I know." Ruth winced. "I'm not very good at this

friend thing. But I think you could probably use one—a friend, I mean. And a drink, too. And I know I could. So? Drink?"

Now, this was weird.

But weird was okay. Weird might bring her one step closer to being happy. At least with weird she might feel something.

"I thought we were friends once," Maddy said.

"I know." Ruth nodded. "But let's try again. For real this time."

For real. How funny those words sounded. How true.

Maddy stood. "Let's do it."

The next day when they were pitching to a table full of executives, Maddy stood in the middle of a storm. A whirlwind of branding and promotion. Marketing and editorial meetings. Richard sat at the top of the conference room table, his face illuminated by the yellows and greens of the new logo, flashing bright and beautiful across a PowerPoint presentation.

She watched his every facial reaction, knowing that a frown would signal that this new effort of theirs—the blood, sweat, and tears that she and Ruth had put in over the last week—would die before it even had a chance.

But there were no frowns. There weren't any smiles, but there also weren't any frowns.

She and Ruth exchanged panicked looks as Ruth turned on the lights and everyone blinked like owls in a barn.

"Nice work," Richard said and Maddy watched Ruth let out a deep breath. But Maddy had the sinking feeling they weren't out of the woods yet.

"Billy's your first guest?" Richard asked.

"We can tape on the new set on Monday."

"And after that?"

Ruth listed the other guests they'd contacted.

"We could just as easily have them on the old format," Richard said.

"But the new format—"

"Loses money in advertising dollars," he said. "And costs in promotions. You want me to double the budget—"

"Just for the next few months," Ruth interrupted.

There was more discussion, but Maddy heard it from a great distance. This was it, her dream dying.

Connect, she thought. Maybe he just didn't feel the connection. And that was her job.

"Maddy?" Ruth said, her tone pinched. Her eyes had that wide *help me out* look.

"It's this format or I'm out," she said, surprising even herself. "Let's stop informing our audience, Richard. They get information everywhere, the Internet, magazines, and their friends. Let's educate. Let's entertain. Let's change lives. Let's matter to the people of Dallas, in a way that isn't just weather and traffic. Let's make an impact."

How about that for a fight!

But blank looks greeted her around the table.

Oh, what a mistake. What a giant, career-ending mistake. She looked over at Ruth, her friend with a drinking problem, and to her great surprise Ruth winked.

"Me too, Richard," she said. "This is the show, or I'm out, too." Slowly Richard pushed away from the table and stood.

"Then this is the format." He looked around the room, at all the folks from PR and marketing, legal, and HR. "Let's make it work."

Richard left and everyone in the room filed out, people walking by Maddy and shaking her hand. Congratulations all the way around.

She accepted them all, feeling like she was floating three feet off the ground. It had worked. It had actually worked.

"You've got big giant brass balls," Ruth said when the room was empty.

No, Maddy thought, *I'm just looking for a reason to care. A reason to give a shit about my life.* Billy blew it apart when he came back and nothing was ever going to be the same, she couldn't pretend that it would.

"Yours aren't too shabby either," she said.

"Let's get to work," Ruth said. "You want to contact Billy, or should I?"

"You."

Ruth didn't audibly sigh, but it was there just the same. "Maddy?"

She wanted to be oblivious to the concern, but she'd spilled the whole damn story yesterday, halfway through the third round of vodka sodas, so Ruth knew everything about her and Billy.

"Just . . . you talk to him."

"You know you're going to have to interview him, right? Talk to him for, like, an hour?"

"I know," she said, and she also knew she had no idea how she was going to make it through that.

chapter 29

Sunday morning Billy was putting syrup on Charlie's toaster waffles when Victor called.

"You little minx," Victor said. "Going behind my back to talk to Hornsby."

Billy slapped the syrup top down with his palm before putting it in the fridge. "I'm sorry I didn't tell you."

"Damn right you're sorry. But Hornsby and the GM want to have a meeting with us."

"What does that mean?"

"It means you're not dead yet."

Billy watched Charlie eat the waffles, shoveling them in two pieces at a time, syrup running down his face. He bounced in his chair, more excited than anything to have another bite.

I used to feel that way about hockey, he thought. *A million years ago. Before the scar. Before I was really any good at it, I just wanted to play. Just play.*

And he wanted a chance to play that way again. "Let me know, man. I'll do whatever they want."

"Billy? Billy Wilkins? Is that you?"

"It is. But there's some other stuff going on you should probably know about."

"What's the story with *AM Dallas*?"

Ice settled over his body, the ice he was going to need to survive tomorrow morning.

"I tape the show on Monday."

"Tomorrow."

"Yep."

"And Dom?"

"I'm going to talk to him tomorrow afternoon."

"And what's . . . ah . . . what's happening with the kids?"

"We filed the paperwork on Friday," he said, running his hand over Charlie's hair. His pinky got caught in a giant clump of syrup. Billy was going to have to take this kid out back and hose him down. "We just need to wait and see."

"You've been busy," Victor said, recrimination in his voice.

"I know, man, and I'm sorry I didn't call, but some of this stuff I had to handle on my own."

"I understand. But from now on, let me do my job."

"Happy to, Super-Agent Man." They said goodbye and Billy hung up.

"Where's Becky?" Charlie asked for about the hundredth time.

"She's sleeping." Billy had checked on her just a few minutes ago, half expecting to find an empty bed and a curtain fluttering in the breeze from an open window, but instead she was sprawled out over half the bed. Snoring.

The last five days had been like that. He didn't want to think about how long it had been since she'd slept through the night.

And the thought that she was catching up on it here, under his roof, made him content.

"Can I wake her up?"

"Nope, buddy. After breakfast we're going to the bathroom."

Charlie got mutinous. His little face screwed up tight. Bathroom wasn't anything he liked discussing. "Diaper."

Billy reached under the counter for the candy he'd bought yesterday. "Not if you want these." He lifted the bag of M&M's and Charlie looked sideways at it.

"What are those?"

"Bribes. Come on, Charlie, let's go pee like big boys!" He corralled the unhappy, sticky three-year-old and headed for the bathroom, feeling for the first time in years like his life was heading somewhere. Somewhere good.

"Are you nervous?" Becky asked as she and Charlie sat backstage while Billy got his makeup done. He was glad that Gina was taking care of him and not that other girl, the one who had been so eager with the mascara.

"No." He lied, his leg bouncing, the fabric of his gray slacks shimmying with the motion.

Becky slapped her hand on his knee and he worked harder to bounce it. She laughed and pressed harder to hold it down, until Charlie joined in and suddenly the two of them were holding his leg down, laughing.

This was the strangest game, but they seemed to love it.

A little over a week with Becky, and her laughs were becoming a common occurrence.

"Hi, guys." It was Maddy coming around the corner, and he stiffened. Jerked actually—the sound of her voice was like a knife to his throat. Becky stood, staring at Maddy like an angry guard dog.

Charlie, who was three and clearly had no loyalty, ran over to Maddy to hug her legs.

She wore a red dress with a purple belt at the waist and purple high heels that made Billy want to hug her legs, too.

The pain that came from looking at her was nothing new. He'd ached for her since he was a kid. But there had always been something sweet tempering it, a hope or an understanding that made the ache bearable.

There was nothing making it bearable right now. Her beauty cut him to the bone. And so he looked away.

"How are you guys doing?" Maddy asked.

"I peed in a potty!" Charlie cried. They were tempting fate by going without a diaper today, but that's what all the websites told him to do. Whole hog.

Maddy seemed suitably impressed.

"How about you, Becky?" Maddy said, coming to stand closer to the girl, who shrank back, her guard dog look turning to a sneer. The thirteen-year-old had picked up on his feelings and maybe she was hurt herself because Maddy hadn't called once over the last week. Ruth had been the one to contact him with all the details about the show.

"Fine," Becky said.

"Your hair looks great," Maddy told her with a tentative smile he remembered so well from when they were kids. Like she was sidling up to something that might rip her hand off at any moment. That's how she used to look at him.

Becky was totally impervious.

"I brought you something," Maddy said, pulling a book from behind her back. "I just finished it a few weeks ago. It's about killer horses."

Becky's head came up and Billy realized that with all the fun they'd been having—the Chuck E. Cheese and the potty training and the swimming—he'd forgotten about things like books. He'd forgotten that Becky really liked them.

He tried not to think about what a team they could be, he and Maddy.

"You can take it," he assured Becky. He wanted to tell her that she wouldn't be betraying him, or herself. That being angry because she was hurt would only hurt her.

Talk about a lesson he could learn.

"Thanks," Becky said and took the book, opening it immediately.

"Are you ready?" Maddy asked him and there was something slightly eager about her smile. Something hopeful.

"Ready as I'll ever be to talk for an hour."

"It's more like thirty-eight minutes, actually."

"Why doesn't that make me feel better?"

She reached out to put a hand on his shoulder and he flinched away. There had to be some rules if he was going to survive this.

"Please, Maddy," he whispered. "Have a little mercy."

She clenched her hands together, holding them still. "I'm sorry," she said.

Sorry, he thought, getting angry despite himself. *Fuck your sorry.* "Yeah. Me too. I'll see you out there."

He pulled Charlie close, the kid clambering up into his lap like a monkey. For a moment it all registered on Maddy's beautiful face—she was on the outside and she was cold and lonely and miserable there and he wanted to reach for her. To welcome her in.

All the family he'd ever need.

But it wasn't worth it. He knew the pain her lack of faith brought.

"I'll see you on the set," he said.

Maddy composed herself and walked away.

Around the corner from the dressing area, Maddy stopped. She stopped and leaned against the wall, her knees liquid, her lungs cramped.

Oh my God, she thought. *What is wrong with me?*

Billy was okay. She'd broken his heart again and he was okay. And the kids . . . oh, the kids, they looked so good. The last week had changed them. Billy had changed them. Just like he'd changed her.

Sabine came walking past. "The audience is arriving," she said. "They seem pretty lively. Lots of excitement."

Maddy didn't care. She didn't care about any of it. She'd fought for this new job, this new show, and it was good. She was proud. But looking at Billy, at those kids . . . she realized exactly what she'd thrown away. The chance to have everything.

She could connect all over the place, with the guests, with her audience, with the stories. She could be amazing at her job but part of her would continue to die. Just like it had been dying for fourteen years without Billy.

No, she thought, trying very hard to stem the tide of these thoughts, to convince herself that allowing the possibility of pain back into her life was tantamount to getting hurt.

But something different was happening in her body, something beautiful and strange, painful and sweet. Like spring.

Faith was returning to her. After a fourteen-year-long winter, faith was fighting its way free from the dark mud she'd buried it in.

In a riot of color it exploded into her heart. Into her body.

Purples and reds and oranges.

"You okay?" Sabine asked.

Maddy stepped away from the wall, her knees rock solid, her lungs working. Her heart making plans her brain struggled to translate.

"No. But hopefully I will be."

Sitting in front of the live studio audience Billy was plenty nervous, but what was really freaking him out was Maddy.

She was sweating.

As Billy got mic'd during the first commercial break, a girl came out and powdered Maddy. But the sweat was still there.

"You're doing great," he said to her, and she glanced up from her cue cards.

"You think?"

"Yeah. The new style, it's . . . great."

It was true. The music and set, the logo. The live audience was responding to all of it. Responding to her.

But Maddy didn't seem like a woman who was reaping the rewards of her hard work. No, she seemed like she was about to jump out of a plane or something.

He glanced offstage to where the kids sat. Becky had her head buried in that book Maddy had given her and Charlie was mastering another level of Angry Birds. Beside them sat Gina, who gave him a thumbs-up.

Billy had warned her about the no-diapers situation, but she'd volunteered to take care of them anyway.

"We're on in five," Peter said.

Billy took a deep breath and ran his hand over the white shirt Becky had chosen for him.

"I love you, Billy," Maddy said, and he spun to face her.

Oh, she was a mess. Sweaty and panicked.

"What are you doing?" he asked, his stomach replaced by a storm of nerves.

"I'm not sure."

The red lights came on the cameras and they were live.

chapter 30

"Billy, walk us through that fight at the end of the last Mavericks game," she asked. So far, so good. Five minutes in and there hadn't been any more surprises, and whatever freak-out Maddy had been in the middle of seemed to have passed. He still felt jittery with adrenaline, waiting for some kind of ambush.

"I . . . I was angry. I was angry that our team had played so hard and still lost. The guys are young but they've got so much heart and they were coming off that ice beaten. You know? Defeated. And I was defeated. I had a crappy season last year, which was all my fault and I had no one to blame but myself. And, well, sometimes a fight can cheer you up better than anything else."

"So you fought to make yourself feel better?"

He smiled. "I never said I was very smart."

Her eyes snapped and he remembered how she hated it when people called him stupid. Even him.

What's going on? he thought.

"You have a history with fighting, though." She leaned forward in her chair, her whiskey eyes sucking him in. When she looked at him like that the studio audience fell away and he tried to resist, but he knew it would make for a better show if he followed her lead.

He'd had this plan to keep himself removed. To just barely answer the questions. To do his part and then get the hell out of there.

But she'd been so sweaty.

And the *I love you* thing. Was it another trick?

"It's a part of hockey," he said with a shrug. "I think the culture is changing, though."

"Do you think it should?"

"You know, I might be putting myself out of business, but yeah, a fight is one thing—two guys, center ice, agree to drop gloves; fine—but the guys that play dirty . . . there's no place for that anymore. We've lost too many guys to crap like that. The crap I used to do. It's got to stop."

"You played dirty. That cheap shot at the end of the last game."

"You're right." He nodded, taking full responsibility. "And I don't want to play that way anymore."

"Even before hockey you had a history with violence."

Here we go, he thought, unable to believe he was going to talk about his childhood . . . without mentioning her. It was ridiculous. He couldn't even look—

"I grew up with Billy," she said, turning to the audience, and his mouth fell open. "In fact, many people don't know this, but for about five minutes about a million years ago, Billy and I were married."

The crowd gasped, murmurs rippling through the room. Cell phones were pulled out of pockets—the news of their marriage was going to be all over the world in less than a minute.

If a rock had fallen from the sky he wouldn't have been any more shocked. He could only gape at her while she talked about their neighborhood. His ears were buzzing, his heart pounding.

What the hell was she doing?

"You . . ." He cleared his throat and tried again. "You were the one who handled all the bullies," he said. "You were like the playground enforcer. Anyone so much as looked at another kid's lunch money, and you'd go over there and take out their knees."

"Well," she laughed, tossing that hair over her shoulder, "it was easier to do that when I knew you'd come charging down like a madman if anyone tried to hurt me."

"I would have," he said, and the words came out raw. Honest.

The crowd gasped, some people clapped.

"We'll be right back with more from Billy Wilkins," she said and the lights on the cameras flicked off.

"Is this for show?" he whispered, unable to play her game. He wanted to rip off his mic, but he'd done that before. And he was supposed to be cleaning up his mess, not making it worse.

"I called Dom," she said, "before the show. I told him I wanted to talk to him about you. About us. I'm sorry I was scared. I'm so sorry I pushed you away." Now she wasn't sweating . . . she was crying. And her words were dangerous. Falling down around him like fire. "And if you don't want to talk about us, about growing up or our history, I understand. I can go back to the script. But I just want you to know, I'm not . . . I'm not scared anymore. I'm not ashamed. I believe in you." She glanced backstage. "With those kids, you're . . . you're amazing. I want the world to know. I want people to look at me and think of us. I would be really proud of that."

"Maddy," he sighed, scared to believe it. Worried that in his desire to believe it he was being fooled.

"It's okay," she said, wiping her eyes. "This is crazy. I totally understand. I have no idea what I was thinking. We'll go back to the script. I understand. I do. It's got to be hard to trust me. I just wanted you to know that I have faith. In you."

Gina came running out, and slapped powder on Maddy as fast as she could. "You've got to stop this nonsense. Those kids are freaking out and you're gonna look like a raccoon in front of a million viewers."

Gina vanished and Peter was there with the hand count and the lights were on and Maddy was smiling, calming down the buzzing audience before talking about the New School.

The studio darkened and on the screen behind them they showed the promotional video that Luc and Tara Jean had made. It was slick and emotional and Billy sat there, cold to all of it. His eyes on Maddy.

Faith.

The lights came back on and Maddy turned to him. "What gave you the idea for this school?" she asked.

"You."

She blinked. Sat back, a tentative, hopeful smile flickering across her face.

Faith, he thought, and decided to talk about something he never spoke of.

"Remember the night I got my scar?" He touched it, the familiar thick ridge, the curl at his lip where the blade had bit deep.

She nodded.

"My dad did this to me," he said to the audience, to every person he'd lied to about it. To every guy he'd hit on the ice because he was angry. Because he was remembering that night. "I was twelve years old and he held a hockey skate up to my face. He was a bully, my dad. A mean drunk. And he was just trying to be tough, but my mom got involved and there was a fight . . . an accident, and the blade sliced through my lip, across my face. My sisters were gone, and my dad ran away. I'm not sure where my mom went."

"To the neighbors."

"Of course. But you were there," he said and turned to the audience. "Maddy was ten years old and she called the cops and sat beside me holding my hand. I've loved her ever since."

He turned his hand over, palm up.

Past, present, and future, it was all right here. Right now. Without hesitating she put her hand in his.

The crowd went crazy.

His heart went crazy.

"But Billy," she said, smiling, tears in her eyes, her hand in his, "that doesn't explain the origins of the New School."

Man, she was good, he thought, and squeezed her hand. The rest of the thirty-eight minutes flew by. They talked about the school, his career, and his possible future in the minor league.

"I've made a lot of mistakes," he said. Maddy's hand in his, he looked backstage at the kids, his heart overrun with emotion. The kids were staring at him, wide-eyed. Probably freaking out.

"I'm trying to make things better. For everyone."

"I'd say you're off to a good start." Maddy stood, her hand still in his. "I'd like to thank you all for coming," she said. "For watching, for sharing this hour with us." She glanced at Billy, who winked at her.

Everyone started clapping, coming to their feet. Stomping and whistling.

"Thank you," she said, her voice catching on tears. He tugged her against his side, his arm holding her close. "See you tomorrow," she cried over the noise and the cameras went dark.

"We're clear," Peter yelled and before Billy could do anything, Maddy turned, wrapped her arms around his neck, and kissed him.

Closemouthed and hard. A promise. A stamp. *Mine,* that kiss said. *Mine.*

He chuckled and kissed her back. Claiming her—this magnificent, surprising woman, this queen of her kingdom—as his.

There was a tug on his jacket and he turned to find Becky and Charlie. Becky glared at Maddy.

"Is this a trick?" she asked. "Like that thing with us? Did you do this for ratings, or whatever?"

Maddy shook her head. "No. No trick."

"Then why'd you do it?"

"Because I love him and I want everyone in the world to know."

Billy stepped backward, making a bit of a show of being blown away by her words.

"Do you love her?" Becky asked him.

"I have my whole life. Every minute."

Becky rolled her eyes, clearly he'd gone a bit too far, but he didn't care.

"So," Becky looked at them, "what do we do now?"

"Chuck E. Cheese," Charlie cried, lifting his hands to be picked up.

Billy groaned and Charlie clapped his hands over Billy's face. "You promised! You said if I peed in the potty every time, you'd take me to Chuck E. Cheese."

"I did." He looked over at Maddy. "Want to come?"

"Absolutely," she said without hesitation. Probably because she didn't know that Chuck E. Cheese was the seventh circle of hell. "Let me change." She walked away a few steps and then turned. "Want to come?" she asked Becky, but the girl hung back. Burned a few too many times.

"Go," he whispered, and it took another moment of hesitation but then Becky quickly joined her.

His eyes burned, happiness making a mess of him. There were some tough hurdles ahead of them. The foster parent interviews, the adoption process, his possible career in the minors, the change in Maddy's show.

But right now he had no doubt that they could handle it, together. The stuff that had ruined them before didn't stand a chance against all the things they could do right.

Love was the least of their strengths.

This moment, watching Becky and Maddy walk down the hall, away from him, their heads bent together, Charlie's perfect weight in his arms, this was the happiest he'd ever been. This moment couldn't be improved upon.

He was a man complete.

Charlie wiggled in his arms.

"I need to pee," he said.

Oh, how wrong he'd been. Now it was perfect.

"Let's go, buddy." Billy headed for the bathroom, tears unchecked on his face.

epilogue

Two years later

"*Can you fit* in there?" Billy asked as Charlie climbed inside the sparkling silver perfection that was the Stanley Cup. "Can you get your head down?"

Charlie tried, but the best he could do was stand inside of it.

"Good enough," Billy said and took a picture of his five-year-old, newly adopted son, who was grinning like a mad man, standing in the Stanley Cup.

It was Billy's day with the cup. Every player on the winning team got a day with it and Billy had chosen today—the finalization of the adoption process.

The kids' Gotcha Day.

Perfect.

"You know," Maddy said, sweeping out into the backyard with a case of beer in her arms. She was still wearing her running clothes from her workout this morning. Sometimes he thought she did that on purpose—to mess with his head. He could barely look away from her ass as she tumbled the bottles into a tub filled with ice, which was next to a tub filled with pop. "People are going to be here in an hour."

Becky, fifteen going on twenty-five, more beautiful than there were words to describe, came out with bowls of chips and set them down on the other table. She was already dressed for the party, had been since dawn. A green skirt, a purple top with little spaghetti straps. She reached up a hand to pick at her lips, but then stopped herself.

"You think we have enough food?" she asked, worrying, always worrying. She went to a counselor once a week for help with some compulsive behaviors. It seemed to be helping. But still his heart bled for her, just bled.

"It's five teenagers and a couple of adults," Billy said. He grabbed Maddy's hand and pulled her into his arms. She didn't resist, despite the fact that guests would be arriving in an hour.

During the week, she was the queen of morning television. Her show was more popular than *AM Dallas* had ever been.

But in their home, with the kids and their friends, she was Maddy Baumgarten—a different kind of queen.

"Marry me," he whispered against her lips. "The adoption process is over, we can elope and you can file to adopt and then it's done. We're a family."

"We already are a family," she said, kissing him back, holding his cheeks, brushing his hair away from his eyes. A thousand touches, a million little pats a day—after two years she still seemed to be making sure he was there. "And I'm not eloping again."

"Okay. Marry me in a church with a thousand people. We can televise it."

"Hey!" Luc Baker stepped into the backyard from the kitchen. "I need some help with the gifts."

"Gifts!" Charlie said as he tried to climb out of the Stanley Cup. He tripped and fell and Billy leaned over and swept him up.

"I'm going to take a shower," Maddy said and vanished as Luc walked into the yard.

"Wow," Luc said, coming over to look at the Cup

where it sat unceremoniously on the ground. Charlie lifted the toy car he'd been playing with out of it. "Treating it with the respect it deserves, I see."

"Later we can drink beer out of it."

Luc smiled, but it was bittersweet, and his hands were reverent as they touched the silver, the names of the hockey greats etched in its side.

"You did good," Luc said.

"It was the team," Billy answered, uncomfortable.

"No, man, I watched that game. *Everyone* watched that game. It was you." Luc stared at him. "You lead the shit out of those kids."

Billy laughed. "That was beautiful, man." Uncomfortable and proud and happy, he hurried to change the subject. "Beer?"

"Sure."

Billy grabbed two icy cold bottles from the tub and handed one to Luc. "So, you getting any sleep?" he asked.

"No. None at all."

Tara Jean stepped out onto the lawn, holding a little girl in a serious ruffly pink and white dress. "Chloe!" Becky cried and ran over to take the baby.

"Thanks, Becky," TJ said. "I need to go help Maddy."

"What does Maddy need help with?" Billy asked, already stepping forward. This was supposed to be a party, he didn't want her working so hard she didn't have any fun.

"I got it!" TJ said and waved over her shoulder as she went back into the house. "You guys discuss hockey . . . or potty training."

"Is this stupid?" Maddy's hands were shaking as she pulled up the zipper on her dress. In the mirror she didn't look like a bride, despite the white eyelet lace. She looked like a thirty-six-year-old woman in a sundress.

"This is stupid," she answered her own question.

But Ruth shoved her down into a chair and Gina was suddenly there with her magic toolbox. Tara Jean was in the kitchen handling the caterers.

"Nothing about this is stupid," Ruth said. "It's romantic and awesome. He's going to be blown away."

That was what she thought, but trying to plan a surprise wedding on their kids' Gotcha Day felt a little like overkill. Too much happiness. Too much joy.

Silly, kind of.

"Honey," Gina said. "You've got to stop crying or we're never going to get this mascara on."

The bedroom door creaked open and Becky slipped in, Chloe in her arms, looking red-faced and crabby.

"I think she might be hungry," Becky said. "Have you seen Tara Jean?"

"Here I am," Tara Jean came in behind her. "Come here, baby." She took Chloe and sat on the corner of the bed to nurse her eight-month-old. "The caterers are all set up, and the guests are starting to arrive."

"I'll go help distract the groom," Ruth said and vanished out the door.

Becky blushed at the first sight of nipple and came over to stand beside Maddy.

"You look beautiful," she said.

"So do you. You were right about the green." Maddy touched the sequined edge of the girl's skirt. It was simple and sturdy, that skirt, cotton, with just a little bit of flash and glamour. Not unlike Becky.

"Oh, I forgot—the minister is here," Tara Jean said, stroking Chloe's head. "Luc is trying to keep the guy busy while Victor entertains Billy in the backyard."

"Do you think Billy guesses?"

"He's wondering why the whole team showed up for our party."

Maddy smiled.

"If he goes into the kitchen, he'll know something's up. The caterers have totally taken over," Becky said. "They've got lots of shrimp." Her eyes glowed. She was a shrimp hound, this girl.

"Good," Maddy said, hugging Becky close. "I'm so proud of you," she whispered into her shiny hair.

"I love you," Becky whispered and Maddy closed her eyes against the sting of tears. The words were still rare, and more precious because of it. Not like Charlie, who declared his love every ten minutes. His love for Billy, for Becky, for Maddy, for toaster waffles, for his new skates. You name it, Charlie loved it.

Becky was more reserved in her affections, but deeply, deeply loyal.

She was so much like Billy.

The door creaked open and Ruth stuck her head in. "I can't keep the smoke and mirrors going much longer," she said. "He's starting to suspect something's up."

"We're coming." Maddy got to her feet, the white lace falling down around her knees.

Tara Jean, her matron of honor, had a little spit-up on the front of her pale blue dress. Which, really, when you thought about it, was kind of perfect. On this love-filled, imperfect wedding day, what was a little spit-up?

Ruth, her bridesmaid, was wearing a red and yellow sari-type dress. Like she was making up for all her years without color.

"I'll go get the minister and Billy in place," TJ said and slipped out the door, her baby cuddled up on her shoulder.

"You ready?" Ruth asked.

How did this happen? she wondered. *How did I get*

here? A house full of friends. Two kids. A man who has loved me since we were children. Who am I to have this?

"Come on," Ruth said, tugging her into motion. "Don't get cold feet now."

"It's not cold feet," she said at the door. "I just want to savor it all."

Ruth smiled, this friend who'd come into her life when she'd needed one most. When she'd needed to vent or rejoice or cry or laugh or drink too much vodka in a seedy bar.

Maddy smiled back at her, her teammate, and no words needed to be spoken.

"Let's go." Maddy threw open the door and walked down the hallway. When the guests saw her, they headed outdoors, and soon the backyard was flooded with everyone they loved.

Becky and Charlie were standing beside Billy, holding his hand while he talked to Coach Hornsby. Behind Billy stood a man in a suit. The minister.

Ruth walked outside, leaving her alone in the doorway, looking at her life.

The backyard fell silent and Hornsby tapped Billy on the shoulder and pointed over to her.

She watched him, this man she loved so much, she watched him stumble through emotions. A lot of confusion at all of the people who were suddenly in his yard, and then he caught sight of her and his face had that *what have I done to deserve you?* look that marked him as hers.

And then she saw the moment when he realized what was happening.

He gasped, his eyes flooded.

"Ouch, Billy," Charlie said. "You're squeezing my hand."

"Sorry, buddy." His voice was thick. Rough, full of every emotion that echoed in her heart. He leaned down to kiss Charlie's hand and then he kissed the top of Becky's head.

"Surprised?" Becky asked.

"Always," Billy said.

Blake, who had an angelic voice to match his devilish slapshot, started to sing and Maddy, more happy than she knew was possible, went to join her family.